One Small Voice

One Small Voice

SANTANU BHATTACHARYA

FIG TREE
an imprint of
PENGUIN BOOKS

FIG TREE

UK | USA | Canada | Ireland | Australia
India | New Zealand | South Africa

Fig Tree is part of the Penguin Random House group of companies
whose addresses can be found at global.penguinrandomhouse.com.

First published 2023
001

Set in 12.96/15.36pt Garamond MT Std
Typeset by Jouve (UK), Milton Keynes
Printed and bound in Great Britain by Clays Ltd, Elcograf S.p.A.

The authorized representative in the EEA is Penguin Random House Ireland,
Morrison Chambers, 32 Nassau Street, Dublin D02 YH68

A CIP catalogue record for this book is available from the British Library

Hardback ISBN: 978–0–241–58233–6
Trade paperback ISBN: 978–0–241–58234–3

www.greenpenguin.co.uk

For my grandmothers, Tara and Arati

Lakeerein haath mein thee toh muqaddar thee
Inhein hum band rakhte the
Zameenon par bichheen toh phir samandar, mulak,
Ghar, aangan sabhi ko kaat-tee guzreen!

— *Gulzar*

When lines were only etched on the palm
They told our destiny
We kept them closed in a fist;
When they are drawn on the ground
They cut across oceans, countries,
homes and hearths.

Contents

PART ZERO
Agni / *Fire*

The colours of fire are rather cheerful. I look down to see them all over me. Red on my feet. Yellow on my fingers. Orange on my shirt like meteoric streaks. The shades meld into narangi, dhusar, silait, gerua. Bronze, rust, tangerine, honey, carrot.

Agni, fire. Once used to consecrate beginnings, honour endings.

Agni, now used to immolate innocents.

Agni, so holy, so horrific.

The flames blur my vision. I step back and see what I've done. I look down at my hands, feet. I wipe the sweat off my face. It leaves a gash on my forehead.

The phone buzzes. *Ma calling* . . . But I cannot answer. The colours are dripping from my body. Tip-tip-tip.

I close my eyes and gulp a blob of dried spit. I open them and the sunlight singes through. I squint. That was night, this is day. That was the start of our story, this is the end. Twenty-five years between them.

Come, my friend, stand next to me. Give me permission to tell this story – yours, mine, ours. The story of a billion ordinary people. A billion exceptional stories.

PART ONE
Prithvi / *Earth*

2012

Plop

The body drops with a plop.

The people on the platform waiting for the Mumbai local train were like vultures. They let the first wave of passengers off the train, then rushed in like a deluge, a mass of heads and limbs and bellies, icky, sticky, yucky. He'd got stuck in their midst. The train started to move. Panic gripped him. The next station would be even more crowded. He pleaded to be let out. The sea parted. Someone gave him a light push. Someone held out a hand. Someone pulled him out. On the platform, a spasm went up his body. His injured leg gave way. Plop.

A crowd now gathers around him, leads him to a bench. He raises his hand to thank them.

When the next train arrives, another human scuffle ensues. This time, a little girl is ejected. She falls and bruises her knee. Her mother brings her to the bench. The girl sits, looks at him. Something passes between their eyes.

'What's your name?' she asks, her eyes still teary from the fall. In her curiosity, she's forgotten about her leg hurting.

He shakes his head.

The girl sticks her tongue out, like a friend has been naughty in class. She whispers, 'You don't know your name?'

He shakes his head again. Once upon a time, he had many names, many homes, many friends. Now he has none. Suddenly he wants to tell all this to the little girl.

The girl's mother walks up to them. She was busy picking up the vegetables strewn across the platform when her daughter fell. 'Chalo, let's go home fast-fast. Everyone will be waiting for me to make dinner.' She dusts her daughter down and takes her away. The girl looks back at him and winks before disappearing from sight.

He remains sitting.

It is November already. The ancient Mayan calendar predicted that the world will end on 22nd December 2012. Everyone seems excited, movies have been made, restaurants are offering end-of-the-world discounts, shopping malls have set up themed play areas.

His world has already ended, or at least the world he knew, the one he'd built. He is thirty years old, and doesn't even know what name to call himself by.

1980s

Jejus

'What is your name?' Papa asked in English, the foreign words sounding funny in his mouth.

It was the same ritual every evening. Papa would come back from the office and change into his kurta-pyjama. Ma would bring out steaming-hot chai and Marie biscuits. Then they'd sit him down on a stool, his legs swinging as he faced the three-seater sofa on which Ma and Papa sat at opposite ends, and the interrogation would begin.

'Shoob-uncle Dee-ve-di.'

Ma closed her eyes and shook her head. 'He's three and he can't even say his name!' She wiped beads of sweat off her forehead with the pallu of her saree.

Papa raised his palm, as if to tell Ma he had this under control, then turned back. 'Let's try again, beta. What is your name?' He'd fallen into Hindi but corrected himself to finish in English. His voice was indulgent, encouraging.

'Shoob-uncle Dee-ve-di.' He said it slowly this time. Then, before his parents could react, he pointed to the calendar on the wall, unmoving in the thick summer air. 'One nine eight five,' he painstakingly read out, to show them he could say the numbers.

A smile escaped Papa's lips. Papa found everything he did

9

fascinating, unlike Ma, who never seemed to be impressed enough, always goading him on to do more.

'Yes, beta, the year is 1985. But first, you have to say your name properly, na? Otherwise how will you get admission into the convent school? It is the best in all of Lucknow.'

Ma reached out and straightened his collar, brushed strands of hair off his forehead, then patted his cheek. 'What is your name?' Her English was funnier than Papa's.

'Shoob-uncle Dee-ve-di.'

Papa put the teacup down and sighed. 'Uff, we are Tri-ve-di. Dwivedi is the uncle down the street.'

He couldn't tell the difference; they sounded the same to his ears. 'Who is better? Them or us?'

'Both are high-caste Brahmins. But our ancestors knew three Vedas; theirs knew only two.'

'What are Vedas?'

'They are holy books, son. They have everything one needs to know.'

'Have you read all three, Papa?'

'Okay, enough now.' Ma put her teacup down too, struggling a bit because of her big tummy, where the baby was asleep. She slid across to the centre of the sofa, and the tummy seemed to move slightly after her, like a separate object. She looked sideways at Papa as though she'd given him enough time to do this his way, and was now taking control.

'Don't you want to be like your Nana-ji? He was an *engineer*,' she said to her son, mouthing the word carefully, like she was uttering something holy. 'He used to say – *I have built one of the first bridges of independent India, and I have made sure it is strong enough to keep standing when our dear country turns hundred!*'

He knew this. Ma said it every time they crossed the bridge over the river.

'Shoob-uncle Dee-ve-di.'

'Badmaash!' Papa looked genuinely angry now, his nostrils flared a little. Papa didn't like Ma praising her father, the *engineer*, because Papa wasn't an engineer himself. Just like *he* didn't like it when Ma praised the Dwivedis' twin daughters. *So pretty, so well-behaved.* Their names were even more difficult to pronounce than his own.

Papa gave him a tug on his arm. 'If you don't say your name properly, you will have it from me. Do you know how many people Papa had to put maska on to get you this interview at the convent school?'

'And who stood in queues under the scorching sun at all the English-medium schools to get the forms?' Ma lowered her voice as if speaking to herself. 'Keep working like a donkey, not a minute to even read the newspaper ... Wake up before everyone else, cook, pack tiffins, do groceries, bathe and feed the child ...' Ma always spoke in half-sentences when she had to say something Papa wouldn't like hearing.

Ma wagged her finger at him. 'If you don't go to a good school, you'll be stuck in this village. Little people with their little minds and big-big talk.'

Papa turned sharply towards Ma. 'Lucknow is not a village. It is a city with a thousand years of civilization. It was the capital of the Awadh kingdom. This is where the first rebellion against the British Raj was—'

Ma cut Papa off. 'Well, now it's a wasting small-town. It's no Delhi or Bombay.'

His parents fell silent. The whirring of the ceiling fan took over. All he had wanted was to play with them after a day of picking branches alone on the terrace.

'Shubhankar Trivedi.'

The words formed in his mouth like a chemical reaction. His parents turned, shocked. 'Say that again, beta!'

'Shubh-ankar Tri-ve-di.'

Papa clapped so loudly in front of his face it made him blink-blink-blink. 'Now say your mother's name – Vasundhara Trivedi.' He nudged Ma's arm with his elbow and smiled.

She smiled back shyly. 'And your father's name – Ashutosh Trivedi.'

He burst into tears. 'Why are all our names so long?'

For the interview, Ma chose an off-white shirt and long blue shorts that they'd bought at Janpath Market. Nani was there too, and she wouldn't stop talking about what engineers wear to the office. 'Your Nana-ji always wore a white shirt and black trousers. Starched from top to bottom!' She pointed all ten fingers at herself and motioned from head to toe. 'I polished his shoes so perfectly that I could see my face in them!' She looked up fondly at the sky. 'He'd say – *Subhadra, you keep my head held high*.' She raised her voice to get Ma's attention.

But Ma wasn't listening. She was focused on the clothes and their price tags, going through combinations of shirts, trousers, socks, shoes under the harsh tube-lights in the small dark shop. As he tried them on, Ma and Nani commented on whether the shirt was too loose, the shorts too long, the socks too high.

Ma made her decision. Nani raised her eyebrows and stared at the checked linoleum floor, her look when she disagreed. This led to an argument between mother and daughter, neither willing to give in even though the afternoon heat parched their throats. Nani finally conceded. 'Who am I to say anything? I'm just a poor old widow.'

'You'll see when he wears them.' Ma had the final word, she always did.

But on the day of the interview, Papa thought the shorts

were too baggy, like a police havaldar's, touching the knees, and the shirt didn't look *rich enough*.

'That is because we aren't rich,' Ma said. 'I wanted to buy good fabric from Siyaram's and get the clothes stitched by Master-ji, but that would have been double the price.' Ma looked like she was going to cry. 'Now they'll reject him for his clothes, na?'

Papa rushed to pacify. He said they could keep the shirt but swap the trousers for the brown ones Panna-chacha had gifted last Diwali.

Ma oiled his hair and bathed him with the Palmolive soap that was otherwise kept only for guests. Papa drew a straight partition with a sharp comb, making sure not a single strand of hair stood out, then sprinkled Pond's talcum powder over his neck and massaged it into his skin.

'I don't like this white-white,' he protested.

'Arre, how will you smell good otherwise? What will the principal-madam say?' Papa teased.

At the school, they waited outside the principal's office. He wandered around the long stone corridors, but Ma ordered him not to stray too far. 'When they call your name, smartly raise your hand.' Her bump was larger now, and she was always short of breath.

When they were finally called in, he saw that the principal's office was crowded. The walls were covered with shields and certificates. There was a large photo of a woman frowning at them. A plaque underneath announced her name – SISTER BENEDICTA. Did no one in Lucknow have a short name?

Next to the photo was the statue of a bearded man on a cross, quite naked, little red streams flowing down parts of his body. He couldn't take his eyes off this person. Ma noticed this and whispered in his ear, 'If the principal asks who that is, remember to say Jejus. It's their god, okay?'

He wanted to ask why the gods at home looked so well-fed and content while this principal's god looked so sad and thin.

Just then, the lady in the photo entered. She was shorter, though the frown was the same. She wore a grey saree tightly draped around her petite frame, pleats pinned in places. His parents half-lifted themselves from their seats. The lady waved, and they let their suspended bodies drop back to the chairs. They held their breaths while she ruffled through some papers. Then she looked up at Papa.

'What is your profession, Mr Trivedi?' The principal's English was different, smooth and rounded. A large cross with the same Jejus hung from her neck. Shubhankar worried that all this dangling would make the god bleed more.

'I am foreman at fertilizer factory,' Papa replied, stuttering mid-sentence. Shubhankar had never heard Papa's voice so soft. Papa's face went red and little streams of sweat flowed down the sides. He added 'dear madam' as an afterthought.

'And what was your father's profession?' The principal seemed very interested in their family.

'He was freedom fighter, dear madam. In fact, he fought with Gandhi-ji in freedom struggle.' Shubhankar knew Gandhi-ji. He'd seen photos of the bald, weak-looking man, a white cloth around his shoulders. Papa shifted in his seat. 'After independence, he was in railways, dear madam.'

Ma leaned forward and cleared her throat. She had sat with her mouth half-open, anticipating a question. But the principal looked surprised, as if she'd only just noticed this woman in the room. 'My father was chief engineer in Public Works Division. He made all roads and bridges in Lucknow.' Ma glanced with pride at Papa, who mouthed something. Ma got the hint and quickly added, 'Dear madam.'

The principal made some notes, then asked them to wait

outside. She said she wanted to talk to the child alone. He held on to Ma's hand, but she disentangled his fingers and perched him up on the chair.

'So, son,' the principal said. 'What is your name?'

Here it was. The ultimate test. He took a deep breath and opened his mouth.

'Shoob-uncle Dee-ve-di.'

His heart sank. He opened his mouth to try again, but the principal was already asking, 'And your parents' names?' His mind went blank. He looked up at Jejus for help. But no, he seemed to have lost all sound in his throat. The principal now picked up a block. 'What colour is this, son?'

This he knew. He felt more confident. 'Red.'

'It's maroon.' The principal sounded disappointed. He felt deflated. Was this woman going to report his failure to Ma and Papa? She played with the tips of her fingers trying to decide what to ask next. Then she pointed to the statue on the wall. 'Do you know who that is?'

'Jejus!'

A smile appeared on the principal's face. She nodded her head several times, then rang the bell for her assistant, who escorted him out into the arms of his parents. 'What did she ask? Did you answer all the questions?' Their voices were high with hysteria.

He felt a hollowness in his stomach as if his body were in free fall and would hit the ground any minute. 'I want to do potty,' he cried.

The assistant laughed at this. His parents squirmed. 'Let's go home first, okay?'

On the rickshaw ride home, when he was feeling better, he asked Papa, 'Did Dada-ji really know Gandhi-ji?'

Ma burst into a laugh. 'He once saw Gandhi-ji at a rally, and told the whole mohalla that Gandhi-ji waved at him.

People of that generation – everyone thought they were a freedom fighter!'

Papa wasn't happy. 'Your Dada-ji *did* fight for independence. Otherwise we'd still be polishing the shoes of the British.'

Ma's reply came quick. 'Yes, your Dada-ji drove out the firangs, then brought me into the family to polish everyone's shoes.'

Shubhankar looked this way and that, as his parents stared out on both sides. Ma's locks were flying wildly in the hot wind. He wanted to reach out and tuck them behind her ears.

A few days later, a neatly sealed letter arrived in the post – a brown envelope with Papa's name typed on a white sticker. Ma placed it on top of the fridge, out of Shubhankar's reach. But she brought it down every few minutes, turning it around, holding it up to the sunlit window, washing and drying her hands before she touched it, careful not to smear turmeric or chilli powder.

Nani came in the afternoon as usual. When Ma told her about the letter, Nani went straight to the puja-room, where her gods were sitting pink and pretty, covered in flowers and ornaments. She lit incense sticks and walked around the house, motioning for the fragrant smoke to reach far and wide. 'This here is God's blessing,' she told Shubhankar. 'It must touch every corner of the house.' He followed Nani around, directing the smoke to parts that had gone neglected.

Ma must have called Papa from the neighbour's new phone, because as soon as he came home, he drew out a long sharp thing from his bag like he was pulling out a sword. A *paper-cutter*. He'd borrowed it from the office stationery. He cut through the top of the envelope, blew for the brown paper to part, then pulled out a crisp folded sheet. As he read it, Papa's lips turned upward in a full smile. He put his arms around Ma's large frame, barely reaching her shoulders across the bump. Shubhankar had never seen his parents hug before. 'Our son is going to go to an English-medium convent school!' Papa's voice quivered. He paused after each word to let it sink in.

Ma bent to pick Shubhankar up, then realized she wouldn't be able to, her bump coming in the way. Nani popped her knuckles over her ears to ward off the evil eye. She said through tears, 'How much I've heard from everyone all my life for bearing a daughter and no son! Now *you* will make me proud, won't you?'

Shubhankar pointed to Ma's bump. 'But what if she's a girl? Will Ma hear from everyone too?' He was sure there was a sister inside.

Ma scowled. 'Don't mind Nani. She's so old-fashioned! Boy or girl, Papa and I will be very happy either way.' Nani laughed it off, then ran to the puja-room to get a box of sweets. They broke one and stuffed it into Shubhankar's mouth.

That evening, they dressed him up in the interview clothes, saying these were auspicious. They bought sweets for Papa to distribute in the office, and planned the dinner they would host for relatives, acknowledging the role of Panna-chacha's gifted trousers. They went to the Hanuman temple in the mohalla, where Papa shoved a large donation of ten rupees into the box, and Nani shoved another ten rupees into Shubhankar's pocket. They rang the bell furiously, Papa lifting Shubhankar up so he could reach the gong.

As they were leaving, Shubhankar said, 'From now on, we should pray to Jejus.'

Nani jumped. 'Chhee-chhee, no need to pray to Christian

gods. Remember we have so many of our own. Keeping them happy only is a full-time job.' She looked away and muttered, 'What-what these parents of today will do to teach their children English. What was the point of fighting the British if all we wanted was to be like them?'

Ma placed a conciliatory hand on Nani's back. 'Relax, Amma. At least it's Jejus. Not some Allah-vallah.'

2012

Macro

'It's like Mr Dwivedi's car.' Ma's voice is chirpy, even though she's trying to hush.

Papa's voice arrives in static waves on the phone.

'Yes, then I guess it's not very fancy.' Ma sounds deflated. 'What do I know about cars?'

He can hear Ma and Papa through the wall, though he tries not to listen. They're speaking in whispers about him, like co-investigators discussing a suspect during an interrogation. When he came back that evening and told Ma about the purchase, her eyes lit up, part surprise, part elation. It was her wish of many years, her son driving her around in his own car. From convent education to car ownership, the Indian middle-class dream had finally come full circle.

But Papa is right. The car he has bought is nothing fancy. It is indeed like Mr Dwivedi's. They've seen it parked outside the neighbour's home in Lucknow for years.

Earlier that day, when he walked into a Suzuki showroom, the Sikh salesman danced around him like a child trying to sell India flags at Mumbai traffic signals, the fluorescent-pink turban glowing under harsh white lights. 'Sir, this one is perfect to take the entire family out. I personally own this,' the salesman said, almost leading him by the hand to a big SUV. When he moved away, the salesman pointed to another shiny sedan. 'And that one, sir, o-ho-ho-ho, what to say! Perfect to take your girlfriend out on a weekend drive! I personally own that one too!' The salesman squinted to get a pulse of his customer's needs.

But the customer walked up to a basic grey hatchback, having made up his mind even before he'd entered the shop. He paid the full amount in cash. It depleted his bank account by more than half. But he doesn't want debts, payment plans, anything that carries into the future.

'You will have to sign up for driving lessons, na?' Ma says now, coming to his room after she's done talking to Papa.

He nods. 'Yes, but I just need to get to the office and back.'

'No! Why just that?' Ma dismisses him with a flick of her fingers. 'We'll go on long drives . . . to Matheran, to Maha-baleshwar.' He knows Ma has a list of places in mind, ideas for weekend getaways that never happen. Usually Ma drags him to a newly opened mall, springing up like shrubs across the landscape of Mumbai. Sometimes they spot yesteryears' movie stars and forgotten celebrities, and this leaves Ma very excited for days, something she can tell her friends in the building. He can see that she is trying hard to keep things happy, to keep him energized.

After the fall on the platform that morning, he'd sat on the bench for an hour, waiting for the trembling in his bad leg to stop. Then he'd walked out of the train station and into the showroom. He decided he couldn't endure public transport any more. There'd been a time, back when he was new to this city, when he walked with a heady airiness, his steps springing with confidence, when the Mumbai local train was an adventure. He would lean out of the doors and let the hot winds caress his face, stretch his hand out. One time, he caught bits of paper flying in the other direction, a clandestine love letter someone was tearing up in another compartment. He'd tried piecing it together after he'd come home. It was in Marathi, and he didn't fully understand the local language.

But all that was before the . . . the *incident*.

Not any more. Now his body is broken, his mind a mush. He is *in recovery*, as the psychologist termed it. In one of their sessions, the psychologist asked him to beware of *micro-aggressions*.

But nothing here is micro, he wanted to tell her. This whole country, this city, people screaming, horns honking, vendors hawking, passers-by shoving, dogs barking, coconuts breaking on the ground unannounced, every corner and every moment here is *macro*. Being wary of aggressions here means being wary of life itself.

He looks at Ma as she narrows her eyes on her phone screen. She catches him looking and breaks into a smile. 'Let's call Nani and give her the good news. How proud she'll be! First car in the family!'

He can hear Nani's phone ringing, then a loud, 'Hellooooo?'

'Amma!' Ma says indulgently into the phone and winks at him. 'Listen to what mischief your grandson was up to today! Just like when he was in school . . .'

1990s

Namaste

'Give me a word without vaowls,' Miss Lucy said, her lips sealed in a smile, hands clasping the chalk at her breasts.

It was one of her googlies. First she'd said every word needed to have at least one vowel, then she'd asked this. Not that the boys cared. They focused on the red lipstick, the tight blouse, the pencil skirt, the way she'd said *vaowls*.

Shubhankar thought about how Chintoo would mimic Miss Lucy when they were at home, the English words sounding delicious. *Dah-lingsss, time for some prow-nouns.* Chintoo jiggled his flat chest.

'A E I O U . . . what are these?' Chintoo would ask Ma.

'Vaa-vels.'

Chintoo would laugh. 'Chhee! They're *vaowls*. Like Miss Lucy says!'

This made Papa grin with glee. He was always urging the boys to speak English at home. 'Ashutosh Trivedi's sons are going to become CEOs in America!' The boys weren't sure what a *sea-ee-oh* meant, but Chintoo thought these were people who lived under the sea because they had lots of money.

The thought now made Shubhankar smile. This caught Miss Lucy's eye. 'Shub-ank-ah, anything funny, dear?'

He shook his head, cheeks flushed from the attention.

He'd rather sit in his corner and look out of the window. His eyes fell on the book of hymns. They'd just come back from the chapel, and the little blue book with its crowded words in tiny print was still on the table. A blue cloth bookmark hung like a tail.

'Hymn,' he said without thinking. 'That's a word without vowels.'

Miss Lucy looked disappointed. She liked asking confusing questions and doing grand reveals at the end of the period. 'Well done, Shub-ank-ah!' She managed a pasty smile and threw him an orange lozenge. She had a stash of these locked up inside the desk. She was the only teacher who rewarded correct answers. Unlike Hindi-sir, in whose lessons the only way to know they'd got the right answer was when they weren't being rapped on the knuckles with a wooden ruler.

Shubhankar slipped the lozenge into his bag. He knew he had permission to eat it in class, but he was going to show it off to Chintoo first. Chintoo was always doing big things, like singing onstage during assembly, or making friends with older boys. That baby in Ma's tummy was now five years old. When Ma had gone to the hospital, Shubhankar had been left alone with Nani and Papa. He'd missed Ma, and was scared for her. Nani had said twenty-eight was too old to have a baby. So when Ma came back in one piece, Shubhankar was so happy he didn't care he'd wanted a sister.

It was he who'd named his brother Chintoo, the small, gurgling, burping, farting creature. His parents nodded in approval, but a few days later Papa said, 'Your brother's good name is Chitrankar Trivedi. You can call him Chintoo at home, and at school your names will be matching-matching!' Papa waited for him to show appreciation. He knew of all the effort they'd put into naming the baby. They'd argued, sourced recommendations, consulted holy men, dipped into the epics.

But he couldn't help saying, 'Yet another long name! And why don't *I* have a nickname?'

'Because, beta, you are the eldest son, and your name should carry the pride of the family!' Papa's forefinger pointed upward, like a sage declaring a cosmic truth.

Miss Lucy was now saying, 'Hymn – this is the *only* word in the English language without vaowls. Isn't that delightful?' She threw Shubhankar another lozenge.

Everyone turned to look. He could see they were impressed. These little successes were accidents. Otherwise, Shubhankar was always middling in class, never scoring high, never showing a flair for any subject, even extra-curriculars. *Average.* Ma and Papa riddled him with questions. *Who came first in class? Did you get selected for the school play? Are you in the parade on sports day?* They fed him carrots and spinach, spooned Horlicks and Chyavanprash into his mouth, tested his mental maths on the fly, made him read the newspaper every day.

Chintoo fought back on his behalf. 'Did you come first in class, Papa? Can I see your report card, Ma?' Shubhankar observed his younger brother in wonder. He was eight, yet it had never occurred to him to talk back to Ma and Papa in this way. Chintoo misplaced books, forgot lunch-boxes, soiled his uniform, then stomped around like he wouldn't do it any differently. Their parents brushed it off with a smile. *The younger one's so naughty, so restless.*

Results days were the worst. Ma's anger was like rotting fruit, the stench growing with every passing minute. 'What are we sacrificing for? We don't even have a TV so that you boys aren't distracted from your studies.' And when they finally got a colour Nelco TV that half the mohalla came to watch on Sunday mornings, she changed her scolding to, 'What use is this? Let's sell it tomorrow only.'

Nani joined in. 'I grew up in a house with seventeen-seventeen cousins.' She held up her fingers even though she had only ten of them. 'The boys would eat first before we girls could fight over what was left.' Chintoo tried not to giggle. Nani continued uninterrupted, 'You've never known what it means to go hungry, to pack your things during the night and move into relatives' houses the next morning.'

She repeated the story she'd told many times. 'My father had a successful zari business in Moradabad. But during the Partition, his Muslim business partner decided to up and leave for Pakistan.' At this point in her story, her eyes became distant, wistful. 'Nawaz-bhai. I still remember him. He was so well-settled in this country all his life, but suddenly he was so keen to flee to another country he'd never been to, knew nothing about. And so . . . our zari business collapsed, partly because the shop was destroyed in the Partition riots, partly because my father lost his will to rebuild by himself. And we had to move in with relatives, a small house . . . We were seventeen cousins under one roof!'

By now, Chintoo would move on to fidgeting with something, taking advantage of Nani being distracted. This would snap Nani back to the present. 'And look at you two! So well taken care of. And yet, no gratitude!'

The boys thought they'd got really unlucky with grandparents. Everyone else seemed to have loving ones who bought them chocolates and sang them lullabies. They longed for the other three illustrious grandparents who'd died before they were born. Dada-ji had fought on Gandhi-ji's team for something called *independence*, Nana-ji had built bridges that would never fall, and Dadi-ji must've been a great cook because

Papa was always telling Ma how his mother's food had tasted better.

'God should send them back and take Nani in return,' was Chintoo's assessment of the fiasco.

'Miss Lucy wants to see you tomorrow.'

The plan had struck Shubhankar on the way home. The mid-term results were out and his marks were average again. He'd spent all day thinking about how to stop Ma from getting angry, until this brilliant idea came to him on the school bus. He ran to the door before Chintoo, bag swinging violently this way and that.

'What does that woman want to see me for?' Ma's spine stiffened. She didn't like Miss Lucy much. Shubhankar had seen Ma in previous parent–teacher meetings – how she stood in Papa's shadow, opening her mouth but no words coming out, thoughts forming in Hindi but not translating into English. Ma, who never stopped talking at home, was dumb as a puppet in front of this foreign woman, staring at Miss Lucy's pointy red heels, twisting the pallu of her cotton saree around her forefinger.

The plan worked. Ma spent all evening obsessing about this meeting, forgetting to ask about his report card. When Papa came home, she convinced him to take a half day's leave from work and come with her. 'I don't understand half of what that firang says. Why is she still here? Shouldn't she have gone back to England with her grandfather in 1947?'

Papa smiled indulgently. 'You should be grateful. That woman could've lived a life of comfort in her country. Instead she's stewing in this heat, teaching our children English so they can make something of their lives.' Papa never hid his admiration for Miss Lucy. 'Don't you see how integrated she is into our culture? She starts every meeting with a "namaste"!'

But the next morning, Papa got a call from his boss Mr Kaushik, whose word he treated more dearly than god's word. Ever since they'd got a phone line installed, after a wait of five years, the boss would call at any time, and Papa would drop everything and rush to the office.

So Ma went to meet Miss Lucy alone. Even though Shubhankar had made this meeting up, he knew Miss Lucy would find something to say. She loved meeting parents, speaking away in English, never waiting for replies, most parents struggling to keep up.

Miss Lucy joined her palms, her cleavage peeping out of her blouse. Ma averted her gaze. 'Namaste, Mrs Trivedi. So nice to see you.'

'Hello,' Ma replied, weight shifting from one foot to another.

Miss Lucy didn't disappoint. 'Did you know that Shubank-ah is an excellent artist?' She went to the cupboard, her heels tap-tapping, and brought out the sketches he'd made in art class. She placed them one by one on the table – a giraffe, a village market, and one that Miss Lucy said was her favourite – of Jesus. 'Aren't these just lovely? Who'd say he's only eight? Your son is very talented, Mrs Trivedi!'

Ma let her tense body slouch with relief. 'Thank you very much. Yes, very good.' She squeezed his shoulder and gave him a smile.

Shubhankar didn't care for his sketches or what anyone thought of them. He was just glad that the mid-term results had come and gone without event.

2012

Bridge

He sketches, the soft scribbles of the pencil cutting through the heavy December air. Ma is watering the plants on the balcony. They somehow manage to look lush and vibrant in this dreary place. Ever since she moved to Mumbai three years ago to take care of him, she's been setting up the little garden, buying pots, digging up soil to plant seeds and saplings, trying to grow dhaniya, albeit unsuccessfully.

Papa is here too, reading the newspaper and sipping his evening tea. He is here for the Christmas break. The Mayans fucked up. The world did not end. The restaurants have folded up their discounts, the movies have flopped.

Papa is trying to have a conversation, clearing his throat every now and then, looking at mother and son. Papa comes down from Lucknow every few months, Chintoo does too sometimes. They want to make the most of their time in Mumbai, away from work. But mother and son are used to coexisting in silence. They've been in the same flat every evening, every night, for three years. When he is at work, Ma spends her mornings cooking and cleaning and doing grocery runs. In the afternoons, she watches TV, endless cycles of serials in which mothers-in-law and daughters-in-law engage in one-upwomanship. In the evenings, she goes downstairs to chat to the group of ladies from other flats in the building. At night, sometimes Ma comes to his room, sits next to him, reads a magazine while he stares at his laptop, scrolling up and down Facebook, this thing on which he's just created an account, where people are putting up photos of breakfasts in Bandra, honeymoons in Greece, trips to New York.

'One-hundred-fifty-eight?' Ma once exclaimed as she peeped into his screen. 'See? So many friends you have! Why don't you invite some over? I can cook them a nice meal? And why don't you post something here, like the others?'

He shrugged. He has never posted anything, there is nothing to post, no life updates, no opinions, no airport check-ins.

He now looks at the sketch. They are like child's lines, crooked, shadowy, moody. He has started to sketch again only recently. After the *incident*, it wasn't just his leg; his fingers were no good either. They trembled as he drew, the nerves twinging in his arm. One time, the pencil flew out and hit the wall with such violence that Ma came running, fear in her eyes. She took the sketchbook away, slowly disentangling his fingers. 'Try again later,' she said softly.

'What are you drawing?' Papa now asks.

'Nothing . . . just . . .' he replies, then adds, 'the psychologist has asked me to draw whatever comes to mind.'

Ma grunts as she enters from the balcony, the water-can dripping, leaving spots on the mosaic floor as she walks across the room. She mutters under her breath, 'I don't know what bak-bak he does with this psychologist. And here I am, sitting all day, but he won't say a word to me.' Ma doesn't like the idea of him, *her son*, being in therapy.

Papa turns away. He never asks about the therapy. He avoids asking about things he doesn't understand, lest he not know what to say in response. He finally says, 'Beta, I think it's time to apply for an MBA. You can get in anywhere – Harvard,

Stanford, Yale . . .' Papa has said this before, wanting him to get on with his life. According to Papa, his recovery is complete – he is back at his job, his body is coming together, the limp only slight these days. 'You should think about advancing your career.'

He looks back to his nascent sketch, doesn't say anything.

Papa lets out a laugh to lighten the mood. 'These American colleges, they have funny names, na? Kellogg, like the cornflakes.'

Ma giggles at this silly joke. He smiles too. This is what his parents' courtship would have looked like if they hadn't had an arranged marriage without ever meeting. They'd only seen one another in photographs, a single one of each, black and white, high resolution, clicked in a local studio, the flashlights strong to make their brown skin tones lighter. These two photos are in their wedding album, on the first page, prelude to the story of their union – Papa trying to look smart, head held straight, chin pointing towards the camera; Ma shy and demure, looking down. Nothing like how they are in real life.

Ma and Papa see him smiling and are encouraged. 'Or Carnegie *Melon*,' Papa adds to his previous joke, shaping his palms as though holding a fruit.

His parents think that they are all on a bridge, walking towards each other, keen to meet at a middle point.

He is trying too, to limp towards the midpoint.

But first he needs to forgive them. The problem is he doesn't know how.

1990s

Rye-ot

Shubhankar opened his eyes to mild darkness, and turned to check on Chintoo. The boy was asleep, like a Kumbhakaran, a minuscule version of the sleeping giant. Should he drop something and wake Chintoo up? His eyes roamed for something to knock over. The Ludo board was on the table, the tokens still in place. Last night, Ma had stopped them mid-game, insisting it was bedtime. Chintoo had negotiated that the board remain untouched.

It was warm for a December morning, because Nani had shut all the windows again. Usually on a winter's night, she'd wrap herself in a shawl, and hold a hot-water bottle to her joints, but wouldn't dare shut the windows. Papa's instructions were to leave them open, and Nani never disobeyed her son-in-law. 'If you don't get fresh oxygen while sleeping, you won't wake up any more,' Chintoo had explained to Shubhankar. But these past couple of nights, Nani had obsessively shut all the windows. The brothers were surprised Papa hadn't said anything. 'At this rate,' Chintoo had said last night, 'the windows will never open again. I hope the first one to die is Nani.'

Chintoo was angry because Nani had called Miss Lucy to complain about the role he'd been given in the school Christmas play. 'Arre, how dare she make you some sheep-veep?

My grandson is fit to be a king!' She'd pinched Chintoo's cheek and promised, 'Just see how I whistle the whole time you're onstage.'

But now school had closed suddenly, and they weren't sure the performance was going to happen.

Walking to the dining table, Shubhankar heard Ma and Papa speak in whispers. They split apart instantly on seeing him. Papa put down the newspaper and left the room.

Ma turned to him. 'Just because there's no school doesn't mean you can forget your studies. Brush your teeth, have breakfast and start solving some sums.'

Ma put out four slices of toast with jam and butter. The sides were slightly burnt, and Shubhankar wanted to send them back, like they'd once done in a dhaba when they'd discovered a strand of hair in the saag-paneer.

Absent-mindedly, he opened the newspaper. Sprawled across the front page was a massive picture, like an advertisement. A dome and many men on top. The surroundings seemed hazy, the picture was grainy. The headline read:

6TH DECEMBER 1992 – A BLACK DAY FOR INDIAN SECULARISM.

And in smaller letters – *Babri Masjid demolition in Ayodhya sparks riots across country.*

'What's demolition?' he asked. Within seconds, Ma was at his side, wresting the newspaper out of his hands. A bit from the corner tore in the struggle. He held on to the scrap in surprise. 'What's ree-ot?' he asked as she walked away. He could hear her scolding Papa for being careless with the newspaper.

'Arre, he's ten. He should know what's happening in the world,' Papa replied, then peeped in and winked at him. 'Beta, it's not ree-ot, it's *rye-ot.*' Papa opened his mouth wide to enunciate, then hummed his way to the bathroom.

Shubhankar bit into the toast and watched the crumbs fall on the plate. The buttered ones stuck around his mouth. He scraped them off with his fingers, lost in thought. What had happened to the Babri Masjid? What did a *rye-ot* mean? Men getting on domes? But why were they climbing on top of mosques across the country?

When Chintoo woke, the brothers finished the game of Ludo. Chintoo won and marched around with a victorious air. Shubhankar wanted to tell Chintoo he was distracted because of these rye-ots, but he didn't know enough to answer Chintoo's questions. He didn't want to look stupid.

Later that day, Nani left for her house. She'd been staying with them since school had shut two days ago. 'If I don't switch on the lights, they'll come in and loot everything,' she said. Then she turned to the boys and added, 'Listen to me, you are my two little pahalwans, na? There are some bad-bad things happening out there, so will you stay alert and guard your parents while I'm gone?' She produced two sweets from the pallu of her saree, placing one in the palm of each grandson.

Chintoo happily bit into the sweet, agreeing to a temporary truce with Nani. But Shubhankar followed the grown-ups from the corner of his eyes, trying to read their lips when Papa offered to accompany Nani to her house because it wasn't safe outside.

That night, Ma refused to let them watch *Chitrahaar* on TV. She gave no reason. Chintoo was inconsolable. 'But you promised we could watch film songs every Wednesday!'

Ma gave Chintoo one smack on the head. 'The whole world is falling apart and look at this one!' Papa tried to pacify them, but Ma was adamant. The boys were sent off to bed early. He could hear Chintoo sniffing, but soon those turned into light snores. Kumbhakaran!

Shubhankar heard Papa switch on the TV for the nine p.m. news on Doordarshan. He sneaked out of bed and peeped through the bedroom door Ma always left ajar. Good thing there was no Nani tonight – when Nani watched TV, she looked around herself more than she looked at the screen. If she saw one of the boys peeping, she would act like she hadn't noticed, let the boy settle in, then throw her shawl at him like a bird-catcher trapping their prey. 'Did you think Nani won't notice because she's old?' she would say triumphantly, grabbing the boy's arm and holding her prize up for Ma to see.

Tonight, Papa kept the volume low. Shubhankar strained his ears to listen. Then the video appeared. Hordes of men raced towards the three domes of an ancient monument, made of old greyish-brown stone. The mosque looked worn out, like it needed a coat of paint. Some men were already on the domes. They carried sticks and swords and trishuls, raised their hands and chanted, danced. Their bodies squirmed in the dust. Many had saffron bands around their heads, waved saffron flags. Then they started beating the domes with axes and hammers. More joined in, until there were hundreds, banging, chipping away at the stone. The next shot was of the domes falling – the left one, then the right one, finally the largest and central one.

Shubhankar's feet were riveted to the ground. The newscaster was back on TV, saying something about this sixteenth-century mosque in Ayodhya. She spoke in difficult Hindi, words he didn't understand. *Loktantra. Sangharsh. Jaativad.* Then someone else was speaking, in English. *Disputed site. Hindu nationalist parties. A rally that got out of hand. Police looking the other way. Army called in.* It all sounded like gibberish. He felt light-headed and sat on his haunches, back against the wall.

The newscaster was now talking about the riots, listing fires, damage to property, curfew timings. Her commentary was accompanied by videos of empty streets, overturned carts, rows of policemen. She named cities where violence had sparked after the mosque was demolished. Shubhankar heard *Lucknow*. Sweat broke out on his scalp. Were they coming to his city? If the mosque could crumble and fall, what chance did their house have? He let out half a gasp, gulped down the rest. He thought he saw Ma's head turn. Had he made a sound? He crawled silently back, climbed on to the bed, and covered himself with the quilt.

All night, half-awake, half-asleep, he saw those men, dancing, hitting, banging on the dome. This is why school had shut, why Papa had stopped going to the office, why Nani had to go back to her place. When the children had suddenly been brought back from school two days ago, four packed into seats for two in the school bus, more standing in the aisle, they'd been delighted by the surprise holiday. He should've known something was off.

He now focused on Chintoo's snores to calm his mind.

The next morning at breakfast, Shubhankar blurted out, 'Are those men going to attack us?'

Ma continued to pour cornflakes into the warm milk in Chintoo's bowl, trying to look calm, like she'd been expecting the question. 'Not at all,' she finally said. 'We are Hindus. Those men are also Hindus.'

'So are they going after Muslims?'

'Uff! Eat your food,' she said, giving up her feigned patience.

Malti-didi was doing the dishes in the kitchen. She said as if to herself but loud enough for everyone to hear, 'Who asked Muslims to build their mosque on the very spot that our Lord Ram was born? Don't Hindus have the right to pray there? This is our land, but these Muslims have built mosques at every place holy to us.' For the time Malti-didi was in the house, she made sure her opinion on everything was known, from the price of dal to the politics of the day. Ma complained that Malti-didi had too big a mouth for a maid, but she'd been in the family for too long to let go of.

Chintoo counted on his fingers. 'You're right. I see seven mosques on my way to school.'

Buoyed by Chintoo's support, Malti-didi came to the kitchen doorway. Her teeth shone between her purple lips. 'And how many temples, Chintoo-babu?'

'None,' Chintoo replied in an instant. He always knew what people wanted to hear.

'That's not true!' Shubhankar said, glaring at Chintoo. 'I've seen eleven temples on the way to school; twelve, if you count the holy tree in the middle of the road.'

'Okay, that's enough!' Ma ordered, making a face at Malti-didi. 'We have Lekha-bua's wedding coming soon, so it's a good thing your school has shut. You can now enjoy all you want!' Lekha-bua was Papa's favourite cousin, and the entire family had been waiting eagerly for the five days of festivities.

'But will the Muslims attack the wedding?' Shubhankar was still spinning off scenarios from what he'd seen last night.

'Not at all.' Ma shook her head. 'Suresh-mausa will be there himself, and he will have security guards all over.'

Suresh-mausa was at every family function, always wearing a khadi kurta-pyjama, Nehru jacket, rimless glasses, a vermilion teeka on his forehead. He had a thin moustache, oiled and curled perfectly at both ends. Chintoo found it impressive, once suggesting that Papa do the same. Even the children knew that Suresh-mausa was a bada aadmi, a powerful man who could make things happen.

'Is Suresh-mausa a good guy or a bad guy?' Chintoo asked, dipping his fingers in the milk to fish out soggy cornflakes. 'He is always so glum, and when he laughs, he sounds like Mogambo and Shakaal.' The brothers giggled. They had a joke about Suresh-mausa owning a den where pretty women in gold bikinis danced to save their lives and crocodiles swam in boiling red water, just like the villains in movies.

'He's a good man,' Ma said, trying not to look at Chintoo's milk-stained fingers. 'He keeps his promises. In the last elections, he promised a TV to people who didn't have one, and now Malti-didi has a TV!'

'Can he get me a Walkman?' Chintoo's eyes widened. 'Dhruv's uncle got him one from America!' Chintoo never missed a chance to mention his friend Dhruv and the illustrious uncle. Shubhankar wanted to tease him, but Chintoo looked genuinely sad. 'Why don't we have relatives in America? Then we would be rich too.'

'Arre, Chintoo-babu,' Malti-didi's voice was sympathetic. 'Let us only move to Umrika. Everyone there is rich and happy.' She threw up her hands like a circus clown. 'No Hindu–Muslim kich-kich also!'

At this, Ma broke into laughter, covering her mouth. This was such a rare sight that the boys threw their spoons down and ran to hug her.

Yagna

The flashing light illuminated half of Ma's face, Nani's greying hair, Papa's kurta, dyeing them in red hues one by one. The white Ambassador car trundled through the streets as the siren shrieked. Chintoo tried to stick his neck out. Ma pulled him in and rolled up the window. Then they sat in silence, as if on their way to school on a Monday rather than to a wedding.

Shubhankar leaned his face against the glass. This was the first time he'd left home since those men had brought down the mosque. He'd expected to see rye-ots. Instead, the streets were dead. Sometimes they crossed groups of men with sticks standing at junctions, but they seemed lazy, smoking beedis, their guards down.

'Are those someone's intestines?' Shubhankar asked, pointing to what some stray dogs were fighting over, teeth gnarled. Chintoo slid across, eager to look.

'No, beta, that is a rag-cloth,' Papa said, trying to laugh. He looked nervous himself. 'You can relax. We're in a VIP car with a siren and laal-batti.' He pointed to the roof with the revolving red light. 'Suresh-mausa has personally seen to it.'

Nani tried to distract the boys. 'Now tell me what-what you'll eat at the wedding!' Her printed yellow silk saree gleamed in the dark. When she smiled, the light flashed red on her teeth, making her look like the chudails on *Zee Horror Show*.

*

The brothers walked hand-in-hand to survey the haveli. It was a big mansion – large iron gates with handles shaped like fish, the lawn decorated with strings of lights, a central court-yard where the mandap had been set up, a verandah on the first floor, opening up into many rooms. They were joined by their cousin, Munni-didi, and the twin daughters of their neighbour Mr Dwivedi, Dhwani and Dwiti. Together, they looked like the *Famous Five* quintet.

Ma called the boys into a room. She'd laid out the sher-wanis on the four-poster bed. They'd bought these at the post-Diwali sale in Janpath Market. The silk shone through the plastic covers. She took them out carefully, and the brothers wriggled their thin bodies into the heavy brocade. The stiff collar rubbed against Shubhankar's neck. Ma combed their hair and sprayed scent on their armpits. Chin-too sneezed as the droplets settled on his face, then said, 'In America, they have a scent that you can roll up and down your armpit, no need to spray!'

Ma let the boys go. 'Be good. No badmaashi, okay?' She closed the wooden door behind them. She'd laid out a silk saree and blouse for herself. Her hair was already tied in a fancy bun. Her lips gleamed from the lipstick. Deep black kajal lined her eyes. She looked like those beautiful movie heroines from the 1960s. Like Vyjayanthimala! Shubhankar had never seen Ma like this.

The smell of tuberoses infiltrated his nostrils. The man-dap was still being decorated. Pink hibiscus, yellow marigold, red roses were strewn all over. Manju-chachi, as the sister-in-law of the bride and the hostess of the wedding, sat in the centre of a mattress on the ground, surrounded by other aunties, playing the dholak, singing folk songs like they were reciting multiplication tables. Sounds of shehnai wafted in from the speaker. Shubhankar looked for the waiter. He wanted to grab a Limca while Ma was still getting ready. She didn't allow cold drinks at home. She said it was bad for health, but he'd heard her saying to Papa that they were expensive. Afterwards he would go see Lekha-bua in her bridal dress before she came down for the ceremony. She was his favourite aunt. When Ma was in the hospital for Chintoo's birth, Lekha-bua had minded him during the day. He remembered her being very sweet.

Panna-chacha walked up to Manju-chachi in a huff, sweat shining on his forehead. He was the brother of the bride; managing the event was on his shoulders. He whispered to his wife something about the bride's lehenga-blouse being too tight. They'd sent word to Master-ji to come for an alteration, but given the troubles, they weren't sure the tailor would show up. Manju-chachi passed the dholak to another woman. A bride's blouse couldn't be too tight, it looked indecent, what would people say? She rushed upstairs.

Shubhankar wondered why everyone called the tailor *Master-ji*, as if he were a teacher. Must ask Chintoo, who always had answers to the strangest questions. Shubhankar called for the waiter and picked up another bottle, a Gold Spot this time. Through the arched doorway, he saw two security guards standing to attention, guns perched on their shoulders. At the gate, Suresh-mausa stood straight with hands clasped behind his back, letting most people pass but welcoming only certain old men. Papa stood next to Suresh-mausa, slightly bowed, palms permanently joined in a namaste, head nodding like a wound-up toy's. The bus with the baratis had arrived. The groom would be here soon.

Master-ji's assistant was at the gate. He must've come to fix the bridal lehenga. He was a cheerful guy who joked with Shubhankar and Chintoo whenever they went to the shop with Ma. He was speaking to the guard, who went and whispered in Suresh-mausa's ear, then came back and said something. The assistant looked confused.

Shubhankar tried to remember the assistant's name. Mohsin-bhai? Masood-bhai? One of those Muslim names that started with M. Chintoo would know. He saw Chintoo playing hide-and-seek with the identical Dwivedi twins. *Dhwani Dwivedi, Dwiti Dwivedi, Dhwani Dwivedi, Dwiti Dwivedi* – the brothers had come up with a tongue-twister about them. Shubhankar tried saying it in his head now and still got it wrong.

Guzzling the cold drinks made him burp. He went upstairs, walking from room to room, unnoticed in the hullabaloo. On the verandah, women milled around busily. They seemed to be waiting for Master-ji. Ma looked pretty in her purple silk saree. Someone had stuck a rose in her bun. Shubhankar wanted to tell Ma that the assistant had come, but her gaze glossed over him. He'd never seen Ma like this, not obsessing over her boys, chuckling with her friends. This made him slightly jealous.

Panna-chacha came up the stairs, two steps at a time, declared that they'd found Master-ji's address, Suresh-mausa was sending a car right away. Problem solved! The women rushed to give the bride the good news. Shubhankar wasn't sure why they needed Master-ji when the assistant was already here! But no one was paying him any attention, so he turned right and went down a narrow corridor, then down a rusty spiral staircase, feeling his feet on every step in the darkness.

At the bottom of the stairs, he slipped out into the back-yard, a dank square where the grille from the gate cast long shadows on patches of moss. There was a tube-well with a bucket under the tap, water dripping in a rhythm, tip-tip-tip. He challenged himself to pump water out and drink it at the same time. But his sherwani was too heavy. He began loosening the buttons.

The whole place lit up, like the light-and-sound show he'd once seen at the British Residency complex. He looked back at the wall, the silhouettes of trees dancing in the muted flashes and shadows. He turned to the back gate, caught a movement through the grille, a manic whirl. Instinctively, his fingers pinched the button. The tough thread pricked his skin, making him flinch. He looked back again at the wall, at the gate, at his finger that now had a neat round drop of blood balanced on the surface.

He took a step forward, saw a column of fire with the face of a man on it, flames licking the body, like a mythical creature that had just emerged from the earth in a yagna, an invocation to the gods, features lit up from below and within, balding head, sallow cheeks, large eyes, terrified. He wanted to get a closer look, or run away; instead he stood still, pinched the button harder, felt the wetness on his fingertip as more blood oozed out.

Loud clangs jolted Shubhankar. The man had gripped the grille, was shaking it, trying to climb. He slipped, fell, wriggled vigorously, rolled on the road, rubbed the flames against the mud. Orange dust rose in slow motion. The man stopped and looked at Shubhankar, lips moving, eyes pleading, arms flailing. It was Master-ji's assistant, M . . . How had he come here? Wasn't he inside fixing Lekha-bua's lehenga?

Shubhankar catapulted into action, a million voices whispering in his head and cancelling each other out. *Fill some water in the bucket and throw it on the man. Call for help. Scream. Do something, anything.* His body moved quickly, forcing his frozen mind to thaw. He pumped the tube-well, up-down, up-down, the pinprick on his bleeding finger hurting, water trickling out in weak gushes. He ran to pick the bucket up, kicked it instead. Water splashed all over the ground, wetting his pointed leather jootis, his churidar.

M dragged himself back to the gate, put his hand through the grille, fire passing between the rods like a magician's trick, the flames more violent now. His body hit the gate, a loud metal noise boomed across the yard, overpowering the sounds of shehnai and dholak from the wedding. Shubhankar could only see the eyes now, the nose and chin melting away. M let out a shriek, a deathly, painful, agonizing howl.

Shubhankar screamed too, but no sound came out. He ran, his feet heavy and uncertain; tripped, fell, his face just escaping the ground. He tried to get up, crawled to the gate, sat face to face with M, the crackling of fire on flesh drowning everything else out. He inhaled the stench, pungent, like experiments with sulphur in science class, but also rotten, like the carcass of a dog lying on the street before the municipality cleared it out. They both looked down at the burning arm, both recoiled. Shubhankar looked up at M's face. The eyes were red, like blobs of meat on a skewer held over the tandoor.

Sounds of commotion from the street. Shubhankar lifted himself, banged on the grille. Help was here! Some men appeared, saffron bands tied around their heads. He couldn't tell how many, the flames leaping in front of his eyes. Seeing them, M clung closer to the gate.

The men stopped, surveyed the scene, not surprised, like they'd come looking for M. Had they done this to him? With narrow eyes and knitted brows, they scrutinized the ten-year-old boy in a wedding sherwani, waving his hands, saying something incoherent. One of the men turned around and ran, shouting behind his back. The rest ran too, almost on tiptoes. A lathi fell from a hand, landed on the street, rolled slowly to the drain.

Shubhankar ran towards the haveli. He had to get the grown-ups. Who had the keys to this gate? Who could call in the fire engines? Was there a phone in this rented bungalow? He was halfway across the yard, his foot slipping on the moss, when the gate clanged again. He turned around. M was on his feet, dragging himself down the street. Shubhankar tried to call out, promise he was getting help. But M disappeared around the corner. Spots of light dappled the ground.

Shubhankar walked back to the gate. His stomach churned. A hoarse whimper escaped his throat, a guttural rumbling from inside. The collar rubbed against his neck, the itch of a new rash, fresh, raw. Everything went quiet. Only the sound of water from the tap in slow motion. Tip-tip-tip.

How long had it been? Hours? Minutes? Seconds? He sat through short breaths, heavy from the stench of M's skin. Dried tears and snot on his face. It was over.

The grille was still warm when someone ruffled his hair. He looked up, startled. The security guards had ambled in from behind. They picked him up, one by each arm, walked him to the house, sat him down in the mandap. Lekha-bua and the groom were exchanging garlands. Everyone showered flowers on the newly-weds. He saw Ma's eager face, Nani whistling, Chintoo and the Dwivedi twins competing for petals. He tried to distract himself. *Dhwani Dwivedi, Dwiti Dwivedi*. It didn't help.

In the centre of the mandap, a fire was lit on a pile of crackling wood, the flames greedily gobbling up the rose petals and rice grains.

2012

Vultures

There is a fire burning somewhere far away. From his window in this Mumbai flat, he watches the lines of smoke rise up to the December sky like paintbrush strokes. He wonders whether it is a blaze, or a funeral pyre.

Shraadh, the Hindu funeral rite to bid farewell to the dead, gets its name from *sraddha*, the utmost sincerity with which one is to perform the ceremony. He has never been to one, but he can imagine ghee dripping into the flames, the echoes of chanting mantras.

Other communities have other rituals. Some stand in silence, heads bowed. Some join hands and whisper prayers. Some sit in communion. And some leave their dead to be devoured by vultures, returning to nature what belongs to nature.

But what of those who are never remembered, forcefully forgotten, like they'd never lived, loved, lusted, laughed? What if there is no name to remember them by, no face, just a little something left, a whiff, a crackle, the eyes?

And what of those who have stayed behind with these memories? During the hours he spends on the internet nowadays, he has read up everything he can find on trauma. Seems like there's a theory that those who undergo trauma tend to obliviate the actual moment into blank space, drop it into a crevice between the *before* and *after*.

He wants to ask, but what of those who remember, in every precise detail? What if they can never unsee those few moments, a movie playing in slow motion, on repeat? Those who carry the scars on their bodies, hiding them in expensive fabric. Do the scars not itch when the silk rustles?

He looks up at the few stars piercing through the Mumbai night haze. Now, twenty years later, he knows the answer. He'd tell them, if anyone cared to ask, that those few witnessed moments are what defines everything to come. It sets boundaries around life itself, barbed-wire fences that can never be crossed. Everything he has ever done after that night was because of, propelled by, in service of it, of M.

But that night also freed him, because now he'd seen what no one else had, tasted the world in all its unhinged barbarism.

It is a curse. It is a privilege.

He becomes aware of the scar on his back, his thigh, the nerves tingling in his bad leg, the palpitation in his heart. He walks slowly to the bed. He needs to sit down.

1990s

Shoonya

Shubhankar was slumped on a velvet sofa. The security guards had said they'd found him in the backyard. Ma asked why he was so dishevelled. He mumbled something about tripping and falling, because the security guards were glaring at him, and their look scared him somehow. Then Ma brought him dal-chawal and spooned it into his mouth. He retched, told her he was nauseous. She sat next to him, and he opened his mouth several times to tell her what he'd seen, but Manju-chachi and the other women kept calling Ma over to help with the rituals. Ma whispered in his ear that she'd be back soon and left a water bottle by him. He lay down and closed his eyes. He could feel her hovering now and then, her palm on his forehead, unbuttoning the sherwani, fanning his face with her pallu. He flitted in and out of sleep. When he was awake, he didn't let it show. He tried not to breathe. The air was contaminated. It smelt of burning flesh. When no one was around, he exhaled in gusts, trying to get rid of the stench that had lodged itself inside his nostrils.

The bidaai was nothing like in the movies. It was a rushed affair, no women singing, no throwing of rice back at the family, no tearful goodbyes. Suresh-mausa said times were bad, the ceremony should wrap up soon, standing guard himself at the flowered gateway, supervising the baratis boarding buses. The bride and groom were ushered to their car. Suresh-mausa plucked out the JUST MARRIED sign. Better not to attract attention, he said. A few of his men jumped into jeeps and travelled with the baratis in a convoy. Chintoo and Munni-didi and the Dwivedi twins watched from the first-floor balcony, trying to squeeze in between the grown-ups. Chintoo called for his brother, but Ma said they should let him rest.

Shubhankar must've drifted off, because by the time he registered voices, the bidaai was done, the guests had gone, the shehnai music had stopped. Only known voices of Panna-chacha, Ashok-fufa, Lakki-bhaiyya, Papa seemed in the middle of an argument, speaking softly but with force.

Shubhankar dared not open his eyes. He felt Ma's fingers running through his hair, his head was on her lap. He didn't know how he could tell it was Ma. She hadn't put him to sleep in many years, but who else could it be? He snuggled closer, wanting to catch a whiff of her scent. She hissed and everyone stopped talking. He lay still, not even letting his eyeballs move. It was a sure-shot way of telling if someone was pretending to be asleep. Chintoo did it all the time and got caught. In the lull, he heard jewellery clink. So the women were there too – Manju-chachi, Pushpa-mausi, Aarti-mami, Nani? Though they weren't doing any talking.

Convinced he was still asleep, the men went back to their argument.

'He came to fix Lekha's lehenga!'

'But we called Master-ji! How could we have known that Master-ji would send his assistant?'

'Didn't the guy have any common sense? Which Muslim in these times would come to a Hindu wedding?'

'Such an inauspicious thing to have happened. Please no

one tell Lekha about this. It'll cast a shadow over her marriage forever.'

'So what are we going to do?'

'What's done is done. Suresh-ji has already handled the police. He's explained to Master-ji, who will take care of the rest.'

'Do you think your son saw anything? I heard the guards found him in the backyard?'

Shubhankar's heart tightened. He tried to distract himself. *Dhwani Dwivedi, Dwiti Dwivedi.* Ma's fingers clutched his hair lightly. Her voice was meek when she spoke. She always behaved differently around the other men of the family. 'He's only ten. If he'd seen anything, he would've told me . . .'

'Keep the boy out of this!' Papa's voice filled the room, not at all sounding like the man who was nodding like a wound-up toy just a few hours ago. 'I don't want him involved in any trouble, like the police questioning him or . . .' He paused, like he was trying to think of other scenarios, then gave up.

Someone cleared his throat and the room fell silent. 'The boy will be fine.' It was Suresh-mausa. 'He is a proud Hindu Brahmin. He carries the family name of Trivedi. We are the masters of three-three Vedas. If he's seen anything, he will make sense of it when he grows up.'

Ma drew in a sharp breath, wanting to say something. But it didn't materialize. Shubhankar wanted to open his eyes that very moment and tell Ma what he'd seen. He was suddenly alert after hours of being cloudy. But Suresh-mausa continued, 'Did you not want my men to guard the wedding? Did the groom's family not praise you for pulling this off in spite of the troubles? What *should* we have done – allowed that man in, knowing what mischief he could create?'

'But the man came back later and begged for shelter . . .' Panna-chacha sounded like he was going to cry. 'He told us there was trouble in the next mohalla. We could just have let him hide . . . Instead we turned him away . . .'

'Should we take in the entire town now? Is it for us to save everyone?'

'And if the mob got whiff that a Muslim was hiding here? Wouldn't that put *our* lives in danger?'

Suresh-mausa's deep voice cut everyone off. 'Are we going to sit here and mourn the death of a Muslim? Do you know how many Hindus are being killed by them? Every day I'm getting reports – Ayodhya, Allahabad, Benaras, Bombay. They haven't spared us anywhere!'

His voice grew louder, like he was speaking at an election rally. 'I was in Ayodhya that day. I saw how our Hindu men rushed to the dome and brought the mosque down. I cried seeing the love for their country.' Then his voice dropped to a whisper. 'We won't care about any army or Supreme Court. Enough of this Hindu–Muslim bhai-bhai brotherhood non-sense. We will build temples at every place they've usurped. Even the Taj Mahal will fall for a Shiva temple.'

Goosebumps pricked Shubhankar all over. A lump of vomit bobbed in his throat. But Suresh-mausa wasn't done. 'Wait and watch. In ten years . . . twenty years at most . . . we will bring them down to zero. ZERO! SHOONYA!'

Shubhankar waited for Papa or Ma to say something, maybe Panna-chacha, anyone. This was all wrong. Very very wrong. The mosque shouldn't have been destroyed. Cities shouldn't be burning. Master-ji's assistant should've been home by now, having dinner with his family, watching TV.

He wanted to sit up, look at everyone, tell them they didn't know what they were talking about, because they hadn't seen a man burn, that if they had, they wouldn't be debating, wouldn't let Suresh-mausa spout his political speeches.

Instead, he let his eyelids roam from side to side, even

opened his eyes a sliver, hoping Ma would catch him awake, ask him what he'd seen, then ask everyone to find the men who had hurt M, find M's family, get the police!

But he didn't get up, nor did Ma say anything. The conversation moved on to transport arrangements. Papa picked him up and carried him out of the haveli. He felt Papa's fennel-scented breath on his neck. Their hearts beat against each other's as Papa held him in the car. Dhak-dhak, dhak-dhak.

Shubhankar decided then that he'd never tell them. Ma nor Papa nor anyone. They didn't have the right to know about M, about him. They were cowards, they'd sided with the killers. He wanted to jump out of Papa's lap, crash through the car's door, and run as far away as he could, wanted to get rid of this long Hindu Brahmin name his parents were so proud of, that Suresh-mausa said would help to make sense of everything.

No, these people had let M die, now they'd watch their son suffer, and suffer with him. That was their punishment.

2012

Tethered

'Don't go, na?' Ma says. 'You can smoke here on the balcony.'

He is halfway up the stairs, limping to the terrace on the twentieth floor of the building. He stops, turns to look. Ma's eyes are pleading. She doesn't like him going upstairs every night after dinner. A few people have jumped off the roof before. He knows it is a big deal, asking her son to smoke right here in the house, in front of her. It is a fat olive branch she is offering him.

But he shakes his head. 'The physiotherapist says it's good for me to climb stairs,' he makes up an excuse and continues on his way.

On the terrace, he sits on the rough cement floor. It takes a lot out of him, to lower his body and bend his back and fold his legs. His bones feel brittle, his muscles mildewy. From here, he can't see much except for the night sky. The building management have made the wall higher and embedded shards of glass in it, to prevent more people jumping off. Fireworks appear from time to time, people celebrating New Year's Eve. The breeze is cool in the night. He takes a deep drag of the cigarette, lets the smoke pass through his lips.

Later, standing up, he looks at the twentieth-storey view, the lights hazy, dancing in the polluted air, shifting in space.

Like life in this city, in movement but tethered.

He lights another cigarette, his finger holding down the spring of the lighter, keeping the flame burning. He brings it close to his face, closer, even closer, until the flame dances right on his nose-tip. He watches it cockeyed. He lets go of the spring when it feels like his skin will start to melt.

There are more ways to die than jump off a building, he wants to tell Ma. *You should know.*

1990s

Susu

Hunger shot through his body like an arrow, passing from stomach to throat and back down to his butt, making it tingle. He smelt freshly fried kachoris rescued from the wedding buffet. He stirred to wake himself, call out to Ma, ask what's for breakfast.

Then . . .

Shame washed over. Was he hungry? Did he really get a full night's sleep? He pressed his thighs against his stomach to stop the gurgling, dug his elbows into his knees until they hurt. He lay curled up in a ball, heart beating heavily in his ear, head pushed against the pillow, his breathing quick, hot. If he opened his eyes now, would he find them watching him – Ma, Papa, Chintoo, Nani, Malti-didi . . .

He woke up again. Chintoo was throwing breakfast tantrums. Malti-didi tiptoed around the bed, the broom going swoosh-swoosh. A crow cawed on the windowsill. A fruit-seller hawked his wares at the gate. Yellow winter sunbeams glowed on his eyelids. But sleep clamped down on him, forcing his mind to shut out any sight or sound or thought . . .

His eyelids flew open. Loud thuds of the water droplets from the tube-well. *Tip-tip-tip. Boom-boom-boom.*

Ma's cold fingers on his forehead. Ma calling his name softly.

He looked up at her.

She squinted in the bright sunlight and smiled.

'Are you looking for something?' Ma caught him off guard. Like every morning, Shubhankar had woken early to pick up the newspaper from the balcony. He held it to his nose, the fragrance of crisp paper and new ink an antidote to the news inside. He looked over his shoulder. The stillness of the grey mornings felt deathlier than the nights. Everyone was asleep, still no school, no office.

Turning the pages, his body felt like being pulled downward by gravity and upward by the sky, making him want to shit and vomit at the same time. Towers of smoke, dead bodies, curfews, men on the mosque, domes crashing, a burqa, a saffron band, spears. He checked from front to back, back to front, short blurbs in side columns, obituaries, even matrimonial adverts. Anything about a tailor set on fire behind a wedding haveli? Nothing. Hundreds were dying. News was of deaths, not of the dead.

Ma held out her hand. 'I'm taking tea for Papa.' He handed over the paper. Papa liked to read the news with morning tea. 'Go wake Chintoo up. He'll have a hard time when school reopens.' Ma's voice was soft. She attempted a half-smile. She looked tired even in the early morning.

The boys spent their days playing Ludo and Monopoly. They borrowed Dhruv's Walkman, listened to cassettes of Bryan Adams and *Saajan*. They fought wars with broken branches, dressed as sultans, wearing Papa's shirts for armour and Ma's dupattas for turbans. He kept close to Chintoo all day. His brother's blissful unawareness was contagious. For a few hours, he could behave like nothing had happened, giggle at silly jokes, get into pillow fights, play the piano on coasters.

Their parents left them alone, keeping busy under house arrest, less talkative, going about their days mechanically. Papa was restless, risking safety to slip out to the shops whenever he could. Ma limited herself to the kitchen and her room, sleeping more than usual, as if recovering from a malaise. Malti-didi didn't show up for days at times, depending on the violence, which moved like a lethal beast from street to street, mohalla to mohalla, sometimes calming down for a few days before flaring up again. Through it all, only Chintoo spoke of the wedding, the food, the unchecked flow of cold drinks. Shubhankar wished Chintoo would shut up.

Ma got them sketchbooks. 'You'll draw every afternoon,' she said. Chintoo scrunched up his nose. Then she produced a box of crayons, still wrapped tightly in plastic. It had all twenty-four colours, not the cheap ones that had only six. She handed it to Shubhankar, and raised a finger in warning. 'When you finish, put them back in the box. Don't let them roll off under the bed.' Then she softened. 'You like drawing, hai na?' She ruffled his hair. 'Draw something nice, we can put it up on the wall.'

This inspired Chintoo. He grabbed at the crayons. 'I want my drawing on the wall too!'

The boys were sent up to the terrace every afternoon. They sat in the sun-dappled shade of papaya trees and peeled oranges, citrus droplets spraying their eyes, the tangy smell hanging in the air until it was time to pack up. Chintoo spoke aloud as he drew – names of things, why this subject, why today. In spite of Ma's warning, Shubhankar didn't monitor Chintoo. At least someone was happy through all this.

Shubhankar's sketchbook was mostly blank, a few half-hearted attempts at drawing what he thought Ma would like to see. But all he really wanted to draw was the fire, the man, his eyes. He wanted to fill the sketchbook up, every page, with every single moment of that night, the angry yellow flames leaping out, streaks of red, brown hollow eyes, black char, grey ash.

But he didn't dare. It was all meant to be inside him, never to come out.

In the end, Chintoo's drawing made it to their bedroom wall. He had tried drawing the school assembly, a stick figure denoting the music teacher playing the piano; other stick figures were students standing in line. Papa put it up, using a ruler to mark points so the picture wasn't tilted, cutting out neat bits of Sellotape.

Ma and Nani stood by to watch. Nani whispered in Ma's ear, 'The younger one isn't as talented. Didn't I tell you the elder one is like his Nana-ji?'

'No drawing from you?' Ma tugged at Shubhankar's sleeve. There was a gentleness in her eyes he hadn't seen in a long time. Did she know what he'd seen at the wedding? Was she trying to apologize for what they'd done?

Shubhankar shook his head. No drawing. Ma looked on, not saying anything.

At night, Shubhankar joined Nani in her window-closing exercise. She whispered to her newfound partner, 'Times are very bad. You don't know what-what is happening outside.' He pulled the panes in with all his strength, then pushed them to check.

Chintoo wasn't happy about this. 'If you die from lack of oxygen, don't come crying to me,' he said, smarting from the betrayal.

But neither Shubhankar nor Nani could reach the bathroom window. It was higher up. He could see the dark sky through its yellow frame. 'Should I ask Papa to shut it?' he asked, but Nani dismissed the idea. She was only interested in safety as long as it wasn't too much work.

On nights when he had to pee, Shubhankar tried to hold it in, scrambled in bed, turned this side and that. Then he tiptoed to the bathroom and left in a hurry. He couldn't bear to be there alone, the blackness staring down, as if a face, M's face, could pop out any minute.

One night, he let go. He lay in bed, fully awake, the warm liquid seeping through his pyjamas, spreading under his butt, soaking the sheets and duvet, the sweater sleeves turning wet and wrinkled, the wool getting heavier. The pee flowed unhindered, an unending river of shame. Within moments, the warm liquid turned cold. He was lying on a slab of ice, teeth chattering, body trembling.

It started to smell only a little later. That woke Chintoo up. 'Bhaiyya has done susu in his sleep!'

Ma and Papa swooped in like paratroopers, as if they were just outside the door. They got to work immediately, silently changing sheets, changing clothes, warming water, washing their son's body with a sponge in the middle of the cold night.

Chintoo giggled and teased from his bed, until Ma and Papa sent him away to sleep in their room.

Karma

Nani sat between her grandsons, stroking their legs in a gentle massage, sometimes giving them a quick smack if they misbehaved. She'd taken to telling bedtime stories. She said this would calm whatever was disturbing the elder one, stop him pissing in bed. She puffed like a train, meowed like a cat, screeched like a door with rusty hinges. When Chintoo asked for encores, she chuckled like a VVIP who'd come prepared for her fans.

'A wolf walked to the stream,' she began in a low voice tonight. 'As he bent his head to drink, he noticed a little lamb further downstream.' She switched to a nasal tone. '*Hey, you! How dare you muddy the water?*'

Then meekly. '*Dear sir*, said the lamb, *the water flows from you to me. How can I muddy it?*'

Chintoo giggled.

'Wolf: *But last time, you were upstream and muddied the water all right.*

'Lamb: *Sir, that cannot be. I am a little lamb, this is my first time at the stream.*

'Wolf: *Oh well, it must've been your father then, so I shall eat you up.*'

Chintoo propped his head up on his hand. 'I don't understand.' His eyes were luminescent in the dark. 'If it was the lamb's father's fault, why was the wolf going to eat the baby lamb?'

Nani sighed. 'No one is their own self, my bachchas. We

are all part of a circle of karma. We will be rewarded for the good deeds of our forefathers, and pay the price for their sins.'

'Who are our forefathers, Nani?' It was Shubhankar this time. 'Did they do good things or bad things?'

Nani seemed taken unawares by this question. Then she reorientated herself and smiled. 'You'll be fine, your forefathers did good things.' She spoke indulgently. 'Your Nana-ji was such a gentleman . . . when he saw me at a wedding and sent word of interest, he made sure I was asked if I would marry him! Imagine!' She laughed in amazement. 'Who'd heard of these things back then?'

This was not the answer Shubhankar was looking for, but he made a *hmm* sound, turned around and tried to fall asleep, hoping he wouldn't have to go to the bathroom that night.

Dhak-dhak

'Today we will pay our respects to the dead.' Sister Benedicta looked at the boys organized in height order, hymn books in hand, shuffling their feet as she read from her notes. The principal had become rounder over the years. She still wore the grey saree, pinned in the same places. Jesus still hung from her neck on a cross. 'St Francis Xavier was a great soul. He was one of the first Christian missionaries in the Indian subcontinent. He left the comfort of Europe and travelled to the jungles of India. Imagine how scary this place must have been in the 1500s!' She paused to let the magnitude of the adventure sink in. 'On this day, he was canonized. Let us pray.'

A whisper rose. *Our Father who art in Heaven . . . hallowed be Thy name . . . Thy kingdom come . . . Thy will be done . . . lead us not into temptation . . . but deliver us from evil . . . in the name of the Father . . . the Son . . . the Holy Spirit . . . Amen . . .* Echoes of hands crossing chests and touching foreheads bounced off the walls of the chapel. Shubhankar tried to imagine a muscular white man slaying wild animals and turning cannibals into whimpering converts. But his mind wandered off to those slayed in the more recent past.

It had taken weeks for the riots to stop. Papa was back in the office. Ma had grown out of her exhaustion; her sharpness had returned with more vigour. *Enough time wasted, three months left to your final exams,* she had started her countdown. Nani went to visit her sister in Azamgarh and came back full of praise for her grand-nephews. 'One is already studying to be a doctor, another is sure to crack the engineering exam! But I also said, *my* grandsons are no less. They top their classes every year, and one is even showing signs of becoming a great artist!'

School had finally reopened in late January 1993. In the weeks since then, everyone had behaved like nothing had happened. The atmosphere was charged with talk of Sports Day. Jesus hung limply in the chapel, still crucified, still helpless. Classmates played ball games and traded WWF cards, teachers obsessed over decimals and prepositions. History lessons stopped at independence. And Civics lessons celebrated India's constitution. *Sovereign socialist secular democratic republic.* The Civics teacher said, 'We were one of the first to break from the shackles of colonialism. Other countries looked to us for inspiration, for values.' His voice was shaky with emotion, but the boys were busy flying paper planes across the room.

As they now shuffled out of the chapel, Shubhankar stole a look at Tabrez. For weeks, he'd glanced at Tabrez and Ashraf and Sikandar, the Muslim boys in class. He couldn't look straight at them, scared that if he did, something would give. He wanted to ask them what they felt about the demolition of the mosque, the riots, the violence. What names starting with M could they think of? Did they know anything about the balding man who was Master-ji's assistant? But Tabrez and Ashraf and Sikandar had been like everyone else. They played during PT period, dozed off at the back of the class, peeped into forbidden photos. Either they weren't affected at all, or they were expert at hiding their true feelings. Shubhankar couldn't tell.

Later in class, Miss Lucy asked another of her googly questions. '*Timber* and *timbre*, what's the difference?'

'Timber with E-R is wood. Timbre with R-E is music,' someone replied. Everyone turned to look.

'Very good!' Miss Lucy snapped her fingers and said cheerfully, 'I listened to a lot of music while stuck at home these last few weeks. Did you?' She nodded her head up and down. Some boys started nodding too, as if it were contagious. 'Yeah? Yeah? I had a really good time.' The class began a little rhythmic head-dance.

Shubhankar stood up without raising his hand. The chair made a screeching sound as it slid back. Miss Lucy and everyone else stopped nodding. 'Rhythm,' he said. Air pumped out of his lungs and escaped his mouth with force. Droplets of spit landed on the table. 'That's another word without vowels.' He had thought of this long back, but had never been able to say it to Miss Lucy's face.

'Huh?' Miss Lucy's mouth was left open in a small 'O'.

'You'd said there was only *one* word without vowels – *hymn*. Here's another one – *rhythm*.' He was breathing furiously. He couldn't stop. 'And no one had a good time at home. Some horrible things were happening out there.' He looked sideways at Ashraf, hoping he would say something. Wasn't it *his* mosque that had been demolished, *his* people killed? But Ashraf seemed as surprised and clueless as everyone else.

Miss Lucy curtly asked Shubhankar to sit down, but stopped the head-dancing and finger-snapping.

For days, Shubhankar hoped his outburst would warrant a summons to Ma from Miss Lucy. Maybe then Ma would ask him about the night of the wedding, probe him enough so he could tell her, maybe then she would apologize.

But perhaps the subject wasn't important enough for Miss Lucy, because she didn't call Ma for one of her favourite parent–teacher meetings.

*

It was after the bombs had gone off in Bombay that Shub-hankar took matters into his own hands.

He read about the blasts in the newspaper. On 12th March 1993, thirteen bombs had gone off, almost at the same time. He saw pictures of hotels, bazaars, office buildings, the stock exchange, cars blackened and squeezed, human parts and torn clothes and howling people on stretchers, smoke billowing from windows and basements and drains. Before this, he'd only seen Bombay in the movies. It was by the Arabian Sea, very far from landlocked Lucknow in North India. It took two days to get there by train. Every morning he turned the pages in a trance, addicted to the destruction, transposing the grim pictures on to movie scenes. Madhuri Dixit doing her dhak-dhak dance on a pile of debris, Anil Kapoor pushing a cartload of dead bodies, Amrish Puri surveying the massacre with his villainous eyes.

And then, he read reports of India's most wanted underworld don, who was a Muslim, planning these attacks to avenge the demolition of the mosque. The don himself was on the run, in Dubai or Karachi or Bangkok, but he had people who'd do anything for him, even plant bombs.

A thought seeded itself in Shubhankar's mind. What if M had somehow escaped, lived, made it to the don? Would the don send men to Lucknow? Were they going to come for him, punish him for watching M burn? In nightmares, he saw his school bus ripped apart by a blast, springing up in the air and landing on its head, his body lying dead under dust and smoke, Chintoo crying, blood streaming down his face. He woke up with sweat sticking to the bedsheet, forehead and armpits hot with fever, pins and needles all over.

Sometimes, he opened his eyes to Ma and Papa patting down a cold sponge on his forehead. One time, Chintoo said, 'Bhaiyya, you were saying something about a tube-well in Bombay.' Another day, delirious, he was convinced he'd been kidnapped by the don, that he was in Karachi or Dubai. He shrieked and shrieked until Ma came running and held him tightly to her breast, rocking him back to silence. He dug his fingers so hard into her, his unclipped nails pierced her flesh.

Then one night, he woke up, clear-eyed and clear-headed. The fever had left his body. He walked to the bathroom, peed into the pot, and stared up at the open window. He stood there adamantly as the pee turned yellow, bubbles frothing on the surface.

The next night, he put his hand on the wall and felt the warmth of flames on the other side. His fingertips pulsed, as if in tandem with M's heartbeat.

A few more nights, and he took his face closer and rested his forehead on the cool tiles. He could hear breathing, deep and clear. He opened his mouth to speak, but no sound came out. M's eyes looked back at him, flames dancing in them.

Some more nights passed. When he finally spoke, his voice was a hoarse whisper. 'Hello.' There was no reply, but he could feel the lips curl up in a smile.

Another night. 'What is your name?'

Another night, some more courage. 'I'm sorry.'

Then. 'Can we be friends?'

PART TWO
Ankur / *Sapling*

2013

Teacher

The children are busy, their heads down. An uncanny silence reigns in the little room, so hot that sweat trickles down the scars on his back. He supervises from high up, the children on the floor. The NGO office manager organized a chair when she saw how difficult it was for him to squat.

A few weeks ago, Ma told him about the NGO. She had spoken to a girl in the building who taught at a government school in the Bhiwandi slums. Ma had got to know of the girl from her evening chats with the other women. 'They are looking for a volunteer to run weekend art classes,' she told him. 'Perfect for you!'

He wanted to compliment Ma on how resourceful she was, thank her for always trying to find things for him to do. But he just said yes.

The following Saturday, the girl, whose name he didn't ask and didn't remember when she told him, drove him to Bhiwandi. She opened the small schoolroom. The children stood awkwardly. He took out the supplies he'd bought – sketchbooks, colour pencils, crayons, erasers. He set them down on the floor. The children picked up whatever caught their fancy, sat down and started drawing.

That's how he has come to be *Arts Sir*. The children love him, remain engrossed in their drawings for hours. Sometimes the mornings turn into afternoons. The parents come to ask after them, take them home for lunch. They bow when they greet him, respect in their eyes.

The school principal is all praise for him. 'You're a born teacher. No one can tell you're just a volunteer here,' she says one afternoon, as he is packing up.

He doesn't tell her that he has done this before, throughout his teenage years, though his motivations then were different.

Back then, he had hoped to find answers. But now, he doesn't even care what the questions were.

1990s

SUPW

'Socially Useful Productive Work.' Chintoo chimed in before Shubhankar could speak. 'They help poor people.'

Shubhankar had asked for permission to join the SUPW class. That summer of 1995, he had graduated to high school, and could take an optional module. He'd seen the pamphlet Miss Lucy had put up on the noticeboard.

'What about helping yourself first? Have you seen your marks?' Ma's back was to the boys. She was ironing pillow-cases.

Chintoo said, 'Everyone gets hundred out of hundred.'

Ma turned to face them. 'Really? Full marks? What do they teach?'

Shubhankar knew this. 'They take students to the orphan-age next door, where they give tuition to the . . . orphans. It's just two hours on Tuesday afternoons.'

'What a strange name for a subject,' Ma wondered aloud.

Chintoo grinned. 'It's social, it's useful, *and* it's productive!'

Ma folded the pillowcase, picked up another one. 'Okay, if it'll get you good marks.' She deepened her voice. 'But only for those two hours, haan? If I find out you've been skipping classes . . .' She wagged her finger in warning. 'Remember, you're in high school now!'

*

The students walked through the Wazirganj slums, dodging carts, dogs, children, gunny sacks in the narrow lanes barely the breadth of a human being. Miss Lucy led the way. She still wore her tight pencil skirt and tap-tap heels, but no more cleavage. Her blouses now went up to her neck, frilled at the collars. She looked back to check on the seven students following in single file. The girls had ditched their skirts and wore salwar-kameez, heads covered with dupattas. They were from rich families, where parents understood the value of socially-useful-productive-work. Big cars waited just outside the slums to pick them up afterwards. Dhwani and Dwiti Dwivedi were there; they weren't rich but probably came for the marks. There was one other boy besides Shubhankar.

Dust flew from walls and covered them like shrouds. Shubhankar had to take a second bath when Ma went on her evening walk. He feared that one day she'd ask how come there was so much dust in the orphanage. He hadn't told her the full truth. It was not only St Mary's Orphanage that Miss Lucy took them to. Some days, they ventured into the slums, mostly in the Wazirganj-Maulviganj area. But sometimes Miss Lucy took them all the way to Dalibagh. The further out they went, the more squalid it got, garbage heaps stretching for miles, mangy dogs licking discarded petrol cans, crows picking at decomposed carcasses.

The group reached the community centre, a crumbling single room. Salma-begum came out in a lazy walk, jangling the keys to open the lock. The children followed after her. Salma-begum had organized them. Shubhankar wasn't sure how Miss Lucy knew Salma-begum, but they seemed very friendly, chit-chatting in broken English and sign language.

Once inside the centre, the children sat on the floor, their hair shiny, well-oiled. Their faces were ragged but keen. They wore clothes donated by the school. Shubhankar spotted a

T-shirt that might have been Chintoo's. Today there were ten, better attendance than most days. They took their things out, haggard notebooks and blunt pencils. Miss Lucy promptly passed the sharpener around. She had the same standards here as in her classroom. She divided the children into groups. Two were assigned to Shubhankar for English lessons. This would go on for the first hour. The next hour was meant for art classes. Miss Lucy had put Shubhankar in charge of these. His classmates helped. This was when Miss Lucy disappeared for a while. When she came back, she reeked of cigarettes.

Today, Shubhankar waited for Miss Lucy to leave the room. He took out a drawing of a scene he'd made. It was basic – round sun, straight rays, triangular hills, square hut, inverted-triangle grass. A non-geometric river flowed across the bottom of the page. The children stared at him unsurely. From the corner of his eye, he could see his classmates packing up. The art classes were Shubhankar's domain, the others hardly needed to stay.

He put the scene away. 'Draw what comes to mind.'

'Anything?' a child asked.

Shubhankar nodded and laid out the crayons he'd got from home.

'If I want to draw a parrot? Chalega?'

This cuteness drew giggles from his female classmates. Shubhankar turned to look. Dhwani had been making eyes at him for a while. He felt the hardness in his crotch. But it was Dwiti he liked. She'd grown into a full woman in the space of a year. Dhwani was still catching up. They weren't identical any more. If he were like any other boy, he would use this time to flirt, pull legs, tell jokes. Like in the TV show *Friends* that he and Chintoo sometimes got permission to watch. They ogled pretty white firangs sleeping with each other. How easily people had sex in America!

73

But he was here on a mission. This was his opportunity. Miss Lucy was still away, the children didn't need supervision. He dashed out of the room.

Salma-begum sat on the bench reading a magazine. Squiggly Urdu alphabet ran from right to left on the page. He'd been trying to catch her alone for weeks. 'Madam?'

'Haan?' Salma-begum looked up in surprise. 'Oh, it's you! All good inside?'

'Yes, they're drawing parrots.' He managed a smile, even though his heart was beating fast. He had to get to his point right away. 'Madam, I wanted to ask about someone.' He gulped down his spit. 'There was a man who worked as an assistant at Master-ji's shop . . .' He saw the blank look on Salma-begum's face. 'You know the one on the main road? Mohan Tailors . . .' He tried to sound casual. 'I'm looking for him, or his family. I thought they might live here?'

Shubhankar could see Salma-begum's inner cogs turning. 'What's his name?'

Shubhankar's spirits dropped. He had to tell her the truth before Miss Lucy came back. 'He . . . well . . . died, madam. But his family might still be here?'

'He died? How long ago?'

'Madam, this was during the riots in '92, the ones after the Babri Masjid . . .' He'd been asking people in the slums but everyone had either said they didn't know the tailor's assistant, or walked away when he mentioned the riots. This was his last chance.

Salma-begum's face hardened. She glanced here and there to make sure no one was nearby. 'That was a long time ago, beta. Why are you looking for his family?'

Shubhankar shrugged. He wanted to find someone who'd known M, who could tell him M's name, what had happened to those M had left behind, in the hope that this would help him figure out how to make things right, though he wasn't sure how.

A resolve came over Salma-begum. She stood up straight. 'Listen, beta. You shouldn't be asking about these things. All that is in the past. Everything is okay now.' She tried to smile. 'You have such a bright future ahead of you. You go to a good school. You are so talented. The children love your art classes. Actually, that is the only reason they come every week.' They stared at each other for a while. 'Jaane do, beta,' she finally said softly, almost pleading. *Let it go.*

They could hear the tap-tap of Miss Lucy's heels coming down the lane.

Later, when the local mosque had sounded the azaan and the children left for prayers, and his classmates left too, Shubhankar collected the sheets of paper from the floor and shut the box of crayons. He looked at the drawings. The child had focused on the parrot's beak, deep red lines running in beautiful curves. He showed it to Miss Lucy. It made her smile.

'Oh, Shub-ank-ah!' she sighed. 'What do we do about people like us?'

He looked at her, unsure of what she'd meant.

'Look at you, turning up every Tuesday, never calling in sick, staying back to clean up when all your classmates have left.'

He felt himself blush. He couldn't remember ever being complimented.

'Some of us just don't fit in, do we? We'll always be apart from the rest.'

Miss Lucy looked at him knowingly, then took the drawing from him. 'Ever considered becoming a teacher, Shub-ank-ah?'

He shook his head. That was not a profession on his parents' wish-list.

Habeeb

M is on the floor, massaging the feet of the underworld don, his eyes reflecting embers, the don is smoking a hookah, pretty girls in gold bikinis are dancing, they are in a multi-storeyed building in Dubai, little cars whizz past on a ribbony highway visible through the glass windows, they're both studying a map of Lucknow, pointing at places where the bombs will go off, thirteen in all, it has to be thirteen, the don's lucky number, it worked in Bombay, his dogs are fighting over something, blood drips from their mouths, the thing drops to the floor, it is Suresh-mausa's intestines, a dog turns to look at Shubhankar, gnarls its teeth, its eyes flash red from the siren, it is coming for Shubhankar, he is running but it is faster, almost catching up—

Shubhankar jolted himself into wakefulness. He had dozed off while staring at his books. The most terrifying dreams always came when he was sleeping lightly.

He checked the bedsheet, it was dry. Good.

'G . . . C . . . E minor . . . B . . .' On the next bed, Chintoo strummed the strings, voice crooning softly. He'd recently walked in with Dhruv's second-hand guitar. Ma had made him promise he wouldn't play when his brother was studying in the same room. They were sure Ma could hear every strum. It was just a matter of choice that she hadn't put an end to this concert.

Shubhankar stared at his books. The lamp that Papa had bought on his last birthday bathed everything in yellow light.

A year ago, Papa had had a new table made for him. It was large with three drawers on either side. 'Enough to fit all your books.' Papa had looked very satisfied with the outcome.

Shubhankar hated the table. The space in the room was now so constricted he and Chintoo were always bumping into each other. When everyone was awake, Shubhankar used the table for show, sitting on the bed because there was no room for a chair. But at night, he lay on his stomach on the bed, books sprawled everywhere.

'What's a word that rhymes with *kareeb*?' Chintoo asked. He'd been composing this one song for weeks, insisting that he wanted it to be in Hindi. He'd named it 'Dosti'. *Friendship*. His idol was Lucky Ali, who'd managed to bring the best of both worlds together – Hindi poetry and Western pop. His album was the biggest hit of 1997. Chintoo was always humming his tunes. *O sanam, mohabbat ki qasam . . .*

Shubhankar shrugged. Chintoo didn't need his help to write the song. Even a few years ago, Chintoo's outgoing nature fascinated him. Now he found it irksome. It was unfair that Chintoo could be fun and talented and naughty. Shubhankar often wondered what Chintoo would've done if he was in the backyard that night of Lekha-bua's wedding, if he'd seen M. He'd have come crying to Ma right then, raised hell, stopped the wedding even, made it all about himself.

Shubhankar turned back to his books. The artwork stared at him from the margins – marching elephants, Madhubani designs, flowers in bloom. This is what he did when his brain couldn't absorb valencies and thermodynamics and calculus any more. These books had come all the way from Madras, by post every month, robustly sewn with tough thread. They specialized in IIT preparation. BRILLIANT TUTORIALS, *Masilamani Street, T Nagar*. The address had caught Chintoo's fancy immediately. He said it with a South Indian accent, slipping the vowels and accentuating the consonants. *Masi-lamani Street*. Their parents and relatives laughed. *Do it again, Chintoo*. Until one day, Papa had grown serious. 'Don't make fun of South Indians. Bangalore is going to be the next Silicon Valley of the world!'

All of Shubhankar's classmates were signed up to these Brilliant Tutorials, which taught exactly how one should prepare for the entrance exam that millions sat every year, and only a few thousand got through. Life after IIT was folklore – jobs in California, fast-track to CEO, salaries worth hundreds of thousands. Dollars, not rupees.

Chintoo was done for the night. He put his guitar away. 'Bhaiyya, what's the difference between Hindi and Urdu?'

Shubhankar tried to remember what he had learnt in History class. 'Urdu was born in the barracks a few hundred years ago, and was spoken by soldiers. It gets its grammar from Hindi, and vocabulary from Persian.'

Chintoo's eyes lit up at this information. 'No wonder they sound the same!'

Shubhankar nodded. 'Colloquially, in current times, what we speak is really a mix of the two, Hindustani. You have no idea how many Urdu words we use in daily life.'

'And we think only Muslims speak Urdu!' Chintoo scoffed.

Shubhankar remembered Chintoo's previous question. 'Did you find a rhyming word for *kareeb*?'

'I did! *Habeeb*. It means *beloved, close friend*. Urdu words are so beautiful, na? That's why Muslims have such lovely-sounding names.'

Shubhankar bristled, but Chintoo was blissfully unaware. He yawned. 'Bhaiyya, I'm sleepy. Switch this lamp off soon, please!' Within minutes, Chintoo's light snores filled the room.

Shubhankar turned back to his textbook. BRILLIANT

TUTORIALS. The bold-font block letters betrayed the thinness of the paper. Two years ago, when he'd started high school, Ma and Papa had launched a campaign to get him into IIT, hunting down private tutors who guaranteed success on billboards in Hazratganj city centre, finding question papers from previous years, notes from illustrious seniors, advice from inspirational students. For two years, Ma had said the same thing to him, like she'd forgotten how to say anything else. *We've made sacrifices so you two can have a good life. And forget about us . . . Don't you want success? All your friends will get into good colleges and leave. Do you want to be left behind in this small place?*

Ma's fire was fuelled by Nani. *A boy should study nothing but engineering, and that too, from the best. IIT it will be for you both. If your Nana-ji were alive today, he'd make sure the elder one got hundred-on-hundred in Maths.*

Ma and Nani were always checking the clock, the gilt-bronze one that Ma had brought to this house as a wedding gift. Semi-naked angels twisted themselves around its frame, blowing trumpets, cheeks puffed. The clock's origins were controversial. Ma claimed it had been gifted to Nana-ji by a British engineer, one of those firangs who'd refused to leave after independence, considered India *home*, like Miss Lucy. But Nani had a different story. She insisted that she'd got it from *her* family, one of the few items she'd managed to wrest away from the hawkish eyes of seventeen cousins. Not that it mattered. Now its only utility was to check Shubhankar's comings and goings, why was he late, what had he been doing when coaching classes had finished an hour ago.

Papa bought the annual edition of the *India Today* magazine that published nationwide college rankings. All year, he read these out at dinner, so the boys wouldn't forget what they were aiming for.

And then one morning, Mr Dwivedi, out on his morning walk, had said to Ma, 'You don't know Brilliant Tutorials? Sure-shot way of getting into IIT! I got Dhwani and Dwiti signed up last year only. Even girls are becoming engineers these days!' Ma was drinking tea on the balcony. She rushed in and woke Papa up that very minute. How could Mr Dwivedi of the two-Vedas fame know more than Mr and Mrs Trivedi, who, between them, should've known six Vedas?

The following month, Brilliant Tutorials textbooks began arriving from Madras. These would *sure-shot* get Shubhankar into IIT. Last summer, when the family were in Kanpur for a wedding, they visited the IIT campus. It was like a pilgrimage to temples, dressing up for darshan, queuing for a glimpse of the idol, hungry for a bite of the holy prasad. INDIAN INSTITUTE OF TECHNOLOGY, KANPUR, read the unassuming neon-lit board above the gate. The guards seemed disinterested, but Papa went up to them nevertheless. 'Let's make sure we aren't breaking any rules.' Shubhankar could see Papa having a little chit-chat, probably asking them questions he'd harboured about this place for years.

The campus was large and leafy. The family made their way to the central square, a broad road flanked by well-landscaped lawns leading to a massive pillared building. On both sides were departments and administrative offices. Papa pointed to the Computer Science building. 'The highest of the highest rank study here.' Since it was summer holidays, the campus was mostly deserted. When a group of boys turned a corner, Papa stopped in awe, as if he'd spotted Edison, Bell and Watt discussing their next inventions. 'IIT-ians,' he whispered, so as not to interrupt them.

Chintoo was starting to get bored. He examined the campus map and asked, 'Why are there so many boys' hostels and so few girls' hostels?'

'Because, beta,' Ma snapped, 'in this country, girls only study Home Science and then make rotis and babies, like your stupid mother.' Papa gave her a scowl, and she'd scowled back with ample elan.

Shubhankar now closed the textbook and rested his forehead on the pillow. He thought of Dhwani and Dwiti. Dwiti's breasts were growing at twice the rate of Dhwani's. It was easy to tell who was who. He couldn't tell Chintoo this. Chintoo was only twelve. But he did say this to the boys in school, who pooled pocket money and smuggled in *Playboy* and *Debonair*, taking turns to sit in the last row and flip through the pages of these magazines, their eyes gorging on the naked white women with humongous breasts, then excusing themselves to go to the toilet every now and then. When Shubhankar told the boys about Dwiti, they had a good laugh, asked for more stories from time to time. *Has the flat-chested twin caught up with her sister yet?* For Shubhankar, being known for something, even if it was someone else's breasts, made school bearable. For those few hours, away from home, away from thoughts of M, he felt *normal*, like he had only as many issues as everyone else.

He got out of bed and tiptoed to the bathroom. He locked the door behind him, trying to keep the screeching of the bolt to a minimum. He ran the tap at full force. He reckoned he had five minutes. He knew of the water crisis and the cost of electricity. But water was the only way he could drown his sounds out.

He pulled down his pants. He was already erect. He began stroking, thinking of Dwiti Dwivedi and how she wore her dupatta tightly around her neck like Madhuri Dixit in the movies, making her breasts look pointy, the outline of her bra showing through. He imagined her wearing those blouses that were tied at the waist, how one artful pull could denude her. He was stroking violently now, panting loudly.

He stroked and stroked, looking at the black sky outside the yellow-framed window. Like every night, M's eyes were watching him pleasure himself. The muscles of his forearm ached from the jerks, but he didn't want to climax yet. Every time he got close to peaking, he held back. There was something about M watching him commit these adult acts, as though he wanted M to know he'd grown up. His body was hot, sweat dripped all over, like he was on fire. Dwiti was there with him, flames galloping around her nipples. M was there too. All three of them burning up in their self-destructing perversity.

When he climaxed, he let out a gasp he couldn't muffle. He placed his forehead against the cool tile, dozed off standing there, limp penis in hand.

He was jolted awake by Ma's knock on the door. 'Turn the tap off when you're done. Water isn't cheap.'

He heard her slippers slapping the floor as she walked away.

Kaamchor

The Bata slippers flipped and flopped on the road. Ma's perfect heels peeped out from below her saree. A few years ago, Ma had started rubbing foot cream on her heels. *I don't like cracked-cracked heels.* She'd even persuaded Malti-didi to do the same. *We're not young any more, Malti. We have to start taking care of ourselves.*

Shubhankar now followed Ma like a puppy. He knew he could just walk with her, or do this on his own. But somehow, he needed her to lead him. He stopped as Ma looked this way and that before crossing the road, expertly navigating auto-rickshaws, motorbikes, a bus. He found a spot by a tube-well on the pavement. Children from the slums were showering under the tap. There were enough of them to keep him hidden.

MOHAN TAILORS. That was the shop Ma entered. The board was yellowish-white with red lettering in English. A coat of dust had settled on its rolled-up shutters. The shop was smaller than Shubhankar remembered. Two men pumped sewing machines with their feet in a choreographed dance. A calendar hung on the wall, a picture of goddess Lakshmi surrounded by gold coins raining down from the skies. Beside it was a labyrinth of shelves, fabric rolls stacked up, new and altered clothes wrapped in old newspaper for customers to pick up. Between the passing traffic, Shubhankar saw Ma's profile, smiling and speaking, head bobbing.

There was Master-ji, barely visible in the shadows. He'd grown older, specks of white in his stubble, a frayed shirt hanging loosely on his thin body.

Ma had mentioned that morning she was going to Master-ji's. Shubhankar's ears had pricked up. He'd known all along that she still got her tailoring work done from there. For years, he'd toyed with the idea of confronting Master-ji, stabbing a finger in his chest, telling him that he was responsible for M's death, for sending M to the wedding that night. But Shubhankar's legs wouldn't carry him this way. There was a red line, a laskshman-rekha, not meant to be breached. The shop was the only place he'd seen M as a human being, manoeuvring the measuring tape with a snap of the wrist, flashing a smile, teasing Chintoo, proposing to wrap him up in fabric, so much so that Chintoo had run out and everyone had laughed.

No, it was too much. If Shubhankar ever set foot in the shop, he was scared he'd do something drastic, irreversible, perhaps tear the place down, set it on fire.

Ma stood with her arms stretched out, Master-ji wrote in his notepad, a third person took measurements, holding the tape around Ma's bust, upper arms, neck. Shubhankar stepped forward to look, letting his guard down. The man said something, they all laughed. The sound travelled over the din, shattering like a crystal in Shubhankar's ear.

This was the new M. Master-ji's new assistant.

A wave of hatred washed over Shubhankar. He had to touch the wall to steady himself. No, he couldn't forgive these people. Look how easily they'd fallen back into their old lives. As if M was a disposable item, as if a man melting into flames didn't warrant a change of ways. How dare Master-ji still run his shop? How dare the new guy take over so seamlessly? How dare Ma still get her clothes stitched here? How dare Ma never speak to him about that night? Were she and Papa so blinded by their dreams that they'd flushed everything else out? Did they really believe a good future could cure his nightmares?

He was the only one with a memory of M, the only one who could keep him alive, return dignity to a life that was snuffed out.

He'd been trying, unsuccessfully.

For two years, he'd stood in front of the blue lopsided board that said KOTWALI AMINABAD, tied to the wall in ugly knots of grey wire, the Hindi letters painted in white, partially covered by hardened pellets of pigeon shit. Cracks ran up and down the building. Shubhankar had settled himself next to a tapri who sold cigarettes, paan, beedi, lozenges. The policemen from the kotwali in their khaki uniforms came out for breaks, adjusting their shiny belts under the bulges of their bellies, chatting about wives' demands and children's school fees, feeding biscuits to stray dogs they'd nicknamed Pinky, Burran, Ghassoo.

For two years, Shubhankar had stopped there on his way to and from coaching classes. If this weren't a police station, he would've been suspected of mischief by now. But no one cared for this gangly, acned teenager under the peepul tree. Hundreds came and went every day, waiting on benches, sitting on steps, loitering in the street. Furrowed brows, sweaty armpits, exhausted faces, bowing down to the policemen, begging for attention while the stray dogs hogged the spotlight. One time, a pregnant woman had gone into labour in front of the kotwali. She was carried down the steps and helped into a rickshaw. She'd gripped the wrist of the policewoman, hope in her eyes, promising to return as soon as the baby was born.

For two years, Shubhankar had wondered if he should go in, tell the police about M, about Suresh-mausa and his men. But what was there to say? Was turning someone away from private property a crime? Was there even a file in M's name? Hadn't hundreds died in the riots? And hadn't it been five years already? Half a decade was too long in a place where people were under attack every few days. Shubhankar was a minor himself, an unsure fifteen-year-old with no solid information, no proof. He didn't even know the victim's name.

No, there was no hope. This place was too crowded for justice. He'd have to find another way.

And Ma had led him to it. Mohan Tailors.

The tea was tepid and sweet. Flecks of tea leaves floated on the surface covered by a thick skin of milk. Even the sight made Shubhankar nauseous. But he continued to sip. It was the only way he could stick around for longer.

'This shop is quite old, na?' he asked.

The chai-wallah looked up. Staring at a boiling pot all day had made the man's skin go red. Clear lines ran along his forehead.

'Master-ji's shop? Yes, yes.' Milk frothed up in places. The chai-wallah tamed it with his ladle. 'It was here when I set up my stall fourteen-fifteen years ago . . .'

'My mother is a big fan of Master-ji. She gets her clothes stitched only by him.'

'Master-ji is Number One fan of my tea. He won't order from anyone else. Many have come and gone, but no one could beat my reputation . . .'

Shubhankar crumbled the clay cup and threw it on the street. A passing auto-rickshaw drove over it, grinding the remains to dust. He wished for an iced-gola, but ordered another tea. Ever since he'd followed Ma to Master-ji's shop weeks ago, he'd hovered around here, looking for answers.

'This assistant is new?' He pointed to the fellow in the shop.

'Lakhan? He's been here for some time.'

Shubhankar pretended to jog his memory. 'Wasn't there another guy before this?'

The chai-wallah wiped his forehead with his gamchha. 'That guy was also nice. Quite short, na? Slightly balding?'

Shubhankar tried to hold the cup steady in his trembling fingers. 'Yes. I was quite fond of him as a child . . .' He inched closer. The vapour from the cauldron fogged up his glasses. 'He quite suddenly . . . disappeared, na?'

The chai-wallah's voice dropped to a whisper. He looked around conspiratorially. 'These people, bhaiyya, what to say. They are kaamchor. No one wants to work. They come like that and leave like that.' He snapped his fingers. *Like that. Like that.*

'But that guy . . . he'd been with Master-ji for years. He wouldn't have disappeared just like that?' Shubhankar paused to steady his breathing. 'What was his name?' He pretended to scratch his head. 'Something . . . M . . . M . . . Mohsin? Masood?' He had a whole list. *Mustafa, Mushtaq, Moosa, Mahroof, Munir, Mehmood, Mukhtar, Mohammed, Mehboob.*

'Aren't you the Trivedis' son?'

They jumped at the question. It was Master-ji himself, standing by the stall. Shubhankar felt his body turn to stone. The chai-wallah stepped in. 'Arre, Master-ji. I was going to bring you chai myself. I just got late talking to this bhaiyya.' Then his eyes lit up. 'Lo ji, what a coincidence! This bhaiyya was asking about your old assistant. Where did he go?'

Master-ji spat red paan-juice on the pavement, looking

87

away. 'He went to his village. Never came back. Said he wanted to work on his farm . . .'

The chai-wallah bobbed his head. 'Didn't I tell you, bhaiyya? These people are Number One kaamchor. It's not that easy making it in the city. It takes real grit . . .'

Is that how M was to be remembered then, a slacker, a kaamchor?

Shubhankar straightened. He was a good two heads taller than Master-ji. He stepped closer and stared down into the tailor's eyes. 'Did you never hear from him since? Did he never come back?' He was not going to let Master-ji off the hook that easily.

Master-ji averted his gaze at first, then looked up with resolve. 'Do your parents know what you're doing? Shouldn't you be studying, making something of yourself?'

The chai-wallah, sensing trouble, buried his face in the cauldron's vapours.

Master-ji tried to stand almost on tiptoe. 'That guy used to work for me five years ago. One day he suddenly disappeared. Why would we be in touch? Was he my friend or what? Will he send me telegrams for Eid and Diwali?' Master-ji dropped the clay cup, crushed it with his foot, not taking his eyes off Shubhankar.

Shubhankar's throat was parched, his tongue a dry blob of tissue. He wanted to pick Master-ji up by the collar and thrash him to the ground like a dhobi thrashing clothes. He wanted to curse, tell Master-ji he knew the full truth about M, threaten to report him to the police. Hot water swam in his eyes. He tried not to let the tears fall.

But Master-ji crossed the road and went back into his shop without so much as a second look at him.

Shubhankar walked away too, disgusted by his own cowardice. If he hated anyone more than these people, it was himself. He let the tears brim over, stream down his face. He passed his fingers through his hair, matty with sweat. His legs were tired, shoulders drooped from the weight of his bag. In his head, he couldn't stop reciting – *Maajid. Mujib. Malik. Miyaan. Mansoor. Mobeen. Mahtaab. Mir* – hoping with all his might that he could stop at any one of these and think to himself, *Of course! This was M's name! Why hadn't it come to me before?*

2013

Sunset

The road is wet and slippery from the rain. The upward slope is making things difficult. He is trying his best to walk at speed, conscious of lifting his foot off the ground. Even a few months ago, he would have had to sit down a few times. Now he can do this at one stretch. He wants to tell Ma this, but he feels foolish, calling attention to his broken body on the first holiday they've taken in years. But Ma isn't looking at him anyway. She is staring out into the valley, at the clouds gathering over the peaks of the Western Ghats, the slight fog that is making everything hazy. It is her first time out of Mumbai since she moved in with him three years ago. He lets her be. A little ahead, Papa turns to check, then slows down, waits for mother and son to catch up.

They are in Mahabaleshwar. Finally, after months of Ma planning a weekend getaway. He has driven them out here, and even if the car doesn't meet the definition of *fancy*, Ma's excitement was uncontrollable. She kept talking about it all week, after he came back from work on the Monday and floated the idea. She returned from her adda the next evening and declared, 'I've told all the ladies downstairs I'll be very busy this weekend.' She held it in, widening her eyes every time Papa called. 'Let's not tell him until he gets here on Friday, okay?' She was like a child planning a surprise picnic.

This morning, she woke up early, the pigeons and crows still asleep. He was stirred awake by the ting-tung of spoons and the glug of milk being poured. She made sandwiches for the trip, neatly placing a thick layer of omelette between diagonally-cut slices of white bread, then covering it in pudina chutney that she'd made the night before. She packed it all in a lunchbox. She filled the Thermos flask with ginger tea that they sipped during their drive. She was even wearing a kurti and jeans, something she'd never wear in Lucknow. 'How am I looking?' she asked Papa, giggling. 'In Mumbai, I can be modern.' Papa looked Ma up and down in amazement, like he'd spotted a movie star.

'There isn't going to be much of a sunset today,' Papa says as mother and son now come closer, holding his palm up to his eyes and squinting at the sky, but he knows Papa has one eye on his injured leg. 'It's very cloudy.'

'No, let's go all the way,' he says. He wants to show them that he can do it, that he is all right.

Later, when they have admired the failed sunset and have come down the slope, they find a café. Ma says she wants to drink coffee. But at the counter, Ma and Papa are flummoxed by the menu. 'What's a latte?' Papa asks.

'Sir, it is black coffee with milk on top,' the girl replies.

'And what is . . . cappoo-sino?'

'Cappu-*cheeno*, sir.' The girl is getting restless. 'It is also black coffee with milk on top, but with froth.'

'So latte doesn't have froth?'

'No, sir, latte also has froth, but lesser than cappuccino.'

'Can't I just get black coffee?' Papa is getting restless too. Ma has melded into the background, studying the menu so carefully she might as well be mugging it up for exams.

'That would be Americano, sir.'

Papa pricks up his right ear. 'American coffee? Where are the other ones from then?'

He steps in to rescue his parents. 'Why don't you go and find us seats? I'll order.'

Relieved, they huddle away from the counter in quick steps.

They are finally ensconced at a table with a view, only slightly marred by two fat children trying to mount a heaving mule, the parents running around clicking photos, the mule ejecting projectiles of poop all over the pavement. Ma and Papa sip on their coffees carefully. Ma has a moustache of foam that Papa dabs away with his hankie.

'Is the coffee good?' he asks.

His parents bob their heads. 'This coffee costs one hundred and seventy-five rupees?' Papa is still stuck on the menu, can't believe the prices he's seen. Ma looks guiltily away, like she has committed a crime by wanting to drink coffee and spending so much money in the process.

'How things have changed in the last few years.' Papa shakes his head. 'Air-conditioned car, seat belts, smooth highways, American coffee shops.' Papa looks out at the darkening valley. 'I miss simpler times . . .'

He nods, sips his coffee. He wants to say to Papa, *Isn't this what you wanted, some money and small luxuries, a car and fancy coffee, and when you couldn't get it yourself, didn't you want this for your sons?* But he knows now that this is how human beings are. All we want is to move up the ladder, but once we've gone up, we look back and yearn, those markers of a past time now quaint, *retro*.

In Germany, they have a word for it – the memories of the East that have endured, even though back then people were scaling walls and crawling through tunnels to cross over to the West – *ostalgie*, born out of the need to hold on to something familiar when everything around has changed beyond recognition. He wonders if there will soon be a word in this country too.

'Remember our trips by train?' Papa's voice is wrapped in nostalgia. 'Indian Railways is *the best*! You sit by the window and watch the entire country go by, farms, villages, towns, forests – the *real* India!' Papa smiles fondly. 'And then at the stations, drinking sweet milk-tea in clay cups. Ah! That chai!' Papa smacks his lips, slaps his thigh. 'Remember?'

1990s

Dumbos

'Arre, this girl is studying here also,' Mr Dwivedi said proudly to Papa.

Dwiti Dwivedi sipped her chai from the clay cup, ignoring her father and continuing to stare at the textbook. She was sitting with her feet up on the berth, a massive biology book open on her lap. Shubhankar wondered how she could see all of it from above her breasts. Papa and Mr Dwivedi were on the platform, at the train window, killing time until the signal turned green. There was something about fathers and not getting on the train until the last minute. When they were children, Chintoo would plead with Papa, nearly in tears, and then think it heroic when Papa ran to board the train after it had started moving.

Papa widened his eyes at Shubhankar, signalling that he should be studying too. Shubhankar slouched and sipped his chai instead. He stole a look at Dhwani, who was on the other side of the aisle, focusing on something on the next platform. She'd cut her hair short, curls looping around her shoulders. She'd said it was because of the heat, but Shubhankar wondered if it was an intentional act of distinguishing herself from her identical twin, a distinction she could choose, unlike their breasts.

The five of them were going to Howrah from Lucknow

Charbagh station, but it felt to Shubhankar that everyone he knew was there. He had spotted classmates on the platform, in the other compartments. They had all seen each other so often during their travels that they'd even stopped waving. They sat with fat books and vacant looks, waiting for the month to end.

It was the summer of '99, and the whole country was on a train. Every student finishing school that year was travelling up and down the subcontinent, sitting entrance exams for every engineering college. IIT was the top choice, always, but there were backups, then backups of backups, and so on. They had to make sure they got into an engineering college by the end of the summer, even if it was a two-room space passing off as an educational institution. In the spirit of every child becoming an engineer, the government had approved any place that had a lathe and a circuit board under a waterproof roof.

Mr Dwivedi wouldn't stop talking. 'What to tell you, Dwiti is so diligent, so studious. She wants to write all the engineering *and* all the medical entrance exams! And she's good at everything. Have you seen her dance?' He clicked his tongue in happy frustration, like he would ask Dwiti to do less in life if he could. Everyone could see he was loving it! He turned to his other daughter. 'Dhwani is also very good . . .'

Dhwani continued to look out of the window squinting, like none of this was reaching her, like if she could, she'd push through the window bars and crawl out, head first.

Mr Dwivedi grew reflective. 'You know, Mr Trivedi, my relatives tell me – *If you spend so much on your daughters' education, how will you have the money to get them married? And you have two-two of them!* I say – *My daughters are my sons, they're not a burden, they're my pride!*

Papa finished his chai and aimed the clay cup through the gap between the train and platform edge. 'You're lucky to have daughters, Mr Dwivedi. They're sincere, obedient. My sons are useless! They don't study only. I don't know what will become of them.'

That summer of '99, there were two styles of parenting. One, to praise the child incessantly, pre-conferring on them degrees and titles they were yet to know the full forms of. The other, to berate them publicly like they were decadent delinquents. Shubhankar wished Papa would let him travel alone, like some of the classmates he'd seen in exam centres, without guardians, smoking after exams, partying in the evenings. But Papa had taken leave from work for a month to accompany his son. 'What kind of parent lets their child travel alone in this heat across this mad country?' he'd heard Papa say to Ma one night. Papa's boss, Mr Kaushik, hadn't objected. The only other time Ashutosh Trivedi had taken a week off was when he'd had chest pains.

'Take care of your father,' Ma had said to Shubhankar before they left for the station. 'Make sure he stays hydrated, and takes his medicines on time.' That was the only thing she'd say before their departure, no wishing him luck, no patting his head like the other parents. Ma's face had hardened that summer, tired from organizing the logistics of travel – packing, making food for the trip, washing and ironing clothes, keeping tickets and exam cards ready. She had become a machine.

Nani, on the other hand, had been jubilant. She arrived in good time before father and son left, prayed in the puja-room, made Shubhankar bow his head to the gods, spooned dahi into his mouth for good luck. 'Remember, you carry the family name on your shoulders.' She patted his cheek with her palm. 'Now go and make your Nana-ji proud. What he would've done if he were alive today, seeing his grandson become an engineer!'

Chintoo chuckled. 'He hasn't become one yet. In fact, he hasn't even got into college!' Nani turned away irritated, ignoring her younger grandson who was never up to any good.

Now the engine sounded its horn. They had about five minutes before the train left the station. 'Another chai, Mr Trivedi? This one's on me.'

'Sure-sure, Mr Dwivedi.' Papa bobbed his head. 'When the train stops at Mughalsarai, it'll be my treat.'

The two men walked away, leaving Shubhankar alone with the twins. They heaved a sigh of relief.

Shubhankar leaned forward and cleared his throat. 'Umm, Dwiti . . . you know you can't become an engineer *and* a doctor, right?' He wanted to get Dwiti's attention, impress her with his humour.

Instead, Dhwani turned around and laughed at his joke. 'Don't even try,' she said, pointing her chin at her sister. 'She's gone nuts! As if all the engineering exams aren't enough!' She reached out and brushed a strand of hair off Dwiti's forehead, like a mother would.

Dwiti looked up from her textbook. 'Ha ha!' she said in mock-amusement. 'How can you both be so dumb? Seriously! It's all about increasing your chances, guys. The more exams you take, the more avenues open to you.'

Dhwani rolled her eyes. 'But what do *you* want to become? An engineer or a doctor?'

Dwiti looked at her sister in exasperation, like they'd discussed this many times before. 'Left to myself, you know I'd become a dancer. But since that's not happening, I might as well become something that earns me money and takes me to America.' She raised her shoulders and dropped them. 'Easy-peasy! What's so difficult to understand?'

Dhwani poked Dwiti, eyes dancing with mischief, voice pregnant with an oncoming laugh. 'Tell him why you want to go to America.'

Dwiti giggled, shook her head in embarrassment. 'I mean, that's not the *only* reason, but dude, America is *full* of McDonald's!' Her eyes were wide and watery. 'You can have burger and fries every day, for every meal! Have you been to the one that's just opened in Lucknow? Dhwani and I had to queue for over an hour to even get in!'

They all laughed, so loudly that people in the other berths turned their heads to look. Shubhankar wished Chintoo was there. His brother would surely have many other virtues of America to extol.

Then he grew serious. He looked out to check where Papa and Mr Dwivedi were. He spotted them at the stall, waiting for the chai. 'And what happens if you don't get through any of these exams?' he asked. The thought had come to him many times, but he'd pushed it away. He *had* to get through at least one of them. It was his passport out of this place.

Dwiti stared at him, like she hadn't even considered this possibility. She opened and closed her mouth, once, twice, unsure of what to say.

'Have you heard of Kota?' It was Dhwani, leaning forward and whispering, like she was letting him in on a conspiracy. Shubhankar shifted in his berth so he could hear her better. 'It's this city in Rajasthan. The place is full of coaching centres for IITs. People who don't get into IIT after school go to Kota and stay there for a year or two, dedicate all their time to preparing for the exam, and most crack it in the end.' She winked. 'I guess that's what I'll do.' She seemed happy with her backup plan.

Dwiti shook her head vigorously. 'But that won't happen, trust me, guys. All of us will surely get into a top IIT.' She narrowed her eyes teasingly. 'At least *I* will. You both worry for yourselves, dumbos!'

The train started to move forward very slowly. Papa and Mr Dwivedi were running towards it, the latter's belly jerking up and down. Through the window, they passed the children a batch of freshly fried pakodas wrapped in newspaper, the oil already starting to seep through.

'Take this, fast-fast,' they said, breathing heavily. Then they made a dash for the door.

Bharat-darshan

M's heels are perfect, Shubhankar can see them through the flames, M is walking fast, late for work, Master-ji is waiting at the shop, kaamchor, he'll call M, M doesn't like that, he's not a shirker, he did turn up at the wedding, even if it was dangerous, Shubhankar is running to keep up with M, feet tapping to music on the Walkman, Bryan Adams singing '18 Till I Die', was M eighteen when he died, Shubhankar wants to ask M, he calls out, again and again, but he doesn't know M's name—

A tap on his shoulder woke Shubhankar up. The heat was unbearable, and the fan circulated more noise than air. Out of habit, his hands went to the mattress. The sheet was dry. Good. His heart was still beating fast from the dream. He turned to see Chintoo standing, a finger to his lips. *Shush*. When he'd fallen asleep, Chintoo was still on his guitar, composing.

Chintoo motioned for Shubhankar to follow. He shook his head. He was too groggy. But Chintoo was insistent. 'Come, naaaa,' he pleaded.

Shubhankar dragged himself out of bed. His body was sore. He'd always been thin, but now he could feel his ribs poke against his upper arms. He was finally done with his travels. He'd sat twenty-three exams in the space of a month, sometimes two a day.

The brothers tiptoed through the flat. Out on the staircase, they jumped two steps at a time to the terrace. Chintoo gave the door a small push. It creaked open. They walked to the wall and sat facing outward, legs dangling. There was a slight breeze up here. The leaves of the papaya tree rustled. Shubhankar took a deep breath.

'So, last exam done?' Chintoo patted him on the back, pretending to be grown up. 'What a trip, haan? Bharat-darshan! Incredible India! Roorkee to Rourkela, Calcutta to Cochin!' He spread his arms out, like a slogan for a tourism advert.

This made Shubhankar smile. His jaw muscles strained. It was probably the first time in weeks that he'd smiled. 'It wasn't just me,' he said. 'Wherever I went, I saw my classmates, their friends, cousins . . . It was like all the country's seventeen-year-olds had been packed into one place, waiting for their future to be decided by a handful of exams.'

'Sounds like a concentration camp.' Chintoo shimmied, as if a shudder were passing through him. 'It's 1999! We're almost in a new millennium! And still . . .' Then his voice got serious. 'Bhaiyya, what's the plan?'

'What do you mean *what's the plan*?'

'What do you mean *what do you mean*?' Chintoo mimicked. 'How are you okay with all this? Look at your life! You're under the thumb of these people!'

Shubhankar wanted to say something smart, something that wouldn't cut a sad figure of himself to his brother. But when he opened his mouth, something else came out. 'The plan is to leave. Just get through this and never come back. Never see the faces of these people.' The words came fast and quick.

Chintoo nodded vigorously. 'They will lose not one, but both their sons. They can go write all the fucking exams themselves.'

Fucking. Shubhankar had heard the word only in Hollywood films, and on the tongues of posh boys in school, sons of IAS officers and defence personnel who'd taken an exam called the SAT, pronounced *S-A-T*, to study in America. *Fucking* sounded out of place in this middle-class apartment block with its chipped paint and leaky pipes.

Chintoo produced two cigarettes from his pocket, slightly squished and twisted.

'You smoke? Doesn't Ma smell it on you?'

Chintoo laughed off the question, then lit both cigarettes and passed one to Shubhankar. He took a drag and coughed. It'd been a while. He'd started smoking during the last year of school, but hadn't touched a cigarette the entire month he was travelling with Papa. Soon the head-rush made his body break into a cold sweat.

'I want a life like the firangs.' Chintoo's new Adam's apple bobbed with jealousy. 'Did you know white kids have graduation parties when they finish kindergarten? And their parents celebrate when they get jobs as secretaries? They don't give a fuck about engineering! They're all about what *they* want, how *they're* feeling.'

The brothers sat in silence, imagining the glorious lives of white people.

Then Chintoo said between puffs, 'One day, I want to drive by this street in a Mercedes and not even turn to look at this house.'

Chintoo talked about money, getting rich. But for Shubhankar, just getting away from this place was enough. He didn't aspire to anything more.

Chintoo continued, 'And even if I give Ma or Papa a lift, you know who's not getting a lift from me ever?'

This was easy. 'Nani!' They laughed. Nani and Chintoo were still battling it out.

The scenarios got more bizarre as the night wore on – chauffeurs wearing white gloves, champagne chilling in the car, a sunroof they could stick their heads out of. And they would wear sunglasses – oh, for sure – like the rich people on TV. Maybe they'd give Dhwani and Dwiti a ride, one in each car. Chintoo said with a wink that he preferred Dwiti.

They'd lost track of time. It was in the wee hours that they tiptoed down the stairs. Chintoo stopped at the landing. 'Bhaiyya, is everything okay? Is there something I don't know? Sometimes I get a feeling you're keeping something from me.'

In that moment, Shubhankar was tempted to tell Chintoo everything. Wasn't this what he'd wanted for years, for Chintoo to share the burden? And wasn't it Chintoo's right – to know what the family had done, what they'd *not* done, how they'd continued living like nothing had happened, that the ghost of a burning man stared from outside their bathroom window every night?

But he looked at Chintoo now, his little brother, the creases under his eyes from his dashing smile, his nimble fingers that played the guitar, Chintoo in all his sprightly youthfulness, good-natured rebellion, wisps of a moustache falling gracefully on his upper lip. All very different to Shubhankar's own amoebic adolescence.

Did he really want to taint Chintoo's unsuspecting innocence? And was he ready to share M with anyone else?

He gave Chintoo a light kick. 'Let's go down before Ma wakes up!'

'*Fucking* hell!' Chintoo elbowed his brother away.

2013

Milestone

Dhwani Dwivedi, he types into the search bar on Facebook, clicks Enter, waits for the results to load. He suspected right, there aren't many people with that name. But there are a couple, just not the one he is looking for.

He glances up from his laptop screen. Ma is watching TV. 'What's happening with Dhwani these days?' He tries to sound casual.

Ma is so surprised that she switches off the TV by reflex. She stares at him for a second, then reorients herself. 'Umm, Dhwani, I don't know. Last I heard, she was teaching in a college or something. I haven't been in Lucknow for so long, I've lost touch . . .' She pauses for a response, but he just bobs his head. When she can't stop herself any more, she asks, 'How come you thought of Dhwani suddenly?'

He is irritated, defensive. 'Why? Can't I just ask about an old neighbour?' His voice comes out spikier than he'd planned.

Ma gives it back to him. 'Yeah, because you've been *so very* curious about the world all this time, na? You ask about people every day!' She turns away sharply and switches the TV back on, mutters under her breath, 'Now I've missed the most important part of this serial . . .'

He doesn't want to tell Ma that Dhwani has been on his mind all week, ever since the art class at the NGO last

Saturday when the girl from the building said something about cutting her hair short because of the heat. That one offhand comment had brought Dhwani's voice back into his head, her bright eyes looking at him suggestively.

He shuts the laptop, picks up his towel, and heads to the bathroom. He steps into the shower and turns it on at full force. He looks down as he hardens, his penis getting bigger under the flow of water. His stomach tickles like a little child's. He feels his arms and back while soaping himself, the few bulges in muscle still left. He stands in the shower for longer than usual, holding on to this rare moment, delaying the act he knows he is going to commit. He doesn't care about wasting water. Even if Ma wants to, she will not knock on the door and ask him to turn the shower off. He is a thirty-year-old man now, and she is in *his* flat.

He thinks about Dhwani during the field trips smiling at him from the corner of the room, Dhwani dancing Odissi onstage, Dhwani in the train leaning forward and whispering. He begins stroking himself, his breaths coming up short, in rhythmic sync with his hand. He knows that thoughts of Dwiti and M are lurking somewhere too, but he clinically pushes them out, picking them up with forceps and placing them out of his purview. The psychologist has talked about this at length, separating conscious thoughts from subconscious ones.

Dhwani, it has to be only her tonight. He strokes and strokes, takes his time, building sexy scenarios in his head, him kissing Dhwani backstage after her dance, her chest heaving from the activity, him disentangling the flower-gajra and mukoot from the bun in her dark hair, pulling out the pleats of her saree and shoving his hand in, going down on her in the train's seedy toilet while Papa and Mr Dwivedi are nearby drinking chai, his fingers hungrily squeezing her breasts, her thin warm lips on his.

When he finally climaxes, it comes from deep inside his underbelly. He can feel every nerve in his body alive, the route the semen has taken tingles. His balls are slack from releasing the tension of months. He puts his back to the wall and feels the wet tiles on his body. He is suddenly exhausted. He turns the shower off and reaches for the towel.

In the last few years since the *incident*, he has rarely felt aroused. He may have woken up with an erection in the middle of the night every now and then, and the whole thing would be done in a matter of minutes. No foreplay, no titillation, nothing to fantasize about.

An injured body is a wasted body. Neither does it desire, nor is it desired.

According to the psychologist, today would be a *milestone*. She has asked him to write his milestones down in a journal. Some he does, most he doesn't. There aren't many to begin with. But for today's one, he wouldn't know what to write.

By the time he's out of the bathroom, the spark has died, the cloud has set back in. All he wants to do is fall asleep.

But Ma is standing at the table. 'Dinner's ready,' she says. She looks tired from their little argument.

'I'm not hungry,' he mutters as he tiptoes to his room, leaving watery footprints on the floor that he knows Ma will have to wipe afterwards. He shuts the door lightly behind him.

1990s

Jaago!

Mr Dwivedi seemed the same on TV as in real life. 'Slightly taller,' Chintoo said, looking around for responses. For the last two nights, Chintoo had been in a state of frenzy, running to the window to catch a glimpse of the TV cameras, going up to the terrace for a better view of the street, even reading the newspaper from start to finish, something he never did.

Mr Dwivedi shielded his eyes from the flashlights going off the moment he came out of the gate. Reporters pushed their mics into his face. He mumbled at first, then shouted, 'Please leave our family alone.' But the reporters were like hungry animals. The mics fought like swords to stay at his mouth.

The broadcast cut to the studio where the newscaster took over. She promised to bring the latest as it unfolded. Unlike a few years ago, news wasn't limited to half an hour at nine p.m. on Doordarshan, the state broadcaster – ten minutes for national news, ten for international, five for sport, five for weather. Multiple private news channels now ran day and night – *24x7*. The tabla beats played every few minutes to announce *Breaking News*. Anchors in suits and silk kurtas worked in shifts. The double-decker ticker scrolled furiously across the screen, disappearing before anyone could make sense of the words.

'Look! That's her!' The shot cut to a picture of Dwiti. She looked younger than she had looked on the train ride, face plumper, hair shorter. It stopped halfway down her bust. Shubhankar wondered how the news channel had got hold of this photo. They'd probably bribed the studio where it was taken.

'Can't watch this any more. My heart is palpitating,' Nani said and tried looking away, but involuntarily turned back to the screen.

When the sirens had come blaring three nights ago, waking the mohalla up, Chintoo had jumped and run out of the room. Shubhankar could hear Papa shuffle into his slippers hurriedly and open the door. He tried to doze off for the next hour, but the sounds wouldn't go away. There were more sirens, police cars, ambulances, media vans, flashes. He'd walked out to the living room to find Ma sitting alone, hands cradled, head lowered in sleep, chin folded over inelegantly.

'Where's Chintoo?'

Ma said he'd gone with Papa. 'That boy can never sit still. Now *you* don't go anywhere. Sit here . . .' she looked up at him in a sleepy haze '. . . with me.'

He sat down. 'Do you know what's happened?'

'It's something at the Dwivedis' house.'

He'd wanted to go downstairs too. But Ma had asked him to stay with her, a request so rare that he couldn't imagine doing otherwise. Besides, she hadn't said much to him that summer while he'd travelled for exams. They sat side by side, not touching.

It was six in the morning when Chintoo and Papa came back. Chintoo's eyes were flicking frantically. Shubhankar could tell that the boy wanted to burst out with the news.

Papa's face was ashen. 'Arre, don't ask. Such bad business,' he said, even though no one had asked. 'One of the girls has hanged herself from the ceiling fan . . .'

'Which one?' That was the first question that came to Shubhankar's mind.

'Dwiti,' Chintoo said quietly. 'Apparently she finished her homework last night, packed her bag for school, practised dance steps with Dhwani . . .'

Shubhankar remembered the Odissi dance Dwiti and Dhwani had performed at the Diwali fair last year, organized by Suresh-mausa's nationalist party. The twins had entered the stage from either side, dressed in bright-yellow sarees perfectly pleated down the middle, their expressive eyes lined with kajal. They had worn ornaments made of flowers. Mukoots pointed skyward on their crowns. For the next few minutes, the audience had sat mesmerized as the sisters performed, fingertips joining and parting in mudras, eyebrows quivering. They circled the stage in expert formation, one standing behind the other, arms spreading out like a four-handed goddess, each hand signifying a different weapon to battle evil. When the performance had ended, Dwiti was standing, her ample bosom heaving, and Dhwani was on her knees, in front of her sister, face turned upward. Dwiti had bowed right, then left, then centre, soaking up the adulation. She'd walked to the front of the stage and bowed at Suresh-mausa, who stood up to clap. On his cue, the audience had risen for a standing ovation.

'. . . They're saying the pressure got to her – studies, dance, everything. I guess, with all the results coming out soon, she couldn't bear the possibility of failing . . .' Chintoo's voice trailed off.

Dwiti's eyes looked back at Shubhankar, that day on the

train, how resolute they were, how confident, how ambitious. How could she have given up like this?

Mr Dwivedi was now speaking to the reporters. He couldn't stop himself once he'd broken his silence. 'She was the best daughter. She came first in class, she was preparing hard for IIT, she was a top dancer, she won prizes at the Maths Olympiad. What else could a parent ask for?' He burst into sobs, lips trembling, Adam's apple bobbing. 'Why wouldn't she just tell me if she felt overwhelmed? I never asked anything of her. Everything she did was her choice.'

From behind him, Dhwani appeared, a shawl wrapped tightly around her body, hair in a topknot, eyes confused and empty. The cameras abandoned Mr Dwivedi and focused on her. *Hurry! That's the twin sister!* Dhwani tugged at her father's arm, led him into the house, mumbling inaudibly in his ear the whole time, like a mother to an inconsolable child. She closed the gate behind them.

The shot cut back to the studio where a panel of experts was waiting. 'Is this the price our youth will have to pay for economic development? Every exam season there are so many suicides,' a woman with a big bindi on her forehead was saying. She looked like a professor at one of those arts universities Ma and Papa would never send Shubhankar to. *Too softy-softy, no job prospects.* 'Will we make India a technology superpower over the dead bodies of our kids? How many more lives will it take before parents acknowledge their kids' trauma?' The woman looked straight at the camera and held up her fingers, her manicured nails shining in the spotlight. 'This girl, by committing this brutal act on herself, has sent a message to the entire country. She's saying – *Jaago! Wake up! Listen to the youth! Don't sacrifice them for the dreams of the nation!*'

Ma scoffed. 'There is no message to be sent by tying a dupatta around your neck. People who do these things think they'll change the world in their wake.' Her voice was pointed and bitter. 'In the end, nothing changes. You have to live your hardships out with grace. No one's life is easy . . .'

Ma was looking at the TV the whole time, but Shubhankar knew she was talking to him.

Hinglish

Shubhankar is hanging from a pole, a dupatta around his neck, tightly wound, red welts on his body, M is standing below, the flames warm Shubhankar, like a pot cooking on a fire, Papa says to the reporters, I had no idea, it was all his choice, Shubhankar wriggles, tries to set himself free, M is extending his hand but Shubhankar can't reach it, Miss Lucy tap-taps in reeking of cigarettes, she holds up a drawing, on it written in squiggly Urdu alphabet – jaane do beta, let go—

Shubhankar had nodded off for only five minutes. He'd tried everything these past few nights – sleeping with the pillow over his face to keep out Chintoo's guitar-playing, waking up in the night to sketch, masturbating thinking of Dwiti then Dhwani then Dwiti again. But nothing worked. The only drawings that came out were of Dwiti hanging from the fan, the tightness of the dupatta around her neck accentuated by furious lines. Sometimes the page tore from the pressure of his pencil. He skipped over the breasts, making them shapeless under her nightdress, which is what he imagined her hanging in. In the bathroom, no semen came out, though he was always erect.

Tonight he went up to the terrace. He sat on the wall, legs outward, facing the back garden. He looked down from the fifth floor. In the dark, he could only see his dangling legs, his crooked feet, bones jutting out at the knees, body hair curling gracelessly. He would hate his pubescent body, if it was possible to hate himself any more.

He thought about how easy it would be to slip away. No sound needed. No message to leave behind. Nothing to change in his wake. Just melt into oblivion.

The strike of a matchstick, a flash held up to a cigarette, the flame extinguished with an expert motion of the wrist. Shubhankar flinched, held the wall tightly. Papa's face lit up, then receded into the dark, leaving only a flickering dot, like a light on a distant highway. The smoke curled upward in perfect rings. He didn't know Papa had this talent. He didn't even know Papa came upstairs.

'When I graduated, your Dada-ji packed me off to Calcutta,' Papa started without preamble. '*There is no future in Lucknow. Never come back here.* I still remember him saying that. We were standing on the railway platform.' Papa took a deep drag of the cigarette, followed by perfect smoke rings again. 'But in the big cities, thousands turned up. In the seventies, there were no jobs, no American multinationals. Only public sector. The British had left us with nothing to start from, had looted this country through and through. I waited for hours outside offices. The Anglo-Indian receptionists shooed us away like cattle. In the interviews, Indian men with foreign degrees wore suits and spoke English like they'd just stepped off the ship from England.' Papa laughed. 'And there I was in my simple cotton shirt and trousers, trying to answer their questions in Hinglish.'

Shubhankar knew this story – not finding a job, the eventual return to Lucknow, working as an accountant for no pay in an uncle's shop. Until the job at the fertilizer factory had materialized like a miracle. But Dada-ji had never got over his son's failure. *I fought to free this country, but this country couldn't even give my son a respectable life.*

Papa stubbed the cigarette out and flicked the butt with a flair, then lit another and, while the matchstick was still burning, offered Shubhankar one. He declined.

'You know what's unique about the Indian middle class?' Papa didn't wait for an answer. 'We have no fallback option. The poor can give up. They have nothing to lose in the first place. The rich can pay their way through things, escape the country, go on a retreat. But we middle-class people . . . we have to keep going. We have to work every day to hold on to the little things we've acquired. And we fear that politicians will take even those away.'

Papa came closer. Shubhankar could feel their sleeves touching in the breeze. 'What is worse than not having money?' Papa waited patiently this time, but Shubhankar didn't know the answer. 'Not having a voice.'

Papa put a hand on his shoulder. 'We have nothing to give to our children. No inheritance, no connections, not even our talents, if we had any in the first place. So we can only give you an education. That is the only weapon you have, to break through this ceiling and move up the ladder.' His fingers drummed on Shubhankar's shoulder blade. 'I know you are a sensitive boy, you are affected by things you see. You want to change the world, make everything right. But you'll see later . . . if we don't look out for ourselves, no one else will.' Papa withdrew his hand. 'And poverty is really wretched. If we ever slip into it, there's no coming out. Everything we've built step by step is so fragile . . .'

Papa nudged Shubhankar to turn around and put his feet on the terrace. He obeyed. Papa started walking towards the stairs.

'Can I stay here for a little longer?' Shubhankar asked in a small voice.

Papa's footsteps stopped. 'You'll be all right? No funny business?'

They stayed like that for a few minutes. Then he heard Papa close the door carefully behind him. The rusty hinges echoed in the stillness of the night.

Dashehri

The summer of '99 was also the summer of mangoes.

'Langra is the best variety,' Panna-chacha said. His mouth was bright orange.

'Dashehri!' Suresh-mausa insisted, then made loud noises as he sucked on the gutli. 'That is the king of mangoes, the pride of Lucknow!' He smiled, pulp sticking to his teeth. He smiled a lot these days, ever since he'd been elected to the local legislative assembly on a nationalist party ticket. The orange of the mango matched the saffron of his scarf. Little trishul stickers gleamed in the light, his party's symbol, the trident.

Nani sighed, eyebrows raised, eyes to the floor, making her discontent known. This was not why she'd called everyone here. *Mango conference*, Chintoo had named it. Panna-chacha and Manju-chachi, Lekha-bua and Nandu-fufa, Aarti-mami and Girish-mama, Suresh-mausa and Pushpa-mausi, Kejriwal-sir and the ghost of his dead wife, had all been invited for a purpose. Nani felt the agenda slip away from her fingers, like the gutli itself.

'Mangoes will come every summer, but what to do about *this one*? This is the one and only summer of *his* life.' With a slight movement of her chin, Nani pointed to Shubhankar, who hadn't touched a mango. A hush fell over the room. Juices were guiltily gulped, gutlis put back on plates.

The results of the twenty-three exams had started to come

out like drip-feed. When the first one arrived, Ma had taken the letter from the postman and torn it open gracelessly, nothing like the way she'd preserved the envelope from the school all those years ago. SHUBHANKAR TRIVEDI — FAIL was typed across a sheet of paper. The cheap typewriter ink was already fading.

Others had been lists put up in colleges. Shubhankar and Papa started at different ends of the list, working their way to the middle, until their fingers reached the centre. Then they split and started again. When they were sure Shubhankar's name wasn't there, they rode back in silence on Papa's new scooter.

Shubhankar spent his days at home as Chintoo went to school and Papa went to work. He waited for the postman to bring another letter that said FAIL. News of his classmates making it to colleges trickled in. Sometimes he went to Maulviganj to help Miss Lucy with her SUPW classes. There were many students signed up now and she needed a volunteer to manage them. The children of the slum asked Shubhankar why he wasn't running the arts class any more. They still came up to show him their drawings, disregarding the student who'd taken his place. Whenever he ran into Salma-begum, she greeted him with a big smile and kind eyes, but nothing more.

Sometimes he roamed the streets in the hot afternoons when everyone else had sought shelter. He'd spent six years walking around the city, trying to find answers for what had happened to M, trying to reconstruct him as a person. He'd failed desperately. Someone should type that out on a piece of paper. BIGGEST FAIL.

Every evening, Nani brought news from the mohalla. 'What-what things people are saying! Apparently he was up to some mischief. Not going to classes, walking around the streets aimlessly, like he was . . . high on something.' She lowered her voice. 'They saw him in the slums . . . He was even at the Aminabad police station, they say!' She referred to Shubhankar in the third person, even when he was there. She slapped her palm on her forehead and sobbed, 'What would his Nana-ji have said if he were alive? Why is he dragging the family name through muck? Is this how he repays all our hard work?'

Suddenly she wiped her tears and turned her ire on Ma. 'Didn't I say from the start? One has to be strict with the children. What is this circus? One son is roaming the streets, the other is playing the guitar. People are saying the mother was too lenient.'

'People always find a way to blame the woman, na?' Ma shot back. 'The father can check out of home by going to work. The sons can be disobedient and wayward. It's the woman who has to go around fixing everyone and everything.'

Nani squirmed and looked away. She knew it wasn't her place to gossip about her son-in-law in his own house. This was the most Ma had said in the last few days. She hadn't spoken to Shubhankar at all, even though they'd been stuck together in the flat all day. She'd gone from chore to chore like a robot, her face expressionless, eyes puffy.

The mango conference was Nani's social masterstroke, to get everything out in the open, to collectively commiserate, to get everyone to contribute to the solution.

Now a mango popped up in Shubhankar's field of vision. He turned to find Suresh-mausa holding it up for him. 'Don't be so sad, beta! Today, one can be whatever he wishes!' He jabbed a finger at his own chest to exemplify his comment. 'Look at our India. We're a nuclear power! The Americans said – *You're a poor country, you can't go nuclear.* We said – *We'll show you what we can and can't do!*' Suresh-mausa shook his head in disbelief at the magnitude of the feat. 'Now as we speak, our soldiers are slaying the Pakistanis in the Kargil war. If we want, we can nuke the whole of Pakistan in thirty minutes!' The mango almost squelched as he tightened his grip.

Shubhankar spotted a turtle-shaped paperweight within reach. He wanted to lob it at Suresh-mausa's head. *We can nuke Pakistan but we can't protect our own people.* He held his one itching hand tightly in the other.

Suresh-mausa turned to Papa with an air of business. 'It's not impossible to get your son into an engineering college. A phone call from someone important, a little donation, all this can go a long way.' He looked around the room for effect. 'Let all the results come out. If you still need my help, I'm always here. Serving the people is my duty.'

At this assurance, everyone looked relieved and reached back for their half-eaten mangoes. Suresh-mausa nudged Shubhankar again. At the touch, a static passed through his body. He recoiled, but Papa was staring at him sternly, an instruction to accept the gift from the most powerful person in the room.

Shubhankar relented, made a dent in the fruit, and sucked the juice noisily.

Tamasha

The circle turned against the white screen, emptying and replenishing itself. The sound was of a thousand cats wailing. The wind blew in from the open window, pregnant with the promise of water. It was the day of the first monsoon rain, and the day of the last result.

'It won't take long.' Dhruv sounded apologetic, feeling responsible for the performance of this second-hand laptop that his uncle had brought from America. Chintoo didn't mind the wait – the longer the better. He ran his fingers on the keys, the touchpad, the screen that was also a lid! *What the actual fuck! This is the most gizmo thing EVER.*

The last result was to be announced on the *internet*. It was the newest thing on the scene, like Kwality smoothies a few summers ago, or baggy jeans with six pockets in the new Pantaloons store. The brothers had trekked to Dhruv's place where the laptop was hooked to the internet by a *dial-up connection*, via a *modem*, the black box shining a row of lights like a discotheque and screeching like cats.

Then suddenly, the cats fell silent and the screen went blank. The contents of the page began to appear, line by line, top to bottom, as if from a typewriter – logo, name of institute, name of exam, year, roll number, white space, more white space. Then SHUBHANKAR TRIVEDI: UNSUCCESSFUL. Then white space, footer . . .

Shubhankar turned to the window. He fixed his gaze on

the trees dancing like manic dervishes at the first hint of cool breeze, so he didn't have to look at Chintoo and Dhruv. He wished they'd give him some time alone. But this was Dhruv's house. Surely he couldn't ask Dhruv to leave his own room?

'Wait. I may know how to change this!' Dhruv's voice was optimistic. No one in the mohalla knew the internet better than he did, if at all. 'Now you take the mouse to this circular arrow icon . . .' Chintoo observed with wide eyes. 'And you refresh the page!' Dhruv clicked the mouse laboriously. The circle of life appeared again. The screen went blank. The cats woke up to wail. The page spurted back line by line. Still UNSUCCESSFUL. The laptop started to make loud whirring noises. Dhruv said it needed to be shut down.

On their way back, rain pelted down like stones. People ran for cover, squeezing their bodies under shop shelters and tarp awnings, umbrellas dented downward or blown back upward. Vendors pushed their carts to safety. The brothers waded through the water collecting on the street, the drains overwhelmed by the sudden downpour, still clogged with dry leaves from the summer. Chintoo said if it weren't raining so hard, they could've stopped for a smoke.

Shubhankar knew Ma could tell the moment she opened the door. She saw it in the faces of her bedraggled boys. Papa appeared behind her. Perhaps he could tell as well, although he asked. Chintoo mumbled something, and Papa went back to the living room. Shubhankar slowly took off his wet shoes, soaked socks. Nani came with a cloth and mopped the puddles off the floor in silence, avoiding eye contact.

He went into the bedroom and sat down, not caring that his wet clothes were staining the bedsheet. Ma called everyone for dinner. He heard the ting-tung of stainless-steel plates and silent crunching of bhindi. They didn't call for him. No one could face each other tonight.

After dinner, Ma came in with a dusting cloth. In quick movements, she slapped the life out of everything in her way. Dust sprayed across the room, cobwebs landed on bed-clothes, spiders escaped, dancing on their many legs. The cloth turned black when Ma wiped the backs of the furniture. She made a pile of his books and dumped them on Chintoo's bed. She threw his school uniform out of the cup-board, on which classmates had written farewell messages with multicoloured pens on the last day of school. She stopped at his drawings. He thought she'd tear them up, but she shoved them in a drawer. The corners crumpled. She dragged the guitar out from under Chintoo's bed. A string broke and hung limply. She wrapped it in an old faded saree and took it away. 'No more majlis. Too much singing and dancing has happened in this house,' she said loudly. Chintoo tried to protest, but slunk back when he saw Ma's face.

When she was done, Ma went to her room and banged the door shut. They heard her shout through the walls, 'Didn't I tell you that ordinary people's children also turn out ordinary? How did we even *think* our sons would do better than us?' The words sounded like clouds bursting inside her chest.

Papa knocked on the door. This was the first time he'd been evicted from his room. He didn't know what to do. Ma had never claimed any part of the flat as just her own. 'Vasundhara, don't be like this. What's all this tamasha?' Papa's voice was meek. His pacifying skills had lost their edge tonight. 'Come on, open the door.' Rat-a-tat-tat. 'All is not lost. Didn't Suresh-ji say he had connections? He'll sort something out, get a college admission for—'

Shubhankar took his drawings out of the drawer, walked

to the bathroom and shut the door with a thud. He ran the water at full speed. He didn't care. In fact, he wanted Ma to hear, wanted her to ask him to turn the tap off, to argue with him. *Fuck you, Vasundhara Trivedi. FUCK YOU. Come confront me if you have the courage. Come slap my face. Say something! Don't treat me like I don't exist! Don't talk about me in the third person! Don't shut me out!*

He tore through the drawings, again, again, again, until they were nothing but little bits of paper dropping to the floor. He collected them and put them in the pot, cranked the flush, watched them swirl in the gushing water like tiny particles in Brownian motion. He flushed again, again, again, until there was no sign of them.

Then he splashed water on his face, his red-hot ears. The water landed on his skin in floods, cool from the first rain. So, this is what would become of him, Suresh-mausa was going to decide his future. That man's charity was his only hope. That man, M's murderer, was to be Shubhankar's saviour. And then what? He'd live here all his life, in this wasted town where men burnt men alive, then sat around debating which mango was best. Where people brushed aside a child's night-mares in pursuit of wide-eyed daydreams.

He took deep breaths in and out, in and out. What a mess he'd made of his life! He'd obsessed about the past so much that he'd ended up without a future.

No, he couldn't be another addition in Suresh-mausa's saf-fron favour bank, another trishul on his scarf. He had to seize control.

He would take a year out to study. He would go to Kota, lead the life of an ascetic – no TV, no friends, surrounded by losers who didn't make this year's exams. He'd throw himself into his studies, remember everything – formulae, equations, theories. He'd crack at least one of the twenty-three exams next year and get out of here. He'd never think of M again. The whole world had forgotten M, why shouldn't he? He'd never read the newspaper, never draw. He'd be like everyone else in this country, blinkered, apathetic. That was the only way to survive here.

And when he finally got out of this hellhole – this claustrophobic flat, Papa and his middle-class people-pleasing, Nani and her taunts, Chintoo and his oblivion, Ma, especially Ma and her pin-pricking coldness, in that faraway place – he'd discard all signs of his origins. He'd find his own people, make his own home. That would be the end of Shubhankar Trivedi, and the start of something new, *someone* new.

He turned the tap off. The only sound in the flat was the ticking of the gilt-bronze clock.

PART THREE
Vaayu / *Wind*

2000s

Y2K

'Shabby.'

The man arched his eyebrows in surprise. 'Huh?'

'My name is Shabby,' he repeated and settled into his seat. It was an 'E', neither aisle nor window. He felt foolish not asking for a window seat at the check-in counter. He hadn't even known about checking in. One never had to check in for Indian Railways.

'Subramaniam,' the man in the aisle seat introduced himself, the South Indian name placing him confidently on the map. He still seemed hopeful that Shabby would reveal more about his origins, but Shabby looked away. He was a 24-year-old on his first flight ever. He wasn't going to spoil it making small talk.

Shabby. The name had bounced off his tongue that first day of engineering college as he'd introduced himself to the other students. It gave away nothing – where he was from, his religion, caste, even gender. He could be anything, anyone. As far as he was concerned, Shubhankar Trivedi was dead. The others had been the same. Sunil was Sunny. Kashyap was Cash. Ramesh was Mesh. The ones who didn't rename themselves were named by friends. The dark-skinned was Kaalia, short one was Tingoo, pothead was Ganjeri. Everyone deserved a second chance. It was the new millennium – Y2K. They had left their parents' homes forever. A new life beckoned.

Subramaniam gave up on Shabby and began chatting to the white guy in the window seat. Shabby craned his neck to see if there was a smoking area at the back, but this was 2005, not the 1970s. Nor were the air hostesses, in their tightly draped peacock-printed sarees and silk blouses, any good. They'd welcomed him with a sour face, hadn't offered a drink, and now weren't bringing the food out. Shabby felt betrayed.

Subramaniam rang for the air hostess every few minutes. The lady refused to come out, though they saw her peeping from behind the curtain. 'Too slow.' Subramaniam shook his head in frustration.

'You mean the plane is too slow?' The white guy's wonder seemed genuine, like the Indian spirituality he'd come here for had ways of estimating speed in mid-air.

'No-no.' Subramaniam bobbed his head. 'I meant the service.'

The two men talked about flights and travel, cities and work. Shabby nodded off to sleep as they pulled their wallets out to share photographs of their children. The pilot's voice crackled over the speaker. *Ladies and gentlemen, welcome aboard this flight to Mumbai . . .*

Mumbai. Bombay. A few years ago, the local Marathis had elected to cast away the British hide and embrace the indigenous name. But the city still had the sea, the glamour and movie stars and businesspeople, the freedom to live. This was what Shabby had worked towards for years, a fresh start on his own terms.

That night in the summer of '99, when he'd walked up to Papa and said he wasn't going to ask for favours from Suresh-mausa, that he'd take a year out in Kota and prepare for the exams again, to his surprise, his father had agreed, and even Ma had opened the bedroom door and let Papa back in. The following summer, when he'd got into an engineering college – not an IIT, but still a respectable second-tier one in Vellore – his parents had swallowed their disappointment and thrown a celebratory party before he left. Panna-chacha and Manju-chachi, Lekha-bua and Nandu-fufa, Aarti-mami and Girish-mama, Sharma-uncle and Sharma-aunty, Kejriwal-sir and the ghost of his dead wife, Papa's boss Mr Kaushik, had all gathered, eating mangoes even though the harvest hadn't been great that season. Suresh-mausa was out of town, and Shabby was thankful for that.

For eight semesters, he'd kept his head down and studied hard. He'd stopped reading the papers, turned away from the TV in the hostel common room. He hadn't watched even when the planes crashed into the World Trade Center in New York, or terrorists crashed into the Parliament in Delhi, or the state of Gujarat erupted in riots. After every semester, as his first-class results trickled in, he'd known that he was inching out of the shadow of his past.

And then, the final step – the job interview. Shabby had felt stuffy in the suit Papa bought for him. This was the first time he'd worn one. Ma had suggested getting one stitched by Master-ji, but Papa scoffed. *That guy makes women's blouses.* The next day, they'd gone to the Raymonds showroom in Hazratganj, in Lucknow city centre. Shabby was measured from head to toe. A jet-black suit was delivered within days.

The interview had a panel of three – two middle-aged pot-bellied men, stiff collars holding up the fat around their jaws in a perfect arc, like traditional Kathakali dancers; one lean suave man in a navy-blue open-collared shirt and steel-grey tight trousers. Shabby had already taken a technical written test, and the Kathakali dancers honed in – how had he solved this problem, how did one use objects in programming, the future of Java. They asked about internships, pored over reports he'd submitted. They bobbed their heads at everything he said. He couldn't tell if they were agreeing or disagreeing.

The man in the open-collared shirt was, in comparison, the modernist dancer. He waited until the Kathakali performance was over. His English had a tinge of something foreign, the Rs rolling off his tongue. *Tao-werrrr.* An American version of Miss Lucy. His questions weren't technical. Instead, he'd asked Shabby about himself – how he saw his life in ten years, what his hobbies were, was he in a relationship? Shabby had never been asked such things. No one had ever been interested in *him*. He shook his head, tried to say something modern-sounding, like he was *between relationships*. He'd heard it in some foreign movie. But the words wouldn't form on his tongue. He was aware he was coming across as a villager to Mr Suave.

'What city would you like to live in?' the man in the blazer asked. Another googly, like Miss Lucy. What was with these Westernized people? Didn't they know that in this country, one didn't have the luxury of choices? *Just give me the job already!* 'As an American multinational, we have offices everywhere,' Mr Suave explained. 'In a couple years, you could also move abroad . . .' He looked at Shabby pointedly, aware that he'd dangled the fattest of carrots. *Abroad! Dollars!*

'Mumbai,' Shabby blurted out. It came from deep within. It was the furthest away from Lucknow he'd ever wanted to go. The city of dreams, of nightmares.

'Bombay,' Mr Suave said, stubbornly holding on to the British name.

'Bombay,' repeated the Kathakalis, their flab sinking deeper into their collars.

'Bombay,' Shabby whispered under his breath.

'Yourrr gonna have so much funnnn.' Mr Suave had a glint in his eye.

When the offer arrived, Shabby had stared at the printed words – OFFER, SOFTWARE ENGINEER, SALARY, MUMBAI. He called his parents on his new mobile phone. Papa had bought it for him last winter. It was an expensive one, with a polyphonic ringtone. 'Xerox the letter and send it to us,' Ma said. 'I'll file it with your school admission and engineering college acceptance letters.' His three achievements in twenty-four years of life.

'It's an email attachment, Ma.'

She'd grunted at this.

Now he woke up with a jolt as the plane made a full left turn in mid-air. Every few seconds, it ran into thick grey clouds. The engines revved noisily as if in battle. But after each cloud passed, a little more of the city appeared, a little closer. Long roads snaking through an endless mass of concrete buildings, flyovers twisting and criss-crossing, a sliver of beach, the sea in the periphery at all times.

Subramaniam pointed to his white friend. 'Look, that's a local train. The lifeline of Mumbai.' Shabby leaned in to see a tiny long box on glistening tracks, like a toy.

The white guy jumped in his seat and stabbed his finger on the glass, pointing to an endless stretch of deep blue. 'Is that, like, an infinity pool?'

Subramaniam smiled indulgently. 'No-no. Those are tarpaulin sheets on slum shanties. They use them as cover during the monsoon season.'

The pilot's voice crackled again. *Ladies and gentlemen, welcome to Mumbai . . .*

Bombay Duck

The taxi was clammy. It hurtled down the Western Express Highway, floating on smooth road, bumping over potholes. The strange smell still hung in the air, the same as when Shabby had travelled from the airport to the hotel, pungent, like the stench of garbage, but not quite. His hand went up to cover his nose.

'New to the city?' the driver asked, angling the rear-view mirror so he could look at his passenger. Shabby nodded, then took in the sights. Families living under flyovers, men hawking wares at traffic signals, women rocking babies in hammocks made of torn rags, children selling India flags, garbage stashed in unsupervised construction sites. The parade of life.

'This is a city of smells,' the driver said. 'Now you'll smell garbage. The next moment, perfume. Now public latrines. Then freshly fried vada-pau. In a few months, you'll miss the smells when you're away.' A plastic packet flew towards the taxi and got stuck to the metal meter, flapping noisily as it emptied its contents on the windscreen. Old flowers and bits of rotten fruit blew away.

'Where are you from?'

'Lucknow.' Shabby bit his tongue. Where he was from didn't matter. His life was starting, here, now.

'Ahhh!' the driver grinned. 'I could tell that you're from the north. You don't look like you're from here. Even your

Hindi . . . so pure!' Shabby had only asked if the driver would go to Colaba, but that had been enough to pick up his accent. The driver was from the north too. Allahabad. He slapped his hand on the wheel in excitement. The horn sounded by mistake. A dog crossing the road raised its tail and bolted out of the way. 'The locals don't like us, they say we're taking their jobs, but we North Indians keep this city going,' the driver said with pride.

Shabby observed the insides of the taxi. Even though it was a kaali-peeli, the black-and-yellow painted cabs of Mumbai, the interior was like Bollywood Disneyland on steroids. The walls were covered in puffy plastic all the way to the roof. Madhuri Dixit was on the left and right, Rani Mukerji and Preity Zinta pouted from the top, Aishwarya Rai squeezed a lemon between the windows. 'I drive with all my heart-throbs.' The driver looked shy. 'Fifteen years in this city and I still hope that one day, a movie star will open the door of the taxi and sit beside me.'

Colaba was a long way from Andheri, where Shabby had checked into a hotel arranged for by the company. He'd stay there for two weeks while he found a place to live. A few others were there too, all part of the same cohort. They'd instantly formed a group, had dinner together on the first night, shared useful information on where to get new SIM cards. Tonight, they'd planned to party. 'This is the disco capital, baby,' a boy said, waving his hands to imaginary disco beats. The others rocked their bodies too. Shabby had slipped out for the evening, promising to meet them later. There was something he needed to do first, something he'd promised to do the moment he got to this city.

A new smell infiltrated his nostrils. 'Does the garbage not get picked up?'

'Oh, this isn't garbage. This is the Bombay Duck.' Shabby

tried to imagine a raft of smelly ducks floating in the briny seawater. The driver spotted the confusion. 'But Bombay Duck is not a duck, sir. It's a fish.' He waited for Shabby's reaction. He'd clearly told this story many times. 'During British rule, they transported the fish in the Bombay Mail train. And *mail* is *daak* in Hindi. And *daak* sounds like duck!' He gave Shabby a moment to process this. 'That's how the fish got its name! Ghajjab, no sir?' He seemed proud of his general knowledge.

Every few kilometres, the neighbourhoods grew fancier, leafier. The smell of the Bombay Duck receded. The air was suffused with the heaviness of impending raindrops. They passed buildings several storeys high with solid iron gates and bevies of security guards. When the taxi turned into Marine Drive, the grey sea came into view and ran alongside them. Shabby stuck his head out of the window and let his hair fly.

They passed the Air India building. Shabby craned his neck to count the number of floors, but the taxi zoomed past to the Oberoi Hotel, Inox mall and Churchgate station, finally stopping at the Gateway of India.

Shabby sprang out of the little kaali-peeli car.

The driver smiled, baring his teeth stained red with paan-juice. 'Welcome to Mumbai, sir. It is the best city in the world.'

Shabby inhaled the salty air. He surveyed the iconic Taj Mahal Hotel that Jamsetji Tata had built to stick it up to the British, because the whites wouldn't allow *uncouth* Indians into their haunts. Now white tourists walked in and out of the hotel with elan.

He turned to face the Gateway of India, the central arch flanked by two smaller ones, a solid stone structure looking out to the bay. Little dinghies floated in the grey waters. A muted sunlight broke through the thick clouds. A big boat had just come in from the Elephanta Caves and tourists were getting off. Couples canoodled along the boulevard. A man with a camera walked up to Shabby and asked if he'd like a photograph. Shabby shook his head. The man moved on to the white backpackers, who happily posed as if they were dangling the Gateway from their fingertips. A little girl sat on the ground with souvenirs on a plastic sheet, but the wind was threatening, and she began collecting her wares and putting them away in her bag.

Shabby walked down the narrow lane and turned right into a bustling street market. Colaba Causeway. Chappals, yoga pants, bead necklaces, bathroom fittings hung from the stalls. He walked on, crossing Horniman Circle and Asiatic Society, stopped for bhel-puri by the side of the street, savouring the crispy rice topped with zingy onions and chilli powder. He looped back to the Jewish synagogue, a modest structure bathed in a shade of blue. He knew he was taking his time, preparing himself for what he was about to do.

At Rhythm House, people were leaving with CDs and vinyls. He stepped into a booth to listen to a random CD he'd picked out. 'Prem Joshua', the cover said. A white guy chanted the Gayatri Mantra to atmospheric synthesizer music. Shabby moved his body to the rhythm, holding the large headphones to his ears, like he'd seen in the movies. He smiled at an image of himself in the glass. Later, he bought the CD.

After some more walking, he finally stood facing the Bombay Stock Exchange. The tall circular building was familiar from all those newspaper images he still vividly remembered. He turned to catch the name DALAL STREET on a sign. When Mumbai was still Bombay, and the thirteen bombs had gone off in 1993, the ones planned by the underworld don, one had exploded here. The area was sparsely populated on a Sunday evening. The only sound was of children playing cricket. Shabby looked around this peaceful street, at the children in the middle of their game. The place seemed to have no sign of rupture, ready to open for business on Monday morning. The underworld don was still in exile and had never returned to India.

Shabby wondered what M would have made of this truce.

Could Shabby put it all behind him too? During the riots in Gujarat a few years ago, when he had been in engineering college, even when he'd tried to look the other way, not paying attention to the TV in the common room, focusing on his game of table tennis, he'd been aware of the months of violence against Muslims, slums burnt down, women raped, children slaughtered, families shoved into ovens and baked alive, heads cut off with swords, mosques vandalized. The state government had looked away, just like Shabby and the rest of the world.

But in his dreams, Shabby had seen Suresh-mausa walking with a spear, a saffron band with gleaming trishuls around his head, ordering his men to kill all the Muslim tailors of Gujarat, especially those whose names started with M. Suresh-mausa chanted *Zero, Shoonya.* No matter how many dead tailors were dumped at his feet, he was insatiable. *Zero, zero, zero!* Shabby would wake up with shivers, sketching in the light of a torch, lest he disturb his room-mates. With trembling hands, he drew tailors' heads placed in a line on the street, their scissors and spools of thread and sewing machines and measuring tapes piled high in a corner, like a celebratory bonfire.

A student leader who was organizing a candlelight vigil against the government inaction had urged Shabby to join in, bring his sketches to the protest march. *We can make a slogan out of this. Zero rapes. Zero slaughters. Zero violence.* But Shabby had torn all his drawings up the next morning. They wouldn't solve a thing. He'd failed to do anything for M, who still made appearances in his dreams, visitations that left him depleted for days. He had failed M. Now the only thing left was to try and forget him.

That is what he was here to do.

Fat raindrops fell in large spots on Dalal Street. The humid air and the cool breeze mixed in a strange concoction of temperatures. The children picked up their wickets and ran for cover. One of the boys fell behind, looking for the ball. Shabby spotted it and bowled it over to him. The boy caught it like an expert and flashed a smile.

Then Shabby turned to leave. If he could speak to M, he would have said, *This is where we part, my friend. I couldn't do right by you, but I leave you here to heal, like this city has healed.*

Right then, the stock market disappeared behind sheets of rain.

2013

Onrush

He is back at the Bombay Stock Exchange, eight years after that lazy Sunday evening.

He was in Colaba for a client meeting, at which he'd nodded along to what his manager said. When it was his turn to present, the manager had just kept talking, only glancing at him when it was time for a change of slide. He'd obediently pressed the Next key. When the meeting was done, his colleagues looked away embarrassed, then dispersed, scrambling to catch the local train from Churchgate or hailing kaali-peeli taxis, keen to beat the evening rush. He decided to amble around, not ready to go back to the flat just yet. He walked down Colaba Causeway to the Asiatic Society, crossed Horniman Circle, onward to Dalal Street. His leg ached, the limp becoming pronounced as he covered more distance. But he kept going.

Today Dalal Street is bustling. There are no children playing cricket. Instead, busy traders are investing and selling, food-stalls keeping them fed on vada-pau and pau-bhaji. Cars are clogging up the narrow alleys, suited businessmen jumping out with an air of busyness, files in hand, shouting into their mobile phones. Along the pavements, clerks sit under tarpaulin covers with typewriters, assiduously typing up documents for clients. One looks up at him and asks, 'Sir, you need a typist or stamp duty done?'

He shakes his head, feeling out of place, unprepared for this hecticness. It is as if he has walked on to the stage during a live performance, having previously come here only after the lights had been switched off.

He steps aside, making way for the onrush. He tries to find the exact spot he had stood in that evening, where he'd bid farewell to M.

But he is unable to locate it. *No matter, what's the point anyway?* Back then, he had believed he was on the threshold of a new life, in a new city, with a new name, new friends, and a body strong with the zest of youth.

Now, how much has changed. His body is broken. His promises remain unkept. His friends are gone. He doesn't care for names any more.

But this city is still what it always has been, unrelenting in the face of anything coming its way. And much like this city, M too has prevailed, not abiding by any farewell. M is still here, with him, within him.

2000s

Mach-mach

'Sir, your name?'

'Shabby,' he offered, resisting the question, but the property broker swayed his head like an elephant. 'All these short-forms don't work here. Your good name, please.'

It was a hot Sunday afternoon. The broker was at the gate of the building, alternately screaming into his mobile phone and spitting on the ground. He came forward and shook Shabby's hand. Their sweaty palms made a squishing sound.

At the gate, the security guard tried his best to write down Shabby's full name, scribbling some letters from the English alphabet into the visitors' log, then gave up. The guard asked the broker, 'You know the rules, na?' The broker gave a thumbs-up and spat some more. He had forewarned Shabby – the building was owned by a church, and only Christians could live there. But the broker said he had a *strategy* in mind.

On their way up, Shabby asked, 'Does the landlord know I'm single?' He'd learnt to clarify beforehand. He'd spent the last two weeks looking for a place. The brokers showed him what he could afford and what he was allowed. They were not always the same thing. His bachelor status disqualified him from most accommodation.

'No worries, bro,' the broker winked. 'These are Christians. They are cool. They eat all kinds of meat, play the guitar, drink alcohol. They go out with girls even before they get married. Being single is not a problem.'

The door opened and an elderly lady stepped out. She had short-cropped hair, thick-framed glasses, a frown so deep that only surgery could remove it. A cross hung from her neck, so large it'd put Sister Benedicta to shame. She sized Shabby up and asked the broker, 'Christian?'

'Almost,' the broker clicked his tongue.

The lady kept looking at Shabby but spoke to the broker. 'Okay with non-veg?'

'Okay with everything. He's not a typical Hindu. He's *cool*.'

Now she spoke to Shabby directly. 'No taking down photos of Jesus. No putting up Hindu gods in the house.' Shabby also bobbed his head. At least she hadn't said, *no girlfriends, no daaroo, no parties*, like the others. But then she said what every landlord had said until now. 'No Muslims. Those people sacrifice goats for Eid and the blood flows everywhere.' She scrunched her nose up. 'Four-four wives each man has!'

The broker jumped in. 'Don't worry, madam. He doesn't know any Muslims only. He's just moved to Mumbai from the north.'

The landlady seemed to relax. She opened the door wider to let them in, quickly showing Shabby the little one-bedroom flat. The viewing was over within minutes. Before they left, she told the broker, 'But you will have to manage Father Mendosa. If that old man finds out I'm renting to a Hindu, he will throw a fit.'

On their way down, Shabby asked how the broker planned to *manage* Father Mendosa. 'He likes whisky from foreign.' The broker raised his fingers to his mouth. 'You can arrange?'

Shabby got on a local train. Usually it was human bodies packed into airtight compartments. Breath, elbows, grazes, farts. Babies and bags were transferred to their owners over the heads of other passengers. Prearranged groups held on to seats, singing bhajans, playing cards. In the ladies' compartments, women cut vegetables to get ahead on dinner prep. When there was any space left, beggars crawled, vying for attention, singing in nasal voices so they could be loud. This was not the Mumbai Shabby had imagined.

Today being Sunday, the train was mostly empty. He found a place to sit, the fourth person on a seat of three. He smiled at the thought of the grumpy Christian landlady and the spitting broker, and Father Mendosa's bribe of imported whisky. *You can't make this shit up*, Chintoo would've said.

This would be another story to share during dinner at the hotel. Every night, the new joiners brought back tales from their house-hunting escapades. Just about anything in this city passed off as a place to live. Rooms so small that the only way to move was on the bed, openings between walls that could serve as door and window and wardrobe, basins so minuscule that washing one's mouth could flood the floor. Even their American multinational's salaries couldn't get them a decent home.

'In this city, even movie stars live shoulder to shoulder. They carpet their narrow balconies with artificial grass and call it a garden,' someone said.

'Mumbai is more expensive than Manhattan. I've read in the *Business Times*.'

'One broker showed me a flat with a wall blackened from a leaky pipe. When I asked him to repair it, he said – *Why you need luxury as bachelor? All that after marriage, na?*' Everyone had laughed.

Now sat in the local train, Shabby spotted Ganjeri at the door. The guy was leaning out precariously, head moving to music beats on his earphones. His curly hair blew like a wild bouquet of wires. He noticed Shabby and flashed his famous smile. He claimed to have five dimples. He was one of the new joiners. He'd also been in college with Shabby, but they hadn't been close.

Shabby went up to him. 'I'm getting off here,' Ganjeri said, pointing to the oncoming platform. 'You want to get off too?'

A voice on the PA system announced first in Marathi *pudhil station Dadar*, then in Hindi *agla station Dadar*, then in English *the next station is Dadar*.

They found a spot on the overbridge. Shabby told Ganjeri about his afternoon. As he listened, Ganjeri took out a pouch of weed and balanced it on the railing. His penchant for weed was well-known. That's how he'd got his name. *Ganjeri – the ganja king.*

'What's happening with your house-hunting?' Shabby enquired.

'Arre yaar, don't ask!' Ganjeri fished rolling paper from his pocket, flattened it on his palm, then pinched out some weed and sprinkled it generously along the middle. 'This city is too much mach-mach. People like us, we can only live in ghettos.' He saw Shabby's confused face. 'I'm Muslim, na? My name is Syed Shah!'

'I had no idea,' Shabby said, embarrassed. He'd only ever known him as Ganjeri.

Ganjeri laughed in a series of hiccups. His dimples deepened and shallowed alternately. 'Did you think I'd walk around in a skullcap and soorma?'

'That's not how I meant it.'

'Well, I've found a place. No great shakes but it's all right. Two bedrooms. It's in Parel. Okay-okay neighbourhood.' Ganjeri's brows were knitted as he put the pouch back while holding the paper in place.

'That's good then?'

'Oh well. I haven't told them my name yet. The broker says they'll reject me if I do.' Ganjeri began rolling the paper, the weed staying in a thin line along the middle. The wind, the trains, the crowds, nothing seemed to come in the way of this expert act.

'What if you got a flatmate to sign the contract in his name?' Shabby asked, the idea suddenly coming to him. 'Have you asked anyone at the hotel?'

'I did ask a couple of them. All the guys are Hindus, though. Why would they risk lying to the landlord and all that?'

'I would!' Shabby's voice came out a bit too enthusiastic. 'This is Mumbai! Why does any of this matter here?'

'You sure?' Ganjeri looked suspicious. 'You don't have to talk to your family? A couple of the guys said they had no probs, but their parents wouldn't give permission.' He hiccupped again. Sun shone on his dimples.

'My parents have no say in my life.' Shabby liked the sound of it as he said the words. 'Can I see this place?'

Ganjeri was done rolling. He slotted the joint behind his ear, to be lit once he left the station. 'I'll organize a viewing, okay?' He shrugged in a *who-knows* sort of way. 'You might just like it!'

Shabby nodded. A good feeling swept through him. He hadn't realized how alone he'd felt in this city where everything was utterly dysfunctional, and yet everyone seemed to walk around like they had it all under control.

'Okay, I have to bounce now. But I'll see you later?' Ganjeri did a fist-bump and walked away. Shabby saw him going down two steps at a time, his lithe body finding gaps between people.

Shabby stood on the overbridge for a while. The tops of the trains were rusted and brown. People sat on the platform fanning themselves with newspapers, waiting for a long-distance train. A man was trying to tell a constable that there was a suitcase lying unclaimed, but the constable seemed unsure of what to do. Two happy children ran through the crowds, dressed for a fun Sunday evening, their parents trying to keep up.

Lost in thought, Shabby left the station. He turned a corner into a garbage dump and walked into a family of pigs. The little pink ones rubbed their snouts against his jeans. The mother pig gazed lazily in approval.

Jamooni

Ganjeri poured the beer, tipping the bottle and glass at an angle. He'd kept the glasses in the freezer, and they fogged up as the dark-yellow liquid flowed in, frothing at the top. He waited for the froth to subside before pouring the rest.

Shabby looked on in admiration, wondering how a guy from small-town Surat had learnt these tricks. In the six months they'd lived together, Ganjeri had shown a penchant for alcohol unknown to Shabby. In college, it'd just been cheap Old Monk and Royal Stag.

Ganjeri handed the glass to Shruti. She took it in her left hand. Her right hand was in Shabby's hair, fingers curling through his thick strands. She caressed his locks as she sipped the beer.

'Listen, feroza is a legit colour.' Shruti looked serious. Shabby and Ganjeri tried to stifle a laugh. 'What the fuck, ya!' She took a bigger gulp.

'It's just blue,' Ganjeri said. He handed Shabby his beer. Shabby put the glass down on the floor. He didn't want to sit up yet. Just a little longer with his head on Shruti's lap. On the ledge, the pigeons made goo-goo sounds.

Shabby looked up at Shruti's face. 'You have a name for everything. Earrings are *danglers*, tops are *spaghetti* and *tank* and *cropped*, the balloon pants are *harem*.'

Ganjeri took a swig. 'What was that colour she came up with the other day?'

'Jamooni,' Shabby said. The boys laughed. 'That's just purple.'

'Uff! It is not! Jamooni is so dark it's almost black, but still holds on to those purple hues. These colours are just not the same when said in English. You small-town boys! Get on with the trends, okay?' Shruti was from Bangalore and took pride in her big-city ways, where *ethnic* was making a come-back. She gave Shabby's head a slight tap. He thought it meant it was time to sit up, but pretended not to understand. He had an erection. He was working on getting it down before he could change positions.

Shruti had come home with Ganjeri a few weeks ago. They'd met in a shared taxi. Now she was a fixture in the flat. She held the boys together like glue. Shabby and Ganjeri had done fine before her, but now they couldn't imagine being left alone.

Shabby sat up and sipped the beer. It was already tepid. He hated the weather in Mumbai – hot, hotter, hottest. He caught a pigeon looking at him. It flapped its wings. It seemed jealous of his drink. He wondered if he should leave some water on the ledge for the pigeon family that came and went at will, having found a gap in the wire mesh.

Shruti cosied up next to him. 'I don't want to go back to my flat.' Her voice was tired. She was having trouble with her flatmates, who were fighting about how to split utility bills.

Shabby and Ganjeri had no such problems. They'd settled in well. They went to the office together but didn't see each other all day. They worked for different clients. Shabby was in the Networks division, Ganjeri in Devices. The flat was all right. Shabby was the main signatory on the contract, his high-caste Hindu name leaving no room for questions. Ganjeri had moved in afterwards as a *temporary guest*. Shabby wasn't impressed when he'd first seen the flat, but without him, Ganjeri would have had to live in a ghetto. Now, after a few months, the flat didn't seem so bad. It was home, a place they came back to from the mad city. Yes, there were the slums in front which could get noisy, the aarti every evening for some Hindu god or another. More slums on the other side of the tracks, the azaan from the mosque sounding five times a day on the loudspeaker. And of course the trains hurtling past every few minutes on the Central line.

'You're living with a Muslim?' The surprise in Ma's voice was unalloyed, like this wasn't the story she'd built in her head about his life in the city. Shabby had held off telling her for as long as he could. 'I'm not saying anything, just . . .' She'd searched for words. She had no idea what to say. Their family hadn't socially interacted with a Muslim ever, let alone having one in the house. 'Does he cook a lot of non-veg?' she'd finally asked. 'Their food is very rich and oily, lots of onion and garlic, na?'

'We eat what the bai cooks,' Shabby had replied curtly. It was true. They'd found Shakku-bai who cooked vegetarian food during the week. Sometimes the boys cooked chicken at the weekends. Ma hadn't said anything more.

But Papa had called a few minutes later. He sounded agitated. 'What is this I'm hearing? You didn't even consult us?'

Shabby had felt triumph. From now on, he was going to make his own decisions. 'These things don't matter in the big city. Everyone lives with everyone. No one cares!' He'd never asserted himself like this to his parents. With every step, he was testing the waters for how far he could go.

'Look, you're an adult now.' Papa seemed to have sobered. 'But I'm just worried about trouble. It's always safer to live with your own kind.'

'I thought we were high-caste Hindus.' Shabby knew how snide he sounded. 'Nothing happens to us, right?'

Papa grunted and hung up. After that, he only piggybacked

on Ma's calls, exchanging pleasantries. *Is your work going well? Is your boss happy with you? Anything about that on-site project in America?* Sometimes Nani and Chintoo chimed in too, if they were around. But Shabby never had anything much to say to anyone. His life here in Mumbai was so different, so free, so *cool*, that he couldn't even imagine trying to describe it in words to anyone back there.

Not that he intended to. He wanted to keep Lucknow as far away from Mumbai as he possibly could.

Now the chhan-chhan of anklets came down the corridor and paused. The three of them put their beers down instinctively. Shruti split from Shabby and sat at a distance.

Shakku-bai made an appearance at the door. Her nose-stud shone in the sunlight. She put the broom and mop away, and untucked the pallu of her saree. 'All done,' she said to Ganjeri. Her voice was impassive but strong, as always. She stood straight, like she had authority over them.

'Okay.' Ganjeri bobbed his head.

'You're running out of oil and salt.' Shakku-bai was still speaking to Ganjeri, but gave Shruti a quick glance. 'Should I get tomorrow?'

'Of course,' Ganjeri said. 'Thank you,' he added as an afterthought.

Shakku-bai pointed to the pigeons. 'These are back again! Last week I gave them a good thrashing, but they never learn their lesson.' The three of them looked helplessly at the birds, who strutted proudly at being the subjects of human attention. 'I'll see to them later. They need a proper kambal-pitai.' They'd seen how Shakku-bai held the blanket up like a matador, saree tucked at her waist, inviting the pigeons to a fight, then thrashed them into defeat. Sometimes she used the stiff broom, shouting as she hit them. *Bol, will you come here again?*

Just you wait. You haven't seen the worst of me yet. After each such episode, the pigeons stayed away for a few days.

'Yete . . .' Shakku-bai said in Marathi and walked away, the keys at her waist jangling. The three of them relaxed when they heard the lock turn in the door. Shruti slumped, pulling her knees in, resting her head on them.

'She's less of a cleaner, more of a Mother Superior,' Ganjeri joked.

'I'm sure she thinks I'm a slut, hanging out with two boys, drinking beer.' Shruti pursed her lips. 'Apparently I was supposed to know you're running out of salt, just because I'm a girl. I mean, hello, I don't even live here!'

Shabby gulped the rest of the beer down. 'Shakku-bai can be quite scary. She moves stuff around at will, cooks what she likes, she has even put her own Ganesh idol in the kitchen. She treats this place like she owns it!'

'Can you believe she threw my flowers away and put her own in the vase?' This had happened a few times, until Shruti had stopped bringing flowers to the flat.

'She's been working in this mohalla for ages,' Shabby said. 'I asked the watchman if he could find us a new maid, and he said – *Good luck trying to fire Shakku-bai.* Seems like she's a bit of a don around here.'

'Guys, please,' Ganjeri interjected. 'Give the poor woman a break. She lives in a one-room hut in the slum. She thinks it's two boys here, so she can play lady of the house.'

'But she clearly has a thing for Ganjeri,' Shabby teased. It was true, Shakku-bai seemed to fall for Ganjeri's charms. 'She only speaks to him, like I'm some freeloader second-citizen.'

Shruti sat up and twirled an imaginary moustache. 'Oh, Syed! Man of the house. So sexy, ya!' She always called Ganjeri by his real name.

The three of them burst out laughing.

Kachda

M is rolling a joint on the overbridge of Lucknow Charbagh train station, will you give me a place to live, he asks Shabby, yes of course, Shabby says, but Ma and Papa are in the flat, releasing pigeons into the room, don't live with Muslims, they are saying, their food is very rich, full of onion and garlic—

Eyes still shut, Shabby reached out to feel the bedsheet. Not wet. He was relieved. He wouldn't know how to explain to Shakku-bai or Ganjeri if it ever happened. He'd have to do the washing secretly early in the morning, before the stench pervaded the flat. But today wasn't the day.

He opened his eyes and stared at the pigeons, still asleep, beaks tucked into breasts. He was thankful to have them around. Until he'd moved to Mumbai, he'd never had to sleep alone. In the hostels, first in Kota and then in Vellore, he had had room-mates, and before that in Lucknow, there was Chintoo. He got up and made himself tea, tiptoeing around the flat, not wanting to wake Ganjeri. He hoped to steep in the dream like the teabag steeping in hot water, but the dream was already starting to erase itself.

He grabbed a rough sheet of paper from his work bag. It had some official stuff printed on it, but it would do. He hadn't bought a sketchbook or pencils, still telling himself he wouldn't draw any more. But every time he dreamt, there was something that made him want to put them down on paper, though with little success. Today he got only as far as the curved line of the train track. He scrunched the paper and threw it on the floor, then looked out of the window.

Downstairs, the water-tanker had arrived. People from the slums were queuing; no setting up the market today, which they usually folded up at night and pieced together in the morning, in case the police decided to launch one of their eviction drives. The police always came in the middle of the night, with bulldozers and torchlight. What happened to the people sleeping on the pavements? Did they warn them in advance? Or did they hoover them up into their machines?

Shabby's eyes roved, settling on one person after another in line, waiting with empty buckets. The municipal office sent the tanker at will, depending on how much bribe had been paid and how much water the rich and middle class needed, people like him and Ganjeri and Shruti, leaving their taps running while they brushed their teeth, avenging their aqua-deficient childhoods. He spotted Shakku-bai in the queue, sleepy eyes, swatting away a fly, resigned to standing there for the next few hours.

Could he draw this scene? He picked the paper up and flattened it on his lap, then drew a bucket. He stared at it, then scrunched it up again and aimed it at the waste-paper basket. Kachda. *Garbage.*

He reached for his phone, scrolled down the list. There she was. *Ma.* He'd called her a few weeks ago, the last time he'd woken up from a dream like this. He didn't like that he needed to call her on such mornings. It defeated the effort he'd put into staying away from Lucknow and keeping his family at bay. But there was something about the dreams that made him want to reach out to Ma, like she was the only person in the whole world who would understand, though she'd never hinted at knowing anything about M, never tried to speak to him about it. Still, the dreams left him so exhausted that Ma's stoic stolidity helped to breathe oxygen back into him, give him the energy to return to steering his life away from her.

Otherwise it was Ma calling him on her new mobile, which he'd gifted her, bought in Mumbai and sent with someone going to Lucknow. They were quick five-minute calls asking what he'd eaten, how the weather was, then something new about a relative or neighbour. Someone's daughter got married, someone's son ran off with his girlfriend, someone died. There was always a lot happening in Lucknow. Ma never asked about his life in Mumbai. She seemed satisfied as long as he'd eaten his food.

Now he pressed on her name and heard the digits dialling.

'Hello?' Ma sounded calm. He imagined her reading the newspaper before she'd have to hand it to Papa.

He remembered that Papa had had a small accident. His scooter had lost balance and he'd bruised his right leg, or maybe the left one. Shabby wasn't sure he'd asked. 'How's Papa?' He felt guilty about not calling before.

'He's okay, he's back to work. The bruise is still blue but fading. He's getting old, you know . . .' Then she snapped back to her usual tone. Ma hated painting a sorry picture of themselves. 'And the scooter, my god! They took two thousand rupees to repair! What a loot this country is becoming!'

Shabby wondered if he should offer to pay. Two thousand rupees was less than what he paid for drinks in a bar. But he knew Ma wouldn't like that. *We can take care of ourselves, you know? Your father is still earning.*

'Have you called Nani?' Ma asked. Shabby bit his tongue. He'd forgotten again. Nani's sister in Azamgarh had died, and Ma had asked him to call her. 'Nani is very sad,' she'd said. 'This was the sister who took care of her when she was small, lost among those seventeen cousins.'

'Umm, no . . . It's been so busy lately. I'll call this weekend,' Shabby lied.

Ma didn't pursue the subject any more. 'Will you come home for Holi?' *Home!*

'I'll ask my manager if I can take leave. I'm not sure, though. The project is quite full-on at the moment.'

Ma didn't argue back. 'Okay, we'll speak soon,' she said. The sureness in her voice made Shabby smile. He knew it would be weeks before they spoke again.

2013

Inspiration

Ma is a woman on a mission. She's walking so fast the Nike trainers are hardly visible. She's wearing the track pants and a long T-shirt she bought from Linking Road. Her hair is tied in a topknot.

'How much further?' he asks, huffing-puffing.

Ma turns her head sharply. 'Not too far. Keep up!' He's surprised that she has disregarded his limp. Offended, almost.

'We are going on morning walks from tomorrow,' Ma announced a few weeks ago, after dinner. 'Enough of this sitting around. It's not good for you, not good for me.' His physiotherapist has been asking him to keep to an exercise routine. *Make a chart for the week and follow it.* But he hasn't done much about it, except for the odd walk in the park. He doesn't like people looking askance at his limp. He doesn't like that he can never go too far. He is not happy right now that Ma is speeding ahead of him.

But Ma was adamant. The next morning, she woke him up as the first light was diffusing into the night sky like an unwelcome intruder. 'Come on, drink up some warm water and let's go.' She pulled the pallu of her saree and tucked it at her waist.

On that first day, both mother and son were done in thirty minutes. They came back exhausted, sweat dripping from their brows, armpits dark and wet, heaving deep breaths. They switched on the ceiling fan at full speed and sat down, eyes closed. He tried saying something about the heat being a killer, but Ma interjected, 'Let's not make excuses. We're going every morning.' Then she muttered to herself, 'I don't want to end up like Nani. We women, if we don't look after ourselves, no one else will, and then we end up alone and sick when we're old.'

Over the years, Nani's arthritis has got so bad that she is nearly bound to her house now. He hears that her back is bent, and she can hardly hold anything with her weak fingers. Ma talks to Nani on the phone very often nowadays, probably more often than she speaks to Papa. Sometimes, she passes the phone to him. *Pranaam, Nani*, he says. *Jeete raho, bachcha*, she returns his regards, her voice so soft and quivery it seems like the arthritis has crept into her vocal cords and atrophied them as well.

These last few weeks, Ma has been overcome by resolution. Caring for him has taken its toll on her in many ways. She is plumper now than when she came to Mumbai three years ago. Her hair has more greys. The wrinkles on her face have started to become permanent lines. 'I'm only fifty-five,' she says sometimes. He can't tell if she's excited or scared about her life ahead. But she enjoys the exercise. She has gone out and shopped for the right clothes and shoes to walk in. She pushes herself to walk fast, increasing her heart rate, building strength in her legs. She's learnt to carry a bottle of water to keep herself hydrated. On days he makes an excuse for not going, she goes by herself.

Today is different, though. They haven't taken their usual route of walking to Wadala station and back. Ma is leading the way down an unknown road. 'I want to show you something,' she said before they left, fastening the laces of her trainers. Ma won't allow him to use his phone to check where they are. She wants it to be a surprise.

They have been walking for over an hour when Ma finally stops. He looks at the unfamiliar landscape. Narrow muddy lanes, spare-tyre shops, woodsmoke coming out of a tea-stall. He's never been here before. This doesn't even seem like Mumbai.

'Just a bit more.' Ma points to a zigzag path through some hutments. When they get to the end of that stretch, something like a jetty opens up. It is dusty, derelict, but expansive. Beyond the concrete is a body of water, calm, stagnant, mild ripples competing with each other on the still surface. Mangroves line the sides. And on the water are innumerable little dots. What are they? Birds? Yes, tall ones, standing still on one leg, only moving to dip their long necks into the water from time to time.

He walks closer. His legs are tired, his limp more pronounced, but he is excited. He turns to Ma. 'Flamingos!' he exclaims like a child.

Ma is beaming at her discovery, at succeeding in finding her way here without technology, at managing to surprise him.

'How did you find this?' he asks her.

Ma shrugs. 'The ladies in the building were talking about the flamingos in Sewri, so I got the details.'

Mother and son head slowly to the end of the jetty, and stare at the birds. How many are there? Perhaps hundreds, maybe thousands. Right here in the middle of this mad metropolis! Who would've thought?

'You can come here sometimes to paint in peace,' Ma says softly. 'I thought this could be an inspiration. You haven't drawn anything in a long time.'

He nods, then gets tea from a stall. They sit on a ledge and watch the flamingos in silent amazement.

'This city really does have all kinds, na?' Ma says as she blows on the surface of the tea.

2000s

Firangs

Their breasts jiggled as the girls bent, faces touching. Behind them came the others, playing drums, trumpets, sporting angel wings. Ornate costumes, garish make-up, golden knee-high boots. They threw glitter up in the air. It landed back on them as they gyrated, waved flags, made ululating sounds.

Shabby stood at his bedroom window watching the firangs. Ganjeri and Shruti joined him. The sounds had travelled through the little flat. In fact, the whole mohalla was out to view the spectacle, lining the street. Shop-keepers forgot their customers. People in buildings craned their necks from open windows. The firangs tried to get the crowd to join in, but the audience seemed tentative, shuffling their feet, half-smiles on faces, not fully understanding what was going on. Only a dwarf dived in. And the pigeons on the ledge hopped, making goo-goo noises to match the rhythm.

'What the fuck is happening?' Ganjeri hiccupped.

Shruti pointed to a girl in a pink miniskirt. 'There's Rebecca! She's nice.' Then turned to a tall guy in the parade. 'The guy is called Erik, I think.'

The two Americans had moved into the next-door flat. It had been a noisy affair. Lots of knocking and dragging, a cacophony of foreign accents. Since then, a steady stream of white backpackers had come and gone. Shabby had run into them on the stairs and in the lift. They either behaved like he was invisible, or had a practised smile pasted on their faces.

'Yeah, I know Erik,' Ganjeri said. 'He goes running every morning. Comes back with his face red like a tomato.' Shabby had seen Erik and Ganjeri whisper on the stairs, money and weed exchanging hands. 'He's so tall that when he's standing, he tries to place his feet far apart so he can come down to the height of the person he's talking to.'

Ganjeri was over six feet tall. But Erik was something else. Now Ganjeri stood in front of Shabby and spread his feet out to show what he meant. Shabby was five-feet-nine. He didn't like that Ganjeri was using him to demonstrate the height difference.

'Rebecca never talks to me, though,' Ganjeri continued. 'We're all molesters, you see! I'm sure they're given pamphlets from their embassies before they board flights to India.' He switched to a nasal American accent. 'BEWARE OF INDIAN MEN.'

Shruti rolled her eyes. She didn't appreciate unnecessary negativity.

The parade was over. The firangs were making their way back into the building, their white bodies glistening in glitter and sweat. Shruti ran out and opened the door. Shabby and Ganjeri followed. They saw Rebecca coming up the stairs. Mrs Vashisht, the lady in the third flat on their floor, peeped from behind her door. She shut it quickly when she realized she'd been spotted.

'Today is carnival!' Rebecca raised her hands up in the air, and the rest let out a *woohoo!* 'Everyone back home is having so much fun! So we thought – why don't we bring some craziness out to Mumbai.'

'While being totally culturally sensitive, of course,' someone added over her shoulder. 'No cleavage! No bum-cheeks!'

The group insisted that the three join the after-party. *It's gonna be crazyyyyyy!* Erik opened the door and everyone stumbled in. Mrs Vashisht peeped out again, her curiosity too much to contain behind the walls.

In the firangs' flat, Shabby sat at the edge of a sofa. He'd never been around so many white people before. Their bodies moved confidently, taking off wigs and wings, washing off colour, rubbing off glitter. The men took off their shirts. Muscles rippled down their arms and stomachs. They glided through the space like they owned every square metre of air around them. Shabby felt like he was in an episode of *Friends*, except there'd never been any brown people in that show. He made a note to tell Chintoo all about this party.

Erik put on dancey music on Bluetooth speakers. The bass beats boomed through the room, not giving away the song. The firangs slipped into conversation. Most knew each other. The ones who were new also had enough context to join in. Baseball games at school, the latest dating disaster, a new cocktail trending in Rio right now. An argument broke out about the longest flight – London to Perth, or Doha to Auckland? This made Shabby think of the longest journeys he'd made – from Vellore to Lucknow and back after every semester, three nights in Indian Railways non-air-conditioned compartments, changing trains in Chennai, the grime of summers and shivers of winters. He wished he'd known about this party. He would've worn better clothes at least. Now here he was in shapeless track pants and faded T-shirt.

The firangs were all in India to do something interesting. No one worked in a regular job. They funded organic tomato farms in Kolar, drove auto-rickshaws from Delhi to Mumbai to raise money for causes, learnt to dance Kathak, taught yoga classes. Erik and Rebecca themselves had tried their hand at different things – started a macaroon store in Pondicherry, managed a backpacker resort in Goa, and were now setting up an NGO. How were they affording rent and drinks and holidays? What visas were they on? Shabby knew he couldn't just move to the West for social work. There was no visa for people like him to help poor white people.

Ganjeri had settled by a window with a joint, the centre of a small following. He said something, and the group burst out in giggles. Everyone from Shakku-bai to Erik was in his thrall. Ganjeri definitely wasn't what Shabby's original perception of him had been – the helpless Muslim looking for a flatmate. The more time they spent together, the more Shabby sensed in Ganjeri something untamed yet charming, impish yet endearing.

The firangs were now talking about their hardships in India. They seemed to do this often, referencing each other's stories. *Remember I told you last time?* A guy with a European accent was saying, 'They say five minutes but mean five hours!' His Ts were soft, Hs were pronounced where they shouldn't be.

Another chimed in, 'The clerk at the foreigners' registration office openly asked me for a bribe. And when I showed him rupees, he said – *No-no, giuuu mee daallar!*' He attempted an Indian accent. Everyone laughed, including two brown guys in sleeveless jerseys, their accents as foreign as the others'.

Shabby spotted Shruti dancing on the other side of the room, twirling her mustard-yellow top. This made him smile. That was another shade of colour she'd taught him. Sarson. She seemed happy, immersed in the music and moves.

A tall guy with bulging muscles was now telling his story.

'So, check this out. One time I was in a jam-packed local train, right? I needed to get off at Vikhroli, but . . . like . . . there's no way to . . . like . . . get off. I'm . . . like . . . fucking stuck . . . right? So I just pull myself up by the handles . . .' he got up with his arms lifted, fists curled tightly '. . . and I fucking kick the two men in front of me.' His feet whirled in a pseudo-karate pose. 'And . . . like . . . these puny Indians, right? They're like . . . whoaaa. All of them . . . like . . . tumble down, and I walk out like a fucking boss.' Everyone doubled up on their stomachs, heads rolling on the sofa with laughter. Even the brown ones cackled in their foreign accents.

Shabby sat there, uncertain. Should he laugh too? Or should he keep a serious face, to protest at the open insult to his country on its own soil, a country that he'd wanted nothing to do with all his life, but now felt compelled to defend, because no one else would, because every joke on his country also felt like a joke on him.

'In some countries, they kill crows,' he said without thinking. He bit his lip. He didn't know where he was going with this. His accent sounded uncool, heavy. All those years of English-medium convent education, and yet here he was, sounding like a villager. The firangs turned to look at him. He had to elaborate, there was no going back. 'You know, they kill the ugly things so they can only look at the pretty ones.' He shrugged. 'Maybe that's what we should do, kill our uglies.'

The firangs squirmed. Shabby wished he could just disappear.

Ganjeri sauntered in right at that moment. Since everyone was looking at Shabby, he turned too. 'This guy, my friends, is gold.' He reached his hand out and ruffled Shabby's hair. 'He chose to get a flat with me when no one else would.'

The audience eased up, bodies relaxed, as though Ganjeri's endorsement was an unspoken ticket into their tribe. Someone plonked a drunken arm on Shabby's shoulder. 'For real, bro? Kill crows, eh? That's fucked up!'

Everyone nodded. Someone got Shabby a drink and everyone raised their glasses. 'To the ugly fucking crows!' They emptied out the contents in one swig.

Le Establishment

Shabby felt the buzzing in his crotch. The cascading Nokia ringtone sounded over the din. He dug the phone out from his pocket. *Ma calling . . .* He pressed Accept.

'Hello?' Ma's voice was anxious. 'Why haven't you answered my calls?'

It felt good, having this kind of power. He could go underground and she couldn't do a thing, no gilt-bronze clock to keep track of his ins and outs. He mumbled something about work being busy. An auto-rickshaw passed by, wheels crunching loudly on the gravel.

'Speak louder. I can't hear you.' Ma's voice was a command even in desperation.

He looked at Shruti. They'd come for drinks at Janata Bar, and had stepped out for a cigarette. Shruti arched her eyebrows as she blew out smoke. *Everything okay?* Terracotta jhumkas dangled from her ears. He circled his finger to signal he'd be right back, then crossed the road and started walking up Pali Hill where things were less noisy.

'How are you?' he asked.

'Arre, don't say,' Ma's voice finally caved in exasperation. 'This Chintoo will make my life hell.' Chintoo's results had come out over the last few weeks. His marks in the board exams were average, but like his brother, he'd failed all engineering entrance tests.

Ma continued, 'Papa got him admission in a college here.

164

We thought – *Let him study science and prepare for next year's engineering tests.* But this boy . . . he's so stubborn. He changed his course to social studies. Apparently he wants to be a journalist!' A slight giggle escaped her at the incredulity of this proposition.

There was a shuffle, then Papa's voice on the phone. 'Listen, beta, talk to your brother. He's gone completely rogue. Changing courses behind my back, after I paid the fee for science, which is higher than the fee for social studies! When I asked the principal to reinstate him into science, the principal said he's an adult, he can't be forced!' Papa sounded like he couldn't believe his sons were adults. 'Can you drill some of your good sense into your brother?'

Shabby sat on a ledge in front of one of the posh bungalows on Pali Hill. He'd come quite a way up, to one of those secluded alcoves where only yesteryear's movie stars could afford to live because they'd bought land when it was still cheap. He wished he'd got a cigarette from Shruti.

There was a tussle on the line. Shabby heard muffled negotiation. 'Let me also talk to him,' he could hear Nani haggling, 'just two minutes.' There was more friction. 'My opinion is worth nothing in this house . . .' Nani was saying angrily.

Then Chintoo said, 'Bhaiyya.' He'd clearly wrested the phone off Nani. His voice was hoarse, like he'd been shouting.

'Such a mess!' That's the best Shabby could come up with. No one had had this chat with him when he'd failed his exams. He couldn't be blamed for not knowing what to say.

'There's no mess.' Chintoo sounded calm. 'I'm doing social studies.'

'I didn't even know you were interested in journalism!'

'Arre, that's just something I'm telling them.' Chintoo had taken the phone to the bedroom. 'Actually I just want to make music.'

'You have your band for that, na?' Chintoo had joined a band in high school. They performed at festivals.

'Yes, and now we want to take it to the next level. We want to record an album, play across the country. Big dreams, bro!'

'And what is Dhruv doing?'

'Fuck Dhruv. He's going to America to study computer engineering. His uncle will sign as his guarantor and get him a student loan.'

'And you don't want that? There was a time when you'd give anything to go to America and live like the firangs.'

'Yeah, that was, like, a million years ago. Who wants to go to America now? After 9/11, they're coming after brown people, treating us like shit. They think we're all Muslims . . .'

'Look, you know how Ma and Papa are. They won't get off your back until you've given them what they want. Just do what they say. Once you leave home, you can tell them to fuck off.'

'So you're saying I should waste my years playing their game, and only then I can make music?' Chintoo's voice was lined with acid. 'Look, bhaiyya, just because something worked out for you doesn't mean it will for me. Not everyone can endure. Some people rebel . . . like me . . . some people give up . . . like Dwiti . . .' Shabby shut his eyes to force out images of Dwiti Dwivedi. Chintoo continued, 'Also, I'm not even sure it's worked for you. You may have convinced yourself, but I know your heart wasn't in this shit. I don't know what was going on in your head, but I could tell something was.'

Shabby felt his scalp go hot. What did Chintoo know of what he'd been through? 'Oye, shut the fuck up, okay?' He'd never spoken to Chintoo like this. His voice was thick with aggression. 'You don't get to tell me what works for me and what doesn't. At least I'm earning my own money and living a life of my choice. If you go around playing your guitar, you know where you'll end up? Still in Lucknow, living off

Mr Ashutosh Trivedi, hanging out with Panna-chacha and Suresh-mausa—'

'You know who you sound like?' Chintoo cut him off. 'Like *them*! Ma and Papa and Nani! You are literally *LE ESTABLISHMENT*.' Somehow, saying it in French made the insult more piercing.

The screen went blank. Shabby's head throbbed. He'd fought with Chintoo for the first time. The blue light of the phone hurt his eyes. *Ma calling* . . . Again. Then again. Eventually she gave up.

Shabby wanted to fling the phone into the drain.

They sat on the edge of the world, legs dangling. The sea was so dark they couldn't see anything beyond. Waves crashed against their feet. It was high tide. The floodlights in the distance looked like planets.

Shruti linked her arm with Shabby's. Her alcohol-laced breath smelt sweet. She'd known from the moment he walked back into the bar that something was wrong. She'd paid up and got them out. 'Let me take you to a secret place that'll lift your mood up,' she'd whispered. He'd given her a tight hug, not wanting to let go. Shruti joked that they wouldn't find a taxi if they kept standing like this on the streets of Bandra.

She'd brought them to Mahim Creek, a sliver of rocks by the sea. She said hardly anyone knew this place, but it had one of the best views of the city. They stared at the Sea Link bridge that had been under construction for years, its two ends hanging like an open jaw. It was supposed to connect Bandra and Worli and halve commute times. Even now, work continued in the dark. The floodlights made the sea glimmer at a distance. Sounds of cranes lifting and dropping material travelled with the wind.

'Families are like that bridge.' Shruti's voice was soft against the roaring sea. 'The two ends will never meet.' Shabby knew her parents were separated. She'd grown up with her mother in Bangalore. She never mentioned her father.

He arched his back and lay on the rocks. Shruti lay next to him. They stared up at the sky. He wanted to roll over and kiss her. He would never have come here by himself. Dark places weren't his thing. Dark places always took him back to the night of Lekha-bua's wedding. The thought made him snuggle closer to her.

In these few months, she'd become indispensable. He'd been with a couple of girls before, horny teenagers making out hurriedly in back alleys during college days. But no one had touched him, trusted him the way Shruti did. How she curled her fingers around his when they crossed the road, how comfortably she put her head on his shoulder, how she demanded a back rub and massaged his temples in return.

But she did all these things with Ganjeri too. And Shabby wasn't half as smart or handsome as Ganjeri. If he kissed her now, would he be taking advantage of her trust? Would he be behaving like a small-towner? Would he lose her friendship forever?

'You know that bridge will be complete one day, right? The two ends will meet,' he said. 'Do you think that's true for families too?'

Shruti laughed loudly. In this crowded city, finding a place so isolated was rare, where a girl could laugh with abandon without ten men turning to look. 'Going by the record of this bridge, that would take a *very* long time!'

Suddenly she sat up, as if she had willed herself to snap out of the moment. 'Chal, let's get some food,' she said. 'I know this amazing place nearby that sells kakori kebabs. Absolute melt-in-your-mouth stuff!'

2013

Citizen

A crow shits on the windscreen, then perches itself on the bonnet, pushing its audacity, cawing loudly, daring him. It is truly an ugly thing. He doesn't bother shooing it away, nor runs the wipers. He sits in the parked car for some time, watching the pellet of shit harden, then turns off the ignition, locks the vehicle and walks into the office. The air conditioning makes his shirt graze against the burn-mark on his back. It itches more than it hurts.

He takes the lift to the top-floor cafeteria. He walks in to find chairs lined in rows, tables pushed against the walls. Balloons, streamers, glittering hearts tied to pillars. A small podium with a mic. A number of people have shown up. Someone sees him and whispers to the next person, then the next. The whisper spreads through the room like an audio wave. Everyone turns. Some smile, some purse their lips, some don't quite know what to do, so just look elsewhere.

This is how it has been since he came back to work after the *incident*. The company kept his job, but like everything else, everything has changed. His peers now were his juniors before. The new manager is younger than he is. They try their best to integrate him, share team gossip, introduce him to the client, invite him to lunch and after-work drinks. He mostly says no. When he declines, he sees relief on their faces.

At lunch-breaks, he opens the Tupperware box Ma packs for him, eats roti-sabzi staring at the screen, trying to finish whatever is assigned to him for the day. Later in the mid-afternoon, there is a smaller Tupperware with cut fruit, apples, pomegranate, grapes. And yet another one with sweetened yogurt that he never opens. Ma never asks why. She packs it anyway.

His manager has told him during annual performance appraisals that he should aim for a promotion soon, that he's been Senior Software Engineer for a while now, how about Delivery Manager? He just needs to schmooze the clients a little more, work a little longer, reply to emails at the week-ends, mentor some juniors. He nods, says that's what he plans for next year.

The people in the cafeteria now stand apart as he walks down. For the last three years, they have stolen quick glances at his foot. And at his fingers when he types slowly. At least they can't see the scars on his back and thigh. They fall silent when he enters a room. They avoid talk of politics. Violence is in the news every few months – villages of lower-caste Dalits set on fire; youth in Kashmir blinded by pellets fired by the Indian army; a girl brutally gang-raped on a bus in Delhi, an iron rod inserted into her privates, then thrown out on the highway, left to die. His colleagues discuss these passionately when he isn't around. He knows this because he has heard them before entering meeting rooms or common areas. But the moment they see him, they change the subject to IPL cricket matches or the latest movie in the *Golmaal* series.

He tries his best now not to limp, taking confident steps with his left foot, the good one, and lightly placing the right one. He has practised this many times. *The normal walk.* He finds his seat in the front row.

The managing director coughs into the mic. That settles the audience down. The director begins with the company's long history of supporting corporate citizenship. 'And today, we award one of our esteemed employees for surviving a vicious attack on his life.' The director's voice brims with emotion. 'The company has shown him every support these past few years – full compensation while he was recovering for over a year, thirteen months to be precise.' The director's maths is exact. 'When he was ready to come back, we allowed him to join at the same level despite . . .' he licks his lips '. . . well, challenges . . . We even funded consultations with a psychologist. *That* is how seriously we take mental health in this company.'

Everyone breaks into applause, happy that this event has gone on for longer than usual, kept them away from their desks and drudgery.

'I now invite our very own Shubhankar Trivedi to accept the Citizen Bravery Award.' The director stands to attention, like a soldier. 'Shubhankar, we are humbled by your courage, and proud that you are part of our family.'

Everyone turns to look at the hero, but the hero's foot has fallen asleep. He tries his best to raise himself from the chair, but falls back. A low *oh!* passes through the room. People gather to hoist him. He wants to tell them this isn't the *disability*, just sleepy nerves. But they are already leading him to the stage, his arms around colleagues' shoulders. The director unveils a trophy, polished bronze. The foot has recovered sensation by now so he poses for photos, realizing that these will make it to the company's social media, that he will be tagged, that his 160-odd friends will see this. Seniors take turns to get clicked with him. This photo could get them their next promotion.

After snacks and cold drinks are served and he has stayed

long enough to convince everyone that he is grateful, he excuses himself for the rest of the day, says he isn't feeling well. His manager doesn't look happy but acquiesces. What is there to say? He hasn't taken many leaves in three years, either carrying them over or forsaking them. There is nowhere to go, no one to go with.

He comes back to the car and drives out of the parking lot. On his way, he throws the trophy out of the window into a garbage dump by the Eastern Express Highway. He doesn't want Ma to see it, lest she add it to her museum of his achievements. He doesn't want Chintoo to know, ashamed of what being *Le Establishment* has got him.

2000s

I Black

Pale, pink, olive, anaemic, raw-meat. They came in many skin tones. The white sunscreen lotion dripped from their chins. Mixed with mosquito repellent, this gave off a strange homogeneous odour. The women wore white cotton kurtis, heads covered with dupattas. The men wore shorts and hats, breaking into light jogs to combat restlessness.

Shabby stood slightly apart. The others looked at him with raised-eyebrow-tight-mouthed smiles, unsure if he was a guest or a loitering local. Some joined their palms in a namaste, like they were ready to start a yoga class.

Erik and Rebecca were well-prepared. They handed out water bottles and packs of tissues. Rebecca smiled at Shabby warmly. 'So you came!'

She'd chatted him up in the lobby a few days after the carnival parade. 'Erik and I are starting an initiative. We will organize tours of the community around here.'

'You mean the slums?' Shabby had hardly been able to contain his surprise.

'The *community*, yes,' Rebecca had corrected him. 'I meet so many expats who want to understand what it's like to live there. We want to focus on the beauty of life here, powerful stories of resilience and achievement.' She'd given Shabby a card with a discount code. A few weeks later, he'd booked a tour.

'Are you crazy? You're giving money to the firangs to show you around your own neighbourhood?' Ganjeri was upset. 'Why don't you ask Shakku-bai? She can show you how they thrash pigeons there.'

It was true that Shabby could walk into the slums any time. He didn't need a tour. But in the year he'd been in Mumbai, he'd always taken the main road out of the mohalla, never turning into the lanes that criss-crossed through the shanties. And though he wouldn't admit it to anyone, he didn't want to turn Rebecca down. He'd just about made it into their tribe. Out loud, he said, 'The funds go back into the community.'

Ganjeri hiccupped. 'Look at you – *community*. Next is what? Third World is *emerging markets*? Poor people are *low-income groups*?'

Shruti fought back. 'Why can't you just accept that they have good intentions? In fact, *we* are the lazy ones. What have we ever done for our country?'

'Bullshit!' Ganjeri got serious. 'They only want to feel good about themselves. Real solutions take real work – laying pipes for water connection, bricks and mortar for schools, hiring and training teachers. All this tour business is hogwash.'

'If you know what to do, why not put your knowledge to use?'

'They had ideas then too, when they sneaked in as merchants and colonized us for two hundred years . . .'

Shabby had slipped away, leaving Shruti and Ganjeri to their debate.

Now Erik and Rebecca asked the group to huddle for an orientation. They showed them the right way to do namaste, to view a house, to ask questions. Oh, and a few words of caution, though this was a really polite community – don't express discomfort if the children ask for money, don't freak out if men give you inappropriate looks, don't pet the dogs (they probably have lice), don't eat or drink anything that was being offered, upon which they repeated the oft-told story of the American who had braved pani-puris at a street-stall and ended up in Lilavati Hospital within the hour.

They were welcomed by women in red sarees, who put teekas on the guests' foreheads, garlands around their necks. When it was Shabby's turn, they looked at Rebecca, unsure if this brown guy was also entitled to the same welcome ritual. Rebecca smiled brightly, the perfect host, and garlanded Shabby herself. As they turned a corner, a man in a colourful Rajasthani turban stepped out and blew a bugle. The sudden strident sound sent some guests running, shrieking with fear. Erik ran after them. 'Sorry, we thought he was going to attack us,' the guests explained, shamefaced, as they reassembled. The man asked if he should play the bugle again, but Erik sent him away.

They walked through the narrow alleys, sometimes concrete, sometimes mud, sometimes sludge. Doors were open on both sides. The group respectfully peeped in. Life continued unabated – an old man wheezed, someone cleaned their tongue and made retching noises, spicy fumes rose from stoves, serials played on TV. For a few moments, Shabby felt like he was Shubhankar again, following Miss Lucy through the Maulviganj slums. He almost heard the tap-tap of her heels, smelt the reek of her cigarettes. He decided he'd meet her when he next visited Lucknow.

Erik and Rebecca had placed people at strategic points. At one corner, they met a young man who'd cracked the civil-service exam. At another, there were works of embroidery by local women, price tags in dollars. Then they were shown a shed and asked if they'd like to milk a cow. Children followed the group everywhere, showing off their English. *How*

are you, I am fine, One photo please, You from London, I go one day,
You so white, What cream you use, I black.

The slum was much larger than what Shabby could see of
it from his fourth-floor window. Now he understood it was
an unending network of alleyways, winding, twisting, turning. How did they remember their way through this maze?
The lanes and insides of the houses were sparkling clean. It
was on the peripheries that garbage was dumped, where stray
animals fed and mosquitoes bred.

Just when Erik and Rebecca seemed to have pulled off a
successful tour, all hell broke loose. The locals flooded the
lanes, pushing each other, bumping against the firangs, kick-
ing the dogs. *Tanki aali re*, they screamed into doorways. The
municipal water-tanker had arrived on the main road.

Shabby saw Shakku-bai turn into the lane, running as fast
as she could, lifting the folds of her saree in one hand, a
bucket swinging in the other. Younger women overtook her,
jumped over wheelbarrows and toys. Someone inadvertently
scratched her arm. She stopped to curse, then ran again. But
she tripped on the drooping end of her saree. Someone else
elbowed her out of the way. Shakku-bai hit the wall. Her
bucket fell, denting the plastic. She picked it up to check how
bad it was. Then she saw Shabby.

She looked like he'd seen her naked. This wasn't the
Shakku-bai from their flat, insisting on having everything her
way, thrashing the pigeons. Here, in her home, she was just
an ageing heavyset woman, who couldn't run fast enough to
get the one bucket of water her family was to survive on.

Shakku-bai gathered herself and continued her sprint.
Shabby pinned himself against the wall like the other guests,
waiting for this human tsunami to pass.

Pied Piper

Shakku-bai is dressed in a resplendent red Benarasi silk saree, the pleats neatly fall at her feet, matched by the vermilion sindoor in the parting of her hair, she is carrying a vase, beautiful flowers spring out, hibiscus, rose, lilies, marigold, she holds them out to M, smiling, her eyes looking downward, her face coy, I got these for you, she says, there is no water to fill today, so I went to the market early in the morning, they are the freshest they can be, then she turns to look at Shabby, her silver nose-stud glimmering in the first rays of the sun, will you paint these? yes, Shabby replies, I will paint them now, while they are still the freshest—

The rising sun was pink, the receding night indigo, the spinach and coriander green, the lemons yellow, baskets brown; last night's puddles reflected off golden sunlight; men's hand towels were red; the dust rising from the ground was translucent orange as someone scattered water from a stainless-steel lota. The water was colourless.

The cauliflowers and ginger smelt of earth; early-morning flowers were sweet, woven into garlands for worship; dried leaves swept to one side of the street smelt of yesterday. The freshly fried vada smelt deep; the sea-fish were pungent, lying face-up in tokris. Last night's garbage had a slight stench.

The sounds of teeth brushed, tongues cleaned, tube-well cranked for water. The hullabaloo of children going to school in tri-shaws. The splash of taxis being washed before being driven out for the day. The running engine of the tempo offloading produce in the wee hours, its exhaust sputtering. The muted chatter of fisherwomen. The popping of oil boiling in the cauldron. The plop of dough dropped in it. The fizz of frying. The warm steam from freshly made tea, infused with cloves and cardamom. The goo-goo of pigeons on the ledge, stretching themselves awake.

Shabby's fingers worked relentlessly. His wrists ached as his body turned this way and that to cover the canvas. He'd woken up early for months, dream or no dream, made hundreds of sketches. Then one day, he was ready for the canvas. He hid it behind the bed. He wasn't willing to show it to anyone yet. Not Shruti, not Ganjeri. He hoped Shakku-bai wouldn't find it. He was embarrassed of what it would become.

On the street below, the flute-seller made his daily appearance, ambling through the market-stalls, playing his repertoire of sad Hindi film tunes, shrill notes renting the still air, melody bouncing off decrepit buildings, the only time they were touched by beauty. Shabby mixed and mixed colours until he found the perfect shade for the bamboo of the flute. It was only a thin line on the large canvas. But it was important. It was at the centre of the piece. The flautist himself was an afterthought, his back turned to the artist, the children mere line drawings, following the flautist in a trance, weaned away by his tunes.

The Pied Piper of Parel. That's what he would name this painting.

Shabby stepped back as far as he could in the small room. Yes, it was complete.

2013

Accident

Shakku-bai appears one morning, just like that. The bell rings, he opens the door, and there she is, like she has come for her usual everyday work, keys jangling at her waist. By reflex, they smile, even though they haven't seen each other in four years. For a moment, it seems like nothing has changed, like everything around them, even the air, has re-orientated itself, and they are in that little Parel flat again.

Shakku-bai doesn't explain how she has found his new address, this flat in Wadala where Ma and he now are, a part of Mumbai far away from where he used to live with Ganjeri. This neighbourhood has broad roads, gentrified apartment blocks, stretches of arid land. After the *incident*, it was Chintoo and Papa who'd organized everything. No one asked him where he wanted to live. He didn't care. The further away from his old life, the better.

'How are you, saab?' Shakku-bai asks with a nervous smile.

He bobs his head. 'Come in, please.'

'I'll need help with these.' Shakku-bai points to some panels against the wall in the lift lobby.

He turns to look at the panels, not many, perhaps six or seven, about the size of windows. It takes him a while to understand what they are – his canvases, his paintings, wrapped in old sarees, the dusty Sellotape coming off. The sight of them makes a fizzy sensation in his nose, as if his eyes are going to water any minute. 'You had these with you?' he asks.

As they drag the canvases in, Shakku-bai tells him how she saved them. 'After you left the flat, saab, I used my set of keys to get in. I just wanted to check if the paintings were still there, behind the bed and cupboard.' She hesitates. 'I know you didn't tell anyone about them, but I used to clean the house, na? I knew.' Her silver nose-stud glitters as she speaks. 'I brought the paintings out and asked for permission to store them in the community centre. I didn't know when I would see you again, saab . . .'

But you found me in the end, he wants to say. Her face is flushed from the journey she has made on this sweltering afternoon. He imagines her taking the day off work, lugging the canvases up the steps of Dadar station, across the overbridge, then on the train, off it, then the auto-rickshaw ride to this flat.

Ma appears in a corner of his vision. She was in her room, taking a nap. She squints in the sun, trying to figure out who this local woman is, what she wants. But then she sees the paintings and suddenly understands. Her face becomes stern. He has never told Ma anything about Shakku-bai, but she has always been good at intuiting, she's clever like that.

But there are things one can't *not* do for guests in this country. So Ma gets water and biscuits. Shakku-bai joins her hands in a namaskar. Then, suddenly remembering, she pulls a small box of sweets out of her jhola and hands it to Ma. 'This is prasad. I went to the Siddhivinayak temple to pray for him.' Ma takes the box. 'The main one in Prabhadevi,' Shakku-bai clarifies. There are many temples of Lord Ganesh in this city. She's been to the most auspicious one, where long queues snake along the main road and it takes hours before one can get in for a moment of darshan.

'When I heard of saab's accident, I can't tell you what I felt.' Shakku-bai is now wiping tears with her pallu. She points to his bad leg with her chin. 'It shouldn't have happened.' She shakes her head. 'Bad things shouldn't happen to good people.' She says all this to Ma, as if she doesn't have the courage to face him. 'But now all that is over. I prayed to Ganpati-bappa; from now on, only good things will happen.'

Shakku-bai sits for some more time. Ma brings out tea and more biscuits. She serves the prasad, small cone-shaped bright-yellow modaks that they eat whole after touching to their foreheads to absorb god's blessing.

'How is the other saab?' Shakku-bai asks about Ganjeri. 'Give him my regards.'

He nods, doesn't tell her he hasn't seen Ganjeri or Shruti in years.

Shakku-bai says she misses working for them. The new tenants in the Parel flat are a couple with a daughter. They are nothing like him and Ganjeri. The woman doesn't trust her, follows her around the house, checks the furniture and the fridge. One time, she accused Shakku-bai of stealing limes, made her unfurl her pallu to prove she wasn't hiding them there. Something like bile is forming in his stomach as he hears this. He cannot imagine anyone else living in that flat, in *his* home where he lived with his favourite people.

When Shakku-bai leaves, she waits at the door for an extra minute. 'Come home sometime, saab,' she says. She keeps standing there, as if hoping he will say something, maybe a fond word about old times, maybe a question about Mangesh, maybe a thank you for bringing him the paintings. But he doesn't. He lets the door close of its own accord on her face. He stands on the other side, feeling her breath on the wood, until he hears her feet shuffle, turning to leave.

Come home sometime. Home. The word rings in his head long after she has gone. There was a time when he wouldn't have imagined a single day passing without seeing Ganjeri or Shruti or Shakku-bai or Mangesh. Now it has been half a decade since they've all disappeared from his life. And Ma and Papa, whom he thought he'd see only sparingly, less and less with the passing of years, are now ever-present, Ma right here with him, in this alien flat, his caregiver. How easy it is for people to come and go, enter and leave our lives, like life is a play in acts, and every act has a different cast of characters, with the protagonist having little choice in who they are surrounded by, the power completely vested in the playwright.

In the evening, Ma opens up the wrapping around the canvases, tearing through the old sarees ruthlessly. Dust rises and makes them sneeze. She stands the canvases against the wall and looks at them intently. 'Did you paint these?' she asks, her voice betraying slight disbelief, like there was a possibility that these could be someone else's work.

That night, he sleeps deeply. When he wakes up, he hears market sounds in the distance. He limps to the window, but there is only arid land stretching out to the horizon, plastic bags flying like multicoloured jewels, people defecating before the sun shines too brightly on their unwashed bottoms.

2000s

Moscow

Shabby lay on his stomach. Shakku-bai had just changed the sheet, and the crisp cloth chafed his skin. He heard her anklets move around the house as she swept the floor. He looked up at the ceiling fan, its blades still. Shakku-bai was adamant about turning all the fans off while she cleaned, so dust wouldn't fly and undo her work. Shabby held the magazine he was reading, trying to make sense of the article on global warming, but his eyelids were drooping shut.

A flick of the switch woke him. The fan whirred to life. He turned in surprise. Usually Shakku-bai didn't switch the fans back on, letting the boys do it themselves. But today she was standing by the door. The blades accelerated, sending the pages into a tizzy.

Shakku-bai fidgeted nervously with the pallu of her saree, a slight smile on her face. 'Sab theek hai?' she asked. 'It's been a while since I'm working, so I thought I should ask if everything is okay.' They bobbed their heads in a choreographed performance.

'That day, you came to our chawl.'

Shabby sat up on the bed. 'Yes, yes. The firangs have started a tour, so I thought let's go see what it's all about.'

'They want to use the community centre for activities.

They're asking us to gather there for embroidery. They want to teach music and art to the children.'

'Right. So how's it coming along?'

'Oh, one or two women go now and then. Who has the time, saab? Wash vessels, send children to school, come to work, fill water, clean the house, cook for everyone . . .'

Shabby thought of Ma, how she'd listed her chores out so often. Maybe it was something homemakers did, just so there were witnesses to all that invisible unpaid work.

Shakku-bai was starting to get comfortable. She leaned her shoulder on the door as she spoke. 'The firangs were also asking if we would come to evening classes for adults. I told my husband – *I don't have time, but you go learn something instead of getting drunk every day.*'

Shabby nodded, then they fell silent. Shakku-bai smiled at him coyly. She was a changed person, as though that moment they had shared in the slum the other day, the way Shabby had seen her, pushed against the wall, dented bucket at her feet, had unlocked a tenderness she'd kept hidden from her employers all this time. Suddenly, she had nothing else to hide from him.

'Saab, I have something to ask you.' Shakku-bai hesitated. 'My son is fourteen. He's a good boy. But you know boys this age. I found out things about him recently.' She stopped to breathe. 'Saab, he's been hobnobbing with the bhais. There's a Rocky-bhai in that slum . . .' She pointed at the slum across the tracks. 'That man is no good . . .' Her voice was heavy. 'I don't want my son getting into trouble. His friends got into some police ka locha. I'm very scared for him.'

Shabby tried to make a sympathetic face, wondering what he could do about this.

Shakku-bai pulled herself together. 'I've told him – *no ulta-seedha business, if you get into trouble, I can't save you. We have no power, no connections* . . . I've put him in the satsang. He'll go there every evening and sing religious songs. The Guru-ji who comes there is very good. He says nice-nice things – how to help others, how to stay on the right path.' She smiled at the efficacy of her solution.

'Doesn't he go to school?'

'He goes na, saab!' Shakku-bai's eyes lit up. 'He was doing well until two years ago. Then this Rocky-bhai brainwashed him. He says – *What is the use of going to school, only rich people get jobs, poor people never get any decent work.*'

Then she jumped as if an idea had just come to her, although it was clearly what she had come here to say. 'Saab, will you teach him English? At least he'll get a job as a peon in a big office. His English is weak. He says everyone laughs when he speaks.'

Shakku-bai pointed her chin towards Ganjeri's room. 'I thought of asking the other saab, but you are the more serious type.' Her voice was shy. 'That saab is smart and all, but he doesn't sit still in one place only. Sometimes here, sometimes there . . .'

This made Shabby feel good. Ganjeri was a charmer, touching everyone he came across with his dimpled smile. But just this once, Shabby's reserve had won. He nodded yes.

Shakku-bai beamed. 'You are very kind. My son is just downstairs. I told him – *You sit and do time-pass with your mobile while I go up and speak to saab.* Shall I bring him here?' She didn't wait for a reply. 'The watchman won't allow him in. Can you come and talk to the watchman?' She sounded guilty.

They went downstairs. The lift was even hotter than the flat. At the gate, the watchman sat under a jumbo umbrella, waving a bamboo hand-fan to keep away the flies. Outside the umbrella's shade was a teenage boy playing games on his mobile phone.

'Oi, Mangesh, ikade ye,' Shakku-bai called. 'See, saab has come to meet you.' Mangesh got up and bowed. His large eyes shone through his dark papery skin. His high cheek-bones glistened. He broke into a pearly-white smile. He'd make a good model for a toothpaste advert. His ears seemed bigger when he stood, because he wasn't very tall.

'Why won't you allow him to come upstairs?' Shabby charged the watchman, surprised by his own voice layered with authority.

'What to do, sir? The building secretary has asked me not to let the maids' children in.' The watchman stood up to attention and pinched his crotch. 'They used to come with their mothers and create a ruckus. The residents don't like their children playing with—'

Shabby flinched. Neither Shakku-bai nor Mangesh seemed bothered by this. 'Mangesh will come from now on. Don't trouble him,' he ordered.

On their way up, when they realized the lift could hold only two people, mother and son volunteered to take the stairs. In the living room, Shabby asked Mangesh to sit below the fan to dry his sweat. He poured two glasses of water. Shakku-bai looked uncomfortable. 'Why all this, saab?' She drank the water with the glass held high, trying not to touch it to her lips. She signalled Mangesh to do the same.

'Okay, Mangesh. Tell me something in English.'

After some meek looks at his mother, who was glaring at him to comply, Mangesh stood straight as if he were onstage, arms firmly by his side. 'My name Mangesh Tawde. My home in Ratnagiri. I live in Parel, Mumbai, with my father and mother. My father name Divakar Tawde. My mother name Shakuntala Tawde.' His voice was clear. He said the words with force. 'I am proud Indian. India is great country in the world. Everyone live here – Hindu, Muslim, Sikh, Christian,

Jain. Hindus pray in temple, Christians pray in church, Muslims pray in moscow. We all live happily ever after.'

Shabby clapped. This made Shakku-bai very happy.

'Muslims pray in a mosque, not *moscow*,' Shabby corrected Mangesh.

'But my teacher said *moscow*.' Mangesh looked confused. 'And the spelling is also like that only—'

Shakku-bai stepped in. 'From now on, say how saab teaches you to. Okay?'

'Call me bhaiyya,' Shabby said to Mangesh. Something about the boy's carefree smile and unaware smartness reminded him of Chintoo. Still no text or call from his brother. Months had passed. Ma said Chintoo came and went as he pleased, treated their flat like a hotel, leaving Lucknow for days to tour with his band. Thinking of that last conversation with Chintoo always made Shabby feel like going back to Lucknow right then and making up. But he was waiting for Chintoo to reach out. *Le Establishment* was the worst insult Chintoo could've thrown at him, and he wasn't ready to back down yet.

Mangesh head-bobbed. 'Ho, bhaiyya, yeto . . .'

Shakku-bai nudged her son. 'Bhaiyya doesn't know Marathi. He's not from Mumbai, na? Say in English.'

Mangesh looked at them shyly. 'Okay, bhaiyya, see you toomaro.'

Malgudi

'Bhaiyya, have you ever been to a lighthouse?' Mangesh loved asking questions, mostly about the sea – timings of tides, effects of the moon, how to navigate the surf.

'I grew up very far from the sea.' This was Shabby's meek excuse.

'I haven't been either,' Mangesh said. 'There was a lighthouse we could see from our village. Its light was so strong, like a cone. It rotated all night. Ajji promised to take me there.' His eyes were dreamy.

Shabby was sprawled on the sofa. His eyes hurt from looking at the computer all day. Work was so boring he came home with a headache every evening. Mangesh was at the table, a crisp copy of *Malgudi Days* open. Today was a non-study day, and Mangesh was supposed to finish a chapter. But he'd started talking, as usual.

'Do you speak to your Ajji?' Shabby asked.

'Now she has a mobile phone so we call her at night sometimes.' Mangesh had grown up in a village near Ratnagiri. For a few years, when Shakku-bai and her husband had moved to Mumbai and couldn't afford to bring Mangesh, he'd been left with his grandmother, his Ajji. He told stories of sneaking away to the fort with friends, cycling by the sea in lashing rains, stealing chicken from villagers' backyards.

A few months ago, the first evening that Mangesh came for tuition, Shabby had obsessed all day and come back from work early. He'd set out a notebook and a pen, filled a bottle of water and put it on the table. All the while he'd feared that Mangesh wouldn't turn up.

But Mangesh did turn up, hair smelling of coconut oil, perfectly combed to show the shape of his skull, carrying a box of sweets Shakku-bai had sent. He'd insisted on sitting on the floor, refusing the chair until Shabby said in that case, he'd have to sit on the floor too. They'd done very little that first day. Mangesh was distracted. He looked around the flat, eyes resting on the laptops and headphones and other electronics. He left abruptly at five minutes to seven, saying he couldn't be late for satsang.

'What else did you do with your Ajji?' Shabby loved listening to these stories, even if Mangesh repeated them – his grandma's fish curry steeped in spicy chilli, the head massages she'd give him with warm oil, their walks to the temple beneath the swaying palm trees. These made Shabby think of Nani, her bedtime stories and her taunts. He hadn't spoken to Nani in a year. The last time he spoke to Ma, she'd told him Nani's arthritis had worsened, that Nani was walking with a stick.

'Ajji made pakodas of pumpkin flower.' Mangesh's eyes lit up. 'Those were the *best days*, bhaiyya,' he said in English. 'Then I was called to Mumbai.'

In these few months, Mangesh's vocabulary had improved. Words had turned into sentences. Past, present, future. Nouns, pronouns. Mangesh's English wasn't all that bad to start with. He'd just never spoken it for fear of being laughed at. He said that at school, the students who'd lived in Mumbai from the start were smarter. He was still a villager in their eyes.

The tuition had extended to maths and science. The teaching at school was never sufficient. Mangesh showed Shabby tomes of notes he'd photocopied from others. He said the only way to pass the exams was to memorize them. Shabby spent nights reading up and making notes, jogging his memory from his schooldays. He found this infinitely more interesting than programming in C++, poring over lines of software, testing his code on networks equipment, actioning change requests from the client within a day's turnaround time, working on US hours, EST, PST and whatnot.

'What will be my next book?' Mangesh asked. Shabby had bought R. K. Narayan's *Malgudi Days*, Ruskin Bond's *Friends in Small Places*, Satyajit Ray's *Professor Shonku*, books he thought every Indian teenager should read, books *he* should've read in school, instead of Shakespeare and Austen and Wordsworth waxing eloquent about a land so far away that students couldn't even begin to imagine it. Once in a while, he suspended tuition to let Mangesh read in the flat. There was very little space in Mangesh's shanty. Shabby imagined a single naked bulb, sooty corners, rising fumes from Shakku-bai's cooking.

'Well, you won't get to the next book at this speed,' Shabby said. Mangesh turned back to the pages, looking guilty. He read with his finger on the words, one by one. He was fourteen. To think that there were millions of Mangeshs in this country with this level of reading. Maybe even worse.

'You can take this book home,' Shabby offered, feeling bad about his snideness. It was how he'd felt when he told Chintoo off, angry with himself for being angry with his brother.

'No use, bhaiyya. Once Baba comes home, it's a ruckus.' The drunk father who Mangesh only mentioned in passing, who Shakku-bai never blamed when she showed up with bruises on her wrists. 'Everything was fine in Ratnagiri. Baba was very well-behaved. It all changed when we moved to

Mumbai.' Mangesh hated everything about the city. *Have you noticed how foul the city smells? They say it's fish, but it's just rot*, he'd once said.

The key turned in the lock and Ganjeri walked in. Mangesh stiffened. Ganjeri went to the gym every evening. In a way, it was convenient that their paths hardly crossed. For some reason, Ganjeri had never warmed to Mangesh. There was a pressure-cooker atmosphere in the small flat when the two were there together. Ganjeri laughed at Mangesh's mispronunciations, not to his face but his scorn was still apparent. He didn't like Mangesh coming over for lessons too often. *The kid is always here, we don't get time together any more*, he'd tell Shabby. He was disparaging of Shabby's ambitions for Mangesh. *How's your new project*, he'd ask, doing air quotes, *how's the Mother Teresa act going?*

Shabby had confronted Ganjeri about this, but Ganjeri had laughed it off.

'Maybe he's just jealous that Shakku-bai asked you and not him,' Shruti had told Shabby when he shared his annoyance with her. 'Syed *loves* to be the centre of attention. Don't you see how much he enjoys Erik and Rebecca inviting him to their parties, even if he doesn't necessarily agree with their work?'

Shabby had marvelled at how well Shruti perceived the inner workings of people. She was probably right, Ganjeri could be ubiquitously charming and impishly mean. He had the aura to control his surroundings without uttering a word. He could make someone feel special just by casting a smile at them, and someone else feel small by not deigning to give them even as much as a glance.

Now that Ganjeri was in the flat, Mangesh quickly closed the book, inserting the bookmark that Shabby had given him. 'Bhaiyya, done for today. It's almost time for satsang.'

'And what will happen if you're late or you just skip sat-sang today?' Shabby challenged.

Mangesh looked incredulous. 'I can't miss satsang. All my friends are there. And the Guru-ji gets very upset if people aren't punctual.'

'Surely Guru-ji would agree what you're doing here is more important than chanting religious hymns? If singing bhajans got people jobs . . .'

'Guru-ji says spiritual education is very important. People who don't know their culture, who don't connect with their god, they lead empty lives even if they have full pockets.' There was a confidence in Mangesh's voice.

They could hear Ganjeri's chuckles from his bedroom. Mangesh packed his bag as fast as he could and left. Even his dark skin couldn't hide the red flush of his cheeks.

2013

Tangent

It is a cool Saturday afternoon. There are raindrops in the air though the clouds are still forming. After the art classes at the NGO are done, he tells the girl from his building he won't go home right away. He has plans. Then he drives out.

He travels north on the Eastern Express Highway to Thane. Once upon a time, this used to be Mumbai's *twin* city. Now Mumbai has sprawled over, neighbourhood after neighbourhood springing up all the way north, the only direction it can grow, being surrounded by the sea to its west, east and south. Thane is not a twin any longer, just a poor cousin hanging on to Mumbai like a parasite.

He makes a U-turn and drives back, through Mulund, Bhandup, Kanjur Marg. At Vikhroli, he turns right, then cuts through Jogeshwari. He makes a right on the Western Express Highway, goes all the way up to Virar, crossing Goregaon, Malad, Kandivali, parts of the city he has never been to, confused neighbourhoods that look exhausted and shiny in equal parts, slums and high-rises, chawls and malls, old and new, poor and rich sitting side by side, looking down and looking up at each other. How big is this city? How many thousands of lives does it subsume every day, chew up and spit out? How many millions does it sustain? How many dreams does it fuel and set alight?

At Virar, he makes another U-turn and drives back along the highway. Rows of billboards block out the sky on the right and left, movie stars selling singlets, cricketers selling mint, property developers selling flats in apartment blocks, stacks of matchboxes with foreign names – *casa, maison, polis* – and photos of firang families hanging out by the pool, broad-shouldered dad, petite mum, two snow-white children. A slight wind kicks up, dust rises from the numerous construction sites, overbridges, bypasses, metro, all those mega-projects that will take this city into the future, make Mumbai the next Shanghai.

He switches the radio on, then turns it off, nervous of what song it will play, what memory that will bring. The psychologist has asked him to beware of *triggers*.

At Mahim, he turns left, then straight to Worli. He is heading towards the Sea Link bridge. He hasn't been on it yet, though it opened a few years ago. At Worli, he joins a long line of cars. He takes his glasses off to wipe the salt from his face. The row of brake-lights blur into a single red line.

And then suddenly, he is on the bridge. Someone in the office said it is like the Golden Gate Bridge in San Francisco. He hasn't been there, so he wouldn't know. But this is unlike anything else in this country. Broad four-laned stretches in both directions, held up by taut cables, the open sea on one side, Worli fishing village on the other. There aren't many cars this afternoon. He cranks the gear up and presses his foot on the accelerator. The little car wails like an unwilling child being dragged to school. The slanting cables whizz past, making him dizzy. He rolls the window down so the wind can hit his face, get into his hair, make it fly in all directions. He turns to look left at the sea gleaming in the rays that have made it past the dark clouds. He looks right, trying to spot Mahim Creek where he and Shruti had sat on the rocks, the water grazing their feet, watching this bridge being built in the dead of the night, where they'd nearly kissed. But the scenery is moving too fast for him to make anything out.

He picks up speed, takes his foot off the brake. For a few seconds, he is flying. What if he let the car go off on a tangent, crash through the railings, drop into the sea?

What if this was the last thing he saw, the calm sea waiting for rain? What if the last thing he felt was the tingling ache of love? What if the last memories he had were those of his best days in this city?

Would that be such a bad thing?

2000s

Manja

They ran as fast as the kites in the sky. Sand sprayed with every kick, landing on their clothes, arms, faces, specks going into their eyes. They picked up speed, butting up against the gusts from the wild sea at its peak in the afternoon high tide. When they were out of steam, they stopped, hinged on their stomachs, tongues out, tasting the salty air.

Shruti was a pro. She said she'd flown kites in childhood when she visited her family home in Cuttack. She and her cousins would do nothing else all afternoon. Mangesh was less of a pro, but he was a fighter, his teenage fingers nimble, pulling at the string, unafraid to cut his fingertips, droplets of blood that blew away in the wind. Sometimes he ran into the water, hopping over the crashing waves. Anything to keep his kite flying.

They'd scoured Crawford Market for kites and string. Finding kites was easy. It was the string that wouldn't satisfy Mangesh. *Manja*, he called it. 'Back in the village, we made it ourselves, with sticky rice glue and gum from the trees.' Finally, he'd grudgingly settled for the synthetic manja. 'This will take the kite only half as high.' But once on the beach, he'd forgotten about it, turning round and round as the manja wove a web around him. It took Shabby and Shruti to free him, loop by loop.

After Shruti had defeated them, they sat on Chowpatty beach, the warm sand of a winter's day caressing their butts, bodies sore, little welts forming where the fine stones had pricked their soles. The city had surrendered to post-monsoon stupor, letting its harsh sun go limp, a haze descending to eye level. They sucked on iced-golas, throats hoarse from the slush. Shruti and Mangesh made sand-castles, patting the mounds gently, telling stories as they went. *This is the Ratnagiri fort, this is the high wall around it, surrounded by a moat. This is the lighthouse where Ajji and I will go one day.* Shabby lay on his side, head on his palm, elbow dug into the sand. They were like a family on a picnic.

That Saturday morning, Shabby had woken up to a nip in the air, and thought a day like this shouldn't go to waste. He called Mangesh on Shakku-bai's mobile, and they picked Shruti up. She'd run out of the gate like a child, quilted jhola swinging at her side, giving Mangesh a high-five. The two had a tussle about who'd sit next to the taxi driver. 'Girls don't sit in front,' Mangesh said.

'Say that again and I'll show you what girls can and can't do,' Shruti replied in feigned anger. They settled on Shruti taking the outward journey, Mangesh the return.

Shabby had left Ganjeri out. He'd wanted this day to be pure, unadulterated, without the tectonic collisions of Ganjeri's and Mangesh's relationship. Recently, Ganjeri had told Shabby, 'No matter how much you try to educate Mangesh, he's never going to rise above a certain level. In this country, his fate is sealed. His studies will only take him so far. And by telling him he can be more than he ever will, you're no different to the firangs.' This had irritated Shabby; Ganjeri could keep his big words and theories to himself. Shabby was determined to open up opportunities for Mangesh that would otherwise never happen. He'd failed M, but he wouldn't fail Mangesh.

The taxi had brought the three of them to Marine Drive. They bought tickets to the Taraporewala Aquarium. 'We are now in India's oldest aquarium,' Shruti whispered in Mangesh's ear as they entered. Mangesh's eyes widened. He drew lines on the glass as he walked through the goldfish and starfish and sharks. He stood still when he saw the jellyfish. 'I could eat them up just like that.' He flashed his pearly-white smile, the skin below his eyes folding in youthful creases. A swordfish swam up to him and rubbed its nose on the glass. He rubbed his in reply.

The iced-golas still dribbling down their chins, they walked up Malabar Hill. Coconut and banyan trees made a lush canopy over paved streets that wound all the way to the top. The three of them peeped over boundary walls, gawked at bungalows of millionaires. At a twist in the road, they spotted the shimmering blue of a swimming pool, a perfect rectangle, the water peaceful until someone dived in. Mangesh reached out and touched Shruti's arm, his mouth open in wonder. 'Didi,' he said under his breath. 'Look how rich these people are!'

They climbed further up, the lanes becoming narrower. They had to step aside for the long shiny luxury cars to carefully turn corners. Through the dark-tinted windows, they could see chauffeurs in uniforms, black-rimmed caps and white gloves, giving them irritated looks, unnecessary pedestrians in a neighbourhood where no one walked. In the back seats were older men with laptops, women in chiffon sarees touching up their make-up, young boys and girls playing video games.

They walked up to the Hanging Gardens at the top of the hill. The entire length of Marine Drive stretched out in front, Chowpatty beach at one end, the Air India building at the other. It reminded Shabby of the taxi ride on his first evening in the city. It had been a year and a half since then. So much had changed. This heaving dysfunctional city was now home. *Home.*

As evening fell, the lights came on along Marine Drive, all at once, flooding the buildings and street and sea in yellow. Headlights of cars zigzagged along the promenade. The sea was a deep grey, ready to retire into blackness. Just then, big drops of rain sputtered out of the sky, unusual for winter but welcome nevertheless. Mangesh ran for cover under the shoe-house in the children's playground, peeping from the little windows. 'The view is even better from here,' he called out. But Shruti stood steadfastly on the grass, barefoot, sandal-straps dangling from her fingers. Shabby took his jacket off and covered their heads. He put an arm around her shoulders, hugged her close. A stray lock of her hair nuzzled his face. He let it. Then he kissed her cheek. She didn't move, but smiled, signalled with naughty eyes at Mangesh behind them.

Mangesh called from the shoe-house. 'Bhaiyya, Didi, listen to this poem I just wrote. It's in English.

> *'A swordfish became my friend in Bombay*
> *It rubbed its nose and said – Come every day.'*

Govinda

Mangesh points from the shoe-house, that is my father, he doesn't drink, Shabby follows the finger to see M standing next to him, on Chowpatty beach, waves raining fat droplets on them, his jacket covering their heads, Shabby is shivering but M's body is on fire, Shabby is drawing warmth from it, M takes off his T-shirt, muscles ripple, flames lick his arms and flat stomach, Shabby kisses M's cheek, M turns to him and smiles, eyes aglow—

The pit of the chawl seemed enormous, though it was smaller than it looked. People lined the balconies that ran around the courtyard on all floors, little dots bobbing. *Govinda Aala Re . . .* The song played in a loop, all versions of it, the older devotional one, the latest with techno-beats, another from the nineties with passionate dholak-beats. Children danced until an organizer shooed them away. Streamers and bulbs ran across the top. A small stage had been set up in a corner. A few local leaders sat with unsmiling faces. Behind them hung banners, pictures of more politicians with unsmiling faces.

Shabby spotted Shakku-bai on the second floor. She waved. She was in a yellow cotton saree, the starched pallu making a sharp angle at her shoulder. He nudged Ganjeri and Shruti. The three of them waved back. Shakku-bai said something to the man next to her, who Shabby assumed was her husband.

When she'd first told them about the Janmashtami celebrations, her voice was a blend of worry laced with pride.

'This year, for the first time, Mangesh will be a govinda. You know, last year, a few govindas fell and broke their bones. But Mangesh is stubborn. All the boys at the satsang are govindas this year. He's been practising hard.'

Shabby knew. Mangesh had been skipping lessons for practice. But Mangesh had also invited Shabby to the celebrations and he'd said yes. The boy had jumped up in the air with excitement.

Shabby now looked up at the dahi-haandi, a large clay pot of yogurt hanging from a tightrope that the boys would have to reach. Such an ingenious way of celebrating Lord Krishna's birthday. The story went that the god's boy-avatar spent all his time stealing yogurt from the neighbours.

A tap on his shoulder. Shabby turned to see Rebecca and Erik and a few of their friends. One had a pro-looking camera with a protruding lens, with which she clicked a series of shots in quick succession. Another was wearing a dhoti. How he'd managed to walk through these crowds so efficiently was a wonder.

Volunteers gently pushed the spectators to the sides. It was almost showtime. Two men blew bugles. One by one, the govindas entered the courtyard in a single file. There were about thirty of them. They looked like the Indian cricket team at a World Cup final. They stood around the quad, facing the audience. They wore white vests and blue shorts, saffron bands tied around their foreheads. The music from the loudspeakers died down. Two men with dholaks emerged, beating the drums to a celebratory rhythm. The crowd clapped, swaying in a tribal dance. Shabby strained his eyes to find Mangesh, but all the govindas looked alike. They turned and huddled around the centre. Then their journey upward began.

The bottom layer took position in a circle, young strong arms holding each other in tight hugs. The next tier climbed on top of the base, then the third tier, using palms and shoulders as stepping stones. With every tier stabilizing, the crowd went berserk, chanting *Govinda aala re*, clapping louder.

Shabby finally spotted Mangesh in the third tier, his face tense with concentration, steadying himself on the shoulders of a burly govinda, arms reaching across the two boys next to him. He managed to steal a glance at Shabby and nodded slightly. Shabby looked up at Shakku-bai. She was watching her son intently, pallu covering her mouth in anticipation. Their eyes met, and Shakku-bai pointed to Mangesh, in case Shabby hadn't seen him. Shabby nodded and smiled. He felt slightly dizzy.

The spectators chanted, danced, cheered. The firang in the dhoti said in Shabby's ear, 'This is the *real* Indian experience. From where I come, in Norway, I have to drive out miles to even see another human being.' Shabby gave him a polite smile. The man stepped closer. 'Sometimes I go to Bandra station during peak hours and stand facing the oncoming crowds, just to feel the human touch . . .' The rest was drowned out by the bugles.

The penultimate tier was now in place. Four sporty boys, thigh muscles taut, looked up at the dahi-haandi, the destination of this human pyramid. Festivities reached a crescendo. Even the politicians onstage managed to smile. All heads were turned in one direction only, eyes fixed on one place. Just one more tier between the govindas and the auspicious yogurt.

The last govinda began his climb. He was no older than thirteen or fourteen, slightly built, chosen to keep the pyramid light at the top. His eyes darted between the prize and where he was placing his palms and feet. A hush fell over the crowd. The dholaks grew softer. The clapping paused. Shabby looked around him. Ganjeri and Shruti stood in rapt attention, their fingers clasped tightly in each other's, chests heaving in coordinated breathing. They looked beautiful in the early-evening light, frozen in time, sweat forming on their foreheads, mouths agape.

Just then, a low warning sound swept through the crowd. Shabby turned to look. The pyramid was swaying a little. The boy who was to go on top was precariously perched somewhere in the middle. He refused to budge, not having the confidence to go further. The other govindas shuffled their feet to rebalance, but that made the pyramid more lopsided. The young govindas glimpsed around, fear on their faces. Fear of falling, failing. What had looked like an organic culmination of human spirit suddenly seemed like an insane idea – a contraption of adolescent bodies facing an imminent threat of injury.

Shabby's eyes searched for Mangesh – the sweat made his papery skin shine, but he was looking straight up at the dahi-haandi, as though considering breaking the pattern and going to the apex himself. Shakku-bai's lips moved in prayer, her body rocked back and forth. Next to her, her husband stood with hands folded, eyes up to the heavens. Shabby wanted to shout out to Mangesh, ask him not to do anything stupid, for his parents' sake. He'd read in the papers last year that a govinda had died of his injuries.

Another low moan. A govinda in the lower tiers caved and the pyramid stooped further. That was it. The organizers jumped into action. The coach shouted instructions. Volunteers ran, asking the crowds to move further back. Stretchers were carried in. There was talk of an ambulance being on its way. This was a losing game, the arrangements to cope with defeat laid out one by one. It was time to bring the govindas down.

And then, someone in the crowd put their foot forward, dragging others towards the pyramid. One by one, the spectators closed in, reaching hands out to support the bottom tier. Someone shouted a slogan. *Jai Shri Krishna.* Everyone followed. Bugles blared again, dholaks started to play. People in the balconies chanted. *Jai Shri Krishna. Jai Kanhaiyalal Ki.* Their voices bounced off the walls and echoed through the pit of the chawl.

Shabby moved forward in little steps, like everyone else. Together, they formed a cordon of support around the bottom tier. Shabby turned around, flexing his back muscles to give the govinda as much strength as he could. Facing this way, he saw Shruti in front of him, her body pressed against his, face close, the soft mounds of her breasts against his beating chest. She flashed a smile. He smiled back.

Some enthusiastic folk got on people's shoulders to support the second tier. Ganjeri and Rebecca were there, balancing themselves on Erik's shoulders, who stood straight to his full height today. Even the Norwegian in the dhoti had made it up there. Ganjeri reached out to support the third tier. Mangesh looked down and smiled, took Ganjeri's hand and used it as a lever to straighten himself. Using Mangesh's balance, the next govinda straightened too. And one by one, the third tier came back to the centre. The pyramid stabilized.

Everyone's eyes were now trained on the star govinda. The young boy began his climb again. In stealthy movements, he made his way to the pinnacle. He stayed there for a moment, as though he couldn't quite believe the feat he'd just accomplished. Everyone waited with bated breath. Then he reached out to touch the dahi-haandi. He strained a little, the haandi beyond his reach. The crowd tightened around the pyramid even further, allowing every tier to stand on tiptoes, making the pyramid higher. The cheering was maddening by this point, the miracle only moments away. The bugles sounded the final call as the star govinda smashed the dahi-haandi. Yogurt flowed from the pot like manna from heaven, falling in lumps on everyone below, spraying across the chawl. People in the balconies rushed downstairs. They couldn't be contained any longer.

In his frame of vision, Shabby could see Shruti and Ganjeri and Erik and Rebecca and Shakku-bai and Mangesh, beaming, holding their palms out for the blessed yogurt that was now being spooned out by volunteers and distributed as prasad. They turned to look for him, and when their eyes met, they beckoned.

The yogurt tasted like happiness. In that moment, Shabby truly believed there was a place for all of them in this little world, their differences were just distractions. He wanted to rush home and paint this scene on a giant canvas, hang it from his window so the whole mohalla could see what they'd achieved together, live with this memory forever.

Troika

'Cioccolato.' She ran her fingers on his face. They stopped below his eyes, circled his cheekbones. 'When I was small, I went to Italy with my parents. The lady at the hotel reception touched my skin and said, *Cioccolato*.' Chocolate. 'Your skin reminds me of that.' She said it again. 'Cioccolato.'

Shabby closed his eyes as Shruti's fingertips reached his lips. He gulped. His blood was still pumping from the high of the dahi-haandi celebrations. He could feel her trembling too. The energy filled the small bedroom in their little square flat, as though they were on the pyramid themselves, swaying, chanting, a mass of bodies come together to achieve something bigger than the sum of their parts.

Her finger pushed against Shabby's mouth. He parted his lips, only slightly. The finger slipped in. It was salty. His tongue, dry a moment ago, was wet now, the glands working overtime to get the juices flowing. He bit softly. He heard her suck in air, surprised and pleased at the same time. He rolled his tongue to draw her further in. She slipped in another finger. He sucked on them like a child on a nipple.

Shabby's hands were on Shruti's back, stroking the bare skin above her kurti. He went further up to untie her top-knot. Her hair fell in cascades over her shoulders. He traced the locks down to her ears, no jhumka today. He pressed the tender earlobe between the tips of his thumb and forefinger. The lobe resisted, pushed back, tempting him to press harder.

His other hand came up to her breasts, seeking out her heart. It was beating in doubles. Dhak-dhak. Dhak-dhak. She pulled her fingers out of his mouth. He leaned his face in and kissed her. A peck on the lips first, then venturing his tongue in between her teeth. It was met by her tongue, strangely strong and grainy. The tongues rolled on each other like two kids in the sand.

Shabby felt firm fingers rest on the curve of his slim waist. He'd never been touched there before. His skin broke out in goosebumps. The fingers went up his side to his armpits, stroked the hair gently, caressed the strands. He felt the weight on his back. Shabby had felt a wild energy enter the space even though he hadn't known what it was. Now Ganjeri's broad shoulders engulfed him from behind, his hand around Shabby's flat stomach. The muscles in his abdomen tightened, locking in the oxygen he was voraciously inhaling. The length of Ganjeri's body against his, Ganjeri's front against his back. The frizzy scattering of hair on Ganjeri's tight chest against Shabby's triceps, the messy wiry curls on the nape of his neck, the sharp tip of Ganjeri's nose nuzzling the back of his head, seeking out the smell of his hair.

Shabby massaged Shruti's softness with his left hand, slipping it into her kurti, finding his way through her bra, stopping at her nipple. It was supple, moving in directions he willed it to, yet finding its centre every time. His right hand travelled to behind his head. His face breathed into Ganjeri's. Shabby let his fingers travel on it, stopping at the five dimples, two just above the lips, visible only when Ganjeri smiled in a certain way, then one on each cheek, deep, Shabby could stick his finger in them, then one on the chin, dividing the face into two perfectly symmetrical halves. This made Ganjeri laugh. A muffled hiccup blew air into Shabby's ear. It tickled him, made him laugh as well, made Shruti laugh too.

This cut through the tension in the room like the manja through their inexperienced fingers. Shabby kissed Ganjeri hungrily. This kiss was different to Shruti's, less exploratory, more confident, authoritative even. Ganjeri bit Shabby's lower lip and pulled it towards himself like a magnet. Shabby tasted blood.

Their three bodies moved closer, until there was no air left between them. Ganjeri's full six feet pressed Shabby into Shruti. Ganjeri's hardness against the soft flesh of Shabby's buttocks. Shruti's soft mounds against the hardness of Shabby's chest. Soft on hard. Hard on soft. Salty on sweet. Sour on heady. Smooth on prickly. Nimble on solid. Feroza. Jamooni. Subz. Narangi. Salait. Surkh. Rani. All those colours only Shruti knew and Shabby could never create, no matter how much paint he mixed on his palette. Wet. Weed. Musk. Must. All those smells only Ganjeri could carry.

Their three bodies moved to the same rhythm. As though the dholaks were still playing around them. As though there was an audience, little head-dots lined along the innumerable storeys across the length and breadth of their lives. As though they were at the apex of the pyramid, held up by this whole city. This mad grimy unruly untamed unfazed uncowering beautiful soft blue-green city. This city of lashing rains, sweeping waves, flying kites, slushy iced-golas.

Their three bodies were on fire. The flames licked their young skins, only their faces visible, embers reflecting off their eyes, lashes touching, lips kissing, one's hair pasted on another's sweaty forehead. Their hungry thirsty unloved bodies that had journeyed to reach this place, this point in time, to converge into each other, to light the spark that will burn down their pasts, their pain, their tears. Calm everything down forever. Scatter the cold ashes over the unforgiving grey sea.

Their three bodies were a troika. They will journey into the future. Maybe they will gallop in different directions, maybe they will never see eye to eye again, maybe the sound of their hooves will drown each other's voices out. But they will carry with them the story of this night, the story of the life they led together, the story of how the manna fell on them from heaven, even if just for this one night.

The story of this country singed on the burning bodies of its young.

PART FOUR
Jal / *Water*

2013

Mirror

The chest sags over the round belly, brown nipples hang low, shoulders slant downward, no angles, no strength. Unruly matted hair starts below the neck and snakes down to where it grows into a jungle. There are greys on his chest. The legs are thin, the good one still showing signs of muscle, the bad one sticking out, a deep cut running from the back of the thigh down to the knee. Little stitch-marks show like embroidery. The feet are podgy. The skin around the armpits droops, folds of fat and flesh. He turns around. A deep-brown mark along the backbone, no signs of fading even so many years after the *incident*. He hunches, feels its pull, as if it is going to tear and ooze any minute.

He is seeing himself naked for the first time in four years. Full frontal.

The mirror in the bathroom shows only the upper torso. That's the one he has used all this time. On his way back from work this evening, he stopped at a furniture store and bought a full-length mirror. He has passed this shop many times, seen this mirror on display on the pavement. But today, something struck. He swerved the car, parked it on the roadside, and asked the attendant to load the mirror into the boot, not even standing in front of it to check whether it was a good one. He paid up in a hurry and drove away.

The moment he got back, he dragged the mirror out, into the flat. Ma was probably downstairs at her adda with the women. He tore apart the packaging, positioned the mirror against the wall, and pulled his clothes off.

He is ashamed of what he sees, of what he has become, of what the *incident* has done to his body, of what he has let happen to himself. Once upon a time, this body used to be a beautiful thing, a bud blossoming into bright colours and crisp petals and taut stamen. A body to love.

When he is done looking at himself, he puts his clothes back on and goes to stand at the window.

2000s

Nawaab

'He doesn't live here any more,' Ma said to the lady. The pride sparkled like the jewels she was wearing. 'He lives in Mumbai, works for an American company. He's an *engineer*.' Ma still said the word like it was sacred. 'He will go to America soon.'

Mother and son were at the gate of Lucknow's poshest five-star hotel, entering the venue for Munni-didi's sangeet. Panna-chacha had gone all out to organize his daughter's wedding. They were walking down a red carpet like celebrity guests, photographers and videographers filming this moment for posterity, flashlights going off every few seconds.

The lady couldn't keep her eyes off Shabby. 'You must've settled down, na? Bought a car, house?'

'Yes, yes. Very big car!' Ma spread her arms to show how big. 'House, not yet. He's looking for a three-bedroom flat so we can go live with him.'

The lady raised her eyebrows. 'Such an ideal son. Like Shravan Kumar.' Shabby was vaguely familiar with the mythology of the son who'd carried his blind parents on his shoulders for a pilgrimage marathon of the chaar-dhaam.

'And what does your younger son do?'

Ma stole a quick look at Chintoo lurking in the shadows. 'He's still studying,' she said curtly, not offering any detail.

215

Shabby opened his mouth to say Chintoo was a musician, but Ma nudged him to keep walking. When they'd left the lady behind, she whispered, 'She must have a daughter or a niece she's trying to match you with. I won't be surprised if she turns up tomorrow with a photo.'

'Why did you tell her I've bought a car?'

'Just because you don't have one doesn't mean you can't buy one. In any case, it's high time. Otherwise, how will we get around when we visit?' Ma had casually mentioned visiting Mumbai now and again. This made Shabby nervous, the thought of Ma and Papa meeting Ganjeri and Shruti! He pushed the thought aside.

They headed into a humongous hall bedecked with ornate chandeliers and vintage lamps hanging low from the high ceiling. 'Hotels are the latest rage,' Papa had said in the car. 'Gone are the days when people rented havelis for weddings. Now it's all about air-conditioned halls, pool parties.' He chuckled. 'They even have open bars!'

'For your wedding, I don't want any of this Bollywood tamasha,' Ma said, scrunching her nose. Over the past decade, weddings in films had got grander and flashier – sprawling locations, brides and grooms sporting designer-wear, firang models dancing to choreographed steps, stylized Sanskrit mantras chanted to DJ beats. The public were catching up, taking out bank loans, throwing money to desperately make their lives look like the movies. But Ma was adamant. 'I want a proper traditional wedding in a haveli, original rituals, relatives singing folk songs. What was wrong with any of that?'

Shabby's plane had landed that afternoon. Papa and Ma had been waiting at Arrivals. Ma had a red shawl wrapped around her. The soft winter sun made the greys in her hair shimmer, though she still had luscious locks around her ears and crowding her forehead. She was holding up a sheet of A4 paper on which she'd written SHUBHANKAR TRIVEDI. She giggled at her little prank. Shabby tried to remember if he'd ever seen Ma being funny and light-hearted. Papa wrested the suitcase out of his hands and patted him on the shoulder, his hairline noticeably driven back in two years. When they got home, they unveiled the 42-inch TV Shabby had ordered for them online. They'd had it fixed to the wall. They said they were waiting for him to *inaugurate* it. Shabby took a deep breath. He had to survive only three days. He'd told them he was in the middle of an important project, made the visit sound like a favour. This is what they'd wanted all their lives, a son who could elevate their status in society, afford things. Now this is what they would get, nothing more. *Day zero and I'm already gagging*, he'd texted Shruti. *You got this, hang in there, mere sher, roar!* Shruti had texted back.

In the wedding hall, Shabby walked down the red carpet. It felt like the last scene of *Titanic*, when Rose walks down the deck, every person she'd ever known smiling at her. He turned to tell Chintoo this, but the boy had disappeared. They'd watched the movie together in the theatre, but only when it had been re-released after winning big at the Oscars. Their parents didn't allow movies in theatres back then; they were unnecessary distractions that would take time away from studies, unless of course it was award-winning American stuff that everyone else was watching.

Now, like Rose, Shabby saw everyone stand up to greet him. Panna-chacha and Manju-chachi, Lekha-bua and Nandu-fufa, Aarti-mami and Girish-mama, Sharma-uncle and Sharma-aunty, neighbours, classmates' parents. They gathered around, waved. The elder son of the Trivedis, back from Mumbai after so long. *Do you remember me? So handsome you've become!* Ma chaperoned him forward. Before leaving the house,

Malti-didi had taken kajal from her eyes with her little finger and dabbed it on the back of Shabby's head. 'Like a nawaab he looks,' she told Ma. 'This will ward off the evil eye. *Buri nazar-waale tera mooh-kaala.*' She sounded like a bumper sticker of a truck.

At the end of this memory lane was an elderly woman. It took Shabby a while to realize this was Nani. She was smiling, the gaps between her teeth showing. She hoisted herself from her chair, wobbled, one hand on the armrest, one on her knee. The skin on her arms was deeply furrowed. Ma had told him about Nani's worsening arthritis. Before he'd left for Mumbai, he'd seen Nani's weakened frame, but this seemed too much too suddenly. Shabby bent to touch her feet. She clasped his arms to stop him, then pulled him to her sagging chest. 'Welcome home, my prince.' She looked up at him from her shortened height. 'My Abhishek Bachchan, my Rahul Gandhi . . .'

This made everyone laugh. Ma rubbed Nani's back in embarrassment. 'Okay now, Amma. Are you going to list out every celebrity from around here?'

Nani popped her knuckles on the sides of her head, then motioned for Shabby to sit in her chair. He shook his head and lowered her back into it. Someone brought him another chair and he sat next to her. She kept her hand tightly held in his.

There was a sudden cheer from the back, like in a rock concert of thousands. Everyone turned to look, only to realize that the DJ was playing a track to gather the audience. He was a skinny youth in a shiny blazer and jeans that were falling off his meagre waist. He flailed his arms in all directions to the beats of the music. *Yo yo yo!*

Everyone settled down for the performances. Panna-chacha said a few words of welcome. Among the special guests who'd come from *very far* was Shabby. Then Suresh-mausa was invited to bless the occasion. Suresh-mausa faced the audience, palms joined in a namaste. His spine was straight as a rod. He hadn't aged at all. In fact, his skin was tauter, his moustache still well-oiled. 'What an honour to be here today.' A beatific smile on his face. 'I know Munni from when she was *this much.*' He lowered his palm to his knee. 'And today she's getting married.'

Shabby sat looking at this man, trying to call up all the hatred of his childhood, all the times he'd wanted to drag Suresh-mausa by the collar into a police station. But he felt nothing.

Suresh-mausa made to wipe tears. 'All these children, how fond they were of me – *Suresh-mausa, buy me a balloon; Suresh-mausa, lift me up on your shoulders!*' He looked like a clown. Here he was, decades later, still hogging the limelight at family functions, still a small-time politician who cooked up lies to feed his fantasies of self-grandeur.

Shabby's eyes roved, looking for Chintoo, spotting him in the back rows, by himself, slumped over his phone. Their eyes met and Shabby winked, trying to get him in on the joke. The Chintoo he knew would've ripped Suresh-mausa's lies apart, made a comedy sketch of everything and everyone at this wedding. But the boy he saw now was disinterested. Chintoo had come home just when they were leaving, said quick hellos. Ma had laid out new sherwanis for both sons, but Chintoo refused, saying he needed to catch the night train to Delhi where he had a performance the next day. Ma and Papa had exchanged exasperated looks.

Now cousins and friends went up onstage and danced to super-hit movie songs. They'd clearly practised for weeks. Ma had asked Shabby to prepare something as well, but he hadn't. Panna-chacha himself wasn't always around. He disappeared from time to time, and came back smelling of whisky and musk. But Manju-chachi sat in the first row like a judge in a reality show. If she were given a mic, she'd happily share her feedback and raise a scoreboard to grade the act.

Shabby felt the rustle of silk on his arm. Dhwani Dwivedi had slipped into the chair next to him. She looked ebullient, a grown-woman version of her teenage self, the gold bindi gleaming like a third eye on her forehead. The last time he'd seen her was when he'd come back for the summer holidays from his engineering college. He was smoking around a corner when she walked by. Their eyes had met for a moment before she'd looked away and kept walking. It had only been a few years since Dwiti's death, and the Dwivedi family had folded themselves into social extinction, appearing outside the house only to shop for essentials and go to work. They seemed to have finally come out of it. Mr Dwivedi was here, and so was Dhwani.

'You've become a hot-shot superstar in Mumbai, haan?' Dhwani now said. 'Everyone's queuing for your autograph.'

Shabby whispered in her ear. 'And what are *you* doing in Lucknow? You'd be a bigger star in Mumbai.' She moved closer to him, their shoulders touching. They sat like that and watched a few more dances.

Finally, the child-DJ announced the bride and groom's performance. The audience were getting restless, sneaking away to the next room, inveigled by the overpowering aroma of pakoras. To keep up spirits, the DJ played more claps and hoots from invisible fans. Munni-didi went up onstage in her elaborate lehenga, taking position, her back to the audience. The DJ played 'Dheeme Dheeme Gaaoon', a rather soft song for a wedding performance. Munni-didi began turning round and round. It looked like she was drowning and calling for help. The groom, half her size, milled around like her pageboy, picking up the end of her chunni and dropping it. This step continued on loop for the entire song.

'If this weren't their wedding, they'd be fast asleep by now,' Dhwani whispered. 'At my wedding, I'm not doing any of this nonsense.'

'So when's the wedding?' Shabby asked.

'Find me *one* cool guy in Lucknow and I'll get married tomorrow. I'll even do this dreadful dance.'

'You couldn't even if you tried. You dance like a dream.' He thought of her Odissi duet with Dwiti at the Diwali fair.

They exchanged glances, eyes bubbling with mischief. 'You want to go somewhere else?' she asked.

Shabby turned to Nani, who was thoroughly enjoying the performances. 'I'll get you some ice cream,' he half-mouthed, half-shouted in her ear and returned her hand to her lap. Then he and Dhwani tiptoed out of the hall. From the corner of his eye, he caught Ma's disapproving glare. In her head, she was already getting them married.

They picked up ice creams from the buffet and headed to the lawn at the back. 'I'd never have thought you'd grow up like this. It was always Chintoo who was stylish.' Dhwani's voice was teasing. 'The big city suits you.'

Shabby took a mouthful of the vanilla-strawberry-chocolate triple-scoop concoction. His tongue froze for a second. When it recovered, he asked, 'So what do you do?'

'I did a computers course. I teach in a college here.' Dhwani dug the plastic spoon into the scoop. 'My father never agreed to let me go anywhere. After Dwiti, he said he wanted me in front of his eyes all the time. All that studying for IIT just went to waste . . .'

Shabby stiffened at the mention of Dwiti, but Dhwani seemed relaxed. She'd probably said this many times over, that's why the mention of her sister had come so easily to her. Talking about the dead helped, something he'd never been able to do.

'But your parents let you go. And now you've become a star!' Dhwani was back to her cheerful self. Her finger passed through the spikes in his hair. He put the ice cream down and touched her bare waist over the pleats of her saree.

They looked here and there to make sure no one was around. Then he led her behind the hedge.

2013

Manoeuvre

Ma is leaving Mumbai, for good. After four years.

It isn't that she is finally convinced he doesn't need her any more. There is no evidence of that. Yes, he has stopped limping, but he hasn't cooked a meal in years, hasn't done laundry, hasn't cleaned the house. When he isn't in the office, he spends hours in his room, staring at the laptop or at the wall, going to bed early, sleeping late. Ma has even stopped debunking the psychologist, who has said he is in *acute clinical depression*, has offered to refer him to a psychiatrist who can prescribe medication. He has said he needs time to think. The thought of any more medicine flowing through his body makes him sick. But what has finally made Ma leave for Lucknow are Papa's test results. His blood pressure and cholesterol levels are through the roof, and Nani is now totally overcome by arthritis, incapable of helping.

At the airport, in classic Vasundhara Trivedi style, Ma picks up her suitcase and walks in, back straight, no hug, no parting words. Before going, she lists all the logistics she has already told him about twice now – food in the fridge, bills to pay, instructions for the maid, where she keeps the spare keys. At the security check, she turns and waves, even smiles, like she's going off on a short vacation. She looks relieved. Once upon a time, she wanted nothing more than to visit her son in Mumbai. Now she can't wait to get back to Lucknow. This has been as much her exile as his.

And he gives her nothing in return. Not even a smile. He holds his palm up to say goodbye, then turns around and leaves. In these years, he and Ma have had their softer moments, but on the whole, they are still playing *angry parent* and *indignant son*. It is a competition, and they are getting better at outmanoeuvring each other.

After Ma disappears from sight, he walks to a café and orders a coffee. He takes it outside and lights a cigarette. He feels as though he has waited for this day for years, as though Ma's presence had somehow stopped him from fully recovering, even though the only reason she was here was to care for him.

He feels as though his life is about to change. But he knows that even though change is good, not all change is for the better.

2000s

Haleem

'Wa-alaikum-as-salaam,' Ganjeri replied to the greeting.

The vendor smiled, showing his yellow teeth. 'So Syed-bhai, you finally came for iftar?' It was strange to hear Ganjeri called by his real name.

'Yes,' Ganjeri laughed. 'I've brought my friends too.' Shabby and Shruti nodded hello. The vendor pulled the sheekh out of the tandoor. The metal made a high-pitched shriek as it came out of the clay oven. He used a giant fork to slide out the glowing kebabs, bubbling in their own buttery sweat. He folded rumali rotis next to them and handed the three plates to his customers.

'You know the guy?' Shruti couldn't help asking these questions.

'From the mosque.' Ganjeri had the same answer.

'Really? A guy from here goes to your mosque in Parel?' She'd make a good investigator.

Shabby stepped in to the rescue. 'How tasty are these kebabs? And how mal-mal is this roti?'

It was Shabby's idea to come to Mohammad Ali Road. This was his third Ramzan in the city, and he'd heard about the food-stalls during the holy month. Now that Ganjeri was fasting, this is where they could break the fast. He watched

Ganjeri wolf down the rumali roti. One could tell the guy wasn't used to staying hungry all day.

When Ganjeri had decided to fast for Ramzan, he'd told Shabby first. He'd said the last time he'd fasted was as a teenager, still living at home. 'Of course,' Shabby had said. 'It's your choice, man!' That had been Shabby's stance from the start. Ganjeri's embrace of Islam had been both sudden and gradual, like how the morning light dabs out the night darkness, a slow process, the transition never too apparent to the observer's eye. One moment it is night, the next it's morning.

'What next?' Ganjeri asked. Now that he'd eaten, he was in a good mood. He put an arm around Shruti. She fitted right into his tall frame.

'I want to try the bheja-fry.' Shabby widened his eyes at the thought of goat-brain fry. There were stalls in Lucknow famous for it, but it would be unimaginable for their Hindu family to go there. Chicken was the occasional delicacy, that too for Papa and the boys. Ma and Nani never touched it.

The three walked down the narrow alley buzzing with people. There was more food than could be sampled in a month. Strings of lights hung from wires. There were a few firangs too, zoom lenses sticking out of large cameras. Shabby wondered if they should've asked Rebecca and Erik. But with Ganjeri's new avatar, they'd seen very little of the firangs lately. The last time they'd been invited to a party, Ganjeri declined. He said he'd quit drinking and smoking, so what was the point.

'When did you quit?' Shruti had asked in surprise. Ganjeri had poured them beer only the weekend before.

'Let's say just now?' Ganjeri's dimples poked into his cheeks.

'It's his choice, na?' Shabby had interjected. 'In any case, we should all quit smoking.' He blew smoke from his mouth.

Shruti had blown smoke into his face. 'You both quit and give me your packs. All this righteousness is too much for me.'

Now they crossed the Minara Masjid. The turret glittered, alternating bulbs made it look like the light was travelling upward, then downward. Men in kurta-pyjamas and pathani suits were coming out of the mosque. Ganjeri scanned their faces, as though looking for one he could recognize.

The first time Shabby and Shruti got wind of the turn of events was when a receipt for Zakat arrived. 'It's just charity,' Ganjeri had tried to explain. 'Something I donated at the local mosque . . .' He was like a rabbit caught in the headlights.

'So you're going to the mosque?' Shruti had sounded both surprised and offended. By then, Shruti and Ganjeri were officially a couple.

With time, there were other displays of religious fervour, awkwardly sticking out in a household that had never had place for religion before, Ganjeri's morning and evening namaaz in the living room where he got a good direction to Mecca, the exercise mat replaced by a zari-embroidered prayer mat, a group of friends *from the mosque* that he never introduced them to.

'Tell me all this isn't weird for you,' Shruti had poked Shabby.

'How can you stop someone from being religious? This is a free country.'

But no matter how much Shruti resisted Ganjeri's transformation, the friction pulled her closer towards him. Even now, in this conservative mohalla of Mohammad Ali Road, they walked with Ganjeri's hands resting on Shruti's tight jeans.

The night of dahi-haandi that the three of them had shared was a year ago. They hadn't talked about it. It was a flame lit by maddened passion, the buzz of that night, an exploration, a tender beautiful moment. Whatever it was, there was nothing to discuss afterwards, nothing to analyse. This wasn't *Friends*.

After that night, Shabby had learnt that Shruti and Ganjeri had been together a few times before. He'd felt a pang of jealousy, because he'd thought he loved Shruti, and because he felt betrayed for not knowing. But that night had freed him, his body, from the labels used to justify attraction. LOVE. RELATIONSHIP. MARRIAGE. He'd been with many others in the months since – new joiners at work, backpacking friends of the firangs, Dhwani in Lucknow. And Ganjeri and Shruti made a lovely couple, like charged particles bound by a magnetic force. Their union was as certain as science. It couldn't have been any other way.

Ganjeri stopped at a stall. 'Haleem!' he screamed like a child. 'It's been years since I've had this.' He stepped forward to peep into the stewing pot. 'It's cooked for hours, probably all night. Lentils, meat, herbs, masala . . .' He smacked his lips.

'Chuck the bheja-fry then,' Shabby said. 'Let's have haleem.'

Ganjeri ordered three plates after the customary *as-salaam-wa-aalai-kum*. The vendor called him closer and whispered in his ear. 'Dude,' Ganjeri said, turning to them. 'This has beef, though.' How did the vendor know who was what religion?

Shabby laughed. 'I've never tried beef but I'd love to!' He looked to Shruti for fellow-Hindu support, but she'd already counted herself in the cool-with-beef camp.

'Are you sure?' Ganjeri asked, his face serious. 'Once you eat it, there's no going back. You'll be going against your religion.'

'After every new thing you do, there's no going back. And

as far as I know, there is nothing in Hinduism about dietary restrictions.' Shabby tried to sound casual and philosophical at the same time.

'Okay then. Haleem it is!'

They raised their plates like shot-glasses, then spooned the first serving into their mouths. Ganjeri closed his eyes to savour the moment, his lean jaws pronounced as he chewed. Shruti made *mmmm* sounds as she bit into the meat. Shabby tasted only curry at first. Even then, the strong aroma filled his lungs like nothing he'd eaten before. When he finally bit into the meat, his mouth exploded, the juice escaping from under his teeth, dribbling down his gums, titillating his glands, into his throat, warming his stomach. They ate in silence, spooning, biting, chewing, savouring.

'Syed?' A group of boys appeared behind them. They wore pathani suits and stood close to each other, skullcaps on their heads. They looked at Shruti inquisitively.

'You boys!' Ganjeri managed a hiccuppy laughter. He took a conscious step away from Shruti.

'We're headed to the masjid. There's a reading . . .'

'I'll come,' Ganjeri said even before they could finish. Shabby and Shruti exchanged glances. Ganjeri looked back at them. 'Guys, I'll see you later, okay?'

Without explanation, he joined the group and started walking towards the mosque. He didn't turn back. They melted away into the crowd. The last thing Shabby saw was Ganjeri taking his skullcap out of his pocket and placing it on his head. His wiry curls stuck out artistically from the sides.

Yeda

Shabby looked at his watch. Mangesh was due in an hour. He got up and splashed cold water generously on his face. His eyes burnt. He had been lazily sketching, and then he'd dozed off. With Ganjeri often out, Shruti's visits had grown rarer. She said she needed more time to connect with her new flat-mates, but it seemed like an excuse. Today, Ganjeri had gone to paint classrooms in a school in Byculla. Shabby had volunteered to join, but Ganjeri had shuffled his feet awkwardly and said it was *a mosque thing*.

Shabby focused his thoughts on Mangesh. What were they going to do today? The tuition sessions had become less regular. He'd lost track of his plan. Mangesh turned up when he wished. He was sixteen now. He'd somehow passed eighth standard but was two years behind the rest of his classmates. When Shabby had lectured him on his marks, Mangesh had looked down at the floor in silence. Shabby couldn't tell if it was embarrassment or defiance.

Shakku-bai had told him what Mangesh hadn't. 'He's taken up a job at the toll-naka on the highway, saab. I begged him not to. I said – *You focus on studies, I'm paying for your school, na?* But the boy wouldn't listen. He said all his friends were working. It's shameful to sit at home.' She'd continued mopping the floor, her feet deftly moving from one dry spot to another. 'Whole day the boy stands in the sun, passing money and paper from car to counter, counter to car.'

Shabby had shaken his head. 'In foreign countries, this would've been done by machines. Only in this country do we hire people for such jobs.'

Shakku-bai grunted. 'Please talk to him, saab. I've asked the Guru-ji at the satsang too.'

But Shabby couldn't bring himself to speak to Mangesh about it. He feared what he'd hear in reply. Had Mangesh lost faith in his studies? Had all their efforts gone to waste? Had Ganjeri been right after all? Had they dreamt up a future for Mangesh that was out of his reach?

Shabby decided to pivot his lessons to more practical things. Today, they would set up an email for Mangesh. He checked availability for *mangesh.tawde1507*, and was pleased that it was available. Next he could teach him how to use the internet, type up a document, print it off. He made some tea while he waited.

But when Mangesh arrived, he laughed. 'Arre, bhaiyya, I've had an email account from when!' His palm went behind his ear to show how far back. 'I use it to chat with girls. Nowadays I've made a firang friend also. She's in Goa but will come to Mumbai to meet me.' There was something lascivious in his eyes that made Shabby squirm.

Mangesh sat on the sofa, legs spread out, posture straight. His skin now pulled over his cheekbones. His sprouting moustache was a bushy growth. The daily shave had roughened his angular jaws. His arms were solid, biceps bulging out of short sleeves.

'When my firang comes, we'll have a party here, okay? Along with your firangs.' Mangesh pointed to Rebecca's and Erik's flat, then leaned forward and said in a whisper, 'You know the things that happen in the next flat? Everyone in the mohalla knows. They do multi-sex – three people, four people. With these firangs, anything goes.' He jerked his knees in and out confidently, buoyed by the gossip.

Then he sprang up from the sofa, his voice high in exclamation. 'Aila! This is new!' He walked up to the wall and touched the framed photo of the Kaaba that Ganjeri had put up – the holy shrine in Mecca with thousands of pilgrims around it, little white dots surrounding the massive black cube. Mangesh patted his gelled hair. 'I still can't believe this one is Muslim. I mean . . . how . . . !' He widened his eyes and let out a gasp. 'Did you know, before he went all yeda?' He circled his forefinger next to his forehead. *Crazy*. That's what he thought of Ganjeri's transformation. He'd been obsessed for months, running his fingers over Ganjeri's new things – the skullcap, the Quran, the prayer mat. It helped that Ganjeri was hardly around.

Mangesh wasn't the only one. The neighbour Mrs Vashisht had complained to the building management. The secretary called Shabby to ask if his flatmate was really a *mullah*, and threatened to throw them out. Shabby told him that the Supreme Court had banned discrimination against tenants on the basis of anything, that he'd take the management to court. The secretary had fallen silent since, though Shabby was sure they hadn't let the matter go. He hadn't told Ganjeri any of this.

'I could tell from the start something was off about him,' Mangesh continued. 'Now I know. He didn't like me because I'm Hindu.'

'I'm Hindu too, so is Shruti. How come he likes us then?'

Mangesh laughed. 'You guys are not real Hindus. You're hip-hop Hindus . . .'

Shabby wanted to pummel logic into Mangesh's head. *A Hindu is a Hindu. What the fuck is a hip-hop Hindu? And if Ganjeri didn't like Mangesh, how come he liked Mangesh's mother? Their equation had nothing to do with religion, it was deeper than that, a human thing.*

232

But he didn't know how to say this out loud, so he changed the subject. 'How's satsang?'

Mangesh stifled a yawn. 'It's tiring, but meaningful. This weekend we'll line up on the highway to distribute water to pilgrims going to the Bholenath temple. They walk barefoot all night. Guru-ji said we should show more support for our religion. Hinduism is fading away.' He clicked his tongue in disappointment, then pointed to the picture of the Kaaba. 'These yedas are taking over our country.'

Shabby wanted to throw Mangesh out, but he knew he could do it only once. Mangesh wasn't going to come back. Maybe Mangesh knew this too, that's why he was pushing his boundaries, testing his newfound theories on Shabby.

'So what do you want to study today?'

'Bhaiyya, I was thinking – do you know this thing called Excel?' Mangesh's eyes lit up. 'You can do calculations on it. If you teach me, I can apply for an accountant's job.'

Shabby's heart warmed. He wasn't ready to give up on this boy. 'Yes,' he said and reached for his laptop. 'Let's do Excel!' The two of them brought their heads close together and looked at the screen.

After a while, Mangesh said, his voice soft, the edge in it having dissolved, 'Do you know, bhaiyya? The Guru-ji at the satsang has been speaking to my father, and you won't believe it, my father is trying to stop his drinking. He even comes to the satsang sometimes!'

Mangesh's teeth shone so brightly that they reminded Shabby of the first time he'd seen the boy and thought he'd make a good model for a toothpaste advert.

'You should come too, bhaiyya. I know you have a fancy job and lots of money. But trust me, the satsang is a spiritual awakening in the way your job never will be.'

2013

Lanyard

There are big ones and small ones, white and pink and yellowish, walking around the swamp, one leg gracefully raised, pecking endlessly in the sludgy water. He can never tell if the flamingos know that he's here. He adjusts his cap to save his face from burning. The sun is journeying to the centre of the sky. He has been here since seven. But his hands keep moving on the paper, long curved necks and cushiony wings.

If there really is something like spiritual awakening, maybe it looks like this.

He has come here, to the mangroves of Sewri, almost every morning since Ma left. At first, he bought tea, watched the flamingos do their thing. Then one day, he asked the chai-wallah for paper and pen. On a crumpled sepia newspaper, he drew a flamingo. The next few weeks, he carried a sketchbook. Back in the flat, he draws the birds out more elaborately, putting colours on them. More recently, he has bought canvases to paint on larger frames. In a way, this was Ma's parting gift to him, an act that needed no words.

He hasn't been to work in a week. He was busy sketching when he looked at the time and realized it was too late to go in. He hasn't answered his manager's calls, then his colleagues', then the HR manager's. There's an urgency with which he works here. There is a lot to do. The flamingos are birds of flight. They will fly away when their time here is done.

He puts down his sketchbook, calls the HR manager and tells her he won't come back to work, that he is resigning. She is surprised, reminds him of all the favours the company has done him, of the notice period he needs to serve according to his contract. He tells her he doesn't care about the money, they can keep it. He will come by to return the company's belongings.

In the afternoon, he drives down to the office. At the reception, he returns the laptop and pen-drive and ID card. 'And the lanyard?' the lady asks. When he looks confused, she elaborates, 'Sir, the company lanyard. We can't release you until we have that.' He grunts, but drives back to the flat, gets the lanyard, goes to the office and drops it off in a cardboard box. No one comes down to meet him, neither his manager nor his colleagues. He is an *ungrateful employee*, an *underperformer*, a *weird one*. It's like he never worked here, never existed.

He goes out to a nearby shop, and buys a greeting card. THANK YOU FOR EVERYTHING, it says. He gives it to the receptionist, who stares at it. 'Who is this for?' He tells her it's for the company, for taking care of him in his time of need. 'But is there any person I should give this to?' she presses on. He shakes his head, leaves.

And then suddenly, he is free, filled with a lightness so uplifting that it is almost unbearable. All his time now is for the flamingos.

He fears that once they fly away, he will be left alone again. But until then, he has found a purpose to go on, just like Ganjeri did.

2000s

Namaaz

M and Shabby are on the floor, sitting cross-legged, in the community centre in Maulviganj, they hear the azaan from the masjid, Ganjeri enters with a bucket, serves them haleem, HALEEM! Shabby's voice is like a child's, M snatches Shabby's plate away, embers in his eyes, no haleem for you, he says, you went to Lucknow for Munni-didi's wedding and forgot about me, don't you remember we met for the first time at a wedding, no, Shabby cries, I didn't forget about you, I never forget about you, Ganjeri is rolling weed by the window, he turns to Shabby and says, as-salaam-alaikum, you are le establishment—

It was very early. The market had just started to make lazy waking sounds. Shabby went into the living room. A cone of light from the streetlamp filtered in through the open window. He felt like snuggling up in a razai. Even in this city, the dawn had a coolness, fighting the heat off for its few moments of glory.

The prayer mat lay at an angle to the wall. Ganjeri came out of the bathroom, his hair, arms, feet dripping with water, track pants folded up to just above his ankles. He walked on tiptoes, wet footsteps making small puddles. He glanced at Shabby for a brief second. Shabby sat on the sofa. He knew he couldn't speak at prayer time.

Ganjeri put on his skullcap and used his palms to fit it

over his unruly curls. He pulled a checked chador over his shoulders, the tassels hanging in straight lines. He stood upright on the mat, ready for namaaz, the left half of his face illuminated by the light. He raised his hands to touch his earlobes, then brought them down to his navel, one palm over another, beginning to whisper his prayers. His flat stomach breathed in and out behind the T-shirt. He bowed, palms on knees, then stood straight up. *Allah-hu-akbar.* He prostrated himself in sajda, his forehead, nose, palms, knees and toes on the mat, then stood and prostrated again. *Allah-hu-akbar.* He sat up, folded one foot, balancing on the heel of the other, held his forefinger out, then folded it back in. *Ameen.*

Next to Ganjeri was the warm glow of a fire, another body bending, kneeling, prostrating. The eyes weren't violent, weren't pleading. They were at peace even within the flames, like the few moments of Mumbai dawn. Silent murmurs from both their prayers wafted across the room. Shabby wanted to catch them like butterflies, hold them to his ears like seashells. The flames rose and fell on the dark walls like waves. With every utterance of prayer, the flames grew, touched the ceiling, but they were muted, harmless, filling everything with warm divinity. The two bodies turned their heads right and looked into his eyes. *As-salamuaileikum-wa-rahmatullah.* Then turned left, away from him. *As-salamuaileikum-wa-rahmatullah.* Peace and blessings of God be unto you. Tasleem.

The azaan from the mosque woke Shabby. He opened his eyes and steadied his breathing. Ganjeri had finished his prayers. He was sitting on the mat, chin on his knee, looking at Shabby, his eyes earnest below the long lashes. The light now lit up the other side of his face. Shabby wanted to touch it. When had their lives become like this, two banks of a river, flowing side by side in full view of each other, but never to meet?

And now, Ganjeri was going away for three weeks to visit his parents, the first time Shabby would be alone in the flat for so long.

'What were you dreaming about?' Ganjeri asked.

'What time is your train?' Shabby answered with a question.

'Will you be all right while I'm gone?'

They sat there as dawn broke and dabbed the shadows away.

Dargah

The waves lashed against the bulwark.

'So how was the trip?' Shruti asked.

'Busy.'

'Is that why you couldn't phone? One call in three weeks . . .'

Shabby didn't know this. He and Shruti had met many times while Ganjeri was away, but she hadn't mentioned anything.

'I was moving my parents to a new house.'

Ganjeri had arrived from Surat that morning, Shruti in tow. She'd gone to the station to meet him. It was clear they'd had a fight, because Shruti was grumpy and went to Shabby's room and kambal-pitai-ed the hell out of the pigeons. Even Shakku-bai had looked on in surprise. Ganjeri said he wanted to take them out for a chat, suggesting the Haji Ali dargah. He bought them juice at the junction. Then they'd made their way to the middle of the sea, the dargah an underwhelming structure with its small dome. They walked in silence along the strip of paved pathway that connected the shrine to the mainland. Beggars, diseased, maimed, eyes gouged out, children with smaller children on their backs, held out bowls for money, tugged at sleeves, sang in high-pitched nasal voices. The three had looked away with practised indifference, out to the sea, like they'd come to admire its deep grey waters.

'My parents were living with relatives.' Ganjeri inhaled. 'We didn't have our own home.' It struck Shabby how little he knew about these two, his chosen family. Neither did they about him. They'd been so keen to wipe their pasts out.

'But I thought your family had a leather business?' From her surprise, Shabby could tell Shruti didn't know either.

'In the leather business . . . we work with animal hides, and that never goes down well with Hindus.' Ganjeri shrugged. 'They say we kill cows, eat the meat, sell the hide. Yeah, we do eat the meat and sell the hide. India wouldn't be among the world's top leather producers otherwise!'

Shabby struggled against the wind to light a cigarette.

'We lived in a middle-class neighbourhood. I went to a good school.' It was clear that Ganjeri was finding it difficult to talk about this. 'During the riots of 2002, our neighbours asked us to leave. Mobs were gathering. They said – *Leave now to avoid trouble, come back when the riots are over, we'll guard your property*. So my parents left, went to live with my chacha in a Muslim neighbourhood.' Ganjeri ran his fingers through his hair. 'And for six years now, they've been hopping around from one relative's place to another.' He let out a hollow laugh. 'Not all refugees live in camps.'

'And the house?'

'A mob broke in, looted, took everything. They gutted the shop, the factory. There was nothing to go back to.'

'So you've moved them to a new house now?'

Ganjeri nodded. 'It's a small flat, but at least it's our own. It was the one thing I wanted to do when I got a job. I've been saving up.'

Shabby placed a hand on Ganjeri's back. Shruti was still looking out at the sea, like she knew this wasn't the end of the story. Ganjeri asked for the cigarette from Shabby, and took a deep drag, breaking his resolve to quit smoking.

'But that's not the fucked-up part.' Ganjeri took another drag. 'I had *no idea* this was happening to them. I was away in Vellore, in college, and throughout the riots, they kept asking me to stay safe and not come home. They said – *Focus on your studies, make sure you become an engineer, make sure you get a job.*'

Shabby thought of his table-tennis games in the hostel common room when he was at engineering college, trying to look away from the TV playing images of the Gujarat riots. Maybe one such scene was of Ganjeri's home.

'Even that summer, they wouldn't let me come back. They said things weren't stable. I found an internship in Bangalore and my chacha came down to meet me. Didn't say a thing. Took me two years to know that my family had lost everything, that my parents were refugees . . .' Ganjeri turned to look at them. 'Isn't that fucked up? What our parents will do to keep us focused on our future?'

Shruti touched Ganjeri's cheek. Her hair was flying wildly. Ganjeri tucked the locks behind her ear.

'So is it done now, settling them down?'

'It's just started.' The old impish smile appeared on Ganjeri's beaten face. 'I quit my job just before leaving for Surat. And I'm leaving the flat.'

Shabby held the smoke in his chest until it made him cough. Shruti removed her hand and looked out at the sea again.

'I can't do this any more,' Ganjeri said. 'I can't behave like nothing's the matter, that I should just lead this happy artificial life as if all problems are solved.'

'So what will you do?' Shabby asked.

'I don't know. For starters, I'm going to work at the mosque, find ways to help. Inshallah I'll see a path ahead at some point.'

'But . . .' Shabby was looking for words. 'Isn't this life giving you the chance to do what you want, buy your parents a flat . . .'

Ganjeri shook his head. 'You know, the problem with this country is that we believe money will solve everything. It doesn't. My family had money, but what good was it?' He smiled. 'Maybe you won't get it . . .' He opened and closed his mouth a few times, then said, 'You both are my closest pals, but you're too far removed from this. You won't understand what it's like to be a minority . . .'

Shruti shot back. 'If you want to change the world, go change it. Do whatever the fuck you want. But don't patronize me.' She grabbed the pack from Shabby and put a cigarette in her mouth, then expertly lit it in spite of the wind. A few men instantly turned to look. She blew smoke in their faces. 'Never seen a girl smoke, haan?' The men lowered their eyes.

'And where will you live?' Shabby asked.

'With someone I know from the mosque. He has a small room in the chawl. I'll be out a lot, working with NGOs, site visits and all that. Plus I can't pay rent.' Ganjeri burst out laughing. 'You know how we always said our flat was so run-down, we'd find a better one when our salaries went up? Now that flat is a luxury.'

Shabby smiled. 'Well, our salaries went up but we never moved out, we liked the flat so much.' His heart was beating fast, but his mind was working faster. His life was imploding like the dome of a masjid. He searched for a last chance to save it. 'I'll pay your rent. Money isn't a problem.' He was aware of how he sounded, superior, desperate. 'Only until you figure things out . . .' he added.

Ganjeri squeezed Shabby's shoulder. 'You've done enough, my friend. I know you've been fighting the building secretary and that Vashisht bitch. They'll probably throw me out in a few weeks anyway. It's better I get out of your hair before then.'

Shabby wanted to punch Ganjeri, push him into the water. He wanted to fall at his feet and plead. *Stay, please, we'll sort everything out. Let's not take apart what we've built.* But what *had* they built? Had they made promises? Had he really thought this would last forever? He felt deep shame at his naivety.

Ganjeri said, 'You know, I went back to see our old house in Surat. It doesn't exist any more. There's a block of flats there now. Some developer must've swooped in and bought the land. No one protested. Some of our ex-neighbours even bought flats in the building. My father says he doesn't want to file a case. He's sure we'll lose. There are Muslims all over Gujarat still fighting for property they've lost in the riots. But that's what I'm going to do first. Get us back our land.'

'So if all this was part of your grand plan from the start, what was all that you did with us – all the fun, games, drinking, dancing, love, sex?' The men around looked up again at the mention of *sex*, especially in a female voice. Shruti let them stare.

'You make me sound like a scheming asshole. None of it was fake. It just took me some time to understand my purpose. I thought I'd buy a house for my parents and that'd be the end of it. But now I want our land back. I want justice. I want the next generation of Muslims to not have to depend on Hindu friends to rent a decent place. Once you're on this journey, there's no stopping. It's fulfilling and destructive at the same time. Maybe that's why most people just choose to live like dumbos – go to work, push files, come home, cook dinner, watch TV. It's easier that way.'

Ganjeri had all the answers, like an ascetic. The sun glowed like embers in his eyes.

'And what about us . . . you and me?' Shruti asked, still looking at the sea.

Shabby got off the ledge. He couldn't bear to be there any longer, couldn't bear to look at Shruti, to hear what Ganjeri would say in reply to her question. The bile rising in his stomach made him want to throw up. This was it, there was a finality to what was happening, Ganjeri moving out, physically separating himself from them, as though the three years they'd had together, discovering this city, discovering life, none of that had meant anything to him at all.

Ganjeri wasn't just going to another city for a new job or further studies, or getting married and moving on. Ganjeri's entire belief system had transformed; he had a new purpose, a new way of living, a new worldview. And in his new world, there was no place for Shabby and Shruti.

Shabby walked down the narrow pathway in quick steps. The waves were sloshing water over it. High tide was here. The beggars had left. In an hour, the pathway would be fully covered by the black water, cutting the dargah off from the mainland. Anyone who stayed behind would be marooned for the night.

2013

Skit

The sex isn't rubbish. It is just too rushed to be anything, good or bad, like drinking tea right after dipping in the tea-bag. But it has become a routine. Anisha comes up to the flat with him after their art class at the NGO every Saturday. They still don't talk a whole lot, but at least he knows her name now. He isn't sure how it started. There was no flirtation, no hints, no making eyes. They keep most of their clothes on, baring only as much as they need to. In any case, he isn't going to expose his scarred body to her. He's still ugly. He doesn't know why she comes up with him, what her reasons are, whether she's in pain or wallowing in self-hate like him or just wants a hit of pleasure to quench her lust from time to time. But he doesn't care, doesn't ask. It seems to work for both of them that way.

They don't even use the bed. She stands with her back against the wall, he presses into her, his face breathing into her ear, their lips far from each other's. He clutches at her curly hair as he thrusts, firmly holds her waist. Her breasts are small but taut. He can tell from the bulges above her bra. She digs her nails into his back, sometimes right on the burn-mark. He doesn't protest. The pain drives him to finish faster. When he climaxes, the release feels like millions of little metal bits in the aftermath of an explosion. That is dope, pure pleasure. In that moment, he travels back to the night of the troika, more than six years ago now, soft on hard, hard on soft.

When they finish, wash and wipe, they sit on the narrow balcony smoking a cigarette she has rolled. Ma never left the balcony door open. She said it smelt of shit from the adjacent field and let mosquitoes in. But Anisha says she likes to smoke in *fresh air*. They sit in silence, passing the cigarette. Then she leaves, ending their little skit.

But today she peeps into the bedroom. He has never taken her in there. She enters without asking and looks at the mess. Plastic boxes of half-eaten takeaway food, unlaundered clothes on the floor, paper and open sketchbooks and palettes, blotches of paint on the bedsheet. She walks through it all straight to the canvases against the wall. Ma wrapped up in clear plastic the ones Shakku-bai had brought. The new ones he has made of the flamingos are unwrapped, already dusty.

She stands and looks at them, her fingers spread out over the small of her back, her bum arched beautifully outward. She twirls her hair with the fingers of her other hand. Her skin is glowing in the diffused afternoon light, carrying the aroma of sex. He is standing behind her, his back against the cupboard, looking at her looking at the paintings.

She doesn't say if she likes them or not. Instead she says, 'You should take care of them?' She turns around to smile at him. 'Like . . . wrap them up, keep them inside the cupboard . . . or . . . I don't know . . . do like . . . whatever people do to preserve paintings?'

He feels conscious of his body now that she is looking at him outside of sex. He starts buttoning up his shirt. 'I can make more if these get spoilt,' he says casually. Anisha is nothing like Shruti, but this female energy in his bedroom after so many years suddenly makes him miss Shruti, makes him want to curl his fingers around hers, lie down with his head on her lap, like he used to.

But Anisha has already turned back to the paintings. 'You never know, these could . . . like . . . be worth something someday . . . or whatever?'

2000s

Superstars

'One by one they've all left.' Rebecca sat at one end of the worn-out sofa, her blonde hair tied loosely, wearing no make-up. 'We never thought we'd live here forever.' She looked at Erik, who was turning a bottle of Kingfisher beer in both palms. 'But I hadn't thought it'd be so soon.'

Erik shook his head. 'Actually I don't know what I'd thought. I just needed to get out of my petty American life and do something *great*.' He used air quotes. He had a shock of white hair in the middle of his head. His illustrious mane had thinned. There were clear lines on his face. Shabby wondered if he even looked shorter.

'Living in a city is like being in a relationship,' Rebecca said. 'When you're in love, everything's fun. When it's over, everything's unbearable.'

The room seemed smaller. There were boxes along the walls, clothes and books peeking out. Shabby and Shruti had come to say bye. One of the firangs was going to throw a farewell party, but they'd declined the invitation. Shabby felt no need to impress any more. He'd rather say goodbyes like this, quietly, in private.

'Is everything all right with Syed?' Rebecca asked, sipping her lemonade, the drink sweating itself into a tepid dilution in the July heat.

Shabby glanced at Shruti, not sure how much she wanted to share.

'He needed to be back with his family in Gujarat.' Shruti was drinking rum and Coke. She'd asked Erik for a stiff drink, and after sipping it, had gone and poured some more rum. 'He'll be back in Mumbai once he's settled some affairs.'

She was lying. Ganjeri wasn't coming back. These last few weeks, Ganjeri had hardly been around. He'd thrown away or donated most of his things. Shabby was at work in the daytime; in the evenings, Ganjeri left for the mosque. Then one day, he was gone, giving Shabby a perfunctory hug before boarding the taxi with two suitcases. Shabby had felt empty, almost relieved that what he'd been dreading had finally happened. He'd come back upstairs to find Shakku-bai sobbing. 'He was such a good boy. He never spoke to me in a raised voice, he gave me extra money on the side. When I got to know his religion, I asked – *Will you still eat what I cook?* He laughed and asked me in return – *Now that you know my religion, will you still cook for me?*'

Now Rebecca continued probing. 'Is it true that the building management asked him to leave?' Word did spread fast.

Erik didn't wait for a reply. 'It's strange that they'd let us stay and have a problem with him. I mean – we've had wild parties, guests, lots of noise . . .'

'You're white. It's different.' Shruti's words cut through the room like static. 'We Indians are held to different standards of morality.'

'And we're held to no standards at all. We're just decadent foreigners with no morality.' Erik and Shruti were in quite the mood today, gloves off.

'What are you looking forward to when you get back?' Shabby changed the subject. He wasn't interested in another confrontation. This was Shruti's new pastime. She'd quarrelled with Ganjeri, screamed at Shabby, been rude to Shakku-bai. This was a different girl to the one he'd met, defiant, resentful, hard-headed. Sometimes he made up lies so he could avoid meeting her.

'Oh, I don't know . . . the regular stuff really.' Erik looked wistfully into nothingness. 'My dad's mashed potatoes. They're the best! And sitting on the humongous couch and watching a baseball game with my brother.'

'And of course the elections.' Rebecca's eyes lit up. 'The actual possibility of having our first ever black president. Can you believe it?' Everyone nodded. 'I want to be there campaigning for him, volunteering in the polling booths, raising funds. Just voting at the embassy here isn't good enough for me.'

Shabby had been following Obama's 'Yes We Can' campaign for America's 2008 presidential election, though he didn't really believe the guy could pull it off.

'What happened to the NGO you guys started?' Shruti asked.

'We had to close it,' Rebecca said. 'It was tough, like giving up a baby. But a lot of resistance had started to build of late.'

'From the people in the slums?'

'Not the *community* per se,' Rebecca corrected Shruti. 'But there are these leaders who have a lot of say there. Like, there's this satsang . . . it's their everything. Cultural, religious, children's hobby, adult education, spiritual training. The whole community turns up there. There's something sticky and familial about it that we couldn't recreate.'

'She's being too nice.' Erik leaned forward. 'Basically they worship the Guru-ji who runs it. His word is god's word. We heard he told people that we're there to convert them to Christianity. Hell, I haven't been to church since I was a child!' Erik narrowed his eyes. 'You know these kind of sat-sang centres are run with political funding, right? We'd never be able to raise that kind of money as an NGO.'

'It's like they're building an army of fanatics . . .' Rebecca's voice trailed off.

Shruti went for a second rum and Coke.

'You remember Sarah from the carnival party?' Rebecca asked. 'She's become a . . . umm . . . sadhvi? She wears saffron and vermilion and is apprenticed to a godman at an ashram in Haridwar. Every evening, she sits next to him and sings prayers in Sanskrit.' Her eyes danced with amusement. 'Apparently the number of devotees at the ashram has doubled because of the firang sadhvi.'

Shabby laughed, reminded of the Prem Joshua CD he'd bought on his first evening in the city, the white man chanting mantras. He wondered where the CD was now.

'That's the kind of whacko I'm scared I'll become if I continue living here,' Erik said. 'White people in India can't lead normal lives. They can only be superstars or crazies. There's something about how we feel about ourselves, and how everyone else makes us feel – it messes with our heads.'

'Well, I've come to the conclusion that India should be left to Indians. It took the British two hundred years to realize that. It took us only two,' Rebecca smiled. 'If there's a way out of this madness, only you guys can fix it.'

'Let's see how *that* goes!' Shruti said with her back turned to them, still mixing her drink.

Faltu

'This is like eating street food in a discotheque!' Shruti shouted over the din, flashing her smile. It reminded Shabby of old times. 'This paav-bhaaji is so spicy!'

Shabby looked around the vast space with its melange of tiny heads, trying to decide if the multitudes made the place look full, or the space made the crowds seem larger. It was a mall, but might as well have been an airport. Never-ending corridors, zigzagging escalators, neon flashlights, red banners announcing SALE. They were in the pit of the mall, the food court. Shruti dipped the paav in the oily bhaji and took a bite. A bit of the butter dribbled down her chin. She dabbed it away with a napkin. 'What do you think was here before they built this . . . monstrosity?' she asked between bites.

'A slum? What do you think happened to everyone who lived here?'

'Oh, they've been given apartments. You know there are secret underground chambers below the mall, right?' Shruti joked. She was in a jolly mood. They'd come out after ages. It was months since Ganjeri had left, and Shabby and Shruti had made many plans only to cancel last-minute. It was strange without Ganjeri. It wasn't like the three had always hung out together. But this was different, knowing he wasn't here any more.

Shabby said, 'Most people aren't even shopping. They're just passing time.'

'It's sad! That people should give up open spaces and the seaside to hang out in this temperature-controlled consumerist place, including us.' The loud beats on the speakers seemed to have everyone in a trance. 'Can someone tell me why they're playing this music, like they expect us to start dancing?'

'There'll be many more.' Shabby had read in the papers that large swathes of land were being auctioned off to build shopping malls. This was the future of the city – glass buildings, endless shops, pretend shoppers. This one was special – a *luxury mall*, it was called, with only high-end brands, Gucci, Prada, Tommy Hilfiger that everyone pronounced *Hill-finger*.

Shruti arched her eyebrows and pointed her chin. 'Look! That's Mangesh, no?'

It was indeed. Mangesh was at the entrance, a little girl in a pink dress holding his hand, her hair braided in matching pink ribbons. 'That must be his cousin,' Shabby said. 'Shakkubai told me her sister's visiting from Kolhapur.' Shabby and Mangesh were having a good run these past few weeks. He'd come regularly for lessons, inveigled by the promise of Excel getting him an accounting job.

'Looks like he's having an argument with the security guy,' Shruti said. They tried to peer through the two layers of glass. It definitely seemed like some trouble was brewing.

Shabby got up and walked out of the food court. Shruti followed, picking up her bag and scarf. The paav-bhaaji remained unfinished. Shruti opened her mouth to tell the cleaner they'd just be back, but he cleared out the plates before they'd even left the table, throwing the food in the bin in one swift action. More people were waiting for tables.

Shabby got to the entrance in quick steps. 'No-no,' the guard was saying, waving his hand at Mangesh. 'Don't waste

253

my time . . .' Beside them, men stood in a queue, shuffling their feet, looking over the shoulder of the ones in front. When it was their turn, they passed through the metal detector and spread their arms. Another guard frisked them from shoulder to toe, patting the buttocks with ceremony. The queue for women was to the right, with a little booth for the ladies to be frisked in private by a female guard.

'What's happening here?' Shabby asked, his voice heavy with authority.

'Arre, sir,' the guard said. 'Don't bother yourself.' He was turning back to face Mangesh when Shabby asked again. The guard rolled his eyes, but knew he couldn't tell off someone like Shabby. 'Sir, these people can't enter the mall, so I'm respectfully asking them to leave. But this boy is so shaana, he's arguing with me.'

These people. 'Who said they can't enter?'

'Sir, the management has told us . . .' The guard smirked.

'How can they decide who can enter the mall? This is a public place.'

The guard scratched his head. The other one answered while patting someone down. 'It's not a public place, sir. If he wants public place, he should go to Juhu beach. This is private. The developer has built this for people to shop.'

'Look at him, sir,' the first guard said, encouraged by his colleague's support. 'Do you think he can shop here? These people turn up just for the AC. They won't buy a thing. They just want to go back and tell their friends they entered a luxury mall.'

'Bhaiyya!' Mangesh's voice was soft. Shabby had got so embroiled that he'd forgotten about Mangesh, like he was arguing for a stranger. 'Leave it. No point taking tension.'

This irked Shabby even more. 'What does that even mean? What's happening here is wrong.'

There was a crowd gathering. Shabby wanted to point to their empty hands and show the guard how most had bought nothing, including himself. But the guard was saying, 'You enjoy na, sir. Why are you spoiling your day for these faltu people?'

Faltu people. Worthless. Shabby felt an urge to slap the guard hard. As if she intuited it, Shruti squeezed his shoulder. On seeing her, Mangesh tried to smile. 'Didi, ask bhaiyya not to create a scene, na? It's fine. We'll go somewhere else.' He turned around and started walking away. The glass doors slid open. The little girl followed obediently, her fingers curled in his.

Shabby ran to close the distance between himself and Mangesh. The rush of hot air hit him like a furnace the moment he stepped out of the building. He gripped Mangesh's arm firmly. 'Come back with me.' It came out more as an order than a request. 'Let's call the manager and get this sorted.'

'Jaane do, bhaiyya.' *Let it go.* Shabby's hair bristled. What was with this country? Why was everyone always letting things go? *Jaane do. Jaane do.* Why wasn't anything worth standing up for?

Shabby held on to Mangesh's arm but lowered his voice. 'Okay, fine, we won't go to the manager. But you can come in as if you were with me, like we'd come together. Then they can't say a thing.'

Mangesh freed himself from Shabby's grip with a jolt. 'That's the thing – I am *not* with you. If I go in with you, then it's like I'm your servant. But I came here by myself. With *her.*' The little girl's kajal-lined eyes were brimming with tears.

Shabby's breath was hot when he spoke. 'You know what? This is why you people won't get anywhere. Because you don't fight for your rights. You just accept all the crap they throw at you.' He stepped back. 'Fine! Go!'

Mangesh stood staring at Shabby, his eyes narrowed, nostrils flared. 'What to do, bhaiyya? We're faltu people, na? No backbone. No confidence. That's why you'll only come here with your hip-hop friends.' Mangesh stayed there for an extra second, as if he had something more to say, then he turned and left, calling out to the little girl, 'Ae chalaa re!' She ran to keep up with him.

Shabby looked at the mall entrance. Everything had gone back to normal. The two guards chatted as they patted the men up and down. The crowd had dispersed, walking around like zombies again, staring at shop displays they couldn't afford.

A click of a lighter, a whiff of cigarette smoke. Shruti stood behind him. Shabby rested his forehead on her shoulder, exhausted from the exchange. 'I fucked up.'

'*This whole place* is fucked up. This city. This country . . .' She blew smoke in Shabby's face. 'Mangesh. The guard. Syed. You. Me. SO. FUCKED. UP!'

Satsang

Mangesh and Shabby are walking beside a row of palm trees, leaves sway in the rough wind, they will get oil later and Ajji can give them massages, Mangesh is happy, Shabby stops and touches his arm, look Mangesh, there's a lighthouse, on the lighthouse there's M, walking in circles, the flames lighting up the sea, filtering out in a perfect cone, M says, do you know what's really fucked up, you can never reach me, even if you keep walking forever, forever—

The darkness closed in on Shabby. The lanes seemed narrower, the walls black. It was only just past seven, but all doors were shut. He moved like a sleepwalker, following the sound of the drums and cymbals and khanjanis, using his hands to navigate the maze, his palms passing over the rough cement and open bricks. Whenever he felt he was moving away from the sound, he turned and made his way back. This is what it must feel like to be blind. *Visually impaired*, Rebecca would've corrected him. This made him smile.

He finally reached the source of the sound, walking faster as he spotted the lights. He stopped at the community centre. The entire slum seemed to have congregated there. The women sat on one side, the men on the other. Children fidgeted on laps. People clapped and sang to the beats. It was a bhajan Shabby knew. *Govinda bolo hari gopal bolo.* Did Nani sing it in her puja-room? It made him think of Lucknow, Ma,

Papa, Nani, Chintoo, that life he'd wanted to escape so badly. For *this* life. A mirage.

The screech of the mic snapped him out of his thoughts. He'd come here to find Mangesh, to talk to him, to apologize. It had been two weeks since that evening at the mall, and Mangesh hadn't turned up for classes. Shabby didn't want to ask Shakku-bai because then he'd have to tell her everything, including how he'd behaved, things he'd said. So today, he'd come to the satsang. He'd find Mangesh here, tap on his shoulder, ask him to step out. They'd speak in hushed tones and everything would be fine.

Shabby's eyes darted this way and that. When he spotted Mangesh, a stab went through his heart, because Mangesh was already looking at him, his eyes piercing, his skin glistening in the light. He sat hunched over, accentuating his chest muscles, nipples pushing against his tight T-shirt. The moustache was now a uniform straight line over his lips. He was already seventeen. When had that happened?

Shabby tried to smile and wave. He felt awkward here. Out of place. Everyone else was a resident of the slum. They seemed so comfortable sitting on the ground, knees over one another's, hands folded, faces devout. Mangesh looked away, eyes focused on the Guru-ji who was starting his sermon.

'My dearest satsangis,' the Guru-ji said in Hindi. 'As you know, I always begin with a reminder of why we're here. What does *satsang* actually mean? *Sat* stands for *virtuous*. *Sang* stands for *company*. So what does that make us? *Virtuous company*, to each other, to ourselves, to the god we worship.' Practised pause, like Suresh-mausa would've done. 'Turn and look at the person next to you, in front of you, behind you.' The swish of moving heads, shuffling bodies. A few men looked at Shabby, the surprise in their eyes unmistakable. 'Look into each other's eyes. *Seek* the truth. *Demand* the truth.'

Pause. 'But also *offer* the truth. *Spread* the truth. Truth is the only thing that god asks us to share. Everything else, the little that he has given us, we can keep. Our lives may not be comfortable, but we will always have truth on our side.'

Shabby stared intently at Mangesh, trying to find a way to attract his attention. He noticed Mangesh's father next to him, palms joined, eyes closed, rocking back and forth in devotion. Mangesh's elbow rested comfortably on his father's knee.

'And when we've shared the truth with our eyes, we become brothers and sisters. We are bound by an unspoken bond. When you look at each other, even if it's in the middle of the day, whether you're rushing to work, or queuing for water, you will know who your brother is.' Guru-ji's voice deepened. 'And using the same reasoning, you will know who is *not* your brother. When you look into the eyes of an outsider, you will spot the lies, the deceit, conceit, lust, greed, all those sins that our god forbids us to commit. The outsiders have been sent to tempt us.'

The tube-light flickered, but no one noticed. Guru-ji continued. 'Centuries ago, the outsiders came to loot us. They destroyed our temples, walked away with riches and jewellery that belonged to our gods, left our people poor and hungry. They came from Persia and Afghanistan. But what did we do? We prayed, then rebuilt from scratch.' Guru-ji muttered a chant. *Deva . . .* 'And then a few years later, they came again, to colonize, to impose their religion on our land. What did we do? We stuck together, bound by our truth, our god. We said to them – *You cannot colonize our minds, our souls.*'

Mangesh's father put an arm around his son's shoulder, drawing him closer. Mangesh obliged, looking happy.

'That is what we should do now too. Dangerous times are upon us. Once again, our faith is under threat, our values are under attack. Women are being brainwashed – they're asked to behave like men, wear clothes like men, work in jobs like men. Men are being asked to intoxicate themselves. Children are being waylaid at a young age by things like video games and chicken chowmein.' Guru-ji drew in a breath. 'But look at all of you here, how regularly you turn up every day. Is that because of me?' Again a question he didn't wait to be answered. 'Na! You come here for each other, drawn by the love we feel for our own. Hold on to that love, my satsangis!' He clasped his palms in a show of solidarity. 'Together, we will get through this darkness.'

Then Guru-ji turned to look at Shabby, eyes calm, like he'd always known Shabby was there, then back to his audience and switched to Marathi. Shabby didn't understand the language well. He could only catch snippets, the words that were common with Hindi. There were mentions of Maratha pride, the greatness of this vast land to the west of the sub-continent. Guru-ji spoke eloquently of their history, their contributions to society even to this day. Babasaheb Ambedkar, the author of India's constitution. Sachin Tendulkar, the world's greatest cricketer. Lata Mangeshkar, the country's greatest singer. Who could tell, maybe one day in the near future, someone from this satsang could be on that list?

Shabby started walking back. Mangesh hadn't looked at him after that first time. This was Mangesh's world, this slum, this satsang, the embrace of his newly sober father. No one here was going to shoo him away. And there was no place for Shabby here.

He felt his way through the dark lanes. Something small but solid scampered over his foot. He told himself it wasn't a rat.

2013

Robot

He is on the Sea Link again. It has become a routine. Weekend mornings, weekday late nights. He drives at full speed, foot on the gas, teasing the brakes, still wondering if he has the courage to crash through the railing and drop into the sea. It is an addiction, the only time he feels high, lives in the present, sparing no thought for the past or the future.

At the end of the Sea Link is the toll-naka. He slows down as it approaches. Here the road broadens, sixteen lanes each ending in a different ticket counter. Today he squints to find the one with the shortest queue, but his eyes have caught something. Before his mind can register, his body knows. The unmistakable dark papery skin, the white teeth prominent even from this distance. Mangesh is collecting money from car windows, passing it to the counter, then passing the receipt back to the car, his body moving in semicircles, like a programmed robot. He hasn't seen Mangesh in five years. Mangesh's shoulders are rounder. A belly shows through the T-shirt, not the droopy type but a tight muscular one, like it used to be flat once and hasn't given up hope.

A car honks, snaps him back. He is heading straight towards Mangesh's lane. He swerves without thinking, cuts through the next lane, the next and the next. Cars screech to a halt. Everyone turns to look at this driver gone awry. He stops four lanes down, keeps his head turned the other way, focusing on the hotel on the hill to his left. At the counter, he pulls with trembling hands whatever money is in his wallet, throws it out of the window, then drives away. The guy shouts back, asking him to take the change and receipt, but he is driving fast now, away from Mangesh.

It is nearly Borivali when he stops by the side of the highway. His breathing is grated, his fingers on the wheel clammy. The scar on his back itches as his skin breaks into pins and needles. He waits. He can't drive in this condition. He thought he was getting his life back on track, making active choices, keeping himself physically mobile, sexually active, creatively prolific.

But it is all a joke. Memories are potent, living things, breathing inside human bodies. One slight brush with the past and his fragile present has come crashing. Even though Mangesh is only twenty-three now, pushes paper at a toll-naka under the burning sun all day, goes back to live in a slum with his parents in a four-by-six-foot soot-coated room, wears grimy rubber chappals on his cracked feet, has no job security and earns a pittance. Even though he, a thirty-year-old man, is sitting in an air-conditioned car, with a wallet full of cash, with clipped fingernails and a neat haircut. None of that matters today. Privilege and power are not the same thing.

A double-tap on the window. 'Barobar, saab?' A policeman's face has emerged, speaking in Marathi. 'All okay? You've been parked here for a while.'

He tries to smile, to get his shivers under control. 'Ho, mee jaato,' he replies in broken Marathi. *Yes, I'll be on my way.*

2000s

Sindoor

The men looked straight at Shabby, the question in Marathi hanging like a cloud. He gulped down his spit, trying to think of an answer, say anything. It wasn't a difficult question. But it wasn't just a question, it was a test.

'Aspirin,' he repeated.

The chemist glanced knowingly at the other customer. Both men smiled. 'Kya, saab,' the chemist said as he slipped the aspirin into a paper sleeve. 'So many years in this city and you still don't speak Marathi?'

Shabby wanted to ask how it had suddenly come to matter, since he'd been buying medicines from this place for four years. They'd always spoken in Hindi. But he paid the money, grabbed the tablets and walked back to the flat. On the landing, Mrs Vashisht's shadow appeared. Shabby felt her eyes on him, so he turned and smiled. She quickly shut her door. Once upon a time, the firangs were the enemy, then Ganjeri was the enemy; now Shabby was too.

In the flat, the TV played on mute. He never switched it off nowadays, left the news on, wanting to stay updated. Sometimes he stared, the breaking news scrolling past the bottom of the screen, in bubbles on the right and left, until his stomach protested and he realized he needed to eat something. Today he served himself a bit of whatever Shakku-bai had made. He couldn't take the aspirin on an empty stomach. There was an arc of pain around his cranium, travelling from his temples down over his ears to form a knot at the back. He could barely keep his eyes open. He sat down on the sofa with the food and unmuted the TV.

There were shots of a train station. Crowded platforms, migrants pressed against each other like ants in a jar. There was a train just outside, stopped at a red signal, people sitting on the roof, hanging from doors, heads out of windows. Given the crowds on the platform, the station manager was probably deciding whether to let the train stop or pass, there was no capacity to take on any more passengers. The journalist, standing on an overbridge, reported how migrant workers continued to flee to their villages in the north of India for the fifth consecutive day. More reports of violence had come in from across the city. Today a cinema that screened North Indian movies had been ransacked, the tapes torn up. As she spoke, the train sounded its horn and began moving into the station. The crowds on the platform let out a roar, inched closer to the edge, then ran frantically, jumping on the tracks. Some climbed on the overbridge, pushing the journalist out of their way. The frame cut back to the studio, where the presenter was waiting with a panel to discuss these developments.

The riots had sprung out of nowhere. Did all riots start like this? One night people went to sleep in peace, the next morning they woke up to mosques demolished, commuters beaten, shops gutted? No, there were always signs. It was people who chose to look away, telling themselves that such things happened only to others, not to them.

For years now, local parties in Mumbai had campaigned for Marathi people to get preferential treatment – land, housing, jobs. They'd found other enemies before – Gujaratis,

South Indians, Muslims. This time they'd chosen people from the north. *Leeches, vermin, living off the locals' entitlement.* There'd been articles by politicians, random attacks, the Guru-ji at the satsang had switched to Marathi to talk about local pride, the taxi driver on Shabby's first evening in the city had lamented the way he was treated as an outsider – the seeds had been sown for a long time. It was only Shabby who'd thought this wouldn't affect him.

'But Mumbai is not for any one group of people,' a corporate-looking panellist argued on TV. 'This is a cosmo-politan city, the financial capital. I don't need anyone's permission to work in my own country.'

A local politician cut in. 'Madam, if people walked into your home and insisted on living there, what would you do?'

The first panellist shook her head vehemently, struggling to come up with a counter-argument. Finally she said, 'I wouldn't beat them up, for sure. I'd say – *Sit down, let's have a chat.*' She spoke in English, slipping into broken Hindi at times.

The opponent laughed. 'Madam, you are so funny. And what happens if they don't leave? Instead, they call their rela-tives and friends also to come live at your place? Will you not kick them out? You have the right to decide who lives in your home.'

Shabby muted the TV. Visuals of other attacks played on the sidelines of the debate. Broken taxis, defaced buildings, damaged media vans. A curfew had been declared in some parts of the city. There was talk of the court imposing a gag order on the local leader. His supporters swore to amp up the violence if that happened.

Shabby dropped the aspirin in a glass of water and watched the fizz form, frothing at the surface. He drank it down in one gulp. It made him sick. He hadn't slept in days and it was starting to take a toll. He stayed up nights, all the lights switched on. He was scared of what he'd dream if he fell asleep. He'd called Ganjeri a few times, intending to ask if he could come back to the flat, but Ganjeri was always travelling for charity work or court appearances in Surat. Shruti came less often now that there were curfews. For the first time in his life, Shabby was truly alone within four walls.

The phone buzzed. *Ma calling* . . . 'Where are you?' This was always her first question nowadays.

'At home, obviously.'

She exhaled in relief. 'Had your dinner? How was today?'

Shabby had no intention of telling her what had happened today. 'It was fine. No trouble on the way.'

A shuffle, then Papa's voice. 'Are you still taking the train, beta?' Shabby grunted yes. Previously he'd take a taxi to work every now and then, but now he was taking only the train. It was one of the hacks his North Indian colleagues had shared in a group email. *There's strength in numbers.*

'And that local maid of yours? Is it safe to let her in?' Papa's voice was shrill with paranoia.

The thought of Shakku-bai turning on him made Shabby laugh. 'I've lived here so long. Everyone knows me. They wouldn't wait for her if they wanted to target me.'

'No-no, nothing of the sort will happen.' Papa tried to sound reassuring. 'The attacks are against the taxi driver, shopkeeper sort. Not people like us.'

People like us. Shabby hadn't told Papa how his colleague from Allahabad was stopped on the road because he was driving a car with a North Indian licence plate. They'd pelted stones and disfigured the car, then roughed the man up before letting him go.

More shuffling, then Nani's voice. 'My dear, what-what things are happening?' Nani had become part of the daily calls. The violence had given the family a reason to gather, watch the news, give him tips on how to stay safe. 'Listen to me, don't speak our pure Hindi when you're on the street. I hear they speak some strange Hindi? Try to sound like them . . .'

Shabby said goodnight and hung up. The headache was starting to subside. His eyelids felt heavy. He fought the temptation to doze off. Staying awake would help him fight off the memories of that afternoon. An email had directed employees to leave early and continue working from home. Peak hours were when the goons were on the prowl. The city was unnaturally calm, and Shabby had decided to walk for a while. He'd run into a procession of devotees with an idol hoisted high on a palki. The palanquin rocked as the devotees raised their hands in chant. They were North Indians, the women wearing orange sindoor, the powder starting at the bridge of their noses and going all the way through the parting in their hair to the crown of their heads. He'd tried to overtake them, but he was only halfway through the crowd when some men with lathis appeared from an adjoining lane. They began pushing and shoving the group. The leaders of the procession begged, saying this was a religious ceremony, it didn't matter which part of India they were from, because they were all Hindus. But the local men wielded their lathis in the air. Blows landed on some devotees. A woman fell to the ground, a trickle of blood mixing with her orange sindoor. Someone was trying to pick her up, but by then everyone else was running, screaming, elbowing their way to find an escape.

Shabby had stood in the centre of it all, ready for a lathi to hit him, bang against his skull. His sight blurred, legs turned to lead, gut dropped in a knot to his feet. A woman brushed past, her sindoor smearing his shirt across the chest. The bamboo arms of the palki veered dangerously close to his eyes, but he couldn't get himself to move.

When it was all over, Shabby was standing there by himself, flowers and sweets strewn on the street. He hadn't realized when the commotion had fizzled out, when the devotees had dispersed, the goons chasing after them. A warm trickle of piss ran down his right leg. Soon he felt it in his sock. He looked down and saw the growing stain on his cotton trousers. More flow pushed against his bladder. He tightened his muscles to stop it.

A taxi slowed down, asking where he wanted to go. Shabby could tell from the driver's Hindi that he was North Indian. He'd heaved his body into the cab and dropped his head back on the torn leather. 'Take me home,' he'd said.

Bhaiyya, how was your day? It was Chintoo. He texted every night now, breaking his silence when news of the violence began spreading across the country. Chintoo had also offered to come to Mumbai, which Shabby had vetoed.

Shabby typed, *It was okay. If I come to Lucknow for Diwali, will you be there?*

The reply came within seconds. *Yes. Definitely. Just come home.*

Eggs

The aroma of mint wafted up from the Irani chai. Ganjeri made a slurping noise as he took a sip, then looked sideways at Shruti's burning cigarette. Shabby could tell he was fighting the temptation. Then he deliberately turned away. 'It's 2008! Sixty years of independence and we still have to explain why we want to move within our own country! I mean, what's next? Apply for a visa to live in Bombay?'

'Mumbai,' Shabby corrected him in a whisper, glancing to make sure there was no one around that they could offend. But they were in the café at Prithvi Theatre, surrounded mostly by struggling actors, some elite artistes, a dwindling audience. It was a haven for liberals.

'Yeah well, *Mumbai*,' Ganjeri acquiesced, not without being patronizing. 'They changed the name after we grew up, though, so we can't be blamed.'

Shabby focused on Ganjeri to calm himself. Ganjeri looked radiant, though he said he was exhausted. He'd returned from Surat just that morning. His curls had grown, and he'd tied his hair into a small bun at the back of his head. Daylight beamed through the open front of the café, casting a late-afternoon glow on his sharp cheekbones.

This was the first time Shabby and Shruti had met Ganjeri since he'd left the flat. It had been months, and Ganjeri had quashed three previous plans on the pretext of being busy. He'd finally come up with the idea of a play at Prithvi himself, booked tickets, sent reminders. Even then he hadn't appeared until the last minute. Shabby and Shruti were waiting at the gate, had almost written off going in, since late entries weren't allowed. But Ganjeri had come running as the final bell rang, hair flying in the wind.

'Can I be honest?' Shruti put her feet up on the chair. 'The play was so meh . . .' The play they'd just watched had been about two couples who'd fallen out of love in their respective marriages, and were reconciling with the loss of a four-way friendship that would never be the same again.

'I quite liked it,' Ganjeri said, his eyes roving through the crowd in the hope of spotting a celebrity. 'Relationships change all the time, it's just reality.'

Shruti settled into the seat and crossed her legs. 'Relationships are so overrated. Does every play or movie or book need to be about them?' She looked away too, as if stopping herself from saying more. The waiter brought her the Irish coffee she'd ordered. She took out a hip flask from her cloth bag and poured some whisky into it. 'Now this is Irish-fucking-coffee done right!' She looked at the boys as if challenging them to say something, poking the embers, knowing that she'd done something illegal, bringing alcohol to a place that probably didn't have the licence to serve it. Ganjeri and Shruti had never officially called off their relationship. Ganjeri had just disappeared, and Shruti was itching to lash out.

The boys looked here and there to ensure a waiter hadn't seen Shruti.

'Anyway, how are you holding up?' Ganjeri asked Shabby, changing the subject. The violence had subsided, the city was limping back to normal. Shabby had told them about the episode with the devotees on his way back from the office, choosing the details he wanted to share, making it sound like a news report. 'I hope you're not freaking out.'

Shabby clucked in a dismissive gesture. *Not one bit*, it said. In reality, though, he *was* freaking out. He had tried to reason several times since that afternoon, reminding himself of how he was spared by the goons, how they had gone after the poorer Hindus. This time, it was his class that had saved him. Once upon a time, it had been their religion that had allowed his family to look away from M.

But he couldn't shrug off the feeling of threat. It was like free fall, like when he was a child, that hollowness in his stomach making him feel like his innards would hit the ground any minute. He kept thinking of how close he'd been to an attack, right there in the middle of the street, like violence was unfolding on the other side of a glass screen that could come crashing at any moment.

Ganjeri reached out and squeezed Shabby's arm. 'You know,' he said in a distant voice, 'I know how you feel. I've felt this before.' Without notice, he weaned the cigarette from Shruti's fingers and took a deep drag, then closed his eyes and threw his head back, letting the smoke escape his lips. He opened his eyes and looked at his friends. 'Do you guys remember the time when the Babri Masjid was demolished?'

Shabby's body stiffened. He felt an energy rise up from his stomach, through his chest where his heart was beating ferociously, up his throat. He was scared it would form words, burst forth in a confession. Was he finally going to tell his friends what he'd seen, about M? But how? What were the words for it? How does one talk about stuff like that? And was this the right place and time?

Instead he said, 'Of course I remember. Some pretty grim things happened back then . . .'

'Well,' Ganjeri shrugged, 'we were still living in our old family home at the time . . .' He passed his fingers through his hair. 'The house was in a Muslim mohalla. Every day, there were stories of shops being ransacked, rickshaws burnt, someone or the other beaten up. We spent all day cooped up at home. At night, we kids were packed off to our grandfather's room at the back of the house. My mother and other aunties slept on the kitchen floor. The men took turns to stand guard. One time, I saw a burqa flying on a pole. I just knew that something bad had happened to a woman. No one leaves her burqa in a public place, just like that . . .' He broke into a smile to release the tension, then took another puff. 'The violence stopped after a month or so. We went back to school.'

Ganjeri's forehead had broken out in a sweat. 'But,' he raised two fingers, the burning cigarette between them, 'something changed.' He stabbed his fingers between his ribs. 'Every single day I would imagine someone driving a knife through me, or cutting my head off, or dragging me into a sack and dumping me in the river . . . or something . . .' This drag of the cigarette took it all the way to its filter. Ganjeri's voice was raspy when he spoke again. 'Before the demolition, we were clueless in our perfect childhoods.'

Clinks of cups and mugs from the counter rushed in to fill the silence. Shabby thought back to Tabrez and Sikandar and all those Muslim boys in school, how they had seemed so unconcerned about the mosque being demolished, the violence in the mohalla and streets, instead obsessing over paper planes and ball games. It must have all been a ruse. They must have felt what Ganjeri was describing now, what M must have felt when he'd been turned away from Lekha-bua's wedding and had to walk through the mohalla rife with rioters, what Shabby had been feeling since that afternoon.

Shruti gave up on waiting for Ganjeri to return the cigarette. She drew a new one from the pack and lit it, narrowing her eyes as the flame came close. A girl at the next table turned and asked Shruti if she could have one. Shruti pulled another cigarette out and helped her light it. The two women nodded in camaraderie.

'Well, speaking of feeling threats in our bodies, I feel it at all times – day or night, crowded or empty spaces, public or private. I'm always aware that someone can harm my body if they had the chance. I know that there is at least one pair of eyes, wherever I go, that is penetrating my clothes . . .' She let out a sigh. 'We women live with it every minute. I knew of the dangers even before I grew *these*!' She raised her arms dramatically, elbows outward, thumbs pointing to her breasts. The jhumkas in her ears jangled in surprise.

Shabby could see she'd made an effort that day, unlike the last few months. Her hair flowed smoothly down to her waist, her eyes were lined with deep kajal, a tight kurti hugged her body, a sliver of soft skin showing between where the kurti ended and jeans started. Did she still secretly hope Ganjeri would come back?

'I wasn't here when the Babri Masjid thing happened.' Shruti's fingers circled the copper-coloured bracelet on her wrist, the pattern of a snake coiled around it. 'I never told you guys, but I spent a few years in America as a child. My dad was . . . is . . . a professor at Stanford. In fact, I have an American passport. I was born there.'

Shruti stopped, as if that's all there was to the story. But the boys looked on expectantly. She twisted her neck, her head moved clockwise, then anti-clockwise, blowing more smoke. 'Well, there's not much to say. My father used to get drunk and beat my mother. So one day, Mom just got up and left. We came to Bangalore. She got her PhD, single-parented me. We've been the two of us since.'

Shabby hesitated, then put an arm around her. How had he not known this all this time? How much about themselves had they kept from each other? Shruti rested her head against his, her hair smelt of something nice. He was sure she'd have a name for it.

Ganjeri looked away, like he was trying not to think whether Shabby and Shruti were a couple now, or if he'd lost the right to wonder. 'How's Mangesh?' He changed the subject again. This is what had become of them, treading on eggshells around each other, looking out for trigger warnings, changing subjects to keep the peace.

Shabby hadn't told Ganjeri about the mall, the satsang. 'I haven't seen Mangesh in a while. He's grown up now, he works at the toll-naka near the highway. I think he's stopped going to school.'

'You know, I've thought about Mangesh a lot,' Ganjeri said to Shabby. The cigarette was on its last legs, and some ash fell into the Irani chai. 'I was quite mean to him. Somehow I just couldn't stomach how happy the two of you were, so full of optimism, as if that one hour of tuition would make everything okay in his life.' He stubbed the cigarette out. 'I guess I was just angry and bitter, trapped in a life I didn't want to lead. Now that I've stepped away from it, I see that . . .'

'Oh, he's changed,' Shruti snapped, moving away from Shabby. She took a big gulp of her Irish coffee. 'Mangesh is quite angry and bitter now. You guys can be best friends, since you've been thinking about him *a lot*.' She did air quotes. 'What else have you been thinking about, Syed?'

'You know what Mom once said to me?' Shruti's voice was acerbic. 'She said – *Women are like eggs for breakfast. Men can order them any way they want – boiled, fried, scrambled, poached. But women . . .*' Her eyes were stretched, the nerves pulling back into her head, trying to fight tears. '*Women have only two choices – to stay or to leave.*'

Ganjeri opened his mouth to retort, but just then, people from the other tables and the theatre lobby got up from their seats and rushed towards them. Shabby's fingers curled into a tight fist, his jaw clenched in anticipation of an attack. But these were fans rushing to congratulate the cast of the play who had appeared from the stage door. The actors were happy to oblige. There wasn't much of an audience left for theatre anyway.

Shabby relaxed his muscles and stared at the Irani chai, little blobs of ash floating, dredges of the mint leaves lying curled up at the bottom, their essence sucked out.

Chakravyuh

M's face is the only thing Shabby can see, above a column of fire, lighting up the dark lanes, the flames playing hide-and-seek on the exposed brick walls, suddenly a deluge of rats comes charging at Shabby, they scramble over his feet, they smell of Bombay duck, they are wearing orange sindoor, from their snouts to between their eyes all the way to the top of their heads, there are more and more of them, released by the Guru-ji, Shabby is drowning under the deluge, he pleads with the Guru-ji to let him go to M, but the rats are in the thousands now, his body pulled down under them, until only his eyes can see M, but M keeps standing, doing nothing, letting the rats devour him—

Shabby placed the tea on the ledge and stared out of the window. The pigeons were nowhere to be seen today. Surprising, because he couldn't remember a morning when the birds hadn't been there, stretching their wings, making goo-goo sounds from the depths of their throats. He looked at the other ledges, at the building opposite, at the wires that ran between lamp posts, even up at the skies. But not a single pigeon anywhere.

He pulled out his sketchbook and started drawing, his hands still in thrall to his subconscious. He drew the slum lane, the deluge of rats, orange sindoor on their snouts, running towards the artist, feet barely visible as they gathered speed. He drew the walls on both sides, outlining the bricks and cracks, crumbling plaster, lanterns and naked bulbs.

Then his fingers went to the end of the lane. He knew what he wanted to draw, but paused. He tried again, but no, he couldn't draw M. He'd been trying in vain for fifteen years.

He looked down at the market. The water-tanker had come early today. The queue snaked all the way to the back of the shops. People chatted, looking bored. Women in nighties, dupattas draped around their bosoms to protect their modesty. Men in lungis, pinching crotches. Some brushed their teeth while in line to save time. They spat not far from where they stood. Even dust refused to move in the stagnant October air.

He spotted Shakku-bai somewhere at the back, her saree neatly pleated, hair tied tightly in a bun, standing straight, two buckets in hand. She was chewing something. Shabby wondered if she'd seen the canvases under his bed. He'd kept them away from everyone, never finding enough confidence to share. Would anyone make sense of the wild depictions of his nonsensical dreams? He'd thought of showing them to Ganjeri and Shruti, but it was too late now. He was all by himself in this flat. Everyone had left.

He put his sketchbook away and got ready for work. Another commute on the crowded train. The thought made his stomach turn. The violence had subsided, now there were only stray reports, but the train was still safer. He looked at his watch. Time to leave.

He was relieved to see fewer people at the station, though that didn't guarantee an empty train, which would come all the way from Thane. There were only a couple of weeks left until Diwali. He'd surprised himself by promptly buying a ticket to Lucknow. This time around, Ma hadn't needed to convince him to come. He was bored alone in the flat, he was scared, the dreams had become more frequent, almost every night. His life as he knew it had come to an end. Two weeks in Lucknow would take him away from this city, give him a chance to clear his head. And Chintoo was going to be there! The thought made his heart rise up and float.

Strains of a hullabaloo snapped him back. At first he thought it was the oncoming train. The sight of the carriages curving around the bend in the distance always did that to people on the platform. They stood on tiptoes, rolled up their sleeves, fastened their bags, like soldiers gearing up for battle. But there was no sign of the train yet. Shabby turned in the direction of the sound. Even before he could fully see, he knew in his gut it was of the bad kind. Flared tempers, raised voices, curses.

Further down the platform, a group – it was difficult to tell how many people – was pushing a young man, his body bending like a feather with every shove. Shabby stepped forward for a better look. Some other passengers did the same. Two men who seemed like the leaders spoke loudly, voices deep, chests inflated, hands moving with authority as one held the young man's collar and shook him, the other landed a smack on his head. The others in the group stood in alert positions, ready for combat, arms away from their bodies, nostrils flared.

Someone came quickly from the direction of the scene. 'That boy is North Indian. He's going for his railways exam.' He clicked his tongue. 'These people want places reserved for Marathis in railways jobs, so they're attacking candidates across the city . . . Bhai, this'll turn ugly before you know it.' The passengers scattered to faraway corners of the platform. Some left the station with a fast-paced gait.

Shabby knew he had to run. But his feet were fixed to the concrete. He watched the frail form fall on to the platform. The group moved in, punching, slapping. They kept his face intact. They were dragging him towards the edge. The young man's screams were hoarse at first, then vanished altogether.

And behind the bulwark of terror was fire, a thin column, playing hide-and-seek with Shabby's vision, now here, now there, now nowhere, now everywhere, trying to climb a gate, slipping on the grille, now horizontal, rolling with the crying man, now disintegrating into charred fragments. He saw the balding head, hollow eye sockets, sallow cheeks. A tube-well, a bucket waiting patiently, tip-tip-tip. He could fill the bucket and throw water at the fire. He could reach out and open the gate. He could scream for help. He could . . . do something, anything, everything. He could save him, before they threw him on the tracks, burnt this city down, brought it all down to zero. ZERO.

Shabby ran, laboriously at first, every step a tremendous effort. But soon he was sprinting, flying, his toes barely touching the concrete, springing into the air. The breeze clawed at the beads of sweat on the back of his neck. And though he was running so fast, his breathing was clement, coordinated, inhaling when he raised a foot, exhaling when he put it down.

Shabby dashed into the bulwark. He punched, kicked, screamed like a madman, tugged at their hair, scratched their cheeks, dragged them by their ears away from the young man now half-hanging off the platform. He pulled the man up, held him by the shoulders, tried to set him off on his escape. But the man was bleeding, crying in inaudible sobs. He was barely twenty. He fought Shabby off at first, couldn't tell he was there to help. Then suddenly he could. He hobbled away on naked feet, leaving his bag behind.

Blood in Shabby's mouth pulsed the gums through short breaths. He turned to face the men. They were angry, bruised, shocked. In all their careers of thuggery, they hadn't seen anyone like him – bespectacled, hair neatly parted, expensive formal shirt tucked into cotton trousers – stand up to them. They were too used to his kind genuflecting, head-bobbing, running away, watching silently. Wrath foamed up to their mouths like acid.

A spray of spit landed on Shabby's face. 'Naam!' One of the leaders demanded his name, pushing him down to the platform. The concrete grazed his arm. Around him, the men were organizing again, having slightly dispersed, surprised by the temporary setback caused by this new enemy. They were forming a solid wall around Shabby, moving slowly in a circle, stepping in and out, heads joined, their heavy shadows blocking off the light, coordinating themselves in a chakravyuh, a circular ambush, an ancient war tactic.

Just then, a teenager stepped in from the outer circle. 'This one's from the north, for sure.' His voice betrayed how keen he was to impress his seniors. 'My friend can confirm.' He reached out and pulled another person forward, a person whose cheekbones glistened, papery skin marred by scratches, a slight line of blood running along his taut jaw. Shabby stared at the boy who had turned up at his doorstep eager to learn, who'd flown kites in Chowpatty, written poems about swordfish, had reached for the dahi-haandi like he was reaching for the stars.

Mangesh stared back into Shabby's eyes. He waited a little, as if confounded by the responsibility placed on his shoulders. What was he waiting for? Was there anything Shabby could do to change the outcome of this moment they were both trapped in? No. Nani was right. *We will pay the price for the sins of our forefathers.* The outcome was predestined.

'I know him,' Mangesh said, his voice ringing out clearly. 'His name is Shubhankar Trivedi.'

No! Shabby wanted to scream. *No, no, no! My name is Shabby. I chose it, I coined it.*

But Mangesh repeated, 'Shubhankar Trivedi!' He paused, seething. 'He's from Lucknow. He has a fancy job that he's snatched from us Marathis. He has strange friends who have no respect for our culture. They drink, dirty-dance on our streets, do unspeakable things. And they hate all of us.'

The mob didn't need to know more. They erupted like a volcano. There was no form to their actions. Punches, kicks, slaps, clawing, flailing of limbs, flogging of flesh, tearing of freshly starched cotton, flying of dust, dragging of bodies, breaking of bones, cracking of glass, shrieks of hatred hollering through the still October air.

Shabby's body felt both heavy and light as it rolled over the edge of the platform. There was no pain, just the heat from the iron of the tracks searing through the shirt into his skin, the column of fire engulfing him.

M cradled him with burning arms, hot breath in his ear. Shabby closed his eyes, the orange glow wild behind his eyelids. He could feel the tremors from the oncoming train.

PART FIVE
Dhaatu / *Metal*

2014

Reincarnated

Chintoo gets him an iPod Classic, a sleek slate-grey thing with a silver back, a half-eaten apple gleaming, loaded with music. Chintoo visits more frequently now that Ma has left. It is like some unsaid arrangement the family has, taking care of him in shifts, like nurses. Chintoo works in Delhi for an online music magazine as an editorial assistant. Papa and Ma still don't approve, but he, their elder son, has taken up all their attention these past few years. The iPod seems more expensive than Chintoo can afford. Sometimes he wonders if Chintoo is somehow grateful to him, for crippling himself and taking the heat off so Chintoo can do whatever he wants.

Chintoo runs him through the playlist he has created in the iPod. He pauses at some songs, then continues. Finally, he takes in a breath and says, 'I played these songs when . . . when we were taking you back . . . to Lucknow.'

He has no memory of it. One moment he was in a hospital in Mumbai, the next he was in the bedroom in Lucknow, covered by a quilt Nani had made when they were children, in the place he had left a triumphant teenager, blazing with the confidence to put his past behind and begin a new life, and had returned to as a refuge for his broken body.

Chintoo says they booked three adjacent seats so they

could lay him down. The air hostesses tried to decide how to put the seat belts on, then gave up. Chintoo sat at the end of the row, his brother's head on his lap, earphones plugged into his brother's ears. His brother doesn't remember any of this.

He does remember some fragments, though. Waiting for the nurse to turn him on his side, sponging the sores on his back caused by the incessant lying down, running wet tissues through his butt crack, the overpowering smell of shit. He remembers the nurse holding the pot under him, another propping him up, both looking at the clock, listing all the patients they still had left to attend, waiting for the pressure in his stomach to pass through his rectum, disappointed when it was just gas. He remembers Ma wiping him clean, averting her eyes from his adult body, sprigs of hair she had never seen before, balls visible through the loose underpants they made him wear for comfort. He remembers Ganjeri's face, a blur through half-open eyelids, voice deep and garbled, strong familiar palm on his forehead. Shruti's locks so close he could smell her hair.

Back in Lucknow, he remembers Nani coming every afternoon, so Ma could take some time off to rest. Nani was quite bent by then, but she hobbled in on a rickshaw without fail, like a soldier reporting for duty. It was the time of day he was awake, his mornings spent in a haze, cloudy from medicines, the evenings in pain with the physiotherapist. Nani sat by the bed and massaged his legs, warming up the oil beforehand, pouring it carefully into a shallow stainless-steel bowl with petal-like serrations. 'This is the very bowl I used when I gave massages to you and Chintoo, when you were little,' she smiled. 'Such cute boys you were!' She ran her fingers softly over his legs, pressing unsurely. 'Does it hurt, bachcha?' she whispered. He said no, not having the heart to say that she didn't have enough strength to be able to hurt him, even on his injured leg.

And later, when he could do a bit of walking, he remembers Nani setting cushions up on the living-room sofa and helping him settle, then watching replays of TV serials she had watched the night before, her mouth agape, her body jerking in surprise, even though she already knew the twists in the plot.

The others came one by one and in groups. They watched him like an exhibit in a museum, human remains of a living being, encased in bandages, embalmed by ointments. Panna-chacha and Manju-chachi, Lekha-bua and Nandu-fufa, Aarti-mami and Girish-mama, Suresh-mausa and Pushpa-mausi, Mr Dwivedi and Dhwani, Sharma-uncle and Sharma-aunty, Kejriwal-sir and the ghost of his dead wife, Munni-didi and her pageboy husband, Papa's boss Mr Kaushik. They held their breaths as Ma asked him to say hello, trying her best to prove that he was okay. Later, in the living room, they asked questions thinking he was out of earshot. *What happened? How? Most importantly, why?* 'No smoke without fire,' Suresh-mausa said.

He remembers Ma and Papa making up their own stories to explain away things they didn't understand, changing versions, picking enemies at random to suit the audience. *He tutored the Marathi maid's son, that must have ticked something off? One of his friends was a hippie-type girl, you know how poor people view these things? His flatmate was a Muslim, we'd asked him not to live with the guy.*

When the visitors dispersed across the city, these stories must have taken on new forms, new plot points, new characters. Like Master-ji had done with M, called him a kaamchor, a shirker who'd run away to the village because he didn't want to work hard.

This is what happens when people can't tell their own stories. Other people tell them on their behalf, spinning what they wished for them, wished upon them. And they, the voiceless, lie silent, witnessing their lives being reincarnated on other people's tongues.

When he was walking again, first from bed to bathroom, then the living room, then up the stairs one at a time, the doctor said he could go back to normal life. *Normal.* He just needed to continue his exercises and physiotherapy. Papa was keen he get back to work. The company had held his job. 'The HR lady has called a few times. It's been thirteen months, after all. They're getting impatient. You should join back immediately.' Papa frowned, as though the worst that could happen was his son losing his job, not what had already happened to him.

He remembers Ma volunteering to come with him to Mumbai. 'I can't leave him alone in this condition.'

Papa looked frazzled. 'But . . . things here . . . meaning . . . of course, I understand . . . but . . .' Papa had never lived alone, never taken care of himself. Nani stepped in to say that she and Malti-didi would fill in for Ma, no worries.

'I'll be back in a few months. It's just to help him settle in,' Ma promised. She didn't know then that she was going away for four years, that her son would never be his old self again, that he could be somewhat repaired but never fully restored.

He remembers, on the night before they left for Mumbai, Papa sitting by the bedside, hand squeezing his shoulder. 'Beta, the doctor says recovery is only a matter of weeks. It's a question of willpower, you know? That's the only thing you need right now.' Papa snapped his fingers. 'Believe you can spring back to your old life, and that's it! Willpower!' He remembers wanting to ask Papa where he could find some of this magic potion called *Willpower*.

And he remembers the empty hours, night after night for the last five years, caught between wakefulness and slumber, trying to summon M back into his subconscious, needing to hear him, see him, touch him. He remembers M's obstinate absence, his refusal to appear. He remembers the dreams having stopped, and never having returned.

Undelivered

He stares at the photo, trying to locate the five perfect dimples. But they are covered by stubble. The hair is cut short, the wiry curls under control. Ganjeri is wearing a kurta and jeans, a light autumn jacket thrown over his shoulders. Blurred fall colours speckle the backdrop. Three other men and a woman are next to him, all smiling. They are the Class of 2014 at Harvard Business School.

He types out a message on his phone. *Congratulations! You didn't tell me you were going to Harvard.* The carpal ligament tingles. The message shows a single tick. *Undelivered.* He realizes that Ganjeri must have moved to a US number. He tries to remember the last time they spoke. A couple of years ago. Ganjeri was in Delhi, helping a professor at Jamia Millia University with field research on malnourishment among Muslims in urban slums. Before that, Ganjeri was in Kashmir, journalling the revolution of the youth, who had turned up in large numbers to pelt stones at the Indian army to protest decades of occupation. 'The soldiers are firing pellets at the students, blinding them! The kids aren't even armed!' The passion in Ganjeri's voice travelled through the phone and beat against his eardrums. 'When a Hindu riots, they're protesters. When a Muslim riots, they're terrorists!'

He wonders now how Ganjeri has gone from being that angry activist to a smiling Harvard student. He would ask him if he could.

The last time he saw Ganjeri in full consciousness was six years ago, that evening at the Prithvi café. Of course he saw him again in the hospital. Ma said Ganjeri and Shruti had turned up every evening for those two months, arriving before visiting hours started. Ma seemed to approve of his friends. 'They helped with medicines and contacts. We knew nothing and no one in the city.' Ganjeri had helped Papa negotiate time off with the company. Shruti had held Ma when she had first walked in to find him scaffolded in casts, tubes sticking out, machines beeping. 'I was so relieved just to see another woman there among all these men. At least I could hold someone's hand,' Ma said.

He was rushed to the hospital by strangers who had picked him up from the tracks, carried him in a kaali-peeli taxi, waving a white hankie for emergency. The police had arrived later, going through his phone for numbers, calling Ma in Lucknow. He didn't know who had informed Ganjeri and Shruti, but they were already there when Ma and Papa and Chintoo arrived on the first flight they could get.

Ma once tried to ask obliquely about Shruti. 'Don't you like her? Is there something between you two?' But when Shruti packed up and left for Bangalore, Ma understood that even if there had been a past, there was no future.

He now looks Shruti up on his phone. They spoke five months ago, over chat. She said she was helping her mother set up an NGO for women facing domestic violence. She spoke at length about the bureaucratic hurdles, no-objection certificates, inspections, licences. He was mostly silent. Shruti isn't on social media, so there is no way of keeping up with her life. No gourmet meals or retail therapy, no MBAs at Harvard. But he does follow the NGO she has set up, *likes* posts about the good work they do.

Suddenly, he smiles at a story Ma had told him. One

evening when the two women were alone in the hospital room, Shruti told Ma, 'Aunty, I know you don't smoke, but if you wanted to, I have cigarettes. It'll help calm you. Just letting you know . . .'

'It was the first time I'd laughed in days,' Ma said. Then she hesitantly admitted, 'To tell you the truth, I was even tempted to try a cigarette!'

Victim

He picks up a drink from a passing tray and plonks himself in an armchair. The cushion receives his body and adjusts itself around him, like a receptacle. From here, he can see the party progressing in full flow. The NGO staffers are having a nice time, sipping vodka and orange juice, munching the snacks on offer, an odd combination of Western canapés and Indian street food, cocktail sausages and pani-puris.

'There's this thing . . . like . . . a party or something?' Anisha had said to him before she left after one of their Saturday sex-and-smoke sessions. 'Sid Gulati is hosting us . . . I mean, like . . . everyone who works at the NGO and the school?'

Everyone at the NGO knew about Sid Gulati. He was the philanthropist who funded the school in the Bhiwandi slum. There were other similar schools his foundation ran.

'I think you should come?' Anisha cocked her head. 'It'll be good for you to . . . you know . . . get to know the man behind the mission . . . or whatever . . .'

The next Saturday, the principal of the school extended a formal invitation. 'Shubhankar,' she said, beaming from cheek to cheek, 'you are an integral part of our work now, even though you're a volunteer. Sid Gulati has personally invited you to the party. It's his small way of saying thanks for all our hard work here.'

The man himself is nowhere to be seen now. He was around at first, a lean suave guy in his forties, wearing a printed silk shirt and an open-collar khadi waistcoat, adjusting his rimless glasses from time to time. He got the party started, making a little speech, expressing his heartfelt gratitude, sharing impact figures of what the NGO had achieved. Then he disappeared behind a set of heavy wooden doors.

'Sid's calling you,' Anisha says as she walks up to him. 'In his office . . . like . . . behind those doors?' When he looks at her nervously, she snorts in a laugh that makes her drink ripple on the surface. 'It's okay . . . Sid's cool and all . . . like, I've known him for ages . . . he's friends with my dad or whatever . . .'

He makes his way through the party to Sid's office, sliding open the wooden doors. Sid is seated in an elaborate leather chair, turning around to see him enter. The table is so wide it makes Sid seem very far away. Sid raises himself slightly. 'Come come, Shubhankar, please sit.'

He makes himself comfortable on the other side of the table. He has researched Sid Gulati before coming here. Grew up in Delhi, went to Harvard Business School in the nineties, worked for investment banks on Wall Street, started his venture capital fund, returned *home* to India a few years ago. He has been donating a long time. The foundation in his name is a more recent thing. They run a chain of schools for *kids from low-income families in resource-poor urban sectors.*

'So what do you do for a living?' Sid asks. 'The ladies said you're a volunteer.'

The ladies. Sid isn't wrong. All the employees at the NGO are women. He reckons the job pays too low and needs too much empathy for men's egos.

'I worked in tech for a few years. I recently quit my job,' he mutters, then feels pressured to add, 'I'm still exploring options for my next step.'

Sid nods. 'I hear you're doing a really good job with the

kids. You've been spending more time at the school, haven't you?'

He can't think of anything to say to return the compliment. But Sid isn't waiting, he's continuing to speak. 'And we need to compensate you for that, don't we? Why don't we get you listed as a staff member and pay you a salary? It won't be much, especially in this city. We all know that most people who work for NGOs are from rich families. They can do good because they don't have to put food on the table.'

But my family isn't rich, and I'm not taking any money from them, he wants to tell Sid. It's pointless to protest, though. He does need the money. He has been spending all his time painting and volunteering. At this rate, he will drain out his savings very soon.

Sid Gulati opens his palms. 'But it'll be something. No one should work for free.'

He stares through the large windows that look out to the dark sea, a view only possible from this posh Bandra penthouse. The little lights below are the only reminder of the neighbourhood around them, the existence of ordinary people who don't even know this heavenly abode exists. *Up above the world so high, like a diamond in the sky.*

Then Sid leans forward. 'Also, umm . . . look, I'm going to cut to the chase. I know what you've been through.' Sid's eyes are so piercing behind the rimless glasses that he has to look away. 'In this country, we pass it off as daily violence. But in the West, they'd call you a victim of a targeted hate crime.' Sid pauses, lets the statement lodge itself in the room, charge up the air.

He straightens his back. This is the first time he has heard an articulate academic definition of himself. He is a *victim of a targeted hate crime.* Good to know. It sounds like something straight out of a social-policy memo by an American think-tank. He wants to ask how Sid knows about his past, but he presumes it's from *the NGO ladies*.

Or maybe it's Anisha. Maybe she's figured him out. He feels like he has let an infiltrator into his home, has been sleeping with the enemy. But he controls his breathing, tries to fight off the demons of mistrust. The psychologist warned him about this, that he wouldn't be able to trust anyone for a long time after what happened. *Calm down, maybe Anisha is just trying to help after all.*

Sid senses the right time to resume, as though practised in the art of perceiving other people's thought processes. 'My foundation works with people like you, people who've been wronged, who find themselves at odds with society and are trying to rise above the hate.'

He wants to tell Sid – *As far as I'm aware, the only thing I'm at odds with is myself, and the only hate I feel is for my life.* But he bobs his head instead. He feels small, like a fool, being told who he is, what he stands for, what others can do to help him.

'I just want you to know that I'm here to support in any way you need.' Sid Gulati slides a business card down the table. 'You have my number.'

Cartoons

'He is the quintessential common man. He was a chai-wallah, sold tea at a railway station.'

'But what about the Gujarat riots? He was chief minister of the state then!'

'He has dedicated his life to serving the country.'

'He was denied an American visa!'

'He brought development to Gujarat. Have you seen the roads?'

'God knows how many more mosques they'll demolish again!'

'He is the only one who can put Pakistan in its place.'

'He believes in entrepreneurship. He'll make India the superpower we should've already been.'

'He's promised to bring all the black money back from Swiss banks and put it in every Indian's account! Fifteen lakh rupees per Indian!'

'Chhee! How can we have a prime minister who can't even speak English?'

It is as if the cartoons on the walls have joined in the debate. He sips the wine quietly, surrounded by Mario Miranda's murals of people having a nice time, boisterous, wholesome, not dissimilar to the real people around him. He cranes his neck to look at the roof of Café Mondegar. There are murals there too! He wonders if he could ever draw on walls. Does he have the skill? And who'd allow him to draw on their wall anyway?

He has been out to restaurants since the *incident*, since he came back to Mumbai, but only rarely – office parties, team dinners, a couple of times with Papa and Ma and Chintoo. Crowded noisy places still make him anxious, make his scalp sweat, his bad leg tremble. Staring at the murals is helping to smoothen the unrest he's feeling inside.

Chintoo's friends continue trading arguments about the upcoming election. It has caught the fancy of the whole country. He can tell they have never felt so strongly about politics before. They have come down from Delhi for work. His brother is staying with him. Chintoo spent all day taking photos of his canvases and digitalizing them, saying he was *borderline offended* that he'd never known his brother was *this* talented. Then he dragged him along to have dinner with his *peeps*.

'What do you think about the elections, bhaiyya?' Chintoo asks now.

He looks down from the ceiling to find eight impassioned faces staring at him. The election news is all over, there is no staying away from it. The nationalist party's campaign is something India has never seen before. Their candidate appears in person before thousands, then holograms his image to thousands more. He promises the country good times, *achhe din*, like a travel agent selling holidays. He speaks of himself in the third person, like a little child. *He does not fear. He will send thieves to jail. He will build roads.* He declares he will lead like a *man*, proclaiming his chest to be fifty-six inches. *Chhappan inch ka seena.*

'Bhaiyya?' Chintoo's friends are still looking at him.

'I think that . . .' he says, 'the country will get what it votes for, and that is what it will deserve. Isn't that why we defend democracy?'

They wait for more, confused. They are expecting answers, opinions, facts, debates. But he puts the chicken lollipop in his mouth and chews noisily.

Bhavishya

The brothers are lolling in bed when Papa opens the door and walks in unannounced, Suresh-mausa tailing behind. Papa offers him the foldable chair. Suresh-mausa's sides spill over as he sits on it. The others sit on the beds. The brothers stand against the table.

They are in Lucknow to vote. Chintoo insisted that as responsible citizens of a democracy, it was their duty. Ma said it had been years since they'd been *home*. He couldn't argue with any of that. It's true that it has been four years since he left Lucknow, limping, on crutches. For four years, he has been trying to find excuses for not coming back. He has finally run out of them.

The summer of 2014 is merciless. Suresh-mausa, face flushed from being outdoors, is panting. He fans himself with his saffron scarf, the little trishuls vigorously jumping. He has come to campaign in the building.

'This AC is strong,' Papa says, pointing to the air-conditioning unit. He has had it installed in anticipation of his sons coming home.

Suresh-mausa pats Papa on the shoulder. 'Arre, Ashutosh, you are always such a good host. I won't stay long.' Papa smiles sweetly, signals to Ma. She leaves the room to get water and snacks.

Suresh-mausa turns to the boys. 'It's good to see you both.' He points his chin towards the elder one. 'And you especially, standing on your feet again. Wah! Last time we saw you, you were . . .' He clicks his tongue as if in sadness, then gulps down the cold water Ma has brought. 'But what are you both doing so far away? One in Mumbai, one in Delhi? You should be here, campaigning with me, working for your country. You are the youth. Everything we are doing is for your ujjwal bhavishya only.' *Bright future.*

He looks at the other men who have accompanied him. 'We've been out since morning, in this heat. Setting up camps, organizing rallies, distributing pamphlets.' He wipes the remnants of sweat from his forehead. 'But no problem. Look at our supreme leader, how he's campaigning across the country. Today here, tomorrow there.' His hand jumps in space to indicate the breadth of the leader's travels. 'That man is so energetic. I'm telling you, once he's PM, he will solve all the country's problems in one day. Wait and watch!'

In the evening, the four of them sit in the living room. The TV is on, yet another debate playing out. *Are India's Muslims Pakistani spies – the nation wants to know.* The anchor screams non-stop at his guests, nine faces in nine little boxes, like nine fish trapped in tanks, opening their mouths to pitch in, only to gulp air and give up. Most are waiting patiently to collect their payments at the end of the programme. But one fish manages to sneak in an argument that throws the anchor off-script. The anchor calls for a commercial break immediately.

Ma is stitching. She has taken to embroidery since coming back from Mumbai, making tablecloths and bags and gifting them to relatives and neighbours, pretty little things, colourful flowers and rabbits and rising suns cross-stitched on pastel backgrounds. The boys had no idea Ma was good at this. When Ma showed them, Chintoo gushed with praise, coming up with ideas for how she can sell her work online. Ma shook her head shyly.

Now Papa digs his phone out from under the cushion and passes it to his elder son. Chintoo shifts closer to look. It is a forwarded message with tables and calculations. It takes the boys a while to read the Hindi alphabet. The message claims that if allowed to grow at its current rate, the Muslim population in India will overtake the Hindus by 2050, become a majority. There is a long list of numbers split across regions and districts.

'This is mathematically impossible,' Chintoo says, voice already raised. 'Muslims are only ten per cent of the population now . . .'

Papa cuts in. 'You are educated and you don't believe in numbers? These Muslims have four-four wives and twelve-twelve babies. At this rate, they'll overtake us by 2030.'

'How many Muslims do you know with four wives?' Chintoo challenges.

Papa looks taken aback. He's trying to think but the boys know that he doesn't know any Muslims with more than one wife; in fact he doesn't know many Muslims at all. 'From what I see, they're everywhere.' Papa changes tack. 'The Guptas sold their house last year, some Rafiq lives there now. Then Ahluwalia died, a Qureishi moved in. Do you remember even one Muslim in this neighbourhood when you were growing up?'

Papa looks to Ma for support, but Ma continues stitching. 'Keep me out of this politics,' she mutters. 'I'm an uneducated woman anyway. In this country, our opinions don't matter.'

'So what if these people have moved in?' Chintoo seems to enjoy these duels with Papa. 'Our family also moved here from somewhere else! And now we've moved to Delhi and Mumbai. Migration is the oldest truth of humankind.'

'Do you have any reasoning left in you?' Papa stands up, like he needs to do something with his body to fight back. 'We moved here to live peacefully. These people are planting bombs, going to fight for the ISIS in Syria, shooting at the army in Kashmir. Half these Muslims are Pakistani spies.' Papa looks satisfied, having answered the burning question the TV anchor has spent half an hour unpacking. As if on cue, the anchor and eight boxed midgets are back on-screen. The ninth who spoke up has disappeared, probably discharged without payment.

Papa mutes the TV. He is not done. His eyes light up as a new argument comes to him. 'And what is wrong with some Hindu pride? We are the oldest civilization of the world. We invented the zero, yoga. Our science was so developed that we flew aeroplanes, performed plastic surgery when firangs were burning books.' Chintoo smirks noisily at these claims the nationalist party has been making about scientific advancement in the ancient world, some true, some specious. But Papa doesn't take the bait. 'Muslims and Christians have invaded us time and again, made us their slaves. 1857, 1758, 1526 . . . And you think the so-called secular governments didn't sponsor riots? 1984, 1975 . . .'

The boys look at Papa in wonder. This is the man who moved mountains to get his sons an English education, who never thought he had enough knowledge to argue back, always bowing down, to his boss, to the school principal, to the local politician. They are almost impressed by what they see now.

Chintoo's breathing is laboured. 'How far back do you want to go? In how many ways do you want to divide people – religion, caste, region, language? It is this kind of hate that almost got your elder son killed . . .'

Chintoo points to his brother, his finger so close it's almost touching his face. Ma and Papa turn to look. For a few moments, they are all frozen. For too long now, they have kept up the charade of everything being back to normal. This is the first time someone has spoken out loud about the attack, not just as an *accident*, or as something to physically recover from, but what it stood for, what caused it, what more could have happened.

He, the elder son, leaves the room quietly, closes the bedroom door, and switches on the air conditioning. He stands in the blast of cold air, letting the sweat droplets erase themselves.

On election day, they wake up early and hurriedly have some tea and toast. Then they queue up at the neighbourhood school to vote. The men they saw with Suresh-mausa stand guard outside, joining their palms in a namaste when they see the Trivedi family, Suresh-mausa's relatives. Papa returns their namaste, bowing down, touched by the attention of important people.

Chintoo returns to Delhi that afternoon, saying this place is suffocating. But his brother stays back, telling Ma and Papa he has a lot of leave left, not ready to tell them yet that he has quit his job. The savings in his account will sustain him for some time, and the meagre NGO salary will help keep things afloat.

When the results are announced, the nationalists win by the biggest landslide in decades. The country erupts in celebrations. Suresh-mausa dances down the street to dholak-beats, waving his saffron scarf, the trishul stickers popping in the hot sunshine. Chants of campaign slogans rend through the air.

The entire country is now a satsang. There is no memory left of a demolished mosque, the bloodshed, curfews, of

Ganjeri's family's displacement, of a tailor's assistant burnt to death, of a young man left to die on the train tracks.

Like the history textbooks in school, nothing after independence matters. The *sovereign socialist secular democratic republic*, for which Dada-ji fought and Nana-ji built bridges, is wiped clean. The project of hate is now complete, sitting pretty at its pinnacle.

And the politicians are its new gods. They will decide where people pray, who can be friends, who can be neighbours, who can marry.

The common people are nimitta-matra, little specks of dust, blips on the timeline that carry them from election to election. They will never be anything more, and there is nothing lesser left for them to be.

Gita

Nani is dozing off when he knocks on the gate. She opens her eyes, startled. She gathers the book on her lap, its sepia pages hanging precariously. When she closes it, he sees it's the Bhagavadgita. She stands up. She is even frailer than he remembers, her back stooped in a perfect arch. She smiles, nearly toothless. She goes in and comes back with the key, which she passes to him. He reaches through the grille to open the lock. She hobbles into the living room behind him. Then she goes to her room and comes back with her dentures attached.

'You should live with Ma and Papa,' he says, settling into the sofa, the dustcovers still folded along the sides.

'Not at all.' Nani is now fully awake. 'Your Nana-ji used to say – *Subhadra, I can't leave you money, but I have built you this small house, live here on behalf of both of us*. And your mother and I . . . it's better we are in different houses.' Nani chuckles. 'She's never been an easy one.'

He opens his mouth to say something, then closes it. Nani grips his wrist. 'Come on! Say what's on your mind. I'm too old to be proper with.'

'Well, you weren't easy either. You know Chintoo and I grew up not liking you much? You were always giving us a tough time.'

Nani laughs. 'Upbringing is all about strictness and discipline. Too much love makes children comfortable. That is

305

exactly how I brought your mother up. And what a brilliant girl she was! If she'd worked, she would've earned twice your father's salary. Instead we got her married at such a young age . . .'

Nani turns to look at her grandson. 'And look where it got you – made you an engineer! Your Nana-ji would've been so proud. I always knew you had a lot of him in you. Not just your brains. That thing you did later . . .' She waits to find the words. 'When they brought you back to Lucknow, you were a bag of broken bones, bandaged from head to toe . . .' She covers her mouth with her pallu. He tightens his grip on her arm. 'But I also knew that's exactly what your Nana-ji would've done. Everything wrong about this country was his responsibility to solve.' She smiles. 'He used to say – *I have two newly wed brides. One is you, one is my country. Both have had sad pasts, but now you've come to me – free and independent. I will pamper you both.*'

Nani points to the *Dainik Bhaskar* newspaper on the table. 'I worry for you, with everything happening.' The news is grim. A young Muslim man returning from work was killed. Hundreds of Muslims are being converted to Hinduism. *Ghar wapsi*, the nationalists are calling it. *Homecoming.* They have taken no time getting down to business after their election victory. A Member of Parliament of the nationalist party has proclaimed, *Every Hindu woman should give birth to four sons – make one a soldier to protect the country, make one an ascetic to protect the religion.* With this proclamation, he's thrown to the dogs the family planning programme the government has run since independence – *Hum do, hamare do* its popular refrain on national television every night. *Us two, our two.*

'You have to be careful not to get too involved with all this,' Nani says.

He wants to tell Nani she has nothing to worry about, that

he doesn't have it in him to do anything any more. He is a *one-time wonder*. Instead he says, 'Can I tell you a secret? Just between you and me?' Nani blinks tightly like a little girl pinky-promising her best friend. 'I've quit my job. It was just too . . .' He can't find the words.

Nani nods like she understands, like she has had a career of her own. 'Are you still teaching art to children at the NGO?' He nods. Nani shrugs. 'Well, then you're not jobless. You're doing better than most people.'

He thinks of the extra time he's spending with the children nowadays, taking them to visit the flamingos in Sewri, the Kitab Khana bookstore in Flora Fountain, to see deer in the Sanjay Gandhi National Park, places they have never been in spite of living in Mumbai. He has brought them to art competitions, where the other children arrive in big cars wearing Nike trainers and Gap T-shirts, their parents feeding them Mars bars.

'But it doesn't pay, Nani.'

Nani balls her fingers into a fist, and opens it in a jerking movement. *To hell with the world.*

'*Karmanye vadhikaraste ma phaleshu kadachana,*' she chants in Sanskrit. 'It's written in the Gita. Do you know what it means?' He shakes his head. 'It means that a good Hindu should only think of doing good deeds. That's your only duty on earth. The truer your work, the more the universe will find ways to reward you.' She turns to look at her grandson over the frames of her glasses. 'Is salary the only reward? What about happiness, fulfilment?'

Nani stares out of the window, squinting. 'You know, we women are taught from childhood to play roles – dutiful daughter, faithful wife, strict mother . . . disciplinarian grandma. It's now, at the end, I realize I've only acted the way society expected of me. Maybe that's why I was so strict with you and Chintoo . . . I was trying to fit into my daughter's family, do what your parents wanted me to do . . .' She strokes his arm. 'But you do what you like, bachcha, that's what's most important.'

They sit in silence for a long time. The sun starts its journey down the other side of the sky. The room gets dark. Surrounding trees cast long shadows. The maid enters and is surprised to see the two figures huddled. She switches on the lights and offers to make tea. 'Arre, you make tea later. First go get malpuas from Ramlal's for my grandson. You know how far he's come from? Bambai!'

The maid smiles at him. 'The train wasn't late, na?'

'You idiot!' Nani shouts. There is still some of the old fire left in her. 'He came by plane. This is not Moradabad that you can sit on a train and come any time!' The maid's smile disappears. She hurries down to the shop.

He starts laughing, his head thrown back on the sofa. This is the Nani he and Chintoo hated growing up, but now he misses the feisty woman who had everyone wrapped around her little finger. He remembers when he was still bedridden in Lucknow, bandaged up, Chintoo came home, said the university wanted to felicitate him, the hero who'd stood up against injustice. Papa rejected the idea right away. 'This isn't a soap opera. As it is, people are asking questions, saying all kinds of things. We don't have connections or power or money. What if making a hue and cry attracts the attention of politicians, who'd save us then?' At the hospital in Mumbai, Papa had done his utmost to bat away the journalists, standing like a shield, refusing to answer questions. And within a month the journalists had forgotten about them when a boat rocked up at the Gateway of India loaded with terrorists from Pakistan, who ran rampage through the city, occupying hotels and stations and hospitals and synagogues, shooting indiscriminately, taking people hostage. His *story* was worth nothing in this new world where channels were spoilt for choice. Taking advantage of the lull, Papa had got them out of Mumbai. And when the police called to say they couldn't progress the investigation because there were no witnesses, Papa was relieved. So how dare Chintoo disturb the calm?

But Chintoo wasn't one to give in. Father and younger son argued in raised voices until Nani stepped in. 'Let the boy recover in peace. That's the least you can do.' She pointed to the door with her arthritic arm. 'Leave the room. Now!' She had never spoken to her son-in-law like that. Papa lowered his head and walked out. There had been no talk of felicitations any more.

Now Nani looks at him with rheumy eyes. 'When will I see you next?'

He reaches out for a pad on the table and starts scribbling. When he looks up, Nani is dozing off. He gently shakes her awake, shows her the sketch – his face, but the hairstyle and glasses borrowed from what he has seen of Nana-ji in photos.

'Now you can see me every day.'

Nani's head bobs up and down in happiness.

2015

Agony

With every step, the tendons seethe like angry protesters. The pain shoots up like cocaine. Then there is a lull as his foot settles on the ground. The muscles adjust themselves in his frame, like fish in an aquarium. If there is such a thing as sweet agony, this is it, every pore of his body forbidding him to continue, and yet something else pushing him on – *take one more step, run until the end of the road, the tea-stall, run until you see the flamingos.* So he runs, his body feeling taller, shoulders broader, legs stronger, arms swinging, cutting through the humid air.

He has called the psychologist and told her he isn't coming in any more, he will not be referred to a psychiatrist, he doesn't need the medication. She grunted in disagreement. But he can't afford her anyway, now that he has quit his job. Mental health assistance is expensive, a luxury only preserved for the rich. Maybe that is why the rest of the country doesn't stop to introspect, ask themselves how they're feeling about their lives, about things happening to them, around them. It is too risky to poke oneself. One never knows where it will rupture, what might come forth, and once the turbulence has tumbled out, what does one do about it?

So the only thing left for him to do is run. This is what he has been doing every morning for a year since he came back from Lucknow after the elections, running like a mad person on the streets of Mumbai, tracing different routes that all end up at the flamingos of Sewri, when they're visiting.

After getting back to the flat, he stands at the full-length mirror, watching his physique rebuild, slimmer waist, tighter chest, flatter stomach.

There is a lot of advice on the internet about the mind driving the body. But no one talks about how the body drives the mind, sends the blood pulsating through the brain, nourishes it, heals it, calms it.

Go, go, go, run, run, run.

Eeeee . . .

The internet is making the whole world bipolar. He smiles at the thought. His cheeks hurt from the effort, reminding him that he hasn't smiled for days. He only smiles when he is with the children in the NGO school. *Eeeee* . . . he says out loud. *Eeeeeee*, he sees himself in the mirror, baring his teeth. If someone were watching this, they'd pack him off to an asylum.

He focuses back on the internet browser. A moment ago, he was fuming, when he read about a Muslim man killed by a Hindu mob, accused by villagers of slaughtering a calf and storing beef, beaten to death with sticks and knives. The report said the meat was probably not beef, just mutton. He scrolled through the few photos, wanting to see more, addicted as he always is to such things. The pictures showed a lean face with a slight beard, a crisp white kurta, standing against a bright-red background, the kind of photo that gets taken in the nondescript studios that still exist in small towns. He died an ignominious death, but at least he was remembered, memorialized, his next of kin all over the news, demanding justice. M, on the other hand, has disappeared from memory, burnt down to a heap of ash behind a haveli, the only witness a ten-year-old child who still can't remember his name, can't sketch his face, can't get himself to tell anyone what he saw, who remembers him by a letter of a foreign alphabet, the colonizer's language.

*

312

But that was a moment ago. While on YouTube, he was prompted to watch a video of the Indian prime minister addressing an audience during his visit to London. The British prime minister gives his counterpart a glowing introduction, beaming at the prospect of opening up British businesses to a billion-people market. It doesn't matter to the British government who leads the country, what violations they've committed, as long as the pounds keep flowing in. The prime minister's wife stands at the back in a not-quite-maroon saree. It makes him wonder what Shruti would've called this colour.

He fast-forwards through the Indian prime minister's speech. The man is a slow speaker, pausing at strategic moments to let his audience chant his name. Every corner of Wembley Stadium is full, the Indian diaspora turning up in all their dollar/pound/euro glory, celebrating a leader in whose governance they have no stake, having left the country years ago, having put all their energies into building a life somewhere far away, yet pining for India every single day. Ninety thousand Indians packed into that place, waving the Indian tricolour, jumping up and down, dancing to dholak-beats. Like they're watching India win a World Cup cricket match. Politics, cricket, same-same, they can't tell the difference from thousands of miles away. Anything that harks back to the motherland is worthy of celebration.

At one point, the prime minister says, *Britain has given the world James Bond. India has given the world Brooke Bond*, referring to the brand of tea in every Indian kitchen, repeating it like a rhyme. *James Bond. Brooke Bond. James Bond. Brooke Bond.* The crowd goes berserk.

A chuckle escapes his throat, like he's watching a stand-up comedy act. There is something about these leaders, their comic timing so endearing one could never imagine them doing anything sinister.

The prime minister is now saying something about how all of India lives in peace and harmony, how the entire world looks up to India for a lesson on unity in diversity . . .

He closes the browser.

The thought of London makes him think of something else. He opens the website of the University of London, browses the list of postgraduate courses, and navigates to the MA in Fine Art. He has been on this page many times before. The application deadline is in two weeks. The two-year course starts next year. September 2016. It costs £5,000 for UK students and £15,000 for international students. A disclaimer in fine-print says that fees for *home* students are fixed by UK government decree, but that for international students could increase without notice. The requirements seem deceptively basic. Academic or work experience, personal statement, references.

He is about to close the browser but something stops him. He has two weeks. He can write a personal statement. He can upload the digital versions of his canvases that Chintoo made. And he can get the school principal to write a reference, though he isn't sure a reference by an NGO worker in the Bhiwandi slums would cut any ice in faraway posh London.

But what the fuck, he thinks. *Let's do this. Let's apply.*

He looks in the mirror and smiles a genuine smile. *Eeee.*

2016

Aaaaa . . .

Dear Shubhankar Trivedi
It is with pleasure that we attach a letter of offer to the MA Fine Art programme at the University of London. On behalf of everyone here – Congratulations!

He shuts the laptop, paces up and down the tiny living room, then opens the balcony door and steps out. The March heatwave is relentless. He can't even smell the shit in this thick stagnant air. He pulls out his phone and calls Ma. 'I have some news. I've been selected for a Masters at a London university.'

A shriek escapes Ma's throat. 'Congratulations, beta! I knew you would . . .' She gulps, surprised by her own inarticulateness. He hears her tell Papa. Papa's voice is on the phone within seconds. 'Wah, beta! This is excellent. What course is it?'

'MBA.' For once, he wants to give them what they want to hear. He has been the cause of too much bad news for too long.

After hanging up, he climbs on to the ledge, the guardrail pressing against his upper thighs. He closes his eyes and draws in a deep breath. He wants to scream. *Aaaaa* . . . He has never done it before. Always too careful, too measured. He opens his mouth. *Aaaaa* . . . *Aaaaa* . . . But no sound comes. Instead sobs pass through his body in waves, like an animal disgorging itself from inside him. He comes down from the ledge and sits on the floor, knees drawn up to his chest. *Aaaaa* . . . He sits there until the sun sets. The tears dry on his face. The sobs mellow down to tiny hiccups. The beast has left his body.

He gets up and dusts off his back, texts Chintoo the news. He picks up a bottle of Old Monk rum, takes the keys and lets the door noisily shut behind him. He goes down the stairs to the floor where Anisha lives. He doesn't know much about her, whether she lives alone or with parents or flatmates. They haven't asked each other these questions. He doesn't even know if she's single. But he takes a chance. He can't be alone tonight, and there is no one in this city he can turn to. Once upon a time, this would've been a party. Ganjeri, Shruti, Erik, Rebecca, Mangesh, the firangs. They were witnesses to his life. And isn't that what everyone is after? Witnesses. To ratify that they exist, they tried, failed, succeeded?

He knocks on a random door. A woman opens it only a sliver. He hides the bottle behind him. 'Does Anisha live here?' The woman points her chin across the lobby, then closes the door, but not before she has seen the bottle when he turns around. He rings the bell of the opposite flat. Anisha opens the door, looks surprised. He holds up the bottle. 'In a mood to celebrate?' She smiles. He notices for the first time that her eyes are dark brown. The curls escape her top-knot and graze her bony cheeks. She opens the door wider and lets him in.

'So what's the price of this Masters?' she asks later, when they have finished the bottle and ordered for another to be home-delivered. She is sprawled on the sofa, he on the floor. They haven't touched each other all evening. Instead, they listened to music, connecting Chintoo's iPod to her speakers. *Don't look back in anger*, one of the songs said.

He tells her the fees, then other costs – flights, visa, accommodation, food.

Anisha turns around, intrigued. 'And . . . none of my business or anything . . . but like . . . who will pay for this? You have a rich dad . . . or something?'

He shakes his head. He doesn't know how, but he will have to find a way to fund his escape.

Bazaar

The jacket fits his muscular shoulders with a snugness only money can buy. Underneath, the T-shirt wraps around his body tightly. A scarf around his neck, knitted in alternate swathes, has the business-school logo embossed on a leather crest at one end. It doesn't say the name, only those who know can tell what it stands for.

Ganjeri has asked all the stock questions. *What's your living situation? Are you seeing someone? Still with the same company? How's your family doing?*

He hasn't asked much back. He scrolled through Ganjeri's social-media timeline before coming, so he's quite updated. Ganjeri has just been to the conference in Davos, the one where everyone who is anyone shows up. He took a train there and tweeted how he cared about the environment. Before that, he stopped over in Budapest. *#HungarianHangover*. Last year, he was in a relationship with a girl so gorgeous she seemed to have a bit of all the good genes on the planet. They hiked up the Machu Picchu trail and vacationed in the Bahamas. *#VacayGoals*. But his relationship status is now back to *Single*. Over the last few years, he checked in at airports in San Francisco, Washington DC, Mexico City, Geneva, Dubai, Mumbai, Delhi and Hong Kong, where he got massages in business-class lounges. His profile lists three simultaneous employers. The job designations don't give much away – *Strategy, Growth, Impact, Development, Leader, Accelerator.*

There are photos of him with CEOs, ministers, billionaires, Nobel Laureates. As a hobby, he is a Thought Partner to youth entrepreneurs. He spent his last birthday talking to aspiring changemakers on AMA panels. *Ask Me Anything*.

Now the awkward silence is an opportunity to do just that. Ask him anything.

'What's your real gig? You seem to be doing everything at once.'

Ganjeri smiles, as if embarrassed. 'There's no *one* job really. Overall, I manage programmes for philanthropists, and I'm trying to ring-fence funding for young Muslim men, giving them entrepreneurship skills. I just got a couple of million pledged in Davos.' He sounds disappointed by the amount.

In Mumbai for three days, Ganjeri texted. *Quick catch-up?*

Nice long dinner? he texted back. *Quick* was the only way people did things any more – *quick* coffee, *quick* run, *quick* shower. But he has all the time in the world. And if he is going to meet Ganjeri after seven years, it can't be *quick*.

They fixed the time and place, a plush restaurant in the Kamala Mills compound. This used to be a thriving cotton mill two decades ago. Now it sparkles from the bling on people's dresses and themed restaurants. The mill workers were either moved to the slums, or have committed suicide or died of poverty. Only the coarse, stained walls are a reminder of that time. *Shabby chic*, the interior designers call it.

'I saw your paintings, man,' Ganjeri says. Chintoo has put some up on Facebook. 'They're amazing. Also, that volunteering you're doing . . . teaching art. Good stuff.' So Ganjeri has looked him up too. It makes him feel less insignificant. 'You should go all out about this. Create social-media buzz, a website, make vlogs on YouTube, document your time with the children . . .'

He shrugs. 'It's not like the art is changing their lives . . .'

'No, man.' Ganjeri shakes his head like a disapproving elephant. 'You're underplaying yourself. Have you ever thought what your legacy will be? What will you be known for? Everyone wants to be remembered for their best selves.' It sounds like a souvenir the business school would sell in its gift shop.

'So which one is *your* best self – this, or the person who worked with victims of earthquakes and police violence and riots?' He hadn't planned on asking Ganjeri this, but if he doesn't now, he will never know.

The waiter brings the food. Ganjeri has ordered the pasta al dente; the waiter didn't know what that means, nor did he. The waiter pours some red wine to taste, which Ganjeri swirls in the glass, holds up to his nose, takes a sip, approves. The waiter proceeds to pour wine into both glasses.

'I still care about the same things. I just decided to take a different route,' Ganjeri replies to his question. 'Let me tell you a little secret I learnt.' His eyes glint. 'You know the difference between successful and mediocre people? The mediocre ones work for life. The successful ones make life work for them.'

'You sound like a TED Talk,' he jokes.

'Well, let's say I've done a few TEDx's,' Ganjeri says with pretend-coyness, then gets serious. 'No, but really. Before I went to Harvard, I was in perpetual fight mode, even with those I was trying to help. I taught children, but they dropped out of school. I built shelters, but they got blown away by the next cyclone. I wrote fiery articles, but no one published them. I hated the world, hated myself.'

Ganjeri takes a sip of the wine. 'But then I saw how success-ful people go about their lives. Man! They don't care about the work. They only care for the noise you make. The more you make it about yourself, the more the world will lap you up!'

He sits back and lets Ganjeri talk. He gets a feeling that Ganjeri doesn't let his guard down often.

'The rich love talking about themselves, and love those who do the same. Look at me! In a world where mullahs are blowing up buildings, they love to see a mullah like me – suited, booted, speaking perfect English, drinking whisky. It vindicates them, makes them cum in their pants!' Ganjeri grunts in self-deprecating disbelief. 'They see me as this clever Muslim boy who has spent years trying to change the world. My anger could have taken me anywhere – I could be lobbing grenades at the Parliament. But no, here I am, rubbing shoulders with billionaires. And that's why they write me cheques.'

He tries to picture Ganjeri in the Parel flat, drinking, praying, reading, smoking a joint, but can't. This is a different man, one who knows exactly where he is headed, no iota of confusion.

'That's what you should do too.' Ganjeri eggs him on. 'You even have a solid story. You dived straight in. You almost lost your life taking a stand. For all my activism, I've never been able to do what you did.'

'I was just stopping someone from getting killed in broad daylight.'

When Ganjeri smiles, his dimples peep out of the well-groomed stubble. 'It's all about how you look at it. Think of it like this – you are a *brand*. Think of what you stand for, what you can say to the world. You don't even have to invent, you're a hero!'

Ganjeri lowers his voice like he's going to share some rare wisdom. 'The next revolution will be the *story economy*. Everyone will come to the marketplace to sell their own story. There's still time for you to be an *early adopter*.' Ganjeri winks and does air quotes.

'And if everyone's telling their story, who's listening?'

'In a crowded bazaar, the one who shouts the loudest shall be heard.'

Ganjeri fidgets with the stem of the glass. 'Look – you can sit at home and . . . Or you can go out and beat the world at its own game. You don't even need the establishment any more. Just flip out a phone, make a short video, upload to social media, tag some important people.' Ganjeri leans closer, his voice a whisper. 'And keep saying the same thing until you've got enough traction.'

They munch in silence. The waiter asks Ganjeri if the pasta is indeed al dente. Ganjeri wags his head, non-committal. The waiter steps away, eyes still on Ganjeri, clearly having figured out who the important one at the table is.

An image hovers over his head. Ganjeri at the firangs' carnival after-party, sitting on a windowsill, lighting up a joint, telling jokes to a group of foreigners, hiccupping with laughter, everyone laughing with him. Ganjeri always knew how to be a man of the world. It is a rare gift.

'Did you ever win back the land your family lost in the riots?'

'I pulled some strings and we got an out-of-court settlement. We got the top floor of the building they built on our land. Now my parents lord over their neighbours, the ones who asked us to leave and didn't protect our house.' Ganjeri shrugs. 'There are many ways to claim your dignity. You have to find the one that works best for you.'

He reaches out and touches Ganjeri on his little finger. Ganjeri doesn't flinch, lets the fingers stay there. In another place and time, this friendship could have been something else, something more. At least there would've been a choice to explore. But this country is not that place, and now is not that time. They can only be *friends*, if they don't want to end up in jail.

But Ganjeri is braver than he is, has always been. He wraps his fingers around his friend's, holds them tightly, in full public view. A couple of heads half-turn to half-see, but Ganjeri doesn't care.

'Listen to me,' Ganjeri says, his eyes deep, earnest. 'In the West, I discovered a new label for our identity – *person of colour from the global south*.' Ganjeri pauses to let his friend absorb the mouthful. 'It's a broad category, but it's kind of true. We're the most populous, youngest, most ambitious people in the world right now, just about learning to find a way out of our colonial pasts, but not sure what the future actually looks like. Have you considered, in most of these *global south* countries, ours is the first generation in hundreds of years to be born to free, independent parents? Yet from birth, we're put into boxes, taught how to think, what to become. And when we grow up, the West just want us to be cogs in their capitalist machinery, do their jobs on the cheap, work their hours, speak their lingo.'

Ganjeri tightens his grip. 'Whatever we *are* today is not thanks to any support from society or institutions, but *in spite* of it. But guess what . . . we have no voice, no respect, no one's curious about us.' Ganjeri is breathing loudly, the warm breath falls on their joined fingers. 'So, my friend, if you have a story to tell, you better fucking tell it.'

They sit with their fingers entwined in a comfortable familiarity, the kind they have both realized is difficult to find out there in the world. Once upon a time, they had found each other. That too was a rare gift.

Angel

The face is so disfigured that her lips are pulled into a permanent smile. He isn't sure if he should smile back. He turns to the other side, where the eunuch is shifting their weight from one foot to the other.

A hush falls over the room as Sid Gulati stands at the mic. 'Ladies and gentlemen, friends and patrons, thank you so much for coming out tonight.'

The children from the Bhiwandi slums are lined up in the front row. Anisha and the ladies from the NGO are there too.

After that evening with Ganjeri, he decided to write to Sid Gulati about the Masters programme. Sid's secretary wrote back immediately, scheduling a call for the next day. 'This is great news!' Sid spoke in huffs, like he was running on a treadmill. Beats from a song thudded in the background, the kind of nondescript music that plays in gyms. 'It is people like you we want to support, people with initiative, people who dare to dream . . .' He ran out of breath. Beeps of the treadmill stopping.

Everything after that happened very quickly. There was a fundraiser in the diary, at the iconic Jehangir Art Gallery at Kala Ghoda. Sid Gulati chalked out what he called a *masterplan*. They would exhibit his canvases, the ones that had won him a place at this prestigious London university. The guest list included the rich and famous of Mumbai – industrialists' wives, money managers, inheritance consultants, tech entre-preneurs, venture capitalists. 'We don't only want to fund your education,' Sid Gulati said. 'We want to showcase your talent, *tell your story*.'

Now here they all are. The masterplan has been a success. The women patrons gasp and gush at the paintings. The men don't care to look; they put their heads together and net-work. When the NGO ladies paraded the children in, the patrons turned their lips upside down in pathos. *Awww, look at them, so cute.* They asked in broken foreign-accented Hindi, *Tumko chocolate mangta hai, bachcha?* All this poverty was too much for them, making them rush to pledge donations to the Sid Gulati Foundation. *That man does so much for society, he's an absolute angel, no?*

Sid Gulati continues into the mic. 'Today we're here to celebrate art.' He waves at the paintings on the walls, which include one of the flamingos, *The Pied Piper of Parel*, one of Mangesh's lighthouse. 'And we're here to celebrate the human spirit.' Sid points to his protégés – one whose face was disfig-ured from an acid attack by a jilted lover; one born a eunuch in the wrong country; one is him. He feels guilty about stand-ing upright in one piece, taking up a spot that could have been someone else's. He wonders if he should remove his shirt and show the scar on his back, to prove he deserves this. He feels the children's eyes on him – their Arts Sir, their hero, standing in line for alms, like they do for water from the tanker every morning. Anisha's eyes are on him too. He dares not look at her.

'The Sid Gulati Foundation is all about supporting people who overcome unimaginable hardships to make something out of their lives.' Sid waits for impact. Heads bob in agree-ment. 'I'm glad to announce that, with your support, we will award scholarships to these three brilliant youngsters.

Madhvi Sathe will start her own beauty parlour. Kusum will study journalism. And Shubhankar Trivedi will study art in London. Some of his work is here today.'

Sid Gulati turns to him and smiles indulgently. 'Don't forget us when you're famous, Shubhankar.'

Low laughter rumbles through the audience. Gold rings clink against champagne flutes. He realizes this is how the rich clap.

Aasmaanee

My dearest Shabby

The name infiltrates his nostrils like an old smell, armpit sweat-patch on school uniform on a hot summer's day in Lucknow.

I'm so sorry I haven't been in touch. I really wish I'd been better at it. But things got really busy once I went back to Bangalore. My mother had always wanted to set something up to help women who face violence at home, but she was too busy with her teaching. And, of course, bringing me up as a single parent! So when I went back, I decided to make this dream come true. And you know I'm not on social media. That would've made keeping in touch easier. I first thought I'd email, then thought – let's do it the old-fashioned way. Let's write a letter.

The letter arrived that morning. He hasn't received one in years. The only letters sent to him have been official – the employment release letter, the university offer letter. He tore the envelope in a hurry, trying to recognize the handwriting. When he saw who it was from, he realized he had never seen Shruti write. Back in school, everyone knew everyone's handwriting. He can still tell Chintoo's from a distance. Now everyone typed. No one wrote.

I'm writing from America. I finally took my dad up on his offer to spend time with him and his new family. He and his second wife got married a few years ago. Their daughter is five. He's been asking me to get to know my little sister. A few months ago, we had to fold up the NGO in Bangalore. The government cracked down on foreign funding, which I'd worked very hard to secure. Networking, grant applications, interviews! But the government says that's how black money flows into the country. Imagine that! Through local NGOs, who struggle to pay their staff even in the best of times. Across the country, NGOs' bank accounts are being frozen, as if we are the culprits, not the industrialists who hoard millions in Switzerland. Anyway, let me not get started on that. My mother was disappointed, but I was devastated. Five years of work, Shabby. And it all ended with a large padlock on the door. I was so broken that my mother went against herself to suggest that I visit my dad in America. So here I am, in San Francisco, for the last three months.

After finishing the letter, he didn't know what to do. He wanted to read it again, but he didn't want to break down, to cry alone. If there is anything more debasing than crying wretchedly, it is to cry alone. So he got into the car and started driving. Snippets of Shruti's words echoed in his head like he had memorized the letter for an exam.

It's not so bad, this life. You know I've always resisted the temptation to use my American passport, to cash in on my privilege. But now that I'm here, I can see why people want to migrate westward. There's something about breathing in clean air, warm water flowing from taps, not walking into garbage dumps. As a woman, it's even more freeing, Shabby. I don't have to look over my shoulder, think about how late I'm getting home, fear when I go out in a short dress. It's like a different world. Even their problems are different. People here complain about the train being late, about the barista not smiling when they served coffee, about there not being enough organic farmers' markets. They get so worked up about these things, it makes me laugh.

He drives down the Eastern Express Highway and turns into Kurla. It rained this morning. The vegetable sellers use bricks to sit on the puddles. People trudge through the water to buy things. The street is clogged with traffic. He inches forward.

But you know what, we will never be a part of this place, never belong here. My dad has been here for decades. He's a professor. Even then, he only socializes with other Indians. He has some work friends, yes, but they're just colleagues. When he wants to invite someone home, it's always the Indian families in the Bay Area. Even after all these years, he's not found a way to integrate. He might live in a posh neighbourhood, but in his mind, he's in a ghetto. Difficult choices, you see. That's what people like us need to make all the time. Clean air or family? Rule of law or festivals? Job opportunities or speaking our own language? We're always choosing – nationalities, identities, accents. We're not like Erik and Rebecca and their friends, who can turn up anywhere and be just white and nothing else, the entire world designing itself to suit their needs.

At Bandra-Kurla Complex, he speeds up, whooshing through the empty roads, only stopping at the red lights.

Even then, there are so many of us here. Sometimes I feel like I'm in India. It's like everyone who could escape, has. Half the people I know in Bangalore are plotting to leave the country, especially Muslims, women, gays, artists, writers, journalists, activists. It was never easy for us, but today, we're targeted, called traitors, anti-nationals, risk being dumped in jail any time or, worse, being lynched on the street. And when we dream of a life elsewhere, we have to queue for visas and show funds and prove our English proficiency. If we're lucky. Otherwise we get on boats and risk our lives on the high seas. Like I said, difficult choices, always.

At the Western Express Highway junction, he turns left towards the SV Road flyover, then on to Hill Road.

But I'm confident we'll emerge on the other side of this with dignity. There's something unique about our generation, in the way we understand the world, our own culture and others'. We can speak many languages, sing songs, dance dances, read books, chant prayers, wear clothes that are ours and others'. We're too rooted to uproot, and too spread out to cage. Our voices will find their way out into the world. I know this in my heart.

He drives through Pali Naka, crosses Janata Bar where Shruti and he drank together, up Pali Hill, down the slope to Carter Road.

I've been thinking about you a lot, Shabby. Our life, the years we spent together. It's been a decade since then. I can now say that I will never have that with anyone else – a chosen family, no rules, no conditions, no boundaries. We were all outsiders – you, me, Syed, Erik, Rebecca, even Shakku-bai and Mangesh – but we made that little corner of the giant city our home. Those years were like how life should be, how we imagined it as children. Perfect! Before the world snapped us back into its ugly reality.

He passes Jogger's Park, then to Mount Mary, Reclamation, Lilavati Hospital.

I've toyed with the idea of visiting you in Mumbai, but that wouldn't be the same, would it? A couple nights of talking and drinking. I'd come back aching for a life we no longer had. Like the celebrities who get Botox and stop eating to hold on to their youthful looks. But in my soul, I'm still there, in Mumbai, the greatest city on earth. We are the city, and the city is us, our best and worst in all its glory and garbage. It's like we were there even before we arrived, and stayed after we'd left.

He is speeding on the Sea Link bridge, his eyes darting this way and that.

You've been through a lot, my friend. I don't know if you remember, but I was in the hospital every evening. I still get nightmares sometimes about seeing you like that. I can still hear your mother cry on my shoulder when she first saw you. I didn't know how to stop her. I've never seen anyone cry like that.

He finds what he is looking for three lanes away. He swerves and cuts through two lanes in between. Cars slam brakes, honk horns. Someone juts their head out and shouts, 'What the actual fuck, asshole? This is Mumbai, not your village!'

You're a champ, Shabby. You need to know that you deserve only the best, nothing less. Don't let what happened hold you back. Don't let anyone tell you that you don't belong somewhere. Forgive them. Let love win over hate.

He waits as the car hums, slowly moving forward, his eyes trained on Mangesh, watching him turn from car window to counter, then back to the car. Someone at the counter must've said something, because suddenly Mangesh's face creases into a smile. In that moment, Mangesh looks fourteen again.

He is levelling up with the counter when Mangesh sees him. 'Arre, bhaiyya?' he says instinctively, as if they'd met just yesterday. Then his face hardens. But almost immediately, the features soften again. As the car draws up next to him, Mangesh asks, 'How are you, bhaiyya?'

'I'm fine. How are you, Mangesh?'

'Just like before only . . . busy with work.' Mangesh takes the money from him, passes it to the counter and turns back. 'I didn't know you were still in Mumbai.'

Your mother knew, he wants to tell Mangesh. *She retrieved and preserved and lugged my art, tracked me down to return it to me.*

Instead he says, 'I've been here, yes. But I'm leaving. I'm going to London.'

'Oho! Big-big news! That is awesome, bhaiyya.' *Awesome.* Mangesh says it in English. The person at the counter is whistling to get Mangesh's attention. The car behind is getting impatient. They have honked already. He begins to inch forward. Mangesh hands him the receipt and change. 'Come home once, na, bhaiyya? I have a son. His name is Ayush. You have to bless him.'

'Badhaai ho!' *Congratulations!*

Mangesh is receding from view, but he wants to ask him so many things. *Did you finish school? Did you read those books I gave you? Did you ever go to the lighthouse with your Ajji? Do you know what happened to me after that morning on the platform? Do you regret what you did?*

'How's your mother, Mangesh?'

'She is well, bhaiyya. She's busy pampering her grandson.'

'Give her my regards. Please tell her I'm all right.'

Now he understands that sometimes Nani's story of the lamb and the wolf also works the other way. Our elders can absorb and atone for our actions, leaving us with a clean slate to start again. *Those paintings Shakku-bai brought me are why I have an admission, a scholarship, a chance at a future. She atoned for your actions, Mangesh. And today, I forgive you, I bless your son, I wish you the best. You're free of me, and I of you.*

He presses his bad foot, which isn't so bad any more, on the accelerator. Soon he is speeding down the bridge, the taut cables passing him by in a blur. The city beyond grows hazy. The sea is a proper blue today, shimmering in the white sunlight that has come out after the morning's rains. Aasmaanee, that's what Shruti would've named this blue.

It's time to start afresh, my cioccolato, whatever that means, on whatever terms.

Lots and lots of love, always your friend, Shruti.

He turns the radio on for the first time. It is playing a song from a decade ago.

> *You are my ocean waves*
> *You are my thought each day*
> *You are the laughter from childhood games . . .*

Gift

It is time to go, he says to M.

There is nothing left to give, to take. Everything has been said, done. All debts repaid. All borrowings returned. All thanks expressed. All sins forgiven. All ashes scattered.

A new life beckons. In a new place. It will never be home, no. But it will be new. It will be oxygen in our bodies, manna in our souls, like the yogurt from the dahi-haandi.

I know now that life is a precious gift. I got a second chance. You didn't.

And for your sake and mine, I promise I will not squander it.

PART SIX
Aakaash / *Space*

2016

No. 93

When the news arrives, it is a text message in broad daylight, not the distant sound of an analogue phone in the middle of the night, like he's always imagined. *Tring-tring.*

Nani no more. Left us this morning, the message says. Papa thinks he's at work, will call back when he can. But he's just lying down, staring at the ceiling fan. He's applied for a UK visa, booked flights, sold the car, donated his paintings to the Bhiwandi school. In the bare flat, he has only clothes and documents to be stuffed into two suitcases. And himself. All waiting for the grand escape.

The pithiness of the text is like a *Breaking News* update, like something's happened to someone he doesn't know. A life summarized in seven words. He dials Papa's number, then cancels it, calls the landline. He is relieved when Ma answers.

'We got to know this morning. The maid rang the bell but got no answer. So she called me.' Ma's voice is steady. 'It must have happened during the night . . .'

'I'll buy a ticket now. I should be there in a few hours.'

Papa's voice interjects, he's been listening. 'You have a lot on your hands, beta. You have to wrap up work, pack things, hand over the flat. Your visa can come any day now and only you can collect it.' So typical of Papa. 'We'll be fine. You can visit a temple in Mumbai and say your prayers.'

He can hear Ma breathing. The gilt-bronze clock next to

the phone ticks loudly. He can see the alloyed cherubs playing trumpets. He waits for Ma to say something, but it's still Papa on the phone. 'Chalo, we'll have to start making arrangements. You call later once you've finished work.'

He opens a travel app and books a ticket on the first flight. This costs more than he can afford, his bank balance is down to a few thousand rupees. He throws a few things into a trolley bag – a couple of shirts, toothbrush, socks, spare glasses. He picks up the sketchbook, but it's too big for the bag, so he puts it away.

The new airport is huge, and efficient. His check-in is done within minutes. He remembers to ask for a window seat. The departure gate is a long walk away. He buys a coffee, drags the trolley bag on the carpeted floor. The designs are of peacock feathers. Massive fluted columns open up into petals on the high ceiling. The airport is the hallmark of *new India*, a proud modern tech-savvy country. Cafés, restaurants, duty-free shops pass by. He walks by a gate, stops and stares at the screen. It is the British Airways flight he will take to London in a month's time. Can he just walk up now, show them the ticket, board the plane, cut to the chase?

He finds a seat at his departure gate. He is early. Only a handful of unemployed people like him have turned up, old retired folk, women with wailing children. He looks at the muted TV playing the news. The new British prime minister is addressing a conference, the ticker playing out quotes from her speech. *If you believe you're a citizen of the world, you're a citizen of nowhere*, she has said. It appears again and again. It's like she's speaking directly to him. He misses his sketchbook, this would've been a delicious moment to capture. A few months ago, Britain voted to leave the European Union. He is going to a country that has decided to purge itself of foreigners.

He is not sure why anyone would *not* want free visas to cross borders and trade without paying tariff. In India, visas are needed even to cross into Bhutan or Bangladesh or Sri Lanka. Pakistan is another story. White people have no idea of their privilege. Shruti was right, even their problems are different.

The prime minister's lips tremble involuntarily, her nostrils puff in and out, a devious smile appears through clenched jaws. What a warm welcome to his new home. Ha! *Home.* In any case, a current Indian student at the university said it would be impossible to stay back after the course finishes. *Don't expect to find a job here. You'll need employer sponsorship, and Britain has the most expensive sponsorship regime in the world! Arts and design firms can't afford it. They only sponsor visas for doctors and nurses and footballers, not artists.*

Home is an oversold concept. Outdated. For people like Ma and Papa who never aspired to live anywhere else, or maybe never had a reason to escape. His generation, on the other hand, was coached to leave. Flight was drilled into their veins – follow the job, promotion, money. And now, they were a generation of rootless souls, life reduced to a series of pit stops. Citizens of nowhere.

An old lady limps up, limbs given to arthritis. She sits down opposite him and smiles. Suddenly he is reminded of Nani. He feels guilty about not thinking of her. He stands up and wheels the bag around to find a smoking room. Inside, he puffs away at two cigarettes, one after the other, lighting the second before the first is done. Others are puffing away too, hardly visible through the dense smoke. The poisonous air stinks. Little grey clouds stand stubbornly suspended at face-height. It is like a global conference of druggies – people who've flown for hours from different corners only to have one smoke together, bleary-eyed, silent.

*

339

The flight is busy. Large families, migrant workers, business travellers, all cramped together in this bauxite contraption that will magically launch them into the atmosphere. Lids of overhead compartments shut loudly, babies cry, couples click selfies, phones make croaking noises as last-minute messages are typed out.

But everything changes when the flight takes off. People doze. Babies make cooing sounds. Phones rest in pockets like limp penises. Light strains of music from earphones escape into the common airwaves. He looks at the man next to him nodding off to sleep. His clothes are cheap. There is a slight run in the trousers. His hands are rough, knuckles dark brown, blue veins sticking out. Probably works in construction in Dubai or somewhere. This is the future Nani had predicted for him when she turned up every evening that summer of '99, when he'd failed his exams. *He'll be a mali, yes-yes a gardener.* The harsh look on her face at the mango conference. *Bheegi billi, slimy cat, people are saying.* She used up all the energy her body afforded her, chest swelling up for oxygen.

The memory makes him smile. Such drivel people say to each other all the time. And then, how Nani vacated her chair for him at Munni-didi's wedding, pulled him to her chest, welcomed him like a nawaab. Had she forgotten everything she'd said? Did she think *he'd* forgotten? Oh, Nani! All that negativity for what? To die alone in your bed and lie there a corpse for hours before they found you. How long were you lying like that? What were your last moments like? Did you suffer? Did your heart do somersaults in your chest? Did you feel regret? Did you call out anyone's name? Your daughter's? Your husband's? Mine? Did you ask for help? For forgiveness? *My* forgiveness?

The man next to him has woken up, looking at him in surprise. But he can't stop the tears, no matter how much he wipes his cheeks with his hands. They keep coming like an ancient spring that has suddenly found its way out of the earth after years of working through layers of soil.

The taxi stops in front of the block of flats. He looks at the walls, the little lawn, the untrimmed trees. They seem tired, groaning under the ravages of time. Are Papa and Ma too old to manage this by themselves, to maintain, supervise, haggle? At what point should he and Chintoo step in to help? Or are they still playing out their childhood vows of leaving Lucknow and never looking back?

Things at Lucknow airport were quicker than he'd imagined. He was at Arrivals long before he'd planned. Booking a taxi was quick too, the queues organized, card payments accepted. A new flyover made sure the taxi zipped over the city. *New India*. He is unprepared to get out. He needs a little more time to adjust to the Lucknow air, the smells, sounds, language. A panic grips him. Has he made the right choice to come? Is he needed here? Everything would go smoothly without him, he knows that. He doesn't belong here, doesn't know the rituals, the things to buy, calls to make, people to invite. Part of him wants to turn around and book the next flight out. But the driver is holding the door open and pulling his trolley bag out. It's time to go in.

There are people all around, spilling out on the lawn, the narrow driveway, the pavement. They whisper, take little steps towards the house as if queuing to enter a temple. A steady stream of more people appear from the house, the women with pallus and dupattas over their heads. Outside the main door, a riot of shoes and chappals stand like a moat around a fortress. Someone says, 'Oh no! I think someone has worn my shoes and left.' Another replies, 'Arre, no problem! You also wear someone else's.'

He climbs up the stairs to the second floor. The doors of the other flats are open, letting the mourners use their living rooms. As he walks into the Trivedi flat, the smell of incense overpowers him. Smoke rises from the sticks and hangs in the air. The crowd parts to let him in. They are all there – Panna-chacha and Manju-chachi, Lekha-bua and Nandu-fufa, Aarti-mami and Girish-mama, Mr Dwivedi and Dhwani, Sharma-uncle and Sharma-aunty, Kejriwal-sir and the ghost of his dead wife, Papa's boss Mr Kaushik, Munni-didi and her pageboy husband whose name he can never remember. It is like the *Titanic* scene at Munni-didi's wedding, except no one is smiling. Malti-didi appears with a tray, offering water to the guests. Everyone looks a little surprised to see him, like they'd forgotten about him in his own house.

At the end of this line-up is Nani. He has dreaded this moment. He has never seen anyone else like this before. On the flight, he tried to think of Nani as a *dead body*, but no image came to mind. Now here she is, yet she isn't. This isn't the same person, the one bursting with energy, telling stories, taunting, whistling, enthusiastically shutting windows during the riots. This person is lying on the ground in the middle of the living room, dressed in a white saree – a colour she never wore, a garland of tuberoses around her neck, cotton wool stuffed up her nostrils, her complexion pale, eyelashes stiff like cat's whiskers. Nani would never approve of such behaviour. *How-how people lie on the floor in front of everyone!* Now look what death has done. It has taken away from her all opinions, all choice. After a lifetime of talking, death has finally shut her up. Forever.

He spots Papa moving busily around, a file of documents in hand. He has the air of an events manager. His greying strands are unkempt, his stubble completely white. He's never seen Papa unshaven. Papa has always been well-turned-out, even on weekends, ready for a call from his boss. A neighbour taps Papa on the shoulder. 'Trivedi-ji, look who's here.' Papa turns, still preoccupied, then walks up, pats him twice on the cheek. 'Your mother is resting in the bedroom. Go meet her. We're going to leave for the cremation ghat in some time.'

He wheels the trolley down the corridor and leaves it outside the bedroom. The door is ajar, narrow enough to keep strangers out, open enough to let insiders in. He gives it a light push. Ma is lying on the bed, her back to him. He is tiptoeing out but the sheets rustle. Ma has turned around. She looks tired, like the house, like everything else here. 'I was waiting for you,' she says.

'How did you know I was coming?'

'I tried calling a few times, your phone was switched off.'

'Why were you calling?'

She shrugs. 'Just wanted to talk.'

'Have you eaten?'

'Yes-yes, Malti said she'll manage the kitchen. Thank god for her. I've been in the room all day. I don't want to see anyone's face right now.'

'I'll go to the ghat. I'll see you when I come back, okay?'

Ma bobs her head. 'I knew you would come. Even when your father was asking you not to.' She looks happy that her premonition has come true.

In the living room, two boys are lifting Nani on to a bamboo bier. They ask who will carry *the body* to the hearse outside. Papa steps forward and looks at him. 'Come. It is auspicious to carry her on her last journey. The men of the house have to do it.' Panna-chacha and Munni-didi's husband step forward too.

The bier feels feather-light. This is what a human body weighs in the end. The rest of the people chant *Ram naam satya hai* under their breaths, the murmurings echoing through the room like a school-assembly prayer. On the street, a small

343

gathering of neighbours and passers-by has formed, everyone trying to catch a last glimpse. Someone whispers, 'She
was unlucky in her youth, lost her husband early. But later,
she led a full life – surrounded by daughter, son-in-law, two
handsome grandsons . . .'

Nani's maid suddenly appears. She is breathing heavily,
like she's run all the way. 'The Agarwals wouldn't let me take
the day off,' she explains to Papa. 'So I had to somehow finish my work and rush here.' She stands on tiptoe to look at
Nani's face, bursts into tears, wipes her eyes with her pallu.
Papa motions to Malti-didi, who deftly leads the woman
away, whispering in her ear, senior maid to junior maid. They
join the bystanders.

Nani is lowered into the hearse, the glass lid open. More
hands come forward. By the time Nani has settled in, nearly
everyone has earned karma points by helping.

The ghat is chaotic. There are five incinerators working full-
time. With every *body*, at least fifty people have turned up.
Priests chant mantras loudly, as if they can be heard by the
heavens. Relatives sob. Fixers sneakily offer to jump the
queue for extra payments. Attendants shout over the din to
organize logistics. A loudspeaker booms with announcements of who is next in line.

He sits in a corner of the courtyard, eyes fixed on Nani,
who is body number 93, in queue for incinerator number 4.
The place is strewn with flowers, clay lamps, plastic bags, old
newspapers, misplaced footwear, sludgy footsteps. No. 92 is
now being *loaded*. A wave of sobs comes from the relatives.
A man, maybe the son, holds on to a foot and cries inconsol-
ably as the helpers try to disengage him and get on with their
work. The priest chants with more fervour, as if to match
the tears, showering petals and holy water. The metal door

344

of the incinerator noisily opens as if it is Ali Baba's cave. *Khul ja sim sim.* Inside, embers fly around manically over an expansive iron bed, ready to gobble the body up. The helpers count, as if flagging off a race. *Ready . . . one . . . two . . . three.* A crank turns somewhere. The tray on which the body is placed is sucked in, like dirt to a vacuum cleaner. The iron door slams shut, faster this time because of gravity.

Within seconds, he can smell it – the stench of burning flesh, human flesh, flesh of someone who was a person until a few hours ago. The stench rises slowly from the chimney and surrounds the ghat. It sticks to people and pillars and the ground. Even the sound of the loudspeaker seems to carry it.

He knows this stench. He knows it well. He's seen human flesh burn, heard it, nearly felt it.

He is giddy. The air is closing in on him, making him want to retch.

Chintoo hugs him from behind. He turns and hugs Chintoo back tightly. His brother is here, thank god his little brother is here!

'They're taking her inside now, bhaiyya,' Chintoo whispers. From the puffy eyes, he can tell that Chintoo has cried a lot. He sees the helpers picking Nani up, the priest sprinkling holy water, the sound of the crank working, Papa's face expressionless, glasses fogging up from the heat . . .

He can't do this. He can't . . .

He tugs at Chintoo's arm. 'I need to get out of here. Do you have cigarettes?'

Antakshari

He wakes up. Chintoo is asleep, still the Kumbhakaran. It is nice to share a room. He's slept by himself for too many years now. He looks at Chintoo's young effortless body, sprawled on the bed, a crumpled razai half-covering him, half-falling-off. This perfectness reminds him of the scar on his back. It itches to signal it's still there.

He saunters through the flat. It is peaceful early in the morning.

'Hand me the spade, na?' Papa is hunched over the flower-pots on the balcony.

He takes the spade to Papa. 'What flowers are these?'

Papa looks up. Even though there's a nip in the air, his forehead gleams with sweat. 'Hibiscus!' Papa points proudly. 'Those are dahlias, those are marigold.' He smiles. 'My retirement is coming up next year. I need to find something to keep me busy.' He takes the spade and starts digging the soil. Some of it overflows on to the ground. 'I would love to have a house with a big garden, but . . . this is what I have for now.'

He wonders if one day he will have enough money to buy Ma and Papa a house with a garden. Unlikely, since he has spent everything he had and doesn't know whether he will earn anything any more.

He sits on his haunches. 'How can I help?'

Papa points to a string of sachets. 'Take those seeds out.'

He tears the sachet and pours the little bulbous seeds on

to his palm. Papa is saying, 'If all goes well, by winter, we'll have a big garden here. But you won't be here to see. You'll be in London.'

The last few days have passed quickly, the rituals lined up one after the other. As soon as one is done, there's the next one to organize. The puja on the fourth day went well. They are now preparing for the eleventh day. Then there is one on the thirteenth. 'Our ancestors were wise people, beta. They wanted to keep the family busy in this period, for people to come and go, so that we're not left alone in mourning,' Papa explained.

Nani's story again. *We will be rewarded for the good deeds of our forefathers.*

His visa has been granted and is awaiting collection. He hasn't told anyone yet. Papa will go into a tizzy, insist that he go back to Mumbai, as if the embassy will be burgled, the passport and visa will vanish. Sid Gulati's secretary has sent him the schedule for a photoshoot, helping to publicize the scholarship the foundation is giving him. After all, he is the poster-boy of Sid Gulati's altruism. Along with it were campaign ideas to review. FROM VICTIM TO VICTORIOUS, the first slogan read. He didn't scroll further. The secretary has agreed to move the shoot to after the funeral rites are done.

He and Chintoo have joined forces with Papa. They order the flowers, get the marquee set up, the caterer booked. There is always a lot do. Papa keeps them on their toes. They have never worked together on anything before. This sudden teamwork has injected Papa with fresh energy. Plus he knows what people are saying. *Both of Trivedi-ji's sons are here to stand by their father.* This makes Papa's chest puff up with pride.

Ma spends a lot of time lying down. She isn't crying or

sad, just tired. There are days when he sees her go to the phone at around eleven in the morning, wiping her wet hands on her pallu, in a rush like she's late. She picks up the ear-piece, maybe even dials the first few digits. Then she stops, puts it down quietly. One day, she catches him looking. 'This was the time I used to call Nani,' she explains, a bit sheepish. 'It's become such a habit!' He asks what they talked about. A smile crosses her face. 'Oh, just everyday things – what was cooking, did the maid come on time, some relative or the other called . . .'

The smile stays as she stares at the gilt-bronze clock. 'This clock,' she says, 'Nani always insisted it came from her parents' house, and I always said it was my father's gift to me.'

He turns to look at the clock, still in perfect condition thanks to Ma's meticulous cleaning with vinegar and oil.

There is always a steady stream of people coming and going – to offer condolences, help with groceries, drop off food, set up the puja, keep the family company in the evenings. After that first day, everyone has shrugged off their sad looks. The atmosphere is more relaxed now. People share jokes, pull each other's legs, tell stories of Nani. One evening, Nani's cousin pays a visit from Azamgarh. She talks of the feisty little girl Nani was, youngest of seventeen cousins. 'When all the malai in the milk went to the boys, the rest of us girls would stay silent. But Subhadra, she always protested. She refused to drink until a brother gave up his malai.'

There are other stories told by people of the mohalla. The grocer turns up and cries his heart out. 'She loaned me money to build my house but when I offered to pay back, she refused to take even a single penny.' The maid says, 'I told her I lost my neck-chain and next Diwali, she gave me a chain! Just like that!' Even the butcher pays a visit, though Nani was vegetarian. 'Every time I passed the house, she'd say from her balcony – *Ilyas, do you want some water? Your throat must be parched in this heat.*'

At such times, the brothers exchange awkward glances. All these stories make them feel like they were the only ones to misjudge Nani in childhood. That, or they were the only ones over whom Nani felt any ownership, had the right to be mean.

One evening, someone proposes a game of antakshari. Everyone gets excited. Two teams form instantly, one from their mohalla, the other from Nani's. He hasn't played antakshari in years, so he sits silently watching the others belt out obscure Hindi film songs. *Sing with M-uh! Mhare hivda mein naache morrrr . . . Now with R-uh! Roop tera mastaana . . .* They finish the songs at awkward places so the other team get a difficult sound to start theirs with. They remember the songs word for word, the way it is only when there's a special memory attached to them.

Dhwani is here too. She knows quite a few songs, has a sweet singing voice, going into falsetto often for lack of practice. She looks a few years older, but age suits her. She's wearing a well-fitting churidar-kurta. She hasn't got married. He wonders if their making-out at Munni-didi's wedding has stayed with her, but probably not.

Someone says some chai would help to improve the quality of singing. Everyone laughs. Malti-didi dutifully heads to the kitchen. He follows her, asks her to continue playing antakshari. Malti-didi looks confounded. She's not used to men doing kitchen work. She asks if there's something wrong with her chai. He says no, but he can definitely make some without help. Malti-didi goes back to playing, hesitantly. He puts the milk on to boil and stares at its whiteness as bubbles start to form on the surface. He knows he needs to take it off soon, otherwise it will spill. But something inside him wants to see how far up it'll come, if he can stop it just in time from brimming over, from burning. Large bubbles are almost coming up to the rim and bursting of their own accord. He turns the flame up a little more.

A hand shoots past him, turns off the gas knob. It is Dhwani. 'So much for making chai,' she teases, but lets him do the rest of the work. He adds the tea leaves to the boiling milk, then strains the liquid into cups.

'So I hear you're off to London to do an MBA?'

He nods, wanting to tell her the truth about his course, but not sure if he can trust her. 'And you? Still in Lucknow?'

'Where else would I go?' The wonder in her voice is genuine, like she'd rather be nowhere else. Even the suggestion is absurd to her. 'I'm vice principal at my college now. I'm studying part-time for a PhD.' She dances her eyebrows.

He smiles. 'Doctor Dhwani Dwivedi. DDD.' She rolls her eyes at his silliness. 'You know, in childhood Chintoo and I had a tongue-twister. *Dwiti Dwivedi, Dhwani Dwivedi.*' He says it slowly to not make a mistake. Then his face darkens. How foolish! He shouldn't have mentioned Dwiti.

But Dhwani is laughing so loudly he is sure everyone in the living room can hear. 'Oh my god! Why didn't I know about this?'

He starts laughing too.

Chintoo comes in to check what's happening. 'Ssup, people?'

Dhwani tells him the joke, and Chintoo is also laughing. Their stomachs ache so much they have to hold their sides. Some chai spills on the counter.

Majlis

'It's like a body part,' Chintoo says. 'I carry it along everywhere.'

Ma has asked how Chintoo remembered to bring his guitar even when he left in a hurry. The family are alone this evening. There isn't a lot to say, so Chintoo has brought out his guitar. Ma requests songs she claims Nani loved. Then she hums along. These are old Hindi songs and Chintoo doesn't know all the words, so he asks her to take the lead. She is nervous at first, unused to singing for an audience, to singing at all. But once she starts, her voice becomes clearer. *Ohhh sajnaaa, barkha bahaar aayee* . . . The song sounds even better with the guitar, something punchy about the chords. He records a video on his phone of Chintoo and Ma performing, to watch later in London.

Then Papa requests a song. Ma says she doesn't know the words and Chintoo hasn't even heard of it. So Papa sings in an intonation-less voice. *Aa chal ke tujhe, main leke chaloon* . . . When he's done, they all clap. Papa goes into the bedroom and gets a pack of cigarettes, lights one in the living room, something he's never done before. He sits on the sofa with a smile, releasing perfect smoke rings from his lips. Ma tries to look annoyed by this, but the boys can see she's impressed by Papa's skill.

Chintoo says the brothers should perform 'Dosti'. He is shy but Chintoo won't give up, strumming the guitar and starting the song. He joins in, then falls into tune. He remembers

Chintoo composing this as a teenager, in the middle of the night, pushing for originality, looking for rhyming words in Urdu. *Kareeb. Habeeb.* After they finish, Ma says in wonder, 'Why didn't you ever play this for me before?' It's as if she's forgotten how she'd packed the guitar and shoved it away for years. The brothers don't bring it up.

Chintoo says he will move to Mumbai. He wants to be a music producer and has an offer from a studio. There is a glow around him, the aura of a creator, the power to hum a new tune in the shower one morning and turn it into a song by afternoon, a song that the world will sing for years.

Papa gets involved, advising Chintoo like he understands the music business. 'Make sure you meet film people. Bollywood is where the real money is.'

There is nothing left from the years they spent fighting about Chintoo's choices. It is as if Chintoo's blind optimism has finally opened up Papa's blinkered vision, given the man the strength to dream of something bigger than the holy trinity of middle-class existence – *roti-kapda-makaan. Food-clothes-shelter.*

Papa pats Chintoo's back. 'One day, Shah Rukh Khan will be mouthing your songs in super-hit movies.' Chintoo looks pleased.

After the majlis and dinner are done, they watch TV. Chintoo is on his phone, exchanging messages with his many friends. Ma and Papa seem interested in what's playing – a *Bigg Boss* contestant running after another with a knife in hand.

He watches vacantly, trying to look interested when Ma turns to explain.

The news comes on at ten p.m. The tabla beats have become more frenzied over the years. There is always something sensational happening. More cow vigilantes have killed more Muslims. Journalists arrested. Universities stormed, students beaten, activists slapped with sedition charges. The bespectacled anchor and his boxed midgets are back to debate the issues. The anchor's voice has grown louder, now he won't tolerate a word against the government.

'They've even bought the media. That is the one thing we were proud of! A free and fair media!' Chintoo says, lifting his eyes from the phone, then turning to Papa. 'See what you voted for, what it's unleashed. You let them kill one person, you look away, you think – it's just one person. Next thing you know they're killing hundreds!'

Papa stares down at his hands as if the answer lies in the lines of his palms, something that will defend his vote. But he doesn't find anything there. He stays silent.

Chintoo turns to his brother. 'You're doing the right thing by leaving. There's nothing left in this country . . .'

Holika

Chintoo leaves for Delhi after the thirteenth-day rituals, all strapped up, backpack on one shoulder, guitar on the other. The brothers hug. A slight goatie has emerged on Chintoo's chin from not shaving. Something tells him Chintoo will cultivate this look. 'I'll come to Mumbai before you fly out to London,' Chintoo says to him.

But he hasn't bought his tickets to Mumbai yet. The photoshoot for Sid Gulati's foundation is in a few days. He opened the campaign document and read another slogan. I AM SCARRED BUT NOT SCATHED. He closed the document. The visa is still awaiting collection. UoL have sent orientation documents, asked what kind of accommodation he would like. The landlord in Mumbai is asking when's his last day, how he wants to settle the deposit. He has put all these questions aside. He can't bring himself to think.

Papa asks about his notice period, his last day in the office. He mumbles a lie, says he has lots of leave to take. Ma seems happy about this. She enlists him in tasks she's planned. 'Tomorrow we will go to Ahluwalia's to pay for the sweets. And day after to the bank to transfer ownership of Nani's locker.'

That afternoon after lunch, mother and son head to Nani's place. They arrive with bags and boxes like people on a mission. They empty cupboards and showcases and kitchen shelves, drawers and chests and lofts, put everything in the middle of the living room, like a Holika bonfire, a heap of forgotten memories that have left the world with Nani. There are magazines from the seventies, a cassette player that doesn't work, vessels that are overused and those that have never been used, sarees, tomes of books that belonged to Nana-ji, hand-knitted sweaters worn by Ma and him and Chintoo and tucked away for a third generation, rolled-up paintings that were never framed, a couple of sepia photographs of Nani's childhood, some of Ma's youth that have blurred or have blots, a brass temple with little idols of gods. Everywhere he clears, he looks for the sketch he made the last time he met Nani, the one of him smiling, looking like Nana-ji. But he can't find it anywhere.

By the end of the exercise, they are so exhausted they have to sit down. They stare nervously at the pile, like two people who came digging for marbles and have instead unearthed a treasure. Ma says, 'She was so unprepared to die, na? She even made a note to call the newspaper-wallah the next morning. And she'd taken out detergent for the maid to use.' They laugh about how Nani hid her detergent so the maid wouldn't use it all up. They decide to come back the next afternoon.

Over the next few days, they divide up the contents of the bonfire. He helps Ma to catalogue them, decide what to donate, what to give to relatives as souvenirs. They collect the photographs and fold them up in old newspaper, making a note to buy photo albums from the nearby studio. They go through the expensive sarees, and Ma speculates which relative should get which one. They put aside the jewellery to take to the bank. They debate whether to keep Nana-ji's books or donate them to the community library. He elects to keep them. 'Only if you promise to take them when you buy your own house in London,' Ma says.

'What will you do with this house?' he asks.

'Papa thinks we should sell it. By god's grace, we've saved enough to see us through, but Papa says it'll help you and Chintoo to buy your own houses.'

He looks at the heap, reminded of the fact that his parents still think he's going for an MBA.

'Why don't you choose something from here?' Ma says. 'As a memory of Nani.' She points to the silverware, the photographs, a watch, a fountain pen. But he shakes his head, finding excuses. Finally, he shows her something he found and pocketed. It was tucked away in a drawer, wrapped in clear plastic. He was going to discard it, until he looked closely. Ma's school badge – red plastic, her name written in Hindi. वसुंधरा त्रिवेदी | It is still shiny. Nani preserved it as if Ma would need it for her next school term.

Ma extends her hand and takes the badge, stares at it, trying to drag sleeping memories out from deep inside. 'I was in the Red house. I even remember the name – Patel. After Vallabhbhai Patel, the freedom fighter.' She looks up at the ceiling to remember more. 'Yellow house was Azad. Blue was Bose. Green was Ambedkar.'

Ma's mind is still razor-sharp. She runs her fingers over her name carved on the old plastic. He imagines her a little girl in this house, ready for school, books under her arm, hair oiled and tightly braided.

'You know? Amma never let me sit anything out. She wanted me to participate in everything – painting, dance, sports. The number of prizes I won for the Red house!' She shakes her head as if she can't quite believe it herself.

'The last time I was here, Nani told me you were a brilliant student.'

Ma brushes off the comment with a wave. But her smile widens.

'Actually, she said if you'd worked, you would've earned double Papa's salary.'

'She said that?' Ma is intrigued. 'Dhat! Impossible!'

'Really! Qasam se!' He pinches his Adam's apple to swear.

Ma sits silently for a long time, turns away from him towards the open window. 'Maybe that is why I was so hard on you when you were younger, to see you achieve all the things I couldn't.'

Then she hands the badge back to him. 'You want to keep *this*, out of everything here?'

He nods. He can see her chest is starting to heave. He crosses the room and sits beside her, puts his arm around her shoulders. Tears are streaming down her face. She makes no effort to stop them. She clutches his hand tightly. He is crying too. Ma takes his glasses off and wipes his face with her pallu. 'Why are *you* crying now?' she says through sobs, trying to smile.

He pulls Ma close and places her head on his chest. They sit there, her body trembling in hiccups.

Maya

He sleeps long hours, like he hasn't slept in a lifetime. He goes to bed early, wakes up when he feels the pinch of the cool October morning on his skin. Sometimes he goes for runs, before the sun can beat the nip in the air. Before breakfast, he spends time on the balcony helping Papa with gardening, adding manure, watering seeds, inserting sticks for support, misting leaves. When a hibiscus bud appears, he jumps like a child. He rushes to Ma and Papa's bedroom to wake them. They celebrate by drinking the morning chai there.

Sometimes he takes siestas after lunch, dozes off midmorning trying to read a book. Papa is back in the office. Ma has enough to do around the house. Food magically appears thrice a day. He has no idea who's going to the market, who's cooking, who's cleaning up after, who's planning the next day's meals. It is the life of a pet dog – circular, repetitive, predictable, mindless. At peace.

He tries to sketch on leftover paper, but there is nothing left to express.

In the evenings, he goes for strolls, roaming the city that has been both a home and a stranger. He walks the markets, Janpath, Hazratganj, the Gomti riverside, below the arches of the Bada and Chhota Imambaras, past the Charbagh railway station and back.

One evening, he finds himself in the massive new park that opened some years ago – an extravaganza of red sandstone, punctuated with large elephants standing in a row, trunks rolled up in a salute. It is dedicated to the lower castes. The former chief minister, whose idea the park was, has built statues of herself in every corner. Even in her statues, she clutches a handbag. 'She has so much black money that she's hidden it inside these elephants,' a tourist guide is telling his group in jest. 'They say she comes back for it at night.' The tourists laugh at the joke.

He sits in the open space and stares at the statues. *Hathiyon ki maya. The fantasy of elephants.* He takes his phone out, there are calls from Sid Gulati himself. Then a text. *Is everything all right? My office says you've gone incommunicado.* In his inbox, there's an email from the secretary. *We will need to reconsider our offer of scholarship if we don't hear back by . . .*

He needs just a little more rest. He is not ready to leave Lucknow yet, to do the photoshoot, to pack up, to board a flight. He thought he was, he'd escape at the first opportunity. But there is some more of this lamp left. He owes it to himself to let it burn out.

He opens a blank message and types. *Free tomorrow for a walk? I can give you a tour of the elephant fantasia.* He sends it to Dhwani.

The dots ripple as she types out a reply. *I thought you'd left? Was disappointed you didn't say bye. Tomorrow 5.30 in front of my college? I'll make sure I clutch my handbag* ☺

He chuckles and puts the phone down. Suddenly there is something to look forward to.

A thud. An old man on his evening walk has stumbled and fallen. People gather. He gets up to see. The man is moaning. He reaches out, picks the man up, helps him to the side. He lifts up the man's trousers and shines the phone's flashlight. A slight bruise and a swelling. The man gives him his son's number. He calls the son with the details. Then he sets about treating the bruise, asking for water from a tourist, washing the wound. The man flinches but stays still.

Then they sit side by side waiting for the son. The man thanks him, says this is the kind of youth the country needs. If Dada-ji and Nana-ji were alive, they would probably have come here for evening walks too. What would they have thought of the country today? What would they have thought of *him*?

'What's your name, beta?' the man asks.

He is silent for a while, then replies, 'Shubh—'

But the man is saying even before he can finish, 'Shubh? Wah! Such a nice name. Do you know what it means?'

'It means *good*.'

The man smiles. 'It also means *auspicious*.'

Gau-mata

He hears the cackle as he enters. He knows who it is even before he can see. He walks into the living room, stumbles on a big bouquet of white lilies. Suresh-mausa is on the sofa, flanked by his wife Pushpa-mausi and Papa. Ma is on a chair, slightly away.

They spot him at the doorway.

'Arre, look who's here! Come sit, beta.' Suresh-mausa is acting like the host. 'I was in Delhi for important meetings.' And then in a whisper, 'With our honourable minister of agriculture.' Suresh-mausa waits for a reaction to this supposedly confidential news, then continues, 'So I had to miss Subhadra-devi's funeral.'

He sits down on a stool, at a distance. The TV is playing on mute. He tries to focus on the screen so he doesn't have to engage in conversation.

'She was a very good lady, your mother,' Suresh-mausa is telling Ma. 'Every time she saw me, she used to say – *You are doing the right thing by protecting this country. You are doing us proud.*'

He hears Suresh-mausa speak in his direction, so he turns. 'I hear you are going to London to study? At this age? Most boys your age have two-two children. Anyway, when you're done, come back to serve your country, okay? We need young people.'

His face is deadpan. Papa is squirming, wanting his son to be polite, chit-chat. This is not how guests are treated in their house, he's been told from childhood. But he can't put up a show for this man. He won't.

Suresh-mausa notices the TV and turns up the volume. There are reports of another killing. Two Muslim boys going home by train, accosted by a group of Hindu nationalists, accused of carrying beef, dragged down to the platform, beaten to a pulp. One dead on the spot. The body splayed all over the platform, people watching at a distance.

Suresh-mausa is upset, continuously clicking his tongue. 'This is what happens when you don't respect the country you live in. Arre, bhai, if you want to eat beef so badly, just go to Pakistan, na? If you live in India, you have to respect the cow as a holy animal.' He joins his palms as if in prayer. 'Cow is our mother. Gau-mata! This country has prayed to her for generations. Did you know cow's urine cures cancer? It's written in our Vedas. I've drunk cow-urine every morning for the last—'

'I've eaten beef,' he says softly, but the words come out clear and cut through Suresh-mausa's harangue. 'I've eaten beef,' he repeats, to make sure he has really said it. 'I've eaten beef at Mohammad Ali Road. I went there for iftar during Ramzan.' Stunned silence in the room. 'So should I go to Pakistan or will you kill me right now?' Suresh-mausa's face is hardening, but he can see the man doesn't know how to respond, is not used to being spoken to like this.

'It was delicious. I would eat it again. I don't think diet should be controlled by religion or governments.' He raises his finger though his voice is still calm. 'No one can take a person's life for what they eat, who they pray to, where they pray, whether they pray or not. You can't bring down a mosque. You can't let a man burn . . .'

There it is, everything he has been waiting to say all his life.

Suresh-mausa's face is red and sweating. Ma is staring at him. Papa is looking down at his hands again.

'If you support the killing of this boy,' he points to the TV, 'then you should leave my house.' This is the first time he has ever said it. *My* house.

Suresh-mausa looks to Papa, as if expecting Papa to slap his son, put the deviant in his place. But Papa continues to stare at his hands.

'You heard my son, Suresh-ji.' It is Ma's voice, shaky, like she wasn't planning to speak, has somehow blurted this out. She glances at Papa unsurely, then at her son. She thinks she's an uneducated woman, doesn't understand politics, her opinions don't matter in this country. But then she steadies. She cannot unhear the words she has said, cannot unfeel the confidence she has felt, speaking out in front of the men of the family for the first time. She sits upright, palms firmly on her knees. 'Too many people have died, Suresh-ji. Too much damage has been done. We won't sit here in our house and condone these any longer. No religion, no god will forgive us for this.'

He walks to his room in quick steps and shuts the door. Ma is still speaking, her voice now clear. 'And I know for sure my mother wouldn't condone this either. So I request you, please don't drag her name into all this . . .'

The lamp has burnt out. Now he is ready to leave.

Behosh

Ma pushes the door lightly to check if he is awake. He has been up since before sunrise. He has confirmed the photo-shoot dates with Sid's office, replied to Sid's text message, sent an email to the landlord about the logistics of moving out, taken a UoL induction survey. He has even chosen a campaign slogan, the cheesiest one. IT IS NOT JUST THE PHOENIX THAT RISES FROM THE ASHES. If he's going to sell out, it might as well be full-on. Like Ganjeri. And he has booked tickets out of Lucknow for the next day.

He tells Ma all this. She looks surprised, as if she weren't expecting any of this to happen. She sits down. 'Of course, you can't stay here forever.'

'Is Papa upset about last night?'

'No-no, he's on the balcony gardening. We never liked Suresh-ji, you know? But to live in a community, you need to fit in, keep the powerful people happy. You do it for so long that it becomes a habit, until you forget you disliked them in the first place.' She smiles. 'Now you children, free as birds, no ties to the community. You can speak your mind, stand up for what you believe in. Achha hai.' *That's good.* She nods. 'This is the courage we didn't have, now we're learning from our sons.'

He wants to tell her he doesn't know which is better – bound by community, or alienated by freedom. There is a price to pay either way.

Ma sits up like she's remembered something, then opens the folds of a piece of paper. 'This is yours, na?' She is holding the sketch he drew for Nani. Clear lines run through the middle – one vertical, one horizontal. 'I found it in Nani's handbag. We forgot to look in there.'

'You can keep it.'

'I saw your other paintings too. The ones on Facebook, at the exhibition. You didn't tell us about them, but Chintoo showed me and Papa.'

They sit in silence. 'Chintoo also told us you're not going for an MBA. You're going for an arts course. Papa is just worried you won't get a job. But I said – *This boy has come back from* . . .' She gulps, then continues. 'I told Papa our son is a fighter. A job is the last of our worries. He'll make it, no matter what.'

She looks at him. 'When we brought you from Mumbai, Papa and I didn't know if you'd . . . But you know who blindly believed you'd be fine?' She laughs. 'Chintoo and Nani. Those two never got along, but they're exactly the same. They never back down. Nani at least had her gods to pray to. But Chintoo, I don't know where he gets his optimism from.'

'Chintoo is an artist,' he says. 'That's its own kind of faith. Belief in something bigger than just us and our little lives.'

Ma bobs her head. She seems jollier now. 'You're an artist too. Don't underestimate yourself. I told Papa that if you don't get a job after your course, that's fine. You can come live here. After all, whatever little we have is for our sons. Who else have we worked so hard for all our lives?'

A vision flashes through his mind. Nani's house, a studio, an arts school for children, he and Chintoo and Ma and Dhwani working there, Papa gardening in the back, doors open for whoever wants to join in, maybe Shruti could start something too. SUBHADRA DEVI HOME FOR THE ARTS. His heart warms at the thought. He wants to shrug it off as a fantasy. It is too good to be true, too filmy. But he can't. Dreams are sticky things.

'Can I tell you a little secret?' Ma's eyes twinkle with mischief. He blinks tightly, smiling. 'Nani was right about the clock, the gilt-bronze one. She did bring it with her when she got married. I just never wanted to admit that I was wrong.' She sighs. 'So many things we keep from each other all our lives, and then suddenly one of us is gone . . . Will you tell me everything from now on?'

There are so many things I've wanted to tell you all my life, Ma. But he doesn't say anything, just nods.

Ma draws in breath, as if she's preparing to make the first move in this new pact of theirs. 'You know, I was thinking . . . let's not sell Nani's house. It can be a place for you and Chintoo to spend time whenever you want. This flat is small for two grown men.' Her eyes light up. 'Meanwhile, I can go stay there from time to time. If not anything, I can sit and read all of Nana-ji's books. My whole life, I've read on borrowed time. Even the newspaper came to me after all the men in the house were done with it.'

Ma looks at him. Her face is earnest, like Chintoo's. 'Your Papa and I have been together a long time. He is a good man, an honest man. He has always done the right thing, always treated me with respect. We made a good team, bringing both of you up. But now he's obsessed with gardening. And I need something to obsess over too. Spending some time away will be good.'

He can tell this is the first time Ma has spoken this idea out loud. It is a brave idea, especially for a woman of Ma's age, in this place. But Ma seems happy with herself. He is happy for her.

Ma hesitates. 'Will you do me a favour, beta? Can you go to your school and meet Miss Lucy? She's the principal now. She came to see you when you were . . . Remember?'

He shakes his head. No, he doesn't remember.

'You were asleep . . .' Ma stops herself. She is searching for the right word. She doesn't want to beat around the bush any more. She is pushing herself to name what happened to her son, to pronounce the word on her tongue. She is done with euphemisms and half-sentences. He can see it is a struggle for her.

'You were behosh,' she finally says. *Unconscious.* She has at last found her word for her son's state after the *incident.*

'I ran into Miss Lucy in the market a few years ago.' Ma adjusts her bindi. 'I used to think she's over-smart, but now I know that working women are smart like that. If I had worked, I'd be like her too.'

'But who says you aren't smart?' He looks into Ma's large eyes, beautiful, like the actresses of the sixties. 'You took care of us, this house, since you were in your early twenties. You came to a big city like Mumbai and took care of me all by yourself, without any help. Then you came back and took care of Papa and Nani. You've been smart all your life, Ma. It's *our* fault that we never made you feel that way.'

Ma doesn't know what to say. She is not used to compliments. Her lips curl in a smile. She balls her fingers into a fist and opens it in a jerking movement, chucking air at the world, just like Nani.

'Anyway, you should meet Miss Lucy. She has something to tell you.'

Ma closes the door softly behind her, and he gets up to get dressed. It is time for school.

Assembly

The walls are different. The certificates and awards in black frames have gone. In their place are drawings by children, some skilled, some scribbles, all a riot of colours.

'Shub-ank-ah!' Miss Lucy tap-taps in, her pencil heels still pointed. She is the same except her hair has gone completely grey. She wears it well. She opens her arms out. He stands up. They embrace. They have never embraced before, but this feels the natural way to greet each other after all these years. 'My god! How long has it been?' She looks at the ceiling to think, then gives up.

She sits in her chair. She looks settled in her role as principal. It has been five years now. So she did make it then, found a way to create a place for herself here, a foreign woman in this foreign land, on her own terms, not the outsider any more.

Suddenly he feels pride at being her student.

He tells her about the arts course, London, the NGO work with the children. She is beaming as she listens. 'I always knew you'd do great things. I am so proud. We have a lot of students working in big jobs, you know? CEOs, CFOs, this, that . . .' She rolls her eyes. 'But only a few follow their hearts. You're one of them.' He doesn't know about that, but he takes the compliment with gratitude.

'My mother said you had something for me.' He knows it is almost time for assembly. That is why he has come first thing in the morning, before Miss Lucy gets busy.

Miss Lucy's face changes. 'Oh, Shub-ank-ah! It was just something . . . small, from long ago. I don't know why I even told Mrs Trivedi about it when I ran into her.' She dismisses it. 'It's fine, you're leaving for London, going on to do big things . . .'

Suddenly he knows what it is all about. He is staring at her, and she knows that he has understood. She exhales loudly. 'You remember Salma-begum? Our community partner in the Maulviganj area?' Her voice has changed, lost its cheerfulness. 'Well, Salma-begum told me . . . this was a long time ago . . . that you'd asked her to look into something . . . a man you knew?'

Blood has rushed to his ears.

'She got the information, but she wasn't sure whether to . . . so she came to me, but you'd left school by then, so I . . . but when you came back and I went to see you . . . you were in no condition to . . .' She wipes her palm on her forehead. 'Oh dear, look at me! Blabbering away!'

'Did she find him, the man?' His voice is hoarse. Somewhere deep down he is hoping that Salma-begum found M, the man, not the body. A man living a full life somewhere far, far away. A man who, like him, was violated and left to die, but somehow made it through, got a second chance.

But Miss Lucy is saying, 'Well, she found out *about* him.' She presses her lips together. 'He didn't make it, Shub-ank-ah. He died that night.'

His body goes slack. He is trembling, the shivers coming from deep within like an earthquake has erupted in his gut. His breath is a series of staccato beats. He is holding on tightly to the arms of the chair.

Miss Lucy tap-taps her way to the door, closes it, bolts it from inside. She stands there so he can't see her. She will let him have his moment, take his time.

When he has stilled his body, she walks to him, places a hand on his shoulder. 'His name was Mudassir.'

Mudassir. Of course, Mudassir. Mudassir with his bright smile, his measuring tape, his spools of thread and rolls of fabric. Mudassir hopping around the little tailoring shop, hands moving quickly, mouth even quicker. Mudassir showing tricks to him and Chintoo with his fingers, jumbling the order up, pretending to cut his thumb off. Mudassir . . .

'He wasn't married, he only had his mother,' Miss Lucy is saying. 'The mother was given his remains by the police, though there wasn't much to give. She buried him in their native village close to Muzaffarnagar. She lived there until a few years ago. She died quite recently, I think . . .'

He looks up at her. There are tears standing in his eyes, accruing, refusing to fall. 'Were you in touch?'

Miss Lucy shakes her head. 'Salma-begum was. She sent money to the mother once she'd tracked her down. I think she went to the village once to meet her. I organized some donation from our school's charity fund after I became principal.'

So he was not alone in this. All these years, M's mother, Miss Lucy, Salma-begum, they were all holding up M's memory in their own ways. Like the disparate flickers one sees from the aeroplane at night, collectively lighting up a city below.

'How old was he when . . . ?'

'Oh, I don't know exactly. But he was young. Maybe midtwenties? Salma-begum tried to find a photo for you but there wasn't any. He'd come to Lucknow to work only a few years before that.'

'And Mudassir's grave . . . do you have the address?' The name sounds soft and musical when he says it. Miss Lucy nods yes. 'Thank you, Miss Lucy. Where can I find Salma-begum?'

'She's not with us any more, dear. We lost her to cancer a

couple of years ago. She worked with us for as long as she lived. Her student has taken over now . . .'

He lowers his head and lets the tears fall, fat drops on his trousers. He is not sobbing. This is just the calm draining of a dam inside him.

Miss Lucy squeezes his shoulder. 'I have to leave for assembly, dear. But you stay here and take all the time you need. I'll ask my staff not to disturb you.'

He looks up. 'Can I come too?'

The chapel is smaller than he remembers. The statue of Jesus is still as it was, curved strokes of red paint on the body. There is a dank smell in the room. Motes of dust fly in the sunlight filing in through the windows. Melting wax from candles makes random shapes. The pews are lined up symmetrically, the wood bent from years of pressed knees.

Miss Lucy is on the stage, facing the students. He has followed her unquestioningly. Miss Lucy is saying, 'This is one of my favourite students, Shub-ank-ah Trivedi. Today community service is a compulsory component of your study. It wasn't like that before. Twenty years ago, when I started, it was called SUPW and it was optional. But Shub-ank-ah here was the first cohort. He taught art to the children. He is an artist today.'

The students look at him in awe. He hopes Miss Lucy will not ask him to make a speech. But he can trust her with that, he knows she won't. He waits for her to say that he is an engineer, that he has worked with American multinationals, that he is going to London, all the things schoolchildren in this country are told about role models.

Instead, Miss Lucy turns to him and says, 'But the most important thing is, he is a good person.' She looks back to her audience. 'And over here, in this school, that is what we've all come to be. Good people first. Everything else comes later.'

There are a couple of announcements, a student gets up onstage to collect a prize for a quiz competition. He stands in the wings and watches.

Then it is time for a hymn. A teacher brings him a hymn book. It is still the small blue thing it was twenty-five years ago, the cloth bookmark hanging like a tail. He accepts it and searches for the right page. By the time he has found it, the assembly has started singing.

> *What a friend we have in Jesus*
> *All our sins and griefs to bear*
> *What a privilege to carry*
> *Everything to God in prayer.*

He murmurs the tune at first, mumbling the words. Then he is singing loudly, confidently. His body has goosebumps all over. The scar on his back is pricking against his shirt. He is not looking at the hymn book any more. He is standing straight, like he is a proud student of this school again, feet planted firmly on the ground.

For the second verse, the music teacher amps up the piano, her fingers striking the keys with graceful force, just like before. Sometimes years go by, yet the little things change so little.

> *Oh what peace we often forfeit*
> *Oh what needless pains we bear*
> *All because we do not carry*
> *Everything to God in prayer.*

Fantasia

On their walk that evening, there is no elephant fantasia. Instead, he takes Dhwani to the Maulviganj main road. They walk up and down trying to find Mohan Tailors. She doesn't ask why he has brought her here, this polluted potholed street. Instead, once he tells her what they're after, she joins in, asking shop-owners and vendors, Google mapping, slowing down to read shop names on worn-out boards, until they conclude that Mohan Tailors doesn't exist any more. Maybe it shut down after Master-ji died. He can ask Ma, but no, it's a closed story. They stand in front of what he thinks was Master-ji's shop, opposite a tube-well. It is now an electronics mini-mall. The owners must have bought the whole complex because it is at least twenty times larger than Mohan Tailors.

They stand there on that noisy road as he tells Dhwani everything. He always imagined it would be different, the first time he speaks about the night of Lekha-bua's wedding, about M. But here they are, cars honking, buses spewing black smoke, children shouting in the middle of their game. Dhwani doesn't say anything, doesn't ask questions, just listens. It sounds banal to his ears, being said out loud like that, like the plot of a B-movie. In the end, he says, 'I'm a coward. It took me twenty-five years to get here, to even know his name, to talk about it.'

'You're not a coward. You carried this inside you all by yourself. You protected Chintoo from it.' Dhwani's eyes sparkle. He can't tell if they're tears or lights from the passing traffic. 'I couldn't protect Dwiti,' she says in a whisper. 'I could see she was struggling, she couldn't bear the pressure of having to be the best at everything, but couldn't *not* be the best either. It was all in front of my eyes, but I didn't know what to do, until it was . . . too late.'

He wants to take her in his arms, but this is a crowded street. That is no way to behave, not here, in this place.

Dhwani exhales in half-laugh, half-scoff. 'Twenty-five years is long, yes. But sometimes it takes a lifetime.' She turns to look at him. A teardrop escapes her lashes and sits on her cheekbone. 'And sometimes it never ends. You know, when I found Dwiti like that, hanging from the fan, my first thought was to protect my father, not have him see her in that condition. I got up on a stool, untied her dupatta, brought her down to the bed. Only then I called Papa.'

Her eyes are the calmest he has ever seen, eyes that have known a loss bigger than he can imagine, witnessed a twin ending their life.

'But in hindsight,' she says, gathering herself up, 'I should've let him see. At least there'd be someone else to share it with. Now I'm the only one with that image in my head, and it'll be like that forever.'

Yes, there are stories bigger than his own. It is important to remember that.

Dhwani touches his arm. 'Sometimes I feel like it's our mediocrity that saved us. Our averageness made us hold on to a centre, in a way that brilliant people can't. You know, unremarkable but solid?'

He nods in response. He understands it well.

They walk back home in silence, stopping to say bye before she goes into hers and he continues walking to his. 'Take care of yourself,' she says.

'I'll see you when I visit again.' His voice carries a promise, even though she hasn't asked for it.

Then, as he is turning to go, she calls out, 'Shubh?' It is the first time anyone has called him by that name. 'Will you see a therapist in London? No one even suggested I speak to someone after Dwiti died. But things are changing now. Will you please see someone? Just think of it as a chat with a stranger.'

He goes up and hugs her. They stay like that for some time. A neighbour's shadow appears in a window. This might be top mohalla gossip first thing in the morning. *Little people with their little minds and big-big talk.* But no one cares any more – neither him, nor Dhwani, nor Ma or Papa or Mr Dwivedi.

Then they let go of each other and start walking their different ways. Suddenly he turns and asks, 'Do you still dance the Odissi?'

Dhwani looks back in surprise, then shakes her head. 'Haven't danced in decades. It's something Dwiti and I used to do together.'

'You should start again. You were really good.'

Dhwani lowers her eyes, bites her lip, blushes like a teenager. It makes him wish they could go back to the Maulviganj community centre, their SUPW field trips, make eyes at each other, that he had been her friend sooner, maybe something more.

Makes him wish he'd had a *normal* childhood, teenage years, a normal life. It has been a privilege. It has been a curse.

The stone chips crunch under his feet as he walks home. The light in the flat is on. Ma is waiting patiently to serve dinner. He has thought about Ma all day, how she knew about M, about what he had witnessed that night at Lekha-bua's wedding. She had an inkling right from the start, but she has known for sure for years now, since Miss Lucy told her. He has asked himself if he should be angry with her, confront her about why she hadn't spoken to him before, why she had let him deal with it all by himself.

But no, he can't shame her, reopen old wounds that have fossilized under the weathers of time. It is Ma who sent him to Miss Lucy to find closure, when she intuited that he was ready for it, when she herself was ready for it. It has been as much her journey as his.

He and Ma are done with their game. They are accomplices now, they have a pact for the future.

All of them, Ma and Papa and Nani and their lot, did the best of what they knew. Sometimes they learnt and yielded, sometimes they stood their ground. But their time is over. It is now for him and Dhwani and Shruti and Ganjeri and Chintoo and Mangesh to do what their previous generations could not do, undo what they did wrong, and honour what they did right.

As he enters the flat, he can tell from the aroma that Ma has made parval-ki-sabzi, not because he loves it, but because she thinks she makes it really well. She always has to be the best at everything she does.

Classic Vasundhara Trivedi, his dear mother.

PART ZERO
Agni / *Fire*

Govinda bolo hari, clap-clap of khanjani, what a privilege to carry, allah-hu-akbar, stand straight, jai kanhaiyalal ki, allah-hu-akbar, bend and touch knees, gopal bolo, what peace we often forfeit, allah-hu-akbar, prostrate in sajda, govinda aala re, foreheads and noses touch the ground, our father who art in heaven, ameen, sit up with knees folded, lead us not into temptation, allah-hu-akbar, turn right, om jai jagdish hare, allah-hu-akbar, turn left, tasleem, but deliver us from evil, allah-hu-akbar, everything to god in prayer, jai shri ram—

I tie the shoelaces tightly. I don't like them coming undone while running. It is still dark outside, but the crows are cawing. They're here every morning, announcing the sunrise, like the azaan from the mosque, the bells from the temple. In this country, we don't kill our uglies. We are them, they are us. There is a place for everyone here.

Someone else in the mohalla has woken up too, making retching noises as they clean their tongue. The shadows from the streetlamp fall on Chintoo's bed, making it seem like he is there. If I stare long enough, I might just catch the shadow breathing, the outlines moving up and down. I wonder where Ma has kept the Ludo board. Maybe she has donated it, like Nani's things. I am tempted to search the cupboards, but I get up and leave. I want to have a nice long run. My flight to Mumbai is in the afternoon. Ma said we are going to pack all morning. I heard her announce to Malti-didi that she will be busy today. I didn't bring much with me, but Papa went out last night and bought a lot of things for me to take to

London – cashews, pistachios, pickles, sweets, rice, lentils. He said it is always wise to arrive in a new country fully prepared to cook the first meal. The look on his face when he lugged the stuff home! It made me want to go up and hug him.

Out on the street, I stretch, feel the pull in my calf muscles, a slight pain in my shins, throb in my triceps. The sweetshop in front is opening. The shopkeeper pours water from a stainless-steel lota on to his palm, then sprinkles it on the ground. It is meant to clean the shopfront, but the water lands in scattered drops. Dust rises in slow motion, then settles back down. It is like most things in this country – little rituals, ineffective but meaningful, that keep us going from one day to the next, draw a common thread through us billion people. The shopkeeper waves. 'After exercise, come for sweets, beta!' I smile and bob my head, he bobs in response, both unsure if we've agreed or disagreed.

I start running out towards the main road. I can feel the heat building inside my body, pores opening up, allowing the cold air in. I jump over mounds of last night's leaves collected by the sweepers. The newspaper-wallah comes at high speed on his bicycle. I step aside to dodge him. I run by the Dwivedi house, wonder if Dhwani is still sleeping.

At the chai-stall, radio waves cackle as the knob turns to find the right frequency. Other sounds file in – creaks of opening windows, crackle of hot oil as the first batch of jalebis is fried, dull thuds of clubs and dumb-bells from the wrestlers in the akhada. It is almost full daylight now. Old men at nukkads drink chai and discuss politics, debating the country's pressing issues, finding solutions that will never be heard. The milkman is on his rounds, two aluminium canisters hanging from his bicycle. He greets the old men as he passes. *Salaam, chachaa.* The men raise their hands in greeting. *Ram-ram, Gangadhar. Kaise ho?*

I run where my feet take me. I turn right and left, go up and down slopes, cross the bridge over the Gomti river, Nana-ji's tribute to his independent nation still standing strong at seventy. I run through the rows of sandstone elephants in the park, past the school campus, through open fields, the dew forming a thin translucent layer over the grass, waiting to melt in the sunlight. I run past morning walkers, early lovers, schoolchildren, their mothers forcing on them the sleeveless cricket sweaters. I run and I run, through galees and mohallas, aangans and chowrahas, ghats and maidans.

I stop running. I'm breathing heavily. Strains of old music playing on All India Radio waft up to chorus with the birdsong.

> Jo guzar gayee, kal ki baat thi
> Umr toh nahin, ek raat thi
>
> *What has passed, is a thing of the past*
> *Was it a lifetime, or was it a night?*

I turn a full circle to look at the haveli. The gates aren't locked, so I walk in. I pass through the hallway into the courtyard and to the back. Everything looks smaller, shorter, lower, narrower than I remember. The tube-well is still in the same place, but there is no tip-tip of dripping water. The gate leading to the back alley is shiny and black, as if someone had a lot of leftover varnish. This is a different gate. There are no grilles, the ones that M had tried to climb. M!

'Mudassir – what does it mean?' Dhwani asked yesterday. I shrugged. She pulled out her phone and googled. 'Engulfed. Wrapped. Enveloped. It's another name for the Prophet.'

'Well, he died wrapped in flames,' I said.

I look back at the wall where the flames had played

light-and-shadow. It is whitewashed now. I try to recreate the scene from that night, M's hollow eyes turning amber, the flames licking his body, how he clanged the gate, rolled on the road, whirled in and out of vision. Instinctively, my hand goes to touch the scar on my back. It doesn't itch, doesn't hurt. It is like a lifeless snake wrapped around me. An unwitting companion. A harmless foe. A reluctant friend.

But no image from that night sticks. Instead, sounds of the present waft in – auto-rickshaws honking, street vendors announcing their wares in high-pitched voices, parents rushing children to school. I squint as the rays hit my eyes. The sun is up properly now, has flooded the courtyard in bright-yellow warm light. A bit of the nip in the air still hangs back like old memories.

'Do you need something, sir?' It is the caretaker. He has appeared from one of the narrow corridors. 'Are you looking to rent this place for a wedding?'

'No.' I smile. 'I came to meet an old friend.'

He looks confused. 'Here? This is a shaadi ki haveli. Only meant for weddings. No one lives here. People just come and go.'

'You're right. My friend, he doesn't live here any more.'

The caretaker scratches his head. 'What to do, sir? Everyone's leaving this place. Going to the big cities, to foreign countries.' He looks upset on my behalf. 'The only ones left are old people, and us poor people.'

I turn towards him. My brain is active, ideas bouncing off the cerebrum and cerebellum. 'Listen, I need to do something for my friend. I won't be long.'

'But, sir, I have to start preparing for tonight's event—'

I rush out. I know what I'm looking for, it doesn't take too long to find. The paint shop is in the galee right behind the haveli. The owner is just opening up. He seems pleased that a customer has come this early, although he looks at my exercise clothes with suspicion. 'All this paint . . . is for your house?' I shrug. I load the cans on a trolley, place the brushes carefully on the side, then wheel it away, whistling to myself. An attendant from the shop runs behind me so he can bring the trolley back. 'Why didn't you bring your car, sir?' he asks between huffs and puffs.

Back at the haveli, I unload the trolley and open the cans of paint. I grab a dented bucket and fill it with water from the tube-well. The phone is buzzing in my pocket. I take it out. *Ma calling* . . . She must be waiting to pack, worried I will miss my flight. Sid Gulati has texted – *Excited to see you tonight at the photoshoot*. His secretary has emailed the details. Everyone thinks I'm done here.

But I'm just getting started, beginning to tell my story and M's, *our* story, in the first person, in the way that I know best.

The caretaker stands under an asbestos shade. He's too stunned to say anything. A few children have gathered. People stop to look on their way to the market. The shop attendant holds the trolley but can't bring himself to move away.

I dip the brush in the yellow paint first. When I take it out, I can feel its weight. I splash the paint on the wall of the haveli. A vibrant yellow streak shines in the centre of the whitewash. A gasp goes up from the onlookers, but everyone is holding their breaths, not wanting to stop what is about to unfold.

A little girl comes up. 'What is this, bhaiyya?'

'It is fire,' I say. Agni, used to honour endings, consecrate new beginnings. I know my eyes are glowing like meat on skewers.

'But for whom are you making this? This is the back wall. No one even comes here.' Her voice is despondent.

Maybe. *In a crowded bazaar, the one who shouts the loudest shall be heard*, Ganjeri had said.

Maybe no one will see this mural I'm about to paint. Maybe this story won't make any difference to anyone, to these people, to this country.

Maybe.

But maybe not, because I also know that . . .

What matters in the history of time is not the story that dazzles today, but the one that sparkles with so much honesty it survives. Even if it is told by only one small voice. No gatekeepers, no censors. It will be recovered, restored, repeated generation after generation, by grandmothers to grandchildren at bedtime, maybe just a new song here, a new rhythm there.

'So what's the story then?' a little boy questions.

I ask his name.

'Shubh,' he says. 'It means *good, auspicious.*'

Acknowledgements

They say it takes a village to raise a child. I say it takes a community of ardent believers to turn an idea in the author's head into a book. Thank you . . .

Jessica Woollard, for believing in this novel even before you'd read the full manuscript.

Helen Garnons-Williams, for falling in love with the characters and knowing exactly what I was trying to do with them.

The hard-working and passionate team at Penguin – Hayley Cox, Ella Harold, Natalie Wall, Sarah-Jane Forder, Olivia Mead, Becky Wallace and everyone else.

Jon Gray, for the striking cover.

Max Porter, for your mentorship and friendship.

Spread The Word, Mo Siewcharran Prize, Blue Pencil Agency, Michael Green, JJ Bola, for championing the novel at pivotal points in its journey.

Natasha, Dipto, Jo, Gerald, Tissa, for reading the very rough early drafts and taking it seriously, then and since.

Anne, Eleanor, Sharanya, Gabrielle, Tom, Simran, Ajay, Devyani, Ayush, Kat, Saim, Kshama, Sushant, for all our workshops and your honest engagement.

The late VD, whose one act of kindness changed my entire life.

My grandmothers, I didn't get nearly enough time with them, but their stories of resilience and dignity continue to light the way forward.

My parents and my sister, for never asking of me to be anyone but myself.

Shiny, for everything.